"A well-written tale—full of action, adventure, and deceit—with an unusual heroine looking for her rightful place in the world."

—Anne Bishop,
author of *The Black Jewels* trilogy

"You don't find many books like this, never mind first novels. Hetley's *The Summer Country* is like an old Irish whiskey—dark and smoky, abounding in flavor and detail. For the jaded reader of Celtic fantasies such as I've become, bone-weary of all the pale and limpid novels that try to pass themselves off as the real thing, it's such a treat to find a book as strong as this. *The Summer Country* is all things a good novel should be: a tightly-written, resonant, single-volume story rich with flawed characters, dark visions, and quiet joys, with a whisper of true mystery, lying there in wait at the very heart of it all."

—Charles de Lint,
World Fantasy Award–winning author of *The Onion Girl*

"A wonderful debut novel, by turns beautiful and utterly brutal. There's nothing soft and fuzzy about this fantasy land. Hetley gives us a raw, gritty world of hard edges and merciless determination, peopled by characters who live and strive with complete veracity regardless of which side of the mystical veil they hail from. His mix of 'real world' elements with the Celtic mythos is a delight."

—Lynn Flewelling,
author of *The Bone Doll's Twin*

# THE
# SUMMER COUNTRY

JAMES A. HETLEY

ACE BOOKS, NEW YORK

THE SUMMER COUNTRY

An Ace Book / published by arrangement with
the author

PRINTING HISTORY
Ace trade paperback edition / October 2002

Visit our website at
www.penguinputnam.com
Check out the ACE Science Fiction & Fantasy newsletter!

Library of Congress Cataloging-in-Publication Data

Hetley, James A.
    The summer country / James A. Hetley.
    p. cm.
    ISBN 0-441-00972-7 (alk. paper)
    I. Title.

PS3608.E65 S86 2002
813'.6—dc21

                            2002018683

ACE®
Ace Books are published by The Berkley Publishing Group,
a division of Penguin Putnam Inc., 375 Hudson Street,
New York, New York 10014.
ACE and the "A" design are trademarks
belonging to Penguin Putnam Inc.

PRINTED IN THE UNITED STATES OF AMERICA

10  9  8  7  6  5  4  3  2  1

To Merle, my "enabler," and the RECOG group folks who helped to polish this and patch the holes.

# one

—⁓—

THAT MAN WAS still following her.

A gust of sleet stung Maureen's face when she glanced back into the night. *Winter in Maine*, she thought, *you'd at least think the weather would have the decency to dump snow on you.*

February had been a run of sleet and freezing rain, no damn good for skiing or anything—it just made the sidewalks into bobsled runs and the roads into skating rinks. People always pictured New England with those picture-postcard mounds of fluffy white stuff. Instead, most winters plastered the city with yellow-gray ice full of freeze-dried dog shit and dead pigeons.

She hated it. She ached to be out of it.

And that bastard had followed her through four turns to head right back toward the Quick Shop. He kept his distance, but he was still there. It wasn't chance. She hadn't seen another person, or even a car, in the last fifteen minutes. What were her options?

The midnight streets vanished in a vision of green grass and trees, sunshine, warm breezes, and streams of peat-stained water the color of fresh-brewed tea. She breathed summer country, a cabin-fever dream she wanted so much she could smell the clover.

*Wish*, the whisper came, out of nowhere. *Wish*. And hard on the back of the thought came a memory of Grandfather O'Brian's voice, "Be careful what you wish for, my darlin'. The gods just might be givin' it to you."

The thought brought tears to her eyes, or maybe it was the sleet. She had been far closer to the old man than to her own father, and now Grandfather was fifteen years dead. Funny such a devout Catholic should talk of the gods in plural. Funny she should think about him, slopping through the dark streets of Naskeag Falls and thinking dark thoughts about the entire male race.

Maureen's nightmare still followed her, half a block back—a squat black shadow under the streetlights, framed by the double rows of dark storefronts and old brick office buildings. Everything was closed and silent, brooding over her search for someplace warm and dry and public.

The scene reminded her of a hodgepodge of old movies—Peter Lorre stalking the midnight streets with a switchblade in his pocket. For some reason, the movie image relaxed her. Maybe it made danger seem less real, the sleet turning the night into grainy black-and-white flickers on a silver screen.

Maureen pulled her knit cap down tighter on her head and went back to concentrating on the ice underfoot. She was reading her past into the future. No self-respecting mugger or rapist would be out on a night like this. The voices in her head could just take a fucking hike.

Besides, her mood matched the foul weather. She'd had a rotten evening at the Quick Shop, and the chance to blow some scumbag to hell carried a certain primitive attraction.

Maybe while she was at it she should put a slug through the carburetor of that damned rusty Japanese junk-heap that had refused to start and left her walking. And pop the night manager with the roving hands who had reamed her out and docked her pay for being late, before suggesting they could maybe arrange something if she chose to be a little "friendlier."

Hell, go big-time and shoot all the paper-mill cretins from upriver who stomped in for their six-packs of beer, steaming their wet-dog smell and dripping slush all over the place so she spent half her shift mopping up after them.

Definitely blow away the oh-so-precise digital register that had refused to tally when she closed out at midnight. She'd ended up putting in ten bucks out of her own pocket, just to get the hell out of the place. Two hours' pay, before taxes.

### CONVENIENCE STORE CLERK
### GOES BERSERK, MURDERS 20.

Again, Maureen checked on her shadow. He was still there, still half a block back. The way she felt, she almost wished he'd make a move.

She kicked a lump of slush and yelped when it turned out to be frozen into place. Adding insult to injury, her next limping stride found a pothole in the sidewalk, and she sank into ankle-deep ice water.

*Screw this psychotic winter weather,* she thought. *Psychosis: a mental disease or serious mental impairment, a medical term not to be confused with the precise legal implications of the word "insanity."* Psych 101, second-year elective for distribution requirements in the forestry program.

She had reasons to remember the definition, reasons for such a personal interest in the ways and means in which human minds deviated from the norm. Fat lot of good college was doing her now.

A snowplow growled around the next corner and headed

in her direction, fountaining out a bow wave that washed up over the curb and sidewalk to break against the dark line of buildings. Maureen ducked back into the entryway of the nearest storefront, trying to dodge the flying muck. It spattered icily across her jeans, and she stepped back out into the storm, elevating her middle finger at its retreating yellow flashers.

NASKEAG FALLS DEPARTMENT OF ROADS AND BRIDGES, the sign on the dump gate said, YOUR TAX DOLLARS AT WORK.

The man following her ignored the truck, and the slush seemed to ignore him. Hairs prickled along the back of Maureen's neck. Without speeding up or even looking at her, he'd halved the distance between them. The paranoia kicked in, elbowing her anger aside and substituting cold calculation. She needed some defenses.

"Enough of this crap," she muttered, or maybe it was her voices. The next alley offered places where a small woman could hide, places where muscles wouldn't help him. If he came in after her, he was history. She thumped the pocket of her wet ski jacket and felt the reassuring weight of metal.

She ducked around the corner. Dumpsters lurked in the shadows, two of them, jammed right up against brick walls and just close enough together to leave space for a single person. She ducked into the bunker they formed and waited, remembering her lessons.

*Smith & Wesson Chief's Special,* she heard the instructor lecture, *thirty-eight caliber. Five shots, short barrel, not very accurate—don't ever shoot at anything beyond ten yards. Light, compact, reliable—perfect weapon for close-range self-defense.*

*If you ever really need your gun, don't give warning. Don't wave it around. Don't make threats. Just shoot as soon as you show the weapon. Shoot twice. Shoot to kill. He's trying to kill you!*

Her gloves jammed in the trigger guard. She slipped them off and stuffed them into her pants pockets. The wood and metal of the pistol grip actually felt warm compared to the sleet.

The squat shadow turned the corner, outlined against orange streetlights. "You stupid ass," she whispered, "you just voted for the death penalty."

She crouched between the Dumpsters, took the two-handed stance she'd learned in the firearms course, and centered on the shadow's torso. Her senses switched into overdrive, and the world slowed down. Kill or be killed, just like the instructor said.

She wimped out. "Stop, or I'll shoot!"

The man kept coming. He didn't speed up, or slow down, or flinch, or anything. Was the sonuvabitch *deaf*? She aimed at the bricks across the alley and snapped the trigger as a warning shot.

Click.

Her belly froze. She hadn't checked the cylinder before tucking the gun in her pocket. Had Jo been frigging around with the gun, dry-firing in their apartment?

Her hands trembled as she flipped the cylinder open and saw the glint of cartridges. It was a goddamn dud. She'd never had a misfire before. She snapped the gun shut.

Click. Click.

Two more duds, centered on his chest. She ran the whole cylinder around again.

Click. Click. Click. Click. Click.

Clear in spite of the shadows, the man smiled in slow motion. He inhaled deeply through his nose, as if he had been tracking her by smell. His mouth opened and spouted gibberish.

*"Na gav aygul orsht. Ha an dorus foskulche."*

That's what her ears pulled out of the air. God only knew what he'd actually said. Maureen started to scream and found she couldn't. She started to throw the useless gun in his face and found she couldn't. The alley was nowhere near as dark as it had been a few seconds earlier.

The slow-motion unreality continued. The man had a face now, not just a shadow, and his eyes were fire under heavy brows and a mop of coarse black hair. What she had thought was the drape of an overcoat was his square body, short but muscled like a Bulgarian weight lifter. He radiated power and compulsion.

Maureen flashed back to childhood Sundays in church, and she grabbed the crucifix she wore as jewelry rather than a statement of faith. She started to mumble the "Our Father," offering it as a prayer against witchcraft.

The alley seemed as light as day, and the sleet had vanished from the air. Somebody must have dumped flowers in the trash because Maureen could smell them, lilacs or something sweet like that. The brick walls looked more like fieldstone masonry now, like the peasant cottages in Grandfather O'Brian's yellowed photographs of County Wicklow.

Something flashed in the end of the alley, and Maureen saw another man striding easily through the molasses-slow air. Steel mail rippled across his shoulders and swung heavily as he struck the dark man from behind. Gold crowned the second man's head over honey blond hair.

She'd stepped into a tale of knights and mages. Swords. Sorcery.

*Bullshit!*

Maureen gasped at the renewed sting of the sleet. The metal of her pistol burned cold. Shadows swirled in the darkness and resolved into one man standing and another stretched out at his feet. Her scream finally escaped into the storm, sounding more like the squeak of a mouse.

Steel flashed again, hacking at the fallen mugger. The light-haired man swung some kind of heavy bent knife, almost a short machete. Sour bile clawed at Maureen's throat, and her bladder burned like she was going to soak her pants.

A severed hand scuttled through the snow, sideways like a crab, searching for its wrist. Blood flowed black in the shadows. The meat-cleaver chunking seemed to go on forever. Her rescuer kicked something into the heaped snow across the alley, and Maureen gagged when she recognized it as a head. It hissed at her and clacked its teeth.

The light-haired man dropped his knife and pulled a can from his jacket, sprinkling something over the corpse. It writhed across the filthy snow and seemed to spit steam.

He looked up at her and nodded as if she'd asked a question.

"Lye," he said. "Drain cleaner. It prevents healing, blocks the tissues from connecting back together." His voice was bright and cheerful, with a faint accent she couldn't place. He sounded like a TV chef assembling lasagna.

The whole scene was insane. His teeth flashed a savage grin from the shadows, as if killing a man was a public service like emptying the rat traps in the basement laundry room of her apartment. Then his smile vanished as he stared at her shaking hands.

"You tried to fire that gun. Give it to me."

She hesitated and shrank back against the bricks.

"Quick, you fool! Killing him hasn't ended the danger!"

She handed him the .38.

He swung the cylinder open and spilled the duds into the nearest Dumpster, muttering something under his breath. Then he grabbed her wrist and dragged her around the corner onto the sidewalk. Two steps down the street, he slowed and took a deep breath, handing back the empty pistol.

"He stretched time for the cartridges. That's sloppy,

temporary. Never take shortcuts with your spells: Murphy's gonna bite you, every time."

Maureen's mind chased after the surreal concept of slowing the laws of physics. Her thoughts were punctuated by a muffled pop behind them. Two more followed after a short pause, then two more.

"What the *hell* was that?" she asked. "A .38 makes a lot more noise!"

"Not enough pressure. Smokeless powder just burns in the open air. You have to confine it for an explosion."

She shuddered and stared at her hand. Five cartridges in the cylinder . . .

He grabbed her wrist again and pulled her back to the entrance of the alley. The body still twitched in the slush, trying to push itself erect with the stumps of its arms, as if it was searching for its head. It couldn't balance and fell, again and again. Maureen slapped a hand across her mouth and turned away, desperate for a place to run, a place to hide.

"You need to watch." His voice was quiet but implacable. "You must never talk of this. You'll see why, in about a minute. That man did not belong in your world."

He turned her around. He didn't squeeze, didn't hurt, but she could feel the power in his grip and realized, with a shock, that he was built as solidly as the other man. He was immensely strong. Those hands gave her no choice.

What she had seen as chain mail was a gray anorak of tight-woven wool. Splattered blood glistened black in the reflected streetlights. The gold crown was a yellow ski cap, equally worn and stained. His pants looked like army surplus. He must be soaked. *She* was soaked, and she started to shiver with the cold rain and reaction. Her gaze darted around everywhere except at the slowing jerky spasms of the corpse.

Blue light flickered in the corner of her eye, and for an

instant she thought it was the flashers of a police car come to rescue her from this madness. The light strengthened and steadied. Terror snatched her breath again and froze her pulse.

It was the corpse.

It burned with a blue flame like gas, smokeless, with flashing tendrils of copper green or cobalt or strontium red like the flame test for salts in chem lab when she waved the platinum wire over the Bunsen burner. The alley filled with a quiet hiss and sizzle that must be the rain and the slush boiling, because she could feel the heat of the burning twenty feet away through the storm. Her mind locked on the horror, and she barely noticed when her rescuer let go of her.

Bits of flame showed her where the severed hands lay. A blue ball consumed the head and melted the snow bank across the alley. Liquid fire like gasoline floated on the water and licked up splashes of blood from pavement and wall. It even outlined her rescuer, eating the blood off his sweater and pants.

Flesh dissolved. Organs dissolved. Bones glowed into ash and hissed into the flowing water of the melting. The skull popped, spattering gouts of flaming skin and brain across the slush.

Acid rushed up from her belly, and Maureen vomited.

When she could see again, the alley was dark. Wisps of steam floated upward and vanished in the freezing rain. The only evidence of the fight, of her terror, of the corpse, was a scattering of holes melted through the snow to the brick pavement of the alley.

She staggered out into the pale orange light of the street. Her teeth chattered uncontrollably.

"You need warmth and light. I'll buy you a cup of coffee."

The voice startled her. She had forgotten about the

knight dressed like a street bum, out wandering in a storm.

She ought to scream and run. Part of her mind *was* screaming. But whenever he came close to her, she felt calm radiating from him like heat from a sunlamp. She remembered strength, and grace, and a sense of protection. She remembered a tantalizing smell.

"God, what the Mob would pay to be able to get rid of a body like that," she blurted. "Was that magic? Did you do that?"

"Define magic. That was spontaneous human combustion, well documented in scientific literature. Of course, the subject wasn't exactly human."

She staggered into a recessed doorway and squatted down, trying to clear her head. The apartment was at least a mile away. Maureen didn't think she could make it.

She needed coffee.

She needed warmth.

She needed explanations.

She stared up at the stranger. Silhouetted against the streetlights, he looked too damned similar to the man who had been following her. And he hadn't really answered her question. He had just killed . . . something. Something "not exactly human."

All the bone seemed to melt out of her legs and spine, and she huddled back against the doorway. Maureen's memories ran off with her, fleeing the alley. Buddy Johnson had looked like that. Squat, strong, hairy, broad nose and powerful jaws like the Christmas Nutcracker and a forehead that looked like the business end of a battering ram. Java Man walked the streets of coastal Maine. He grew up to play pro football. Brutal aggression fit in there. Steroid rage. He'd bought off a couple of rape and assault charges with his earnings.

Maureen shivered and curled tighter into her ball. She was suddenly ten years old, cold and wet and frightened, hiding from the neighborhood bully who insisted on playing "doctor" with her when he came over and Jo wasn't home yet. It *hurt*. Every time she met a man, she had to fight down *those* memories. She kept wishing Buddy Johnson was dead and buried along with her Barbie dolls and tap shoes.

Something touched her shoulder, and she flinched back. Words flowed around her, gentle, barely louder than the sleet rattling against the storefront glass. She shrank back into the deepest corner but felt implacable hands lift her and guide her back out into the storm.

"You need a chance to dry off and something hot inside you. There's an all-night coffee shop a few blocks from here."

Those were her own thoughts, pulled out of her head and spoken. The man knew what she needed. He wanted to help her. He was concerned. And now that he was close, she smelled him again. He was the first man she'd ever gotten close to, who smelled right. He smelled safe.

"Prefer. B-b-b-booze. Need. D-d-d-drink." Her teeth were chattering too fast for coherent speech.

The apparition in the yellow ski cap shook his head. "The only bar close to here is no place for a lady. Let me buy you coffee."

"S-s-strip joint. Next b-b-block. Open. Serve booze. Walk by it every n-n-night. Seen naked women b-b-before. M-m-mirror."

Besides, she was much too cold to be affected by the atmosphere of sex. And she was used to aggressive, wanton women. She lived with one.

# two

BRIAN THOUGHT HE'D just as soon skip anyplace calling itself The London *Derrière*. At least it had a vestibule, and the vestibule was warm. It was dirty, yes, with cracked and peeling wallpaper, water-stained ceiling, and a smell of unwashed bodies, but warm. It was also bright after the stormy streets, as if the management liked to get a good look at its customers before letting them in.

Oh, well. He'd seen worse in his many decades of soldiering for God and King. Bangkok came to mind, a place called Wong's in the Chinese slums where the bouncer carried an Uzi. He shook sleet out of his hair and gave himself a quick once-over for evidence of the brawl.

He couldn't see any blood—only a little dirty slush to show for his night's work. The burning and his own powers had cleaned up the gore.

Call it luck. Skill. Art. Mostly luck. Liam hadn't sensed him coming up behind. The bastard had been too busy concentrating on the woman and her gun.

Speaking of the woman . . . Brian finally got a good look at this distraction who had wandered into his shark hunt.

Thin. Medium short. Almost skinny, but you couldn't tell any figure under that drenched yellow ski jacket and soaked, baggy jeans.

She pulled off a green wool cap and revealed curly wet hair, burgundy red and cut short. Her eyes were green, and a cloud of freckles stood out like they were painted in dried blood across the white skin of a ghost.

Well, she had an excuse to look a little pale. Brian fed more Power to his calming spell, soothing her thoughts while wondering just how much of her memory he was going to have to edit. That was as tricky as playing around with primers, and he'd rather skip the process.

The bouncer at the inner door was also studying her as they dripped Maine winter all over his floor. Brian gave him a professional look-over and decided to behave. The guy was a little fat, but he could probably bench-press Brian with one hand.

The vault door shook his head. "I'm going to have to ask you for some ID, miss."

That was understandable. She looked like she was about seventeen, maybe one of those homeless waifs. That would explain why she was out after midnight with a .38 in her pocket. It'd be God's own joke if she'd been trying to mug Liam rather than the other way around. He reminded himself that he was in America, the Wild West, where people carried guns all the time.

She fumbled for her wallet and handed over her driver's license. Her fingers were still shaking from the cold or the shock or both. It made her look even younger and more afraid.

The bouncer looked at her, at her license picture, at her again. He took the license over to a light and peered at it carefully, shook his head, and then studied Brian for a moment before handing the bit of laminated Polaroid back to her.

"Kid, I'll give you a C-note if you tell me who did that for you. It's the best job I've ever seen."

"Department of M-m-motor Vehicles," she stuttered between her chattering teeth. "S-s-secretary of S-s-state Office."

"Yeah. And if you're twenty-eight, I'm the mayor of Boston."

The man opened the inner door and waved them through into a tunnel throbbing with canned techno-pop. Strobe flashes lit up the blue glow of a set of stairs leading down. Brian's instincts twitched, and he started looking for exit signs. Life had taught him the old rule of the fox: Always have at least three ways out of your den. He followed the girl down, warily.

*Girl,* he repeated, in his mind.

*Sixteen, seventeen,* he thought, *with an ID saying she's twenty-eight. What in hell has Liam been up to?* The Old One might have authored a list of sins as long as a hangman's rope, but random rape and mugging weren't on it.

*It doesn't really matter, after tonight. Now Mulvaney can sleep, in whatever grave he's found.* Brian felt tension drain out of his back, as if he'd dropped a burden he'd been carrying for years.

The stairs spilled them into a gloom of empty tables and stabbing theatrical spotlights. A fog of cigarette and cigar smoke warred with the tang of sweat and lust and spilled booze. It looked like a thin house: either a lousy show or the lousy weather. Probably both. There was one exit sign, floating in its red glow through the haze. And another. Plus the way he came in. Good.

The music pounded at him, squeezing just behind Brian's eyeballs. It was worse than firing his FAL full-auto on an indoor range. He scanned for the speakers of the sound system and steered the girl toward the corner farthest away. The table also had a clear view of all three exits. It was well away from the stage, but Brian didn't consider that a problem.

The dancer was totally nude except for an incongruous pair of ballerina's toe-shoes. Her body glistened with sweat or oil and jiggled in about five directions at once as she did various obscene things with her hips, but if *she* had ID saying she was twenty-eight, it would be about twenty years too young.

"How do they get away with this?"

Brian thought he'd been muttering to himself, well under the noise level, but he must have spoken louder than he thought.

"F-f-fix. Newspaper says, woman who owns this p-p-place, lives with a cop."

Her teeth were still chattering, even though the room felt hot after the winter storm. The house kept the furnace at full blast for the dancers.

The table sat right by a hissing radiator, and Brian thanked blind luck. Now he could get that soaked jacket off her and let the heat go to work while he figured out some explanations—ones he could sell whether they were true or not. He pulled out a chair for her and held the shoulders of her coat while she wriggled out of it.

Her body smell steamed up from the sweater underneath, and Brian's nostrils flared. Doors clicked open in his brain, and he felt as if someone had picked him up and moved him across a chessboard into an entirely new game. He suddenly knew why Liam had been stalking her.

Brian hung her coat on the radiator to dry and fumbled for a seat. His brain and his hormones tumbled over each other, racing along in overdrive as his mind followed tangled connections and his body responded to genes older than the human race.

*And* it explained her apparent age. Twenty-eight was still nearly a child, for her kind. . . .

A waitress wiggled her way toward them through the flashing strobes. A topless waitress, he noticed, wearing nothing but a pair of high heels and skintight purple Lycra pants that molded her legs and butt and showed no trace of a panty line.

"Get you anything?" The way she hung her painted breast just in front of Brian's nose, it looked like an open-ended offer. The joint was more than a bar . . . no cover charge for the show. They must make money the old-fashioned way.

"Coffee, if you've got it."

The waitress lifted an eyebrow. "Cost you as much as a drink. Four bucks."

"Irish coffee," the girl said. "Two. Make that doubles on the whiskey."

"Six bucks for the doubles."

The girl handed over a twenty. "Make it three of them and keep the change."

The waitress threaded her way back through the maze of empty tables. Brian's gaze dismissed her in its ceaseless prowl of the shadows: He wasn't all that interested in her or the dancer. This redheaded stranger, on the other hand . . .

And if she wasn't interested in *him*, she would still draw Liam's brothers, cousins, and nephews like moths to a pheromone trap. Did she realize it? Could he use her again . . . ?

The sound system was too loud for talk. He studied her in silence, as she soaked up heat and expanded from her knot of fear and cold. She could be pretty or even beautiful, if she made the effort. She definitely wasn't dressed for sex appeal, not with those loose jeans and baggy green sweater. Either she wore no makeup or a powerful understatement, and he hadn't caught any hint of perfume in that wash of her musky smell. He saw no rings, no jewelry except a crucifix.

She didn't know who she was, what powers she could summon.

Brian's thoughts spun, leading him nowhere. His only anchor was the need to watch the exits and the entry stair. Nobody declared truces in the ancient war he fought.

He had followed Liam. Someone could be following him.

The waitress reappeared from wherever the coffeepot lived. She set three steaming mugs in the center of the table, taking no sides in the division of three drinks between two people, eyed Brian, and aimed her breasts at him again as if firing a broadside from a frigate.

Brian wasn't interested. She shook her head at his lack of response, gave the redhead a searching stare as if trying to figure out what *she* had, and wound her way back through the tables again. Her rump twitched irritation at the wasted effort.

The girl swiveled around and poked through the pockets of her jacket, pulling out the .38 and a speed loader. Five fresh rounds clicked into the cylinder, and the gun disappeared under the table rather than back into her pocket. Suspicious little witch.

The noise stopped, and the dancer vanished through one of the exits. So. The blessed quiet meant it was time to use that tale he hadn't manufactured. The redhead had already inhaled half of one mug and sat there, one hand hidden, glaring at him with hard distrust.

"Okay, Galahad, talk! Who are you, who was that in the alley, and what *exactly* happened back there?"

Her attitude was reasonable, given what she'd just been through. However, if he spent any more time with her, he'd have to persuade her that firearms could be unreliable in the wrong company.

He kept his hands on the table and tried not to think

too much about where those chunks of lead were aimed. The ones he'd dumped in the trash had been hollow points—nasty little things.

Send her off on a tangent. "Pawn to Queen Four."

"Huh?"

"Chess. I just thought it was time to try a different opening."

She smiled. It was the first time he'd seen her smile. Granted, she hadn't had much reason. And then a shot of mischief flashed through her eyes, and she became a different person, a person he definitely wanted to know better.

She nodded and sipped her coffee. "Pawn to Queen Four."

"Pawn to Queen's Bishop Four."

*You haven't played mental chess since you were shivering in a captured Argie trench outside Port Stanley. Where have the years gone, since that Falklands balls-up? And why in hell did you try that as an icebreaker with this woman?* Sergeant Major Terence Mulvaney spoke up from Brian's memories, offering his sardonic digs as the price of a mug of tea in the regimental tent. Brian and the big Irishman had bled together in a dozen ugly little wars. Two Pendragons in the entire British army, and they'd both ended up in the SAS. . . .

"Pawn to King Three."

Ah. "Queen's Gambit Declined. It leads to interesting variations, but you're going to find yourself locked in a prison of your own pieces if you aren't careful. You must play a lot of chess, to even try it."

"Used to." Then the light went out of her eyes, and her face hardened again. "The rules never change. Your opponent stays safely on the other side of the table. And the action is purely mental." Her mouth clamped shut, and her eyes narrowed, as if she felt she'd let some secret loose.

It was Brian's turn to blink. *Take it easy, Captain Albion.*

*You've got a casualty here. Check the vital signs.* Those three sentences told him the woman had problems that went far beyond Liam. And then he laughed at himself.

*You're at least bright enough to recognize your own buttons, me laddie. You're hearing her say she needs a knight in shining armor, and your nose wants you to be the chosen champion. Engage your brain and switch the balls off-line.*

She seemed to shake a memory out of her eyes. "Who the *hell* are you and what the fuck's going on here? Did I walk onto a goddamn movie set?"

He winced at her language. "My name is Brian Albion. That was Liam in the alley. It wasn't a movie set, or a David Copperfield illusion. I hope Liam's dead now, although I really can't be sure, and I can't come up with any reason why you should believe me. That's up to you."

She sucked up the rest of her first coffee and started on a second. Maybe she intended to drink all three by herself. One hand stayed under the table. With the gun.

"Saying he's dead, saying you hope he's dead, doesn't tell me *shit*! What the hell happened back there?"

She had a lilt to her voice, slight but noticeable in spite of her anger and crude words. Third- or fourth-generation Irish, he guessed, from a close family where she would have talked a lot with the grandparents. She might have heard tales. . . .

Brian quietly claimed the last mug, guessing she'd at least growl at him rather than shooting him out of hand. Except first thing in the morning, most people won't kill you for taking their coffee. Besides, she didn't have a silencer.

"What did *you* see?"

She muttered something into her mug, then looked up at him. "It's crazy."

"I doubt it."

"That . . . Liam . . . came into the alley and things

started getting brighter, warmer, as if the sun was shining. It smelled good. There was some kind of round stone tower, like a castle."

Ah. "You're Irish, yes?"

She stared at him as if he had just sprouted an extra head. "Grandparents, yes. Some Scots on my father's side. What the hell has that got to do with anything?"

"He was taking you to Castle MacKenzie in the Summer Country. The British Isles have rain eight days out of seven. Trust the Celts to create a fantasy world where the sun is always shining and the wind is at your back."

"Jesus, Mary, and Joseph! Next, you'll be telling me he really *did* burn up when he died. Magic. You claim to do *that*, too?"

"No. Liam did it. The fire wasn't a spell so much as the ending of a spell. He cast it on himself before he came here, and kept it from happening as long as he was alive. When he died, the spell completed itself."

"Bull*shit*!"

Brian frowned. Maybe it was old-fashioned, but he didn't care for that kind of language from a woman. Un-ladylike. But then, he *was* old-fashioned. Or just plain *old*.

She finished up her mug and started eyeing his. She'd downed two doubles in less than ten minutes: equally un-ladylike. Brian slid his mug back to her. He'd gotten maybe three sips out of it.

"You said something about him not being really hu-man."

A drunken *cailín* pointing a gun at his balls did not make for smooth conversation. Brian tried a delicate nudge to her thoughts and relaxed slightly as her hand strayed back to the jacket and came away empty.

"Anybody ever tell you about the Old Ones?"

There was that two-headed look again, with a slight lack

of focus around the eyes. She didn't have a lot of body weight to absorb that much whiskey.

"You mean the Little People? Leprechauns, fairies, elves?"

*Oh, Lord.*

"No. The mages, the witches, the war wizards, Merlin and Gorlois and Morgan le Fay. Merlin was supposed to be the Devil's child. He was an Old One. So was Liam. Technically speaking, Liam was not *Homo sapiens*. That's why he traveled this world with a burning spell set on his body. It destroys the evidence, the bones that aren't exactly right. Cuts down on questions."

"Holy Mary, Mother of God. You are fucking crazy." She stared fuzzily down into the bottom of her last mug, disappointed with what she found there.

Call it five ounces of whiskey now, in fifteen minutes. Or a bit less, since they probably watered the drinks in this dive. That was still heavy input. Maybe the booze helped her to live in a world that belonged to another species. Brian grimaced in sympathy, but that was about all he could do. If she was lucky, she might live the rest of her life without one of *them* brushing by her on the street and smelling that sharp musky sweat.

Liam's blood had been nearly pure. He'd had no more choice in what he did than she had. Put the right scent on a trap, and even the wiliest animal loses all caution.

She looked up again, eyes totally unfocused. "Merlin," she whispered. "Arthur. Lancelot. *The Once and Future King.* Malory. Tennyson. Is that the Summer Country you're talking about?"

*Bloody hell!* Now she was going cloudy on him. Next thing, she'd be chanting "The Lady of Shalott."

"Don't get any warm-puppy feelings about this: The legend of Arthur has to be about the most depressing tale ever told in the English language. It's an endless stream of people you like doing their damnedest to doom themselves and knowing it every step of the way.

"Besides, with Liam you're looking at the other side. Mordred. Nimue. The tangled dysfunctional family of Clan Orkney. Pain for the fun of it."

Pain for the fun of it, like what Liam had done to Mulvaney seven years ago. Well, that debt was paid, although Liam's nasty little cousin still wove his traps. Wait a minute. . . . Maybe *Dougal* had been after this girl.

She started to hum a tune from *Camelot*. Even allowing her the twenty-eight years, she wasn't old enough to remember that show. He was. It had made him sick.

"Do they still hold tournaments in the Summer Country? I hung out with the S.C.A. in college, even learned to fence a bit. We held medieval banquets and mock duels."

Brian had swallowed enough fantasy for one night. "They have dungeons in the Summer Country. They have slaves in the Summer Country. Camelot is dead. Arthur is dead. Law is dead. Power rules."

He wondered how much of this was slipping past the alcohol. Time to get crude. "Liam had power. He wanted a woman, either for himself or for his master. He saw you and wanted you and was about to take you. For life. For rape. A bed slave to bear his children. You wouldn't get a vote. 'Women's Lib' never came to the Summer Country. A woman is either a sorceress or a slave. A bed slave while she is young and fertile and pretty, a drudge in the kitchen or farmyard afterward. Much the same is true for men, unless you have the Old Blood and the Power."

Brian stopped and realized he'd been ranting. Her mug was empty. He wanted a drink or two of his own, to settle his stomach. The next round was his. If she got too drunk, there were things he could do about it.

That waitress was what they wanted in the Summer

Country: a sex toy with no brain. Where the hell was she? His glance scouted the corners of the room.

A slim woman, dark-haired and dark-skinned, stood at the bottom of the entry stair. A man who could have been her twin held her arm. The gray-clad pair scanned the smoky room like a pair of elegant cobras, their expensively understated dress warping the strip club into a Parisian *demi-monde* cellar.

*Damn! Fiona and Sean. Here. Now. Bloody, bloody hell!*

Brian couldn't waste the time to figure out what *that* meant.

The redhead blinked fuzzily at him when he draped her coat over her shoulders and dragged her through the nearest exit. He turned and had a few words with the door, hoping the walls were stronger than they looked. They probably weren't.

Shouts echoed through the room behind them. Customers weren't allowed out back. Brian leaned a little harder on his control, and the girl finished shrugging her arms into the sleeves of her jacket. He slipped her gun out of her pocket before she could think about reaching for it.

*He* could make it work, if he had to, no matter what Fiona or Sean tried to say to the little grains of nitrocellulose.

He pulled her down the corridor past three curtains, dogleg right, up a flight of stairs flanked by flaking cinderblock walls to a door with a crash bar and one of those idiot red flags that said ALARM WILL SOUND. He held another quick discussion with locks and electrons.

They pushed through, not into the storm but into another passageway with doors and stairs and exit signs. The place was a bloody fire marshal's nightmare. The door clicked shut *without* an alarm, and he told it to be a good boy and stay closed. Not that Fiona or Sean couldn't also talk to locks. It would just take them a little while.

A dull thud shook the floor from below, probably Sean or Fiona showing off. That *did* trigger the alarms—electronic horns rather than the metallic snarl that would have been the door. Brian hauled the girl up another flight of stairs and slammed the door open with his hip, dragging her out into freezing rain. He'd expected stairs down, but they were in an alley. The place must be built into a slope.

Another alarm cut in, a mechanical ringing clatter overhead. A sign under it said SPRINKLER ALARM. That meant fire. Must have been Sean: Fiona tended to more subtlety. She wasn't less dangerous, just quieter about it.

*Rain,* he thought.

*Scent.*

Fiona would follow *him*. She wouldn't pay much attention to the girl's smell: wrong circuitry. And Sean wouldn't notice her, either, being what he was. Liam had been the one who'd tracked her.

He looked for water—rain and slush and the running gutters—things to kill his scent. He had to get the girl home without a fight. She was a deadweight, a drunk, a distraction. She'd almost gotten him caught down there.

Mental chess. Fiona was such a devious little bitch, twisting Dougal's plot to her own ends. The bloody girl had been bait for a trap, Fiona's own trap using Liam's hunt as cover.

He slowed down, the clamor of the alarms blocks behind them in the rainy darkness. Sirens wailed in the distance, stringing together the great braying horns of the fire trucks as they plowed through intersections against the lights, and he winced at the thought of a panic stop of one of those metal monsters on the ice and slush. At least there wasn't much traffic at this time of night. Or morning.

Maybe Fiona and Sean would get tangled up in that, get squashed flatter than bedbugs. Faint hope. They'd be more likely to wreck the truck. And Fiona had the persistence of a saint, even if nothing else about her was holy. *That* book wasn't closed.

He slipped the gun back into the girl's pocket. He had better ones. Then he smiled at her and turned on the charm. "You never told me *your* name."

She blinked back, still dizzy from the drinks and the run. "Mau-reen," she said, stumbling over pronouncing her own name. "Maureen Pierce. I don' know if Grandma'd call this a formal in-tro-duc-tion."

He took her hand and kissed it, gravely.

"I won't presume upon it."

Now, to adjust her feelings a little further . . . Any woman who could take what she'd been through and come back with Queen's Gambit Declined was someone he wanted to know better.

A touch of the glamour wouldn't hurt anybody.

# three

MAUREEN'S THOUGHTS REMINDED her of some of the test drugs the doctors had tried on her. She felt the same detached unreality, as if she were a normal woman walking home with a normal man after a normal night on the town. The sense of horror and terror had exhausted itself like a moth fluttering against a lighted window.

Only this strange man remained, a courtly knight guiding her to shelter from the storm. She'd never felt *protected* by a man before. They'd always been the threats.

*I'd like to invite him in. I'm afraid, but I'm not afraid of* him. *A normal woman would invite him in.*

Maureen repeated her mantra as they slogged the last block to her apartment. She ignored the faint voice that whispered fear of any man, that whispered of the fire and death behind them in the cold rain. The mantra shoved that voice back underwater and held it there to drown. She felt bewitched by this man, and by a longing her body hadn't felt outside of dreams.

The rain rattled on her jacket like dribbles of soft gravel, half sleet, still soaking in rather than just bouncing off.

She thought it was about the most miserable weather a
Maine winter could produce.

Brian's hand was warm through her sleeve, no gloves.
Maybe the same powers he'd used in the alley also protected
him against the shitty weather. Calm and safety seemed to
flow from his touch, almost like an electric current.

*A normal woman would invite him in—to chat, to warm up,
to have a cup of coffee or a drink. Not necessarily to stay the
night. It would be simple politeness, on a night like this.*

He was good-looking, quiet, strong, and he reacted fast.
He smelled right. He played Queen Pawn openings in his
head. He had saved her from *something*, tonight. Twice.

*A normal woman would invite him in.*

She swiped a curl of wet hair off her forehead as if it
was a fly tickling across her skin. Caffeine and alcohol tangled in her bloodstream and left her with a detached
twitching high that ignored little things like slush soaking
through her boots and icicles forming in her hair and a
three-alarm fire lighting up the downtown sky. Instead, she
paid attention to that warm hand on her arm and the fact
that he seemed content to keep a polite distance.

*A normal woman would invite him in.*

And her cynical inner commentator answered her in the
second person singular it always used. *You are not a normal
woman. A normal woman doesn't take a month of foreplay to
work up to a kiss. A normal woman doesn't feel like vomiting
from fear when a man comes within smelling range. A normal
woman doesn't keep waking up clammy with sweat, eighteen years
after that monster crushed her to the grass and forced pain between
her legs.*

And yet she wasn't doing any of these things. Maybe
the night's weirdness had burned out the necessary connections.

*A normal woman doesn't see a rapist in every man she meets.*

It wasn't *fair*. After enough psych classes to take a minor in college, she damn well knew what her problem was. That didn't solve it.

It hadn't "made a lesbian out of her," like some of the idiots she'd met might have said. Sexual attraction didn't work that way. Those strippers did nothing for her. She still dreamed about men—gentle men with gentle hands that never went anywhere without permission. She still would *really* like to find out what it meant, to do those things with somebody she loved.

And every time she tried, Buddy Johnson elbowed his way into the scene and tore up the script.

She dragged her thoughts out of the filthy slush. Even with all the crap running through her head, she could still find her way home in a storm. They were slogging across a gray-rutted parking lot full of white car-lumps, up to a three-story tenement with rotting balconies and cracked tan vinyl siding. Highland Apartments: the place she hung her hat.

*Yeah. Home is where the hat is, she thought. The world hasn't offered you too many places to leave your heart.*

Sometimes she wished she could *kill* that inner voice. She covered her turmoil by walking over to one mound of snow and kicking its bumper, hard. The wet snow slid off its hood, revealing a rusty green Toyota with, if memory served, 145,407 miles on the speedometer. She'd nick-named it Musashi, after the samurai who never took a bath. Up to now, it had been crude but reliable, like him. Judg-ing by this week, though, it might never turn 145,408.

"Sonuvabitch won't start." She kicked it again, and more snow slumped down off the roof to pile up against the wipers. There was also a metallic clunk that sounded like a piece of rotten tailpipe expiring. Classic rust bucket. It was all she could afford.

Brian sloshed through the puddles to her side. He leaned

over with hands flat on the hood, closed his eyes, and started muttering to himself.

Maureen shivered at the sight of his bare skin touching cold wet metal. *My God,* she thought, *he's just like one of those Southern preachers, laying on the hands. Faith healing. This man is seriously weird.*

"You've got a cracked distributor cap," he said, after about two minutes of communing with Jap steel. "It also needs a new air filter and new plugs, but the distributor cap is what's killing you. And remember to use the parking brake more: The cable's going to rust up and seize on you if you don't."

Bull*shit*! "You expect me to *believe* that? I've heard about wizard mechanics before, but at least they have to open the hood!"

He shrugged. "How else do you think the British Empire survived Lucas Electrics? It had to be magic 'cause it sure wasn't engineering." He straightened up and dug a rumpled scrap of paper out of his pocket.

"You should be able to start it in the morning. It won't last more than a couple of days, so you'd better get it fixed. This should cover it." She caught a glimpse of Ben Franklin in the streetlight's glow. A hundred-dollar bill.

"But . . ."

"I don't need it. You do." He shoved it into her pocket, next to the .38 Special.

Good-looking, quiet, strong, smart, reacted fast. And, apparently, rich. She hadn't seen a hundred in years. The Quick Shop wouldn't take them.

*Taking money from strange men, Maureen? Like those women in the club?* But her critic's voice sounded like it came from the far side of a brick wall, and the thought of comparing her life to an exotic dancer's or prostitute's almost made her laugh. The closest he'd come to making a pass at her was keeping her from falling on her butt when she'd slipped on a patch of ice.

"Why don't you come inside and dry off for a few minutes?"

Brian nodded, as if her question was totally normal instead of the summation of a formal debate. They stomped their way up the front steps, shaking off winter again like a pair of wet dogs. The outside door was never locked, and half the bulbs in the hallway were dead or stolen. A chill returned to the pit of her stomach, but all the shadows seemed to be empty.

Besides, Brian could protect her. He'd proven that.

She covered her fear by sniffing the wash of warm, damp air in the stairwell, her usual game of guessing who had what for dinner. It was the only use she'd ever found for a hypersensitive nose that could tell the difference between white and red oak by the smell of their leaves. Otherwise, a good nose was a liability in the city.

All the apartments had their kitchens near the stairs. First floor, pizza with mushrooms and pepperoni overpowered whatever the other unit had. Second floor east smelled like KFC again, and west had whipped up a pot of chili. West's cooking was a fire hazard, real five-alarm. They loved Cajun, Tex-Mex, Thai curries—anything to steam your eyeballs out. The couple had grown up in Jalisco.

Fires kindled in her head—dismembered chunks of body burning in the alley, flames exploding out of the cellar club. Old Ones. Summer Country. Hunters. Terror dragged her into myth: visions of sleek gray cobras, man-sized and spitting fire.

Maureen started to shake again.

Brian shifted his hand, circling his arm gently around her waist as they creaked up the stairs to the third floor. It felt safe, as if he was comforting her instead of putting on a move. A memory from Girl Scout camp floated up, a skilled trainer running her hands along the flank of a skittish horse, smoothing out the mane, talking quietly to calm the frightened animal.

The trainer's hands were magic. Brian would make a good trainer. His touch was gentle, reassuring. He had a feral, furry smell with a touch of acrid male to it, vaguely fox or skunk, unlike any other man she'd known. It roused a sense of rightness, weirdly soothing. It might not take her a month to kiss this man.

She fumbled with her keys, her fingers cold and shaky. A man she'd known for an hour or so, and she was letting him inside her apartment. One step from letting him inside her body. Magic hands.

"You say you're English?"

"British. Welsh ancestry, anyway. Most Yanks don't know the difference. England, Scotland, Wales, even Ireland, it's all the same to you."

"You don't have much of an accent."

"I spent a few years in a place where a British accent could be hazardous to my health. Yanks were more welcome. Habits change fast with incentives like that."

She flipped on the lights. The kitchen looked presentable for once: Jo hadn't left dinner dishes all over the place, with plates of petrified spaghetti sauce or gnawed chicken bones looking like the remains of a voodoo ceremony.

Maureen hung her jacket on the coatrack over the radiator. If the furnace didn't die again, even the quilted batting should be dried out by morning. Boots went in the tray, where drips couldn't spread across the floor and ambush her bare feet when she stumbled out to make breakfast. That was a *real* rude way to wake up.

"Get you a drink? We've got Scotch or Irish whiskey, rum, or brandy. Cup of tea, or I could make some coffee."

"Tea would be nice."

Such a prosaic end to such a surreal evening: tea for the British visitor. She set the kettle on the rear burner and cranked up the gas. It even lit. How novel.

"Uh, take a seat. I've got to powder my nose."

She'd drunk a *lot* of coffee in the last hour. Plus there was the question of that warmth she'd felt back in the alley. If she was thinking of letting a man inside her pants, they damn well ought to be clean.

Maureen blinked three times, shocked at her own thoughts. The farther she got away from Brian, the less sane the whole night seemed. Her fingers started to tremble with delayed reaction.

She almost tripped over a pair of black engineer's boots in the hallway, next to a battered hard-shell guitar case. Jo's door was shut.

*Shit!*

She stumbled to the end of the hall, past Jo's door and David's damn guitar, past her own door and into the john. She shut the door. Leaned her head against the cold mirror. Stared cross-eyed at the freckles that looked like they were painted on white paper.

The night's load of shit had totally driven David out of her mind. He'd been as close to a boyfriend as she'd ever found in years. She'd forgotten he would probably come over, after practice. And go to bed with Jo.

*Jo.*

*David.*

*Bedroom.*

*Goddamn whore.*

*Goddamn man.*

The teakettle whistled in the kitchen, snapping her out of her misery. She must have been leaning there for a couple of minutes. She wiped her eyes, blew her nose, flushed the toilet for camouflage.

Walking back past the bedroom door and the evidence,

a muffled giggle slapped her in the face. She heard bed-springs creaking.

Brian had shuffled around in the cabinets, had two mugs out and the box of Earl Grey. Now he waited for her to pour, like a gentleman. Maureen swallowed a scream.

"I think you'd better leave. I don't feel so good, all of a sudden."

He stood up and touched her cheek. She flinched.

"I understand. You've had a rough night. Try to get some sleep. Can I call you in the morning, make sure everything's alright?"

Maureen gritted her teeth, forcing herself to behave like a halfway-normal woman. "Phone's in my sister's name. I'll write it out for you."

She turned away, pulled a piece of paper off the phone pad, and scribbled against the refrigerator. She could feel his warmth behind her and squirmed away, practically crawling up on the kitchen counter.

Their fingers touched as she handed him the paper. She desperately wanted to wash her hands, scrub off the touch. *Goddamn nutcase. It isn't* his *fault!*

His eyes searched her face. "You don't mind if I call you? I can see you again?"

"Fine," she snapped. "Just leave. Call me in the morning. If you don't get out of here fast, I'm liable to puke on you."

"Maureen, what's wrong?"

"Nothing's wrong, goddammit! Just, if you come to see me, don't go to bed with my fucking sister!"

He backed away, and the door clicked between their faces. She set the bolt and chains and leaned her forehead against their metallic coldness. Her gut still churned its mix of hatred and longing. Half of her, mind and body, wanted to rip the door open and chase down the stairs after

him. The other half of her remembered his resemblance to
Buddy Johnson.

The kettle screamed on, behind her, and she turned to
shut off the gas. It subsided into a serpent's hiss, then
crackled quietly as it cooled.

She wondered how much Jo had heard, how much David
had heard. They were awake. Probably deaf to the world,
thinking any noises were the earth moving under their bed.
Then they'd try another position and see if the stars fell.

She put one of the cups away, grabbed a bottle, and filled
the other one. She gulped, and straight whiskey etched her
throat. She wanted to heave the bottle across the room,
watch the golden liquid splatter and hear the glass explode
into little transparent knives. Walk on them, cut her feet,
leave bloody footprints in the snow as she ran away into
the storm. Disappear into the night, into the cold, into the
sleep of winter.

She still had thoughts like that. One time in high
school, she'd stabbed a tattoo into her left arm with an art
pen and India ink. She ran her fingers over the faint scars
left by the cosmetic surgery. Self-mutilation, the shrinks
had called it, itemizing another symptom. They hadn't
liked what the message spelled out, either.

She took another swallow. Fire slid down her throat and
burned in her stomach. Maybe it would cauterize the
wounds.

Dammit, David had been *hers*!

She'd met him after a set when his neo-Celtic group
played in a local bookstore, for Chrissakes, worked up her
courage for a month, talked to him again and again. He
was thin. Quiet in a strange, intense way. Gentle. Patient.
Insane subtle sense of humor. Delicate strong guitar-spider
hands. An obsession with music that defused the whole
man/woman scene and made him safe.

Everything Buddy Johnson wasn't. Maureen had invested three months in letting David past her boundaries. He'd come over, and the three of them would talk music, and Maureen would chisel another brick free from the wall around her, working on opening a door. And Jo wiggled a finger in her sexy way and took him.

*Bitch.*

She stared down into her cup, following the patterns the whiskey traced along the surface of the porcelain.

Patterns. Jo wanted something, Jo took it. That was Jo—confidence personified. She took clothes, took books, took food from the refrigerator, took makeup. Sisters were supposed to share. They were the same size, same color, enough alike to look at, they might as well be twins. Only difference was Little Mo's screwed-up head.

It was all her own fault, anyway. She couldn't blame David. Two identical women, one with a psychic chastity belt and the other who'd drop her pants at noon in the middle of Haymarket Square. Which one would any normal man choose?

*Neither. A normal man would run away and hide from either of you.*

*You're drunk,* said the cup. *You're a drunk*, said her empty cup next to her nearly empty bottle.

*Come by it honestly,* answered Maureen. *Maureen's a weepy drunk. Jo's a sluttish drunk. Dad's a mean drunk. Grandpa O'Brian was a happy drunk.*

She remembered how her brain had pulled Grandpa's voice out of the night wind. Maybe that had been the connection. She thought she was twelve again and terror haunted her dreams and the only adult who would hug warmth into her sweat-chilled body in the middle of the night always smelled of Bushmills. Mom just clicked the beads of her rosary, and Dad was . . . Dad.

*Can't blame David. Can't blame Jo, either. Four years older. Made her fourteen at the start of everything. During the two years when It was going on, that four years made a world of difference. Difference between shit-your-pants terror and a kid turned loose in the toy store.*

Jo had been old enough for Buddy Johnson. She'd wanted sex with the single-minded passion she threw at any obsession. Mo hadn't. Simple as that.

*Buddy was your fault, too. You knew what he was going to do, after the first time. You could have stayed away from him.*

*And if you had told anybody what was going on, Jo would have caught it worse than Buddy. Dad would have killed her with that black leather strap, the one that drew bloody lines across your back.*

*Can't tell anybody: Dad, Mom, Father Donovan, the doctor, teachers, nobody. Never. You promised. Keep Jo out of trouble. Little Mo worships her big sister.*

*Can't tell the shrinks. They'd tell Dad, Mom, the cops, everybody. They'd have to. Can't even tell yourself. It never happened.*

*Lie. Play up the voices and delusions, they'll believe them. Turn the fear of men, the fear of your father, into paranoia to hide the real cause. Leave the real cause buried under the biggest rock you can find.*

Maureen stood up with the exaggerated care of a drunk who knows she's drunk. She put the bottle away, rinsed out her cup, and very deliberately finished up in the bathroom. She stared at the mirror and chuckled with an edge of hysteria. The mirror face grimaced back at her, bloodless and wide-eyed as a startled corpse.

*Those thoughts of letting a man into your pants: Some other woman did that. Not Maureen.*

Back in her bedroom, she peeled off her damp sweater and jeans and underclothes and tossed them with drunken carelessness until she crawled into bed naked. To hell with the open door. Maybe David would get up to pee in the middle of the night and forget which door was which. If she woke up in bed with a man, maybe nature would take its course.

Or maybe she'd kill herself.

The blankets gave no heat, and the sheets felt like they were woven from soft ice. Her body ached for a warm body next to it, someone to gently knead the terror out of her shoulders.

Bed squeaks whispered through the wall between her room and Jo's. She'd seen Jo in bed with a man before, seen her learning the tricks of her trade with Buddy back when the world was young and innocent. That woman'd do *anything*. No way Maureen would ever pry David away from her. And if Brian ever *did* call, Jo would take *him* away.

*Patterns.*

*If he comes back. Slap a man hard enough, he doesn't come back.*

She forced herself to relax, willing her eyelids to quit squeezing their way down through her cheekbones. *Count breaths. Visualize the calming light of a candle flame, an altar candle flickering at the feet of the Virgin. Concentrate. Chant your mantra. Trigger the relaxation response the shrinks taught you, the only thing they ever really did for you in all the sessions through all the years because you swore you'd never tell. Relax.*

The candle turned into flames gushing from the second-story windows over the strip club, then metamorphosed into blue ghost-lights licking a slush-filled alley clean. Her eyes snapped open, and she clamped her jaws to stop her chattering teeth. She was just coherent enough to recognize the symptoms of shock, and just suicidal enough to not care.

Jo's bed squeaked, again. Maureen grabbed a set of headphones from her bedside and blocked out the sounds. The caffeine still warred with the whiskey in her veins, and the whole shitty day left her twitching.

If sleep wouldn't come, she'd try music.

She punched the CD player and came up with Altan, a disk David had given her. They started in on "Pretty Peg," a Scottish reel she'd heard his group practicing once.

She ripped the headphones off and threw the portable player and phones and cables and all across the room. The whole load hit with a muffled thud, landing on something soft in the darkness. Angles and trajectories swirled through her head, and she came up with her bald-assed giant teddy bear, poor bedraggled refugee from her childhood. She couldn't have hit it on purpose if she'd tried.

Insane laughter bubbled up, and she locked her teeth against it. *You fucking idiot, you can't even make a tantrum work! Not with a bang but a whimper. Ought to crawl out and get the .38 and put five slugs through that damned CD. Then sit quietly and wait for the men in white coats to haul you away to the funny farm.*

Pills. Doc Frantz had given her some pills when she couldn't sort out her sleep patterns on the midnight shift. She'd gotten promoted to evenings before she'd used them up. Damned things would stun a horse. Double the dosage, and they even killed the nightmares. They were still on the bedside table.

Her fingers traced the overlapping paper labels on the bottle. Four or five of them, she remembered. They spelled out dosages and warnings. One said something like "Avoid alcohol while taking this medication."

*Screw that.*

She swallowed two pills, dry. Then she thought about night noises and took two more. She didn't want to wake up before David left. Before Jo left. Maybe not before Mo left.

The pills nibbled at her, inch by inch, until she floated away into swirling darkness.

# four

—⚏—

DOUGAL MACKENZIE FORCED himself to keep calm. He didn't jerk on the black leopard's collar. He didn't release it, either. Shadow was too valuable a beast to loose on a mage as wily as Sean. Fiona's pet brother wouldn't stroll into *this* forest without protection.

Instead, Dougal just stood there—a gnarled stringy gnome scarred by the fangs and claws of a thousand beasts. *I've had too much practice keeping calm with Sean and his elegant sister,* he snarled to himself. *When a thorn festers in your skin, you squeeze the wound to force it out. Just a little more patience, and I'll be ready to lance this boil.*

He breathed deeply and concentrated on the earthy smells of the wildwood. They helped him hold his temper, studying the trees and shadowy underbrush rather than Fiona's slim errand boy in gray turtleneck and slacks. The giant cat caught his mood, though. Dougal could feel the tension where dark fur pressed against his leg.

Shadow wanted to kill. His simple predator mind lived for these prowls through the forest—lived for warm blood on his tongue and bones crunching between his teeth.

"And you did *nothing*? The two of you did *nothing* while this Pendragon hacked Liam to pieces? Brian is as much a threat to you as he is to the rest of us! Common sense should have told you to kill the snake when you had the chance!" He glared at Sean, but held his temper. *I'll attack only when I'm sure of winning.*

The Forest of Castle MacKenzie was no place for a casual walk. Dougal had found it, molded it with his magic, and stocked it in the image of a far older and deadlier land. Some of the plants were nearly as dangerous as the animals. Even the bedrock was a living weapon—*his* weapon. If Sean strolled in, alone, to bring his news, his sister *must* have warded him.

"Fiona doesn't want him *dead*." Sean wrinkled his nose, then gave a smirking half-shrug—a feminine move that emphasized how much he resembled his twin sister.

They had the same intermediate height, moderate for a woman or smallish for a man, with slim muscles built for stamina rather than brute strength. Their faces could be masks from the same mold—dark, brooding eyes above high cheekbones, smooth dark skin that would look more natural on Crete than Galway Bay, a nose just short of sharpness. They were sensual predator's faces, dangerous on a woman and incongruous on a man.

Dougal pulled himself out of the anger. Standing in his forest, he couldn't afford such thoughts. Sunlight dappled the shaggy trunks and tangled underbrush, forming mysterious shadows and lumps that seemed to move in the corner of the eye: wild forest, forest with the teeth and claws and danger left in it. Civilization had never touched this forest. Dougal intended that it never would.

Dougal grunted. "So Fiona wasn't ready to move. I was. Your precious Pendragon ruined weeks of planning. My *next* plan is going to include killing him."

Shadow flicked his ears and licked his lips, staring at

Sean with hungry eyes. The cat had felt the thoughts of blood and death. Dougal read his body language clearly: The mutated leopard was thinking about a little snack. The beast-master squatted beside his creature and ran a soothing hand over the coarse fur. The sharp smell of male cat twitched his nostrils.

*Not yet,* his hands said. *This one does not make good prey. It is weak. It is not quick and challenging in its turns. You would find it a boring hunt, and the flesh is bland.*

Dougal stared into yellow eyes. *Wait,* he thought. *We will find a better hunt for you.*

One they were sure of winning. Survival in the Summer Country involved cold calculation as often as it did passionate violence.

Shadow settled at his feet, a sleek pool of ebony fur with coal black paw-print markings where the light touched just right. The cat started licking one paw and nipping gently around his fishhook claws, then lifted his gaze to meet Sean's—coldly weighing potential prey, measuring, thinking hunter's thoughts. Dougal's thoughts.

Sean watched all this with lazy confidence and shook his head. "Fiona wouldn't like that, you know. She'd be displeased if you killed Brian. She has plans for the little boy."

"*Plans?*" Dougal spat on the ground between them. "I had *plans*, too! Your fair-haired *boy* waded right into the middle of my plans and murdered Liam, and the two of you as much as helped him! I ought to string Fiona's ears around my neck for standing by and watching like it was two beasts fighting in a pit! Now she's saying I can't even take vengeance on the Sassenach who held the blade? Your bitch sister asks too much."

A sardonic smile answered him. "As the human children would say, anytime you're feeling froggy, just hop. You won't be troubling my sleep, much less Fiona's. And you'll have a hard time selling that Sassenach label in the Summer

Country. Brian's blood is as pure as yours or mine."

Dougal straightened up, resting his hand casually on his dagger. "Blood is one thing. Mind is another. The Pendragons have the Sassenach mind. Merlin taught them to believe in rules. Merlin taught them to believe in God and King and Parliament. Brian would bind iron chains around your wrists and ankles. Do you want to live like that?"

Sean's mocking smile hardened. "Fiona's plans won't leave Brian much room for God and King and Parliament. Just stay clear of him. Otherwise, my sister will be *most* displeased."

*Interesting,* thought Dougal. *He keeps talking about* Fiona's *plans. His* sister *will be most displeased.* Sean was always slipping little twists into his words, giving one sentence five different meanings. It sounded as if there might be a touch of brotherly dissent brewing, even the jealousy Dougal had noticed more than once before.

"And don't you have any plans of your own, friend Sean?"

"Oh, I like this plan." Sean's drawl carried a slight edge. "We've been playing tag with Brian since he was in diapers. This year, we've decided to win."

"And yet *she* doesn't want him dead. What does *she* want to do with him?"

The half-man shrugged, but a glint of hatred grew in his eyes. "You know Fiona, all scientific and modern. She has an experiment she wants to run."

The thought of being one of Fiona's *experiments* chilled Dougal. She had an evil reputation, even by the standards of the Summer Country. Rumor said that her house-rowan was all that remained of a former lover, showing his blood in the crimson berries. Rumor said that a web spun from human nerves tied her lands together, binding it to her touch.

Maybe she'd decided to make Brian a sentry spirit for

her land. Grind his body into a mush of DNA and spin the warrior genes out in a centrifuge, then splice them into every cell of every tree and sprig of grass around her cottage. She'd take the genetic engineering she stole from the humans and warp it to the uses of the Summer Country. That was the way her mind worked, passion ruled by a logic so cold as to make an iceberg seem like Tahiti.

All Dougal wanted to do was *kill* the bastard.

*Work on Sean's hidden anger. There's something about this that little Fiona's little brother doesn't like. Something more than usual.*

"And are you happy taking orders from your sister? Is your manhood so damaged you enjoy serving as a ladies' maid? What do *you* want to do with Brian?"

Sean's sudden glare made the cold hilt of the dagger feel *very* reassuring. Then the insolent smile was back.

"Touchy, touchy, Dougal me laddie. Killing Brian won't really ease your pain. We both know what the problem is between you and my lovely sister. You're the only man in the Summer Country she's never bedded, never shown the slightest interest in. You're too ugly for her or for any other woman. So you sit up on your hill and stare down at her cottage and wish. I'm surprised that cat isn't female."

Dougal tensed, then relaxed and smiled quietly. There was Fiona's trap: defensive spells wound around Sean, spells that could slip quietly into Dougal's forest without triggering his own defenses. But if Sean goaded him into an attack . . . then the counterstrike would come. Sparring with Sean or Fiona always seemed like that. Feints within feints within feints. Dougal's own magic worked in other directions.

But that would change. *I'll have the Pierce woman soon. She'll rival Fiona in power and beauty. When she's trained, there'll be some changes in the Summer Country.*

Malice sparkled in Sean's eyes. He'd seen the instant

when their trap edged on success, then the failure. "My sister sends her love and condolences with the news. Please *do* come and visit us. It's been *so* long since we had company for tea." He turned and strode off through the forest, ignoring Shadow.

Tea? Dougal wondered what would be in the cup, if he accepted their invitation. He doubted if it would be wholesome. When he had his woman, *then* they could pay a social call. *Her* magics were of Fiona's kind.

Just before Sean disappeared down the trail, he turned back. "We all know you like killing things. Look around for something else to soothe that itch. Stay away from Brian. Fiona wants him." He paused, and smiled. "Besides, I doubt if you could handle him alone. We can."

Then the gray form vanished between the trees. Dougal glared after him. Fiona's pet *had* touched a nerve. Dougal knew exactly why he both hated and feared the witch twins. Yes, Fiona had spurned him. She'd made the reasons clear, in her acid-tongued way.

Certain combinations of the Old One and human genes made the ogres of myth—the kobolds and Nibelungen and other twisted gnomes of earth and forest. Certain combinations made the fairies and the elves, the Sidhe, the fair people of light and air. The earth always desired the air, and the air always rejected and mocked the earth.

Shadow stirred. Dougal sensed restless energy in the bond between him and his killer. The cat was bored with these abstract problems. His was an immediate world built of the smells and sounds and dash of prey. Dougal had promised the cat a hunt.

"Yes, my friend. Your kill is near. It hides somewhere down below us. Wake up your nose, wake up your ears and eyes and instincts. Something is hiding in my forest, and you're the one to find it. You're the one to flush it from its den and kill it."

The cat's eyes glowed. Dougal touched Shadow's mind, placing a picture there: the track, the smell, the shape they hunted. The cat smiled back at him, his tail twitching in a slow snake-curve. Some kinds of game attracted Shadow more than others. This was his favorite.

"Ah, my laddie," he whispered. "You're black death, brought to my hand and tamed. Strange, isn't it, the love we have for deadly things, the love for owning and controlling them? So beautiful they are, so satisfying to loose them on our enemies. You wouldn't be half so fair if you fed on berries or on grass. It's death we love, as much as beauty."

This woman, she would be as beautiful and deadly as a hunting cat. She wasn't, now. She didn't know who she was, either as a woman or a weapon. He would mold her into the mate he needed. Control her weaknesses. Aim her fears. Build her strengths.

Once she was tamed and trained and brought to his bed, he would use her as a rapier to cut the new ways out of the Summer Country, extend his fief, strike his enemies like a thunderbolt out of the cloudless sky. Wipe out Fiona's neat checkerboard of fields and bring back the tangled dangerous wildwood that was the Summer Country's proper face, the face he loved.

And then there would be children, children of the Blood. They would be worth even more than the woman's powers—children with the blending of Old One and human blood, with all the abilities of both races.

She was his perfect mate.

"Not my equal," he whispered to the cat. "No woman is my equal. A woman's position is to serve, my beautiful assassin. To serve as you serve me."

The sister was little more than a prostitute even though her bloodlines were the same. He could never be contented with a whore. Bringing her to bed, controlling her, owning her, would not be a challenge. It would be like taming a chicken to peck corn from his hands. Someone else could have *her*.

Dougal needed a falcon for a mate.

He slipped the leash. Shadow flowed and became his namesake, a moving blackness among the other pools of black under the ancient trees. The two of them crept along the valley, searching through the tangled underbrush of the ridges and the laurel thickets along the clear limestone stream in the depths, testing the air for scent and the ground for tracks. Dougal let the tension and danger of the hunt, of the primitive, hostile forest, wash over him and take his spirit. Shadow lived for the hunt and the kill. So did his master. They became two bodies of one will. Then Dougal knelt and read a track, tracing the thin line of its edge in a single patch of carelessly printed moss.

This would have been the only trace of his prey, if he had been hunting by himself or with a normal cat. Shadow was not normal. Most cats hunt by sight and sound. They have good noses but rarely hunt by smell. Not Shadow. *He* would follow a scent through the brimstone fumes of hell.

"Yes," Dougal whispered, half in his mind. "Yes, my old friend. We have him. We have our poacher."

Dougal scratched the coarse fur between the ears, smoothing it into a slick pelt, then roughening it down to the roots and the fierce heat beneath. His hunters gave him the gift of friendship, of the intimacy that Fiona and the others denied him. Shadow, and the peregrine, and the others, they were Dougal's true lovers.

The Pierce woman would be another, far greater than any of them. Liam had said she even worshiped trees. She would understand his passion for the savage beauties of the wildwood.

"Go. Kill."

Shadow bounded along the line of the track, clearing

twenty feet at a leap, and vanished into the bushes. Dougal's finger traced the track again, a single bootprint in the moss.

Man, human, slave: The fugitive hadn't fled from Dougal's keep. The same beast-mastery that bound Shadow and the falcons also worked on humans. None of Dougal's slaves ever ran away. None of them ever turned on him, or disobeyed, once he'd finished training them.

That was Dougal's magic. That was his gift from the Blood. That would bind the woman to him, once she was brought from the land of humans to the Summer Country.

Thrashing burst out in the bushes ahead, followed by curses and a scream. Dougal pushed himself up from his crouch, straightening kinks in his spine and quietly wiping his hands. He could have moved as fast and deadly as the cat, but he didn't need to rush: Shadow could avoid any weapons a human slave might carry in the Summer Country. That was the other way the cat was more than a normal leopard. A brain sat behind those golden eyes.

Now Dougal smelled fear on the breeze, rank human sweat and blood tinged by thin, sour urine. Twigs snapped, and a scraping sound gave him a clear picture of fingernails clawing bark. Shadow coughed once, a snarling cat-curse followed by silence.

<Treed.>

The thought blossomed in Dougal's head. His smile grew broader. To flee a leopard into a tree . . .

Dougal could feel a plan forming. Shadow measured distances and angles, tensing muscles as his thoughts bounced to a low, heavy branch, then a higher one, switching back and forth and spinning like furred lightning until the frightened human twisted around and lost his grip and fell or dropped his spear. Then the kill would follow, and the hot rush of sweet blood.

<Do it!>

The image broke. Dougal didn't mind. He didn't need to see the details as they happened. The sounds and his bond with the forest gave him what he needed: the scratch of claw on bark, the thrashing leaves as a hundred pounds of cat sprang from ground to limb to limb, the scream of terror, the clatter of a wooden shaft falling to the ground, the crunching thud of a body following it.

There.

Shadow crouched under the tree, paws claiming his kill. His golden eyes blazed with bloodlust. Beast-master and beast read each other's thoughts, respectful.

The human lay twisted, leg broken by the fall. Deep fang wounds tore the throat where Shadow had made his killing bite. Dougal didn't recognize the man, but the Old One rarely paid much attention to slaves even in his own keep. They were fixtures, much like chairs or doors. He only noticed them when they didn't work.

Shadow inched away from the head of the corpse, keeping a possessive paw on the lower back. This meat belonged to him.

Dougal crouched, not looming over the cat and threatening his claim, and drew a short, heavy boning knife. Skill slid the point between two vertebrae and levered, snapping one bone loose from another. Sharp steel sliced through the tough cartilage, the tendons, muscles, arteries, and veins, until the head fell loose. The trophy was all *he* wanted from this kill. It would hang outside his keep, not important enough for a place of honor but a statement nonetheless.

Dougal glanced down at the headless corpse. He felt better about Liam, and the Pendragon, and Fiona, and Sean. The cat had settled down, both front paws pinning one leg to the ground as an anchor against the rip and pull of his jaws. Man flesh vanished in chunks, to the sound of crunching bone and a deep, satisfied purr like an idling diesel.

Dougal shook his head. One thing Fiona didn't understand, one thing none of them understood. It wasn't the killing that mattered to Dougal. It was controlling the killer.

The falcon, the cat, the other beasts, the woman: It was the control that mattered. It was molding them to his will.

"Yes, my love," he murmured to the cat. "I've trained you into what you are. Just like I'll train the woman. One such as Sean would take her with a glamour and expect to hold her. I know better. Her will must be changed. Changed into an extension of *my* will. Changed like you, my lovely one."

# five

—⁓—

SUNSHINE SPLINTERED OFF the ice, turning the
Maine woods into a kaleidoscope of prisms that flashed
with the slightest breeze. Blue sky, white ground, black
and brown and gray and lichen green of the mottled trunks,
all wove together into a world of crystalline beauty and
mystery.

Maureen contented herself with finding beauty in the
shadows; the sunbeams stabbed at her fading hangover.
Waking up, even her *teeth* had throbbed with her pulse.

"Very smart," she said to herself. "*Extremely* smart. Mixing booze and sleeping pills."

The sound of her footsteps crunched out into the hushed
forest and faded away. She barely sank into the crusted
snow, evidence of the cold front that had followed last
night's storm, coating everything with rippled glass. The
scattered pines and firs mixed in among the hardwoods
bent down like penitents under their coating, white and
stiff and crackling. Even their sharp sweet incense seemed
frozen or washed from the sky.

No other footprints marred the path into Carlysle

Woods this morning. Squirrels, snowshoe hares, birds—none of them were heavy enough to mark the hardened snow.

*A candid observer just might have called it suicide, girl. You know, for example, a shrink or the county coroner, they don't necessarily ask for a fucking note to be left behind. Do they, girl? Just ask if the deceased had been acting strange, depressed, had just suffered some personal loss? If they had a history of being, well,* disturbed? *In a clinical sense?*

She glared at a shelf fungus on the trunk of an old birch snag, daring it to talk back. The oyster-shell edge wore a necklace of glittering diamonds, the gift of the storm.

The forest wasn't interested in her problems. Some quirk of ownership had left it here, two miles from the rail yards of downtown Naskeag Falls, a patch of old-growth woods half a mile across and three times that in length. Surrounded by shopping malls, subdivisions, and the regional high school, laced by trails, it sheltered lovers and birdwatchers and the occasional poet.

The city owned it, now. On days like this, Maureen owned it. She had it to herself, sole proprietor. Possession was nine-tenths of the law.

She reached out and ran her fingers over the scaly bark of a hemlock, savoring the slowness of its winter thoughts. Owning a forest would be heaven—talking to the trees, guiding their growth and health, understanding the tangled relationships of all the plants and animals. Even before Buddy, she'd been more comfortable with trees than she had been with people.

*You would fucking think that a fucking honors graduate of the fucking forestry school could get a fucking job in the fucking forest industry in the state of fucking Maine.*

All she had to show for her degree was a degenerate vocabulary from hanging around in beer halls with the sexist-pig machos of the unemployed Forestry Club.

*Supply and demand. It doesn't matter that the sovereign state of Maine is something like 90 percent goddamn trees. Tree-raping paper companies aren't hiring. They don't need a professional forester to tell a woodcutter to nuke a hundred fucking acres.*

So Maureen Anne Pierce worked six to midnight at the Quick Shop and parked her skinny redheaded bod in a cheap two-bedroom apartment with Cynthia Josephine Pierce, similar description, because she couldn't even afford a set of bedbugs of her own, much less a goddamn car that started when she asked it to. Mo and Jo, the sister act.

It didn't help her self-esteem any that Big Sister earned more than twice as much as she did, *with* health insurance and benefits, out of her tech-school associate degree in computer drafting.

So much for education as an investment in her future. But that was Old Business on the agenda, not her current problem.

*Okay, Miz Psychiatrist, what's our next move? Back to square one in our habituation program? Treat our patient with gradually increasing doses of the phobia object? Have our acrophobic stand on a cushion, on a chair, a stepladder, increasing the height bit by bit until she can stare straight down into the Grand Canyon without a tremor? Until she can strip off her clothes and climb on top of a man of her own free will?*

She walked farther in, gradually relaxing, soaking up the silence and the privacy that the forest always gave her. She reached the patriarch beech she used as a signpost, with the hole twenty feet up where a limb had broken off decades ago. For three years now, a female barred owl had been roosting there and coveting small yappy dogs as their unknowing owners walked them on the paths below.

Maureen smiled at the thought and looked up. A faint patch of brown and gray lurked in the depths of the hole. The goddess Athena was home, resting from another night's hunting.

Carlysle Woods was Maureen's sacred grove. She felt like the owl bunkered in her hole, safe here from the mobbing crows of life. She walked among friends—trees and animals she trusted far more than she did any human.

The trees and elusive foxes had seen it all—birth and death, seduction and rape and simple friendship—the forest had seen that life went on, no matter what. Still, Maureen patted her pocket for the .38 she always carried with her. It no longer seemed quite as reliable a friend as it used to be, but she went with what she had.

She crunched her way over the ice, leaving the buried path for her own remembered route. It led across the ghost of a small stream, where summer raccoons washed food and left their dainty footprints in the mud, past a white pine old enough to remember Benedict Arnold's expedition to Quebec, deep into the heart of the woods and the ancient oak that ruled there.

*You know what they say, girl: A doctor who treats herself has a fool for a patient.*

Going to a shrink meant she would have to talk about It. Anything else would be a waste of time. She'd proven that. The oak was the only one she'd ever told about Buddy, about Jo, about Maureen and pain and fear. But she'd *promised* . . .

Besides, shrinks cost money. That hundred from Brian would have covered one session, max. It would take her that long just to fill out the forms. Quick Shop didn't have a health plan, and if they did, it wouldn't cover psychos, and even if it did, this was *definitely* a preexisting condition.

Ben Franklin and the empty speed loader: Those were the only evidence that last night had ever happened. David and Jo were gone when Maureen crawled out of bed, groping for the aspirin bottle. Even the breakfast dishes were drying in the rack.

But the car *had* started and the greasy-fingered mechanic

at the corner garage had found a crack in her distributor cap. He'd also replaced the plugs and the air cleaner. She'd had enough left over to buy a new bottle of Scotch and still have lunch.

Have lunch downtown. She grimaced. There were police barricades all around the smoking hulk of the strip club. Radio news said two women had died. Smoke inhalation. Trapped by jammed fire doors. Cause, probably an electrical fault.

She touched Father Oak. "Northern red oak," she recited to herself. "*Quercus rubra,* specimen tree approximately five-foot diameter breast height and seventy feet tall, struck by lightning about twenty years ago but apparently healthy."

He had already been recovering when Maureen first brought her troubles to him. She sometimes wondered if the lightning bolt had actually struck in the same year as Buddy Johnson. Maybe that was the bond she felt.

Maureen leaned her back against his rough bark and slumped down to squat on her heels. Strength. What Father Oak provided was strength. He could snatch the lightning from the heavens and channel it down his branching arms and give up a strip of bark more than a handspan wide and still survive. A little matter of nonconsensual prepubescent sex must seem trivial after that.

She loved this tree. He was everything her own father wasn't: quiet, strong, sheltering, nonjudgmental, sober. Father Oak would protect her. Father Oak was her friend. She talked to Father Oak. Sometimes He answered questions.

She had gone into forestry because of Father Oak, to return his love to him. Then she'd found out that Forestry, with the capital "F," was more concerned with killing trees than nurturing them. American forestry was an industrial process. It just asked how to get the most board feet of lumber, the largest yield in cords of pulp, in tons of fiber, per acre per year.

That was half the reason she worked at Quick Shop. The two job offers she'd had were as an overseer on the Paper Plantation, whip dem darkies if they don't meet quota.

Maureen shook her head at the memory. She reached into her other coat pocket and pulled out a hand-carved flute, double tubes of dark wood with a surface polished smooth by generations of fingers. She touch-traced the twining leaf-pattern of its decoration, feeling the warmth that had reached out and caressed her hand when she'd wandered into a Junque Shoppe on Martha's Vineyard. The tree that grew it must have had a dryad.

Smooth puffs of breath brought a gentle nontune from the flute—a scattering of paired notes floating out into the crystalline stillness like wind chimes in the icy branches. She never tried to play any music, not with this gift from Pan. As best as she could tell, it had come from Romania and wasn't tuned to a common scale.

The magic of the forest answered her. Jay notes floated back to her in a squeaky echo, the smooth blue-crested thieves gliding from tree to tree, telling her of the night's changes and any other gossip that touched their sense of mischief. Her trills broke delicate tinkles of ice loose to cascade from upper limbs as the sun touched them with its sudden thaw. Maureen conducted a concerto for forest and solo flute, lost in comfort and safety.

A shadow fell across her hands.

"I didn't know there were any Druids in Maine."

Maureen blinked against the sunlight. A slim, elegant woman stood on the ice in front of her, long dark hair in a straight cascade, dark eyes, skin that came from some-where on the Mediterranean. Her outfit of gray fur looked like it had just walked out of a Paris salon and molded itself to her body, and she obviously wasn't worried about animal-rights activists splashing ink on it. Her perfume spoke of dollars-per-gram and said the fur wasn't fake.

Hairs rose along the back of Maureen's neck. The woman hadn't made a sound as she approached, no crunch and squeak from the ice. Maureen couldn't see any footprints on the snow.

"I need to talk to you about my brother."

"Brother?" What the hell . . . ? Maureen had never seen this dingbat before. Or maybe . . . She had a hazy memory, twin shadows in the thick air of the club.

"I think he's calling himself Brian these days, Brian Albion. We saw you together last night."

Maureen's right hand fumbled in her pocket, slipping her finger into the trigger guard of the .38. *Anybody* connected with last night *wasn't* fun.

The woman flipped her hair back with one hand and laughed. "You won't be needing that thing, love. Believe me, I had *nothing* to do with Liam following you. We were following Brian. I know him better than you do. Don't trust him."

"Who the *hell* are you?"

"Fiona. Just Fiona. Most of us don't use second names where I live. There aren't that many of us, to need them. And I promise you we won't be missing Liam. He was a shit."

The obscenity grated in Maureen's ear, out of character with the woman's elegant bearing, out of character with the lilting voice so much a reminder of Grandfather O'Brian that Maureen found herself relaxing against her will.

She fought against the same sense of psychic Thorazine she'd felt the night before. "You burned down that night-club. Two people died."

Fiona shook her head and smiled. "Little Brian burned down the nightclub, love. He set a trap on the door, and it exploded when Sean went through. That started the fire, not us. Brian always was a touch careless with his spells. Ask *him* about how those fire doors got jammed. He doesn't worry much about mere humans. The holy ones never do."

Maureen blinked, distracted by the phrase. "Holy ones?"

"Yes, love. My darling brother is a monk, one of an order that's set itself the task of hunting down the likes of you and me. They've set themselves up as judge and jury and executioner of the Old Blood, in the name of Christ and all his angels. And they don't even see the irony of it. He's hunted the world for decades, under the cloak of various names and the uniform of a British soldier."

"A *monk?*"

"You've heard about the Templars, the Crusaders who protected pilgrims? Religious knights, delighted to separate any non-Christian head from its owner's neck? That's the Pendragons, love, in spades. They've even got their own monastery, tucked away in a dark corner of Wales where the neighbors think the rattle of machine guns is the British army practicing for peace."

"*Monks?*" She hated the stupidity of repeating herself, but Maureen felt the warmth of Brian's hand again and the confused sexual longing he'd aroused in her.

Fiona chuckled, maliciously, as if Maureen's thoughts had been written across her face. "Oh, they're not sworn to chastity, love. Just to obedience and violence. Violence against the Old Blood."

Maureen's thoughts shied away from the mention of chastity and the tangled path to which it led. She forced herself back to Fiona and danger—danger here and now. "He was warning me about Old Ones."

The woman sputtered with laughter. She caught her breath and shook her head again, the black hair swinging heavy across her shoulders.

"Oh, I love that duck! Brian *is* an Old One, dear. Ask

him his age, the next time you see him. Ask him his true name and his purpose in life. He'll probably tell the truth. Most of the Pendragons will. They just won't tell much of it. You have to pin them down."

*Holy Mary, Mother of God.* "Just what the *hell* is an Old One?"

Fiona's dark eyes sparkled in the sunlight. "My brother didn't tell you much, did he? The title means just what it says. The Old Ones are the original people of northern Europe. Scientists like to have everything neatly boxed and labeled, but some of those old skulls they dig up aren't either Neandertal or modern man. We're both and neither, love. The genes give us some interesting powers, including access to the Summer Country. Did Brian tell you why Liam was following you?"

Maureen gritted her teeth. "Something about taking me to this Summer Country."

"And he didn't say why that pea-brained lout would be interested in a random stranger, did he? He didn't say why you could even *reach* the Summer Country, did he? It's the same reason Brian's interested in you. You carry the Blood. You have the Power. You *are* an Old One, love. So much for fearing them."

Maureen decided that "love" was going to get tiresome if she heard it about three times more. Particularly since Fiona loaded it with an edge that turned it into sarcasm.

Maureen was suddenly conscious of the oak bark pressed against the back of her scalp. Looking up, leaning against the tree, the ragged lichen and corrugated bark snagged her hair. She smelled the dry sharpness of Father Oak protecting her, and it drew her back into the moment.

She still squatted against the tree, glad of its support. *Help me, Father Oak,* she prayed, silently. *I'm drifting into dangerous dreams again.* "Old One?" she added, out loud. "I don't look a bit like Brian, like that Liam creature. I don't look like a Neandertal."

"Neither do I, love. Neither do I. Old Ones show sexual dimorphism. Men are big and hairy; women are small and smooth. Goes for humans, too. We're crossbreeds. Hybrids. I *guarantee* you have the Blood. Otherwise, Liam and my beloved brother wouldn't be sniffing around you. I use the phrase literally. You have an effect on them like doe urine on a buck in rut."

Brother. "You and Brian. He's light. You're dark. Not just size."

"Different mothers, love. Same father. Kind of a hit-and-run man, if you know what I mean. It's an old family trait. You didn't find yourself behaving a bit *oddly*, last night?"

Maureen blushed so hard she imagined steam rising from her cap. Oddly was a polite way of putting it.

"It's called a glamour, love. My darling brother was tampering with your head. I don't think he did any permanent damage, but you have been warned."

Maureen felt her blush fade into white rage. She bounced to her feet. Her fists started to clench, and she jerked her right hand out of her pocket before she did *something* with the pistol and blew a hole in her jacket.

*I'll flat-ass* kill *that bastard*!

Besides, Fiona could probably hex the cartridges, just like Liam. It was time to buy a switchblade, or find Granny's old hatpin. She focused her anger. "What the hell do they want with *me*? Don't you have women in this goddamned Summer Country?"

Fiona shook her head. "Hybrids, love. Hybrids. You don't breed mules to mules, to get more mules. There aren't many of us, and most of us are sterile. I'm not. You're not. You write it on the wind. Believe me, dear, it gives you a lot of power. You can make a man do anything you want."

Jesus, Mary, and Joseph! *That* was just what little Maureen needed to go with her tangled sexuality. Talk about sending mixed signals!

"This sterile thing, it goes for men, too?"

"Most. Brian isn't. Liam wasn't. I'm afraid my little pet Sean is, no matter how much he might be wishing that he were not. He still has his uses, though."

*And Brian had the gall to talk about Liam's seeing me as a womb. . . . I'll murder that bastard! I'll stake him out on an anthill in the sun! I'll . . . To tamper with my brain!*

She needed to get away from *that* subject, fast. "Why are you telling me all this? How can I tell if you're lying?"

Fiona laughed again, and her voice turned dry. "Rational self-interest, love. If you know what you are, the rest of us are better off. Less disruption. There's lots of empty land in the Summer Country. We aren't that exclusive."

"Just what the *hell* is this Summer Country of yours? Why should I be interested in it?"

Fiona smiled a Mona Lisa enigma, seasoned with a touch of innocent malice. "Ah, the Summer Country. Alternate reality, love. It's two steps away from you, in any direction. It's what you make it be. It's where I come from, this crystal morning, and it's where I'm going back.

"Think of it as clay on the potter's wheel and you the potter. I have a house there, with gardens ever blooming in the summer afternoon. It's restful when the winter glooms too heavy." She smiled, with a gesture at the ice.

"Another of us keeps hawks and hounds and great hunting cats. For Dougal, life's a sharp thing, full of musk and blood and the threat of sudden death. The Summer Country's what you make it be, love. Sometimes we talk, we drink, we dance. Sometimes we fight. Carve out a space and build the world you want. All it takes is the Blood and Will. You've got the one. Do you have the other?"

Maureen shook her head. It all sounded like absurd escapism, and she wondered if she could believe a word this figment of schizophrenia was saying.

"Why should Ireland follow me here, find me in Maine? Shouldn't we touch the Happy Hunting Ground or whatever the local Abenaki use to take its place? Shouldn't *that* be the blood that matters?"

"Each people has its own world, love, its own spirit land, its place to follow the shaman's talking drum. There are hundreds of them. We only lose them when we try to follow the myths of another blood, when we lose touch with our roots. Why should the ghosts of the Sea of Galilee speak to the people of the Hebrides and Galway Bay? Why should my blood hear the voice of the Buddha? He spoke under different trees and suns and skies. He walked a different earth."

Maureen thought of voices and of lands. "I don't speak Gaelic. The most I know of Irish lore is a few children's tales and songs from my grandfather. I'd never fit in there."

Fiona laughed.

"Don't be for worrying, love," her voice went on, lilting. "The Summer Country changes as the world it touches changes. We're not Brigadoon or Shangri-La, to stay the same while centuries pass outside.

"Do you think we fight the Formorians all day long and sit around all night telling the *Táin Bó Cúalnge*? That you need to know every tale of the Fionn Mac Cuhal, to fit in? That you have to have the Erse? Don't be for worrying. The land translates for you. If it didn't, the Scots would nae be speaking to the Welsh and the Welsh couldn't speak to the Irish and the Bretons couldn't talk to the lot of them. Because all of us are forsaken pagans and damned to old Jehovah's hell, the curse of Babel hasn't fallen on the Summer Country."

Brian had warned her against the Summer Country. Brian, the bastard. Brian, the rapist of her mind.

"Your brother seemed to think the Summer Country is dangerous."

"Of course it's dangerous, love. New York and L. A. are dangerous, too, but that doesn't stop a lot of people from wanting to live there." The dark woman smiled and shook her head at the follies of the world. "*Life* is dangerous. Are you preferring death, so to be safe?"

Fiona shrugged, and went on. "The dangers are the ones we bring with us, the ones we choose to take. Dougal chooses to tame killers to follow him on a leash, to sit on his wrist and take chicken wings from his hand. I train gardens to trap strangers, knowing they might someday trap me instead. Would you rather face a Mack truck than a dragon? At least you can kill the dragon."

Maureen sighed and shook her head. That talk of preferring the safety of death cut too close for comfort. "You never answered me, about lying. Why should I believe you? Why should I trust you?"

"I'm not trying to sell you anything, love. I'll tell you, flat out: Yes, I lie. Whenever it's convenient. Why should I always tell the truth? Do I owe the truth to people who only seek it as a reason to hunt me down and kill me? No way, love!"

"That's getting a bit thick, isn't it? Kill you?"

"What did Brian do last night? He killed a man, attacking from behind. Killed without warning. Had Liam hurt you, threatened you, even touched you? Brian's the one who cast a glamour on you! All Liam did was stop you from shooting him."

The dark woman swept her hair back again, this time with an angry flip. "Beyond that, ask yourself about witches. Ask yourself about drowning, and stoning, and hanging, and burning at the stake. Ask yourself about what always happens to a woman with the Power. And remember, you are one of us! You can join us anytime you want."

She turned away. Maureen blinked, and the woman was gone. No tracks. Two steps in any direction, she had said.

Maureen suddenly noticed that her fingers ached with cold. She blew on them, flexed them, and slipped them back into her gloves. She dusted lichen off her butt. The ice-coated trees crackled with the passing wind. She walked out, unseeing, through her crystal palace, chewing at a fabric of impossibilities and lies.

*Magic.*
*Mystery.*
*Glamours.*
*God . . . damn . . . Brian!*

# SIX

—ɯ—

"Hello?"

"Hi, Mom, it's Jo."

The phone sputtered like an AM radio, nearly drowning out her mother's voice. She could hang up and try again, or just put up with it. That was the famous Verizon service: It cost more to call Lewiston than Seattle, thanks to the jacked-up in-state long-distance charges. And then she still couldn't get a decent connection.

"Everything okay there?"

Mom's generation assumed a long-distance call meant somebody was dead or dying. Otherwise, you'd write.

"Yeah, sure, I'm fine. How's Dad?"

The pause hung over the line, at about a buck a minute. So Dad wasn't fine. Or he was *too* fine, in Mom's opinion.

"He's off on another business trip. You know how this new job is."

Yeah. Days in sales offices, evenings in bars, nights in hotel rooms with the random whore. Jo thought that if Mom gave him what he needed at home, he wouldn't drink as much, sleep around as much. But he'd still hit her. The more things changed . . .

"Mom, it's about Maureen."

Now the silence was deafening. She'd better bull right ahead with it, get it over with. As if she didn't know *exactly* how it would end.

"She's talking to trees again."

Jo heard more crackling and a whining hiss like a B-grade sci-fi movie.

"Mom, you still there?"

"Yes, honey. I don't know what to say. You know she's always been different."

Jo shook her head. Different was *one* way to put it. Paranoid schizophrenia also came to mind.

"Mom, she was dead drunk, passed out half in her bed when I left for work this morning. When I came back, she'd been out to the woods and talked to her sacred grove. She hit me with another one of her rants. *You* know how she shoots off her mouth when she's having one of her spells. This time she threw in some crap about witches following her around, even told me a wizard had laid his hands on that junk Toyota of hers and told her how to fix it. I think she's been mixing her drugs again. You see about that fire last night?"

"Oh, dear. Was she downtown when that broke out?"

"Says she was there when it happened, a goddamn *strip* club! Says it was started by a battle between warlocks."

"Oh."

That was it, just the single syllable. It might be the understatement of the year.

"Mom, I'm scared. David stayed over again last night. Now she's ranting and raving about how I stole her boyfriend. You know how she is about men."

Silence, again. Jo squared her shoulders as if facing a firing squad, waiting for Catholic Mom Lecture Number 25.

"Jo, you shouldn't let a man stay overnight. It's a sin.

Sex is for marriage, for children. Have you gone to confession?"

"*Mom!*"

"Dear, I'm worried about you."

"Worry about Maureen. You know that damned gun Dad got for her? She carries it everywhere she goes. Loaded. God above, I swear she takes it to the shower with her. Why'n hell did Dad ever give that thing to her?"

"Jo, you know he wants her to be safe. She was working nights . . ."

"Mom, just how safe do you think life is, behind bars in the Women's Center down at Pownal? How safe is it in the maximum-security wing over at the crazy house? She's going to shoot somebody, and I'm sure as hell *not* going to jail to keep an eye on her!"

"Jo, you shouldn't swear like that."

Jo shook her head. If Mom ever heard sweet little Maureen's language . . . You'd think she'd trained in longshoreman's school, spent four years in the army rather than in college.

"Look, Momma, Maureen is *nuts*! We all know that. She's dangerous. Can't we get her into treatment again? Make her take that new medicine? I tell you, I'm scared of her. Next time she starts in on me, I'm going to kick her out of here. Before she shoots *me*."

Jo listened to Verizon static for about a minute.

"Jo?"

"Yes."

"Jo, you know we can't force her into treatment. She's an adult. I can't control her anymore. Do you want me meddling in *your* life? I don't approve of the way you live, either. Please, keep an eye on your sister. Please?"

Jo sighed.

"Mom, how many clinics has she been in? How many different psychiatrists and faith healers and just plain quacks has she seen? Not a damn one of them has helped. And you want *me* to straighten her out?"

"Jo, please?"

"Momma, I've been watching out for Maureen for twenty years. I went to tech school. She went to college. I've got a good job. She works part-time for minimum wage. I pay the rent and utilities. She sometimes buys food. More often, she buys whiskey. She practically pees her pants if a man comes within twenty feet of her, but when I meet a guy I'd maybe like to marry, she accuses me of stealing him from her. I've just about *had* it with my baby sister! When do I get to have a life?"

Silence filled the wires again. Jo chewed on her lip until her mother's voice came back, weary with the distance.

"Jo, God gives us burdens to carry. Your father is mine. Maureen is yours. All I can say is, pray for strength. She won't be heavier than you can carry. Good will come of it."

"Momma, I'm just about ready to tell God to carry his own sack of groceries. And if Dad hits you again, I'd suggest you do the same."

"*Jo!*"

"Sorry, Momma, but that's the way it is. I've had it. She's your crazy daughter, not mine."

Jo bit off her next words and hung up. She stared at the instrument, sitting all innocent on the kitchen counter. You could talk all you want, but that didn't mean you'd communicate. It was the main reason why she only talked to her mother about once a month—a kind of predictable catharsis.

Sometimes she thought Momma's delusions seemed worse than Maureen's. Married since seventeen to a drunken, abusive brute who cheated on her every chance he got, and she chewed out Jo for insisting on a test drive before she got serious about a new man. Hell, Dad was probably at the root of half of Maureen's troubles. "Man" equaled "Pain."

And all that treatment their parents had paid for was private, the soul of discretion, no records without a court order. It left nothing to show up on a background check. The little twit could lie when she went for her gun permit.

God.

Jo shook her head. She wouldn't kick her baby sister out. She *couldn't.* Stone-ass crazy or not, Maureen was the only family Jo cared about. Some ways, Mo was still the five-year-old redheaded mirror with smudged cheeks and scraped knees climbing trees and babbling about what the wind in the leaves was telling her. She was still the warm body sitting snuggled up against her older sister while Grandpa told stories he had heard from *his* grandpa, the scared voice in the darkness during thunderstorms when they had shared a room. Maureen had never grown up.

The hell of it was, between these "episodes" they got along as well as sisters ever did. Some of Maureen's spaced-out fantasy world might even be fun. Not the part that had her carrying a gun, or the part that called a phallus a torture instrument.

Those had come early, she knew, prepuberty. 'Way back as far as Buddy Johnson. Whenever Jo brought a boy home, Maureen would cringe away. *That* fear went back as far as Jo's enthusiasm the other way.

But Jo thought she wouldn't mind a world in which the trees talked, in which Grandpa O'Brian's Bean Sidhe howled for the death of a wicked chieftain, in which the Puca drummed his hooves three times on the hillside and a door opened down into the realm of the fairies. It sounded like a nice place to visit.

And the Lurikeen's everlasting pot of gold would be useful as hell.

Fat chance of that. Well, maybe Maureen could just vanish under the Sidhe hill for a night and come back ten years later. Cured. As much as Jo loved her sister, some problems didn't *have* acceptable solutions.

Others did. She picked up the phone again.

Five rings, and a groggy voice answered. A groggy, *male* voice, grunting, and she felt warm all over.

"David?"

"Uh."

"What the hell you doing still in bed?"

"Gotta sleep sometime."

"I didn't get any more sleep than you did, and *I'm* up. Put in a full day at the office, even."

"Um. Takes more out of a man. We give out, you take in. Hard work."

"Look, Maureen's pissed."

"Wha' about?"

"Us. Last night. She still thinks I stole you from her."

"Got no cause. Why last night? Not our first time."

"Wake up, damn you. Maureen's funny that way, you've got to rub her nose in it about five times. She still hoped you were coming over to see *her*."

Sounds of movement came over the phone: a crash of something knocked over, muttered cussing, a few coughs. *Homo sapiens* became vertical on the far end of the line. It had taken the human race a million years or so. There was no reason to expect it would get easier on a daily basis.

"Jo, let me get my head together. Your sister thought I used to be interested in *her*?"

"The man is slow, but it sinks in after a while. Now she's throwing things and foaming at the mouth. You got any suggestions?"

"Jesus."

"He ain't available. Try again."

The phone line crackled, and this time it wasn't long-distance. The noise had to be in the local system—Alexander Graham Bell must have installed the damned wires himself, back in 1883. And done a lousy job of it.

"Jo, I swear I never gave her cause. We talked music and Irish legends. Closest I ever got to her was touching her hand across the table."

Jo sighed. "You don't know Maureen. Holding hands is the equivalent of unprotected sex, to her. I'm surprised she didn't ask you for a blood test. She's scared of men."

"Oh, Lord."

She listened to line noise for a minute, wondering if David was calculating the genetic odds on hereditary insanity passed to any hypothetical children of any hypothetical future union of the Marx and Pierce bloodlines. He wouldn't be the first man scared off by exposure to her crazy sister. Used to be, people kept their skeletons locked up decently in an asylum. Jo had to *live* with hers.

"Jo?"

"Right here."

"Look, I'm not going to give up seeing you just because your sister's screwed up. We can't sleep together over here, five guys living in an open loft. I don't think you're interested in that big an audience."

She giggled. "I don't know. Performance art is big these days. Maybe we could sell tickets."

"Bullshit. Jo, I'll talk to her, try to smooth it over. Look, we've got a gig tonight, down at The Cave. Why don't both of you come over and we can sit out a set. Tell her it's not her fault, not your fault, not *anybody's* fault. She might not throw a scene in public. Look, she's a nice kid, but I'm not interested in hauling that kind of baggage around for the rest of my life."

"You and me both, lover. You and me both." She swallowed the rest of her comments. "I'll try. Maureen's not all that rational."

"I'd noticed. See you tonight. *Manim astheee hu.*"

"Yeah, and my soul's within yours, too. Cut the blarney, you fake Irishman. You know ten words of Gaelic, and five of those are mispronounced. Damn good thing *Dé hAoine* doesn't ask you to sing for them."

"Hey, Marx is a fine old name of ancient Eiru. The group just doesn't ask me to sing 'cause they're jealous of my voice."

"Like I'm jealous of Maureen's way with men."

Jo hung up and stared at the phone again. She felt warm just from talking to him. Maybe David was The One.

She thought The Cave was a good suggestion. It called itself chemical-free, which was a euphemism for drug-free, which was a euphemism for alcohol- and tobacco-free. God knows, they served coffee. She could use a little of that particular psychoactive alkaloid right now.

She'd made fun of David, still asleep at four in the afternoon, but she felt drained. And a little sore in assorted private places. And very, very happy with *some* portions of her life.

So what if Maureen was mad? Mad Maureen was mad. It had a certain symmetry.

The phone bleeped, quietly, an electronic purr intruding into her thoughts. It was probably Mom calling back, not about to let her own daughter get in the last word of an argument. Either that, or one of those click-and-an-empty-line calls she guessed was a computerized dialer that had hooked another fish first.

The phone insisted.

"Hello?"

"Maureen?"

"No, this is Jo. Maureen's out, right now. Can I take a message?"

"Uh, this is Brian, Brian Albion. I walked her home last night, and I wanted to check to see everything was okay. She wasn't feeling well when I left."

Jo filled in the words he didn't say. Like, she was stone drunk, and he wasn't sure she could find the pot.

"You the guy who told her how to fix her Toyota?"

"Yeah. When a car like that refuses to start in wet weather, it's usually the ignition."

He sounded saner than she'd figured, from Maureen's rant. So much for witches and warlocks.

"Well, you were right. She's out driving it now."

Jo paused, gears starting to mesh and turn in her head.

"She won't be back for an hour or so, I guess. She really didn't say. Give me your number and I'll tell her you called."

"Uh, I'm going out again. Maybe I'll call back later."

Meaning he didn't have a phone and was calling from the bus station. Or was married. She'd heard *that* one before. Still, he could serve as a diversion.

"Try about six or six-thirty. We usually eat around then, and she doesn't like to miss the news. We'll probably be going out again later."

"Okay, I'll do that. You're sure she's fine? She was acting a little strange last night."

"Brian, Maureen always acts a little strange. That's who she is. She said some nice things about you, though. That car has been a bitch."

All true statements. Thus she washed her hands of his future problems. It was time to cast a fly over the trout.

"Uh, Brian? Do you like Celtic music?"

"Yes, if it's good. More the traditional performances than the modern fusion stuff, I guess."

"So does Maureen. That's where we're going tonight, a place called The Cave. I think she wants to talk to you. Be polite, and she might invite you along."

"Thanks."

She set the phone down and stared at it. Interesting. So

that was a Welsh mage. He sounded like a normal human being, worse luck for him.

Jo had been raised to believe in lightning rods. Based on a random sample of Maureen's comments, this Brian character could be in for a rough evening. And it was just the sort of thing Maureen would do, meeting the poor bastard in public. The Cave could be a safe chance to sort things out.

Whatever.

That was *his* problem. *If* he came along, Maureen might not spit quite as much venom. She could calm down even faster than she blew up. Hell, supply a substitute, and she might not kick and scream at her "loss" of David, might even start to realize she'd never had him in the first place. Just inviting a man back to the apartment once didn't give her ownership.

Put her and this Brian character together in a public place, Maureen would probably act normal. Jo had seen it happen before. The paranoia seemed to be a one-on-one thing.

And maybe the magic of the fairies would work where modern psychiatric medicine fell short. A man who could faith-heal a Toyota might sort out the tangled web of Maureen's brain.

Or maybe he was just as far around the corner and would never notice.

Whatever.

*If* they could ever get Maureen's head sorted out, the next question was cutting back on her drinking. God help her if they tried to work on both at once.

One problem at a time.

She *couldn't* throw Maureen out. It would be like kicking a puppy.

A puppy with a .38 Special.

# seven

—〜〜—

DÉ HAOINE. IT meant Friday in Irish Gaelic. Brian thought it wasn't a bad name for a Celtic garage band. The group's lead singer had explained it in his opening spiel: Friday had been the only night the band could practice when they'd first started playing together, so the name just sort of stuck—the Friday group.

The Cave was also a fitting name. He'd done a bit of recon after Maureen's terse agreement to meet him here, checking on exits and security. The club was a barn of a place, an old storefront right off the streamside parking lot behind the post office. It smelled musty, like it probably got a bit wet at spring high water. The dominant theme was black: black walls, black ceiling of exposed steel joists and concrete, black carpet, black tables and chairs and snack bar. They'd even slapped black paint on the outsides of the pinball machines and pool tables in the game room. The interior decorator hadn't spent a hell of a lot of time on the color scheme.

Apparently it was mostly a teen dance club, with huge speakers and disco lights hung by chains from the ceiling and a control room that would have done credit to a recording studio. Brian could almost smell the raging hormones over his coffee. However, tonight was an older crowd and *much* quieter: *Dé hAoine* was acoustic.

He hoped Maureen would be as quiet. She radiated tension. He tried to guess the cause, between her glares at her sister and a guitar player in the band, and the way she bared her teeth at him in a parody of a smile.

Touchy. She made him think of sweating dynamite.

The fiddle finished a run, was answered by the penny whistle and the rattling thud of a bass *bodhrán*. The group seemed competent enough. With a little more practice, they could move out of the basements and get some real crowds. They still had some rough edges here and there, but what they *really* needed was a different singer. His voice was good enough, but the accent was pure Downeast Maine. Each time he stepped up to the mike, he spoiled the illusion of a Dublin pub.

*"Grá mo chroí mó cruiscín,*
*"Sliante geal mo mhuarnin,*
*"Grá mo chroí mó cruiscín lán, lán, lán,*
*"Grá mo chroí mó cruiscín lán."*

The music lilted along, innocent enough if you didn't understand enough Gaelic to know it was a man singing a love song to his jug. Brian guessed that covered at least nine out of ten in the audience. He didn't know about Maureen, or that peculiar twin image of her she claimed was her older sister.

He spent the next verse studying the two of them. They made a living case study in how actresses turned chameleon in different roles: No single detail of one differed from the other, but the sum made two totally distinct people. It all lay in their body language.

Jo confirmed his snap judgment that Maureen could be beautiful if she tried. Clothes hung differently on Jo's body, even though they were close to duplicates of Maureen's casual sweater and jeans. The red curls of Jo's hair perfectly framed her face, and whatever makeup she used merely accented those startling green eyes, so deep you could drown in them. Her blend of perfume and natural smell said "sex" to any male nose, human or otherwise, within ten paces.

Her stance, whether moving, standing, or sitting still, said "I am desirable. Look at me." Whether she knew of her blood or not, she definitely was certain of her power.

And every time Maureen caught Brian staring, her face drew even tighter.

Brian swore under his breath. He was much more interested in Maureen than Jo, but that message wasn't sinking in. Besides, Jo was also wearing a sign that read, "This seat is taken." She liked being admired, but she'd found the man she wanted. Maureen couldn't seem to read the signals.

What Maureen seemed to be certain of was her anger. Brian sensed they were actors reading from different scripts. Was her move last night a "go away closer" and he misread it? Not bloody likely; she'd looked physically ill. Was there something between her and her sister and that guitarist?

*Dé hAoine* finished *"Cruiscín Lán"* with a flourish and swapped instruments during the applause that followed. Instead of plunging straight into the next number, the lead stepped up and waved at a corner of the cellar.

"We've got something extra for you tonight. Adam Lester's in the audience, and we twisted his arm to sit in for one number. Many of you know him more as a blues man, but he can make magic out of anything. He gave us the honor of backing him on a couple of cuts of his latest album. If you'll forgive the crass commercialism, I'd suggest you buy it. We need the money."

With the blues reference, Brian expected something along the lines of a big man as black as midnight and showing chain-gang scars on his wrists. He blinked when a skinny white stood up and strode forward, leaving a heavyset black woman behind at his table. The man wore dark sunglasses even in the murk of The Cave. Was he blind? Couldn't be, he moved through the crowd too confidently.

The new guitarist borrowed an instrument from Jo's boyfriend and ran a few exploratory riffs up and down the neck, then nodded at the fiddle. He set a beat by tapping his toe and launched a stream of notes, fingerpicking and sliding with a grace beyond belief.

The fiddle chased him and pounced, and then the two instruments rolled around like a pair of kittens playing with a catnip mouse. A flute joined in, and the ball of fur turned into a rambunctious reel, one Brian had never heard before. And then the deep booming of the drum nipped one of them on the tail, and it leaped up and turned a backflip before diving back into the music.

Music as play. Music alive.

Brian glanced across the table and read peace and joy on Maureen's face, a transformation as brilliant as afternoon sun through the windows of Chartres cathedral. *God,* thought Brian. *If the music means this much to her, I'm not just going to buy the record, I'm going to buy her a system to play it on and a house to keep the system in.*

The beat increased, and the instrumental runs leaped and swirled to impossible speeds and complexities. Brian's mind buzzed just following it all. Playing? He couldn't imagine it. The skill was beyond comprehension.

*Don't think. Don't analyze. Music* is. *Beauty* is. *Just* be.

He flowed with the music, following it as it capered through the green grass of the rolling limestone plains of Ireland. He could smell peat on the wind, and the distant tang of the sea. How long it lasted, he would never know. The Little People came out and danced, and he danced with them, danced with their music, and lost all sense of time.

The music faded out of the sunlight, deeper into the shadows of the Irish forest. It slowed. It dissolved, gently, lovingly into the evening mists, and disappeared underground with the Sidhe. The drum remained, then echoes of the drum, then silence.

Brian blinked into that stunned silence. Speech would be sacrilege. Applause would be sacrilege. The priests up on the small altar-stage laid down their instruments. One of them stepped up to a microphone and shattered the crystal mood.

"Okay, folks, time for a break. We'd love to get Ish up here to sing for you, but that would be a whole 'nother world. We can't compete. All we can do is thank her for the beauty she's brought into our lives and hope it helps to ease her pain."

The words spoke of hidden undercurrents, a reminder that Brian was an outsider in this town and in this world of music. He was *always* an outsider, the ranger guarding the edges of the forest. Problem was, he was never exactly sure which side he was protecting, and neither provided a home.

Memories came at him, unbidden, and again took the voice of a grizzled sergeant major offering advice to a subaltern still wet behind the ears. *You need a home, old son. You've never really had one.*

Last night with Maureen had reminded him of that. She was special. He resonated with her. There must be some way to reach her, to calm the tension. *Not* by using the Power. What he needed was more lasting than that could give, something real rather than a puppet on a string.

Jo deflected David to another table, leaving Brian alone with Maureen and their coffee, waiting for the applause to die so they could talk again. That simmering rage was back on her face.

"I met *your* sister today," she finally said, in a tone warning of hidden minefields.

"The Queen of Air and Darkness?"

"Huh?"

"Fiona. She always wanted to be Morgan le Fay when she grew up. Or Morgause, or one of the three witches in *Macbeth*. Something dark and dangerous, anyway."

"She gave me some questions to ask you."

Bloody hell. "She would."

"How old are you?"

"Oh. That one's a little complicated. The simple answer is, about seventy. Time changes around, between your world and the Summer Country."

"You look about thirty."

"And you look about sixteen tonight. Your sister looks about twenty, only because she dresses differently. We don't age the same as humans do." He held up a palm, to stop her questions. "We do get old, if nothing kills us first. With proper training, you can expect to live about two hundred years. Or you could die tomorrow if you go around trusting Fiona."

"So you know I have the blood of the Old Ones. You're an Old One, yourself. Why did you warn me they were dangerous?"

"Because they *are* dangerous. The fact that you have the Blood only makes it worse." He paused and sipped some coffee as a diversion. How was he going to explain this to an innocent?

"Mostly they ignore humans unless one gets in their way. With each other, they fight and backstab and shift alliances and scheme and connive in ways that make the Balkans seem simple. Meeting you, instantly knowing you for what you are, they will assume you know things you've never learned, can do things you don't even dream about. Those differences could quickly get you dead, or made into a slave."

It wasn't helping. He could read it in the knife-edged line between her eyebrows.

"What's your real name?"

"Arthur. Arthur Pendragon." He grimaced, then shook his head at her obvious disbelief.

"It's a ritual name. There've probably been a thousand Arthur Pendragons since the original flea-bitten tribal chief in an obscure corner of Wales. There are sixteen or twenty of us alive right now. That's why we use other names. Brian Albion means me, just as much as Arthur Pendragon. Fiona's messing with your head."

"And these 'Pendragons' are all Old Ones?"

"Old Ones raised as Christians. We stand between the Summer Country and what you'd call the real world. Our job is to keep the two apart, protect humans from the Old Ones."

"Why?"

"The Old Ones don't have what you'd call a conscience. They keep slaves. They torture. They kill on malice or on whim. Each is an absolute despot in his heart. Fiona isn't helping you, she's using you for some plot she has going."

"And what you did to those fire doors last night proves you have a conscience?"

*Damn. Well, you're* supposed *to be good at thinking on your feet.* "The traps I set on those doors were keyed to Fiona and Sean. The doors wouldn't jam unless *they* tried to pass. And my spells didn't start the fire."

He still wasn't reaching her. This involved something deeper, something more basic to her way of seeing. What he was saying didn't touch that problem.

She shook her head. "So everything's the fault of the Old

Ones? And yet all you Pendragons are Old Ones. I had a logic course in college. Seems to me that your argument is biting itself on the ass. Tell me why I should believe you instead of your sister. Fiona said *you* were dangerous—the kind of man who stabbed strangers in the back."

"Liam was no stranger. He killed a friend of mine— tortured him to death for no other reasons than boredom and the fact that he had the chance. In the years since, I've found five other corpses on his trail. Four of them were women. He followed you into that alley. Would you rather that I'd let him take you?"

He glanced at the crucifix she wore, such a different message than a plain cross. "Why are you a Catholic? I was raised to do this. I don't know why Liam wanted you, but it wasn't for your own good. Not something you'd choose if you had a choice." Brian allowed himself a wry smile.

"Beyond revenge, I killed him because he would have killed me. He would have killed me because he knew I would kill him. It's like cats chasing their own tails. Makes about as much sense, but you can't escape it."

The conversation was surreal. He wondered if any of the nearby tables were listening over the general buzz. This place was "chemical-free." Would they get bounced for being stoned?

He glanced around. The only people looking his way were Jo and David. They were too far away to hear.

He hoped.

"Let me ask *you* a question, now. Why do you think Fiona is trying to split us apart? Why does she want to turn you against me?"

She shrugged. Her face told him she doubted they had ever been together. He bulled ahead with it, anyway.

"For whatever reason, Fiona has decided I'm her mate. The father for her children. She sees you as a rival. God help the woman who stands in her way."

Maureen's eyes bugged out, and she gulped coffee so fast she sputtered. Brian ran through the Heimlich maneuver in his mind before she caught her breath.

"But . . . But . . . She's your *sister*!"

"*Macht nichts*. The Old Ones don't have the same taboos as you civilized sorts. I just *told* you that. Besides, she has ancient precedent. Think of the Egyptian pharaohs, brother marrying sister. More to the point, what sin lies at the heart of the fall of Camelot, no matter which legend you choose? Who were Mordred's parents?"

That reference to fantasy touched her where nothing else had. Her face opened out, shock and curiosity replacing the hard-edged anger. Whatever hid beneath her surface, she wasn't playing to Jo and David anymore.

"Arthur," she whispered. "His half sister."

"By whichever name."

Then something clamped down on her face again, and her lips thinned. She was through with sparring.

"So she's chasing you. She can't rape you, can she? Isn't that a male prerogative?"

*Shit!* Now Brian could see Fiona's bomb, but he was powerless to defuse it. His sister was such a devious little bitch, knowing just exactly what strings to pull and what buttons to push to make others dance like marionettes.

"She can force me if she gets me in her power. She can bind me to her with a spell. I think that's why Liam was after you. To make you a sex slave for his master in the Summer Country."

Her teeth showed now, and with her sharp face it gave her the look of a redheaded piranha.

"A spell to make you want her? A glamour, perhaps? There wouldn't be any connection with my inviting you in, last night? No *tampering* with my emotions?"

"You were in danger and afraid. You still needed protection. I thought it was the best choice for both of us, getting you safely home."

"Bullshit! I came here tonight because I owed you something for saving my butt. I hoped Fiona had lied. But what you tried to do, that's rape. Alcohol, hypnosis, *whatever* the hell you call it, it's still *rape!*" She squirmed in her chair, as if even she was trying to escape from her own words.

Brian squeezed his eyes shut and shook his head. "You told me to stop. I stopped. You told me to leave. I left. 'No' means *no*. That isn't rape."

"If I ever think you're doing it again, I'll kill you!"

"Maureen . . ."

"You go to hell, Brian Arthur Albion. You just go straight to hell. Do not pass Go, do not collect two hundred dollars. Get the fuck out of my life!"

She lurched to her feet and drained the dregs of her coffee. Well, that was better than throwing it in his face. And at least she wasn't screaming.

She *had* been loud enough to get attention. Not just Jo and David, but a dozen faces turned toward them, curious. He had a sudden idiot's vision of passing the hat for intermission entertainment, like jugglers or a pair of acrobats.

He watched her retreating back, rigid as a spear with anger. She marched straight for the door and into darkness. He started to go after her, reason with her, and then decided now wasn't the time or place. She wouldn't be capable of listening. Grenades were like that.

Damned if he knew what she had on her hidden agenda. All he had done was touch her fear of him, soothe her, calm her. Now she was acting as if he was an incubus.

Her musk lingered behind, heavy even in the crowd smell of the evening, bypassing his brain. It ignited a war between his body and his mind. "Go away closer." " 'No' means *no*."

Women.

Particularly women of the Blood. Brian damned Fiona. He damned Maureen, and damned Jo with her confident sexuality aimed at her simple straightforward *Homo sapiens*, and damned Brian Arthur Pendragon Albion while he was at it.

Sex was such a deadly stew.

The musicians wandered back through the crowd, and David joined them, leaving a kiss on Jo's hand. The break was over, intermission act and all. The Downeast lobsterman stepped up to the microphone.

"Well, folks, we've been after the lighter side of Ireland, and it's time to get heavy now. This isn't an IRA song, but rather the contrary. For generations, one of the few ways to support your family in a poor land has been to go for a soldier, to take the king's shilling and go off to fight in foreign wars. And then you come home again. . . ."

The *bodhrán* started to thump a funeral march, and the whistle picked up a slow-paced "Johnny Comes Marching Home." One by one, the other instruments joined, including a *caoine* wail on the *uillean* pipes that would have done credit to the best banshee.

> "*While going the road to sweet Athy, hurroo, hurroo,*
> "*While going the road to sweet Athy, hurroo, hurroo,*
> "*While going the road to sweet Athy*
> "*A stick in my hand and a drop in my eye*
> "*A doleful damsel I heard cry*
> "*'Johnny I hardly knew ye!'*
> "*With their drums and guns and guns and drums*
> "*The enemy nearly slew ye.*
> "*Johnny me dear you look so queer,*
> "*Johnny I hardly knew ye.*"

Brian knew this song. He'd lived it, through long years in the brushfire wars of the death of the British Empire.

He settled his head in his hands. Death and maiming, the arts of war—his life stretched back behind him through the Malay jungles, the heat and dust and stink of Oman, the deceptive civilized streets of Belfast and Cyprus.

Maureen . . . She had no reason to trust him, wouldn't have a reason until it was too late. Just like the young man who marched proudly off to war in his brilliant scarlet uniform, the thousands of young men.

As he'd told her, the circle of killing lived on its own energy. He hunted Old Ones because he knew they hunted him. They hunted him because they knew he hunted them.

*"Where are your eyes that looked so mild, hurroo, hurroo?*
*"Where are your eyes that looked so mild, hurroo, hurroo?*
*"Where are your eyes that looked so mild*
*"When my poor heart you first beguiled?*
*"Oh, why did you run from me and the child?*
*"Johnny I hardly knew ye."*

Each side killed because they feared death. They feared death because they killed. For others, it was the Balkans or Kashmir. For Brian, it was the Old Ones.

One by one, over the years, the war had claimed his friends—Mulvaney had been the last. The enemy had bled just as much. The chess match was a draw. And he couldn't see any way to resign from his current war, any way to negotiate a truce. Nobody trusted enough.

*"You haven't an arm and you haven't a leg, hurroo, hurroo,*
*"You haven't an arm and you haven't a leg, hurroo, hurroo,*
*"You haven't an arm and you haven't a leg,*
*"You're an eyeless, noseless, chickenless egg,*
*"You'll have to be put with a bowl to beg.*
*"Johnny I hardly knew ye!"*

Brian stared down at his cup, finding nothing but coffee. He shook his head.

He was getting old. His thoughts didn't usually start turning this dark until he was at least halfway through a bottle of the Queen's best rum. He didn't start seeing the dead boys and the ones who wished they'd died until the landlord gave out his last call for the night. That was when he saw the blood soaking out between his fingers without the force of a heartbeat behind it, the death blood of another child who'd trusted the old soldier to get him safely home again. That was when he sat in a tent at midnight writing letters to the next of kin.

The grizzled sergeant major was back, whispering in his ear. *You're getting old and your brain is turning soft. Why are you so interested in this barmy little bint? Don't give me that crap about her smell. That's animal talk, dogs following after a bitch in heat. You're only half an animal. What does the rest of you have to say?*

Brian shook his head, slowly, at his inner voice. He saw pain, and he knew considerable about that subject from the inside. When her face opened up with the music, she was the most beautiful woman he'd ever seen. And underneath the pain and anger, he could feel the strength of tempered steel. She didn't even know it was there, but she could be more deadly than Fiona. He didn't want her to ever have to be.

*Speaking of Fiona . . .*

He lifted his head and did his reflex scan of the crowd, of his surroundings, of possible ambushes. Two dark faces sprang out of the shadows, as if they took form before his eyes. Fiona. Sean. His sister winked at him.

*"With their drums and guns and guns and drums*
*"The enemy nearly slew ye.*

*"Johnny me dear, you look so queer,*
*"Johnny, I hardly knew ye."*

The instruments dropped off, one by one, until the tin whistle piped a military retreat and the *bodhrán* finally drummed its funeral cadence into echoing silence.

Brian cursed himself for relaxing his guard. How long had Fiona been there? Had anybody followed Maureen out the door? A minute, two minutes to finish the song . . .

He was outside and fading into shadows before the echoes died.

# eight

—ᴍ—

THERE WERE FIVE of them.

At *least* five of them, Brian reminded himself. He could get killed making assumptions. The darkness could be hiding twice that many. Those were just the ones he'd seen or heard.

He added a mental note to never, *never,* go out in jogging shoes in winter. No matter *what* he thought he was going to do. Now his damned Reeboks squished icy water between his toes with every step.

Brian slid along an alley wall, hugging shadows, feeling the grit and grab of brick against the back of his jacket and praying his feet wouldn't find any noisy junk or ankle-breaking potholes under the snow. This frozen maze of alleys could kill him as easily as the squad trying to pin him down.

There were at least five of them, *and* they were human. That cut back on his options. Times like this, he really questioned the nobility of unilateral disarmament. Things he could do, things he *had* done to Liam, just weren't options against humans. He was supposed to defend humans against Old Ones. That was his bloody *job*.

There were always rules of engagement.

It didn't matter if the damned jackals knew these alleys better than a Jesuit knows the Bible. Didn't matter if they'd sold their souls to Fiona or Dougal, bought and paid for. He couldn't kill them.

A shadow flickered across the end of the alley, short and skinny against the orange of the streetlights. Street kids, who lived in these alleys night and day. Gang kids, with knives and lengths of pipe and probably guns, being Yanks.

How had they found him? He wondered for an instant if the music had called Fiona and her lapdog. That one reel belonged to the Summer Country, that was certain. But this wasn't summer. Far from it.

*Kids,* he thought, and cursed under his breath.

He couldn't kill them, and he couldn't even use the powers of the Blood where there were witnesses. Back when he'd thought Maureen was human, she had been alone. If she'd talked about what she saw, there was no evidence— no other witnesses. The cops would smile at each other and do a little spiral with a finger in the general area of their ears. Just another nut.

He edged deeper into the maze, peeked around a corner, and scanned the shadows for his next move, his next threat. The cheeks of his butt clamped tighter in the ancient response to fear. It didn't matter how many hundreds of times he went into combat; the fear was there. It had better be. When the fear left, you died.

He swallowed metallic spit.

Dark, odd-shaped lumps could be bags of trash or lurking death. Tracks in the snow could be ten hours old or ten seconds. Blackness at the head of a fire escape might be a sentry or only plywood and ice against the sky.

A whistle echoed down the alley: a mockingbird singing

in February in Maine. Another echoed back. That was all he bloody well needed, a street gang trained as Indian scouts.

His glance flicked back to the roof edge: Something moved against the stars. Damn kids held the high ground.

Brian slipped from shadow to shadow, crouching behind transformers humming to themselves under the snow, sneaking around rusty package vans that hadn't moved for at least three storms. The moldy back-alley smells of soaked cardboard, garbage, and cat piss wiped Maureen's fragrance from his memory.

*Welcome to the real world, Brian Albion.*

One of the trash bags stretched, found a more comfortable place to squat, and returned to sentry duty. So much for *that* way out. Brian could step around a corner into the Summer Country and escape, but he had a sneaking suspicion he'd find Fiona waiting for him at the gate.

He still wondered if they were after him or after Maureen. Could be either. Could be both. The kids could just want to help him with the excess weight in his wallet, but he rather doubted that.

Snow crunched behind him along the way he had come. He thought of gamekeepers driving the grouse to the guns. Which way was the weakest line, the escape from the trap? Which way did they want him to *think* was weak? Which alleys led out, and which dead-ended against blank brick walls?

Brian flipped a mental coin and crept right, uphill. Getting pinned against the river sounded really bad. Railroad yards waited down there, too, wide spaces with nothing higher than steel rails to hide behind. No fun.

A shadow peeled loose from a doorway and whistled. Brian spun toward the kid, sensed a club, and took it hard on his left arm before a nerve hold and two spear-handed jabs dumped the brat in the snow. A kick kept him down.

Lying there, he was ragged and scrawny, probably no older than fourteen.

*Cannon fodder*, Brian thought, as he glanced around for other moving shadows.

His arm hung limp and tingled from fingertips clear up to his neck. He tried to shake it out, then scratched it off his equipment list for the evening. The odds were rotten: They had more bodies than he had arms and legs.

Albion's last stand. *How does that saying go? Today is a good day for someone* else *to die?*

More shadows loomed up ahead. Brian glanced around for any promising-looking corners to guard his back.

His chess brain wondered if this welcoming committee had been hired by Fiona or by Dougal. It made a difference. Fiona probably wouldn't kill him unless jealousy had really pinched her on the ass. Dougal wouldn't think twice about it.

The shadows split up. There were two of them, not impossible odds. Both swung clubs in the casual way that said they wanted to terrorize him, wanted him to surrender and save them the effort of beating him into pulp. If they were serious, they would have moved by now.

*Probably Fiona, then.*

*Bugger this!*

Brian stared the closest one in the eyes. *I am not here*, he thought. *You saw a cat skitter across the alley, you saw melting snow fall from the rusty iron of that fire escape, you saw shadows from three different things combined by nothing more than your point of view. I am not here.*

The kid's eyes widened in the thin light reflected from the streetlamps. He swung wildly, probing for the ghost that had just faded away before his eyes.

Brian spun to the second kid, the larger one, turning inside the arc of his club and taking it on his ribs. Something cracked. He managed to tangle the pipe in his useless left arm and hooked an ankle throw. The boy went down, and a heel kick to the head kept him there.

Pain whacked his knees from behind, a reminder from the kid he'd spelled. He'd dropped concentration on that one, lost control. Brian went with the blow, falling, rolling, spinning on his back to bring his feet up between himself and his enemy.

*Down isn't dead.* Brian's legs scissored the kid's right knee and twisted him down into a snowbank. Brian rolled along the contact and whipped a kick to the back of the head. *Three down. Those ribs are going to be a problem, in half an hour or so. Better move while you still can, old son.*

He continued his roll to bring his feet under him and staggered back upright. His eyes locked on the silver shimmer of a blade held low in front of shadow.

*Shit.* He'd left *his* knife at the hotel. The Cave had a metal detector at the door—hard to explain needing a *kukri* for a night of music.

So much for finesse. Bare-handed against a knife, he was going to get cut. He just hoped he could choose where.

Brian kicked snow, trying to startle or even blind his enemy. The kid moved in, knife low and slashing, and Brian spun away. One leg wasn't working right, the one the club got. That wasn't good.

Another slash, another careful crab-scuttle advance. The kid knew what he was doing. No rushes, no stabs, no reaching.

Time. Concentration. Using Power required both. Brian didn't even try. He just watched the knife and fought with the weapons his body still had.

The knife started its starlit arc, and Brian moved forward rather than away. He twisted at the waist to throw his useless left arm against the blade. Something thumped against the meat of his forearm and stuck there, tugging, as he spun up along the kid's arm and whipped a back-fist to his head.

The boy went down, jerking his knife with him as he fell. Brian felt another tug but no pain. If he was *extremely* lucky, it had only cut his jacket.

Snow crunched behind him, and Brian ducked. Pain burst across his right shoulder. He half fell away from it, turning, seeing a blurred form pulling back a club for the finishing blow. Brian's left foot rose by itself, cocked, and snapped out an instep kick. It found the indistinct fork where the shadow's legs converged, and thumped hard enough into the crotch that his other, injured leg shot pain straight up to the base of his skull and collapsed under him.

Five.

If there were any more, they had him.

Brian rolled in the snow, retching. Gasps followed him— the sobbing, choking sounds of a young male kicked so hard in the balls his pelvis had cracked. Sometime soon that kid was going to find the breath to scream.

*Club.* Brian rolled across one of the clubs, fumbled it into his right hand, and half crawled across the churned snow of the alley to gently, scientifically tap a skull. The sobs quieted.

The club served as a brace, as well. He fought his way upright, right hand supporting right leg, left arm dangling useless, blood dripping black into the gray-orange glimmer of the snow.

Five down. They'd probably all live, although that back-fist to the head could have crushed the temple of the kid's skull. Served him right, for pulling a knife. Fiona would have skinned him alive. Or worse.

Not a tidy fight.

Any others?

His blurry eyes sorted shadows and doorways, compared

them against the files of recent memory. *Nada.*

The pause gave him a chance to survey the damage, and the answer wasn't good. Probable broken ribs. Probable cracked leg bone, fibula by the feel of it. Something damaged in his shoulder, God only knows what. Unknown bone or nerve or muscle damage to the left arm. It still had enough feeling in it for him to know that was blood flowing down hot to drip off his fingers.

So much for just cutting the jacket. No light, no time to check it out. Simple pressure bandage. He struggled to force thoughts through the fog.

Belts. He hobbled to the nearest body, using the club as a cane. He knelt in jerky stages that edged on collapse. Shaking fingers coiled the kid's belt around the cut arm, outside the jacket and tight like an elastic bandage, pressure on the wound to slow the bleeding.

More belts. Clubs. He splinted his leg, something to take pressure off his shoulder. That cane trick wasn't going to work more than another five minutes—he didn't have a good arm to use it with.

With his leg bound straight, Brian crawled to a security grill and used its chain-link mesh as a ladder to haul his racked body vertical. His head swam, and the stars dropped down to orbit around the alley.

Sergeant Mulvaney was back. *You're pretty well knackered, laddie. Not good at all. A tyke in nappies could toddle up and push you over with one finger. You've got a problem, old son.*

He didn't need phantom voices to tell him he needed help. Hurt, in a foreign land, with no ID that'd stand more than a passing glance—and how'd he like some blood tests run, before they gave him a transfusion? Maybe a series of X rays? "Interesting, Doctor Jones: Would you have a look at this? Never seen anything like it. . . ."

Brian staggered along the alley wall, stiff-legged, and one shoulder dragging against the bricks for support. The pain was waking up now, the fire of the knife cut and the red-hot nails in his ribs stabbing him with every breath, and a pounding lump on his right forehead he couldn't connect with anything in the fight. Maybe he'd hit it when he rolled.

Mulvaney was trying to get his attention again. First lesson a young officer learned was, pay attention to your senior NCOs. They could save your ass, no matter what the chain of command might say.

*Draw on your Blood. Draw on your Power. Force the pain down. Remember what that bitch Deirdre used to say in training: "Pain is optional. Injury may be mandatory in a given situation, but pain is optional." And then she'd stub out a cigarette on the back of her hand.*

Pain was optional. Easy for her to say. It was what she did to prove it, was a problem. About a dozen of the scars patterning his body had her name signed to them.

Mulvaney shook his head, sighing over the pigheaded nature of young subalterns. *Show you learned what she taught. Not just remembered, but learned. Worry about healing later.*

Brian looked up from the churned slush. Good. That little distraction had moved him about two blocks. Sweat trickled down his nose in spite of the winter air. He tried to wipe it off and found he couldn't lift either hand that far. He couldn't even turn his head far enough to reach his upper arm.

Forget about the sweat. He needed to concentrate on more important fluids. Those hot drips on his fingers—they were blood. He had a choice: take a chance on losing too much of it, or slow the circulation and risk frostbite of the fingers.

Try the middle way: moderation in all things, including moderation. Slow the loss but keep feeling in his fingers.

Meanwhile, he had to keep his feet moving.

Speaking of feet. *Hey feet, where you taking us?*

The answer seemed to be "Maureen's."

The girl with the gun and the attitude. She'd called him a rapist. What made his feet think she wouldn't let him past the door and fill his ass with lead? She could do that in this country. Self-defense. Just like she tried in that alley.

But Maureen was closer. He'd never make it to the hotel. He'd collapse and freeze, if Fiona didn't get there first.

Brian grabbed his thoughts by the scruff of the neck and hauled them back. A wandering brain was one of the fastest ways to die. Where was he?

Fifth and Congress. Well, the thoughts had moved him three blocks farther. Apparently, his feet *had* decided on Maureen's. The hotel was in the other direction. He was committed now, no choice.

Four more blocks. Uphill. And then the stairs. Maureen had that buggering third-floor flat. Stiff leg. Working leg. Stiff leg. Working leg. *A journey of ten thousand Li begins with a single step. What the hell is a Li, anyway?*

Rough bone-edges grated against each other with each step, each gasping breath, shooting fire deep into his side from the broken ribs. Warmth oozed down his arm and dripped into the snow, onto his shoes, his pants. Each slip on the icy sidewalk drove ice picks into his leg and shoulder.

Ten steps of each leg and he leaned on a streetlight. Headlights glinted down the road. He assumed it was the local constable keeping the world safe for democracy, so he straightened up and forced a semblance of a taxpayer out on his lawful business.

Stiff leg. Working leg. Stiff leg. Working leg. A *Li* was a unit of measurement in the ancient Chinese system, length unknown to the current correspondent but probably less than a mile. Irrelevant. Call it a bloody long distance, anyway.

How far had he come?

Not bleeding far enough. A block of flats loomed ahead, it looked right but no parking lot. One beyond, instead. Rusty-bummed green Toyota.

Stiff leg. Working leg. What would he do if she wasn't home? What if she looked through that damned security peephole and told him to bugger off? She didn't love him. She'd made it bloody clear she didn't even bleeding *like* him.

Stairs. He'd thought those buggering Yanks had buggering handicap accessibility laws. Wheelchair access, ramps or lifts, all that sort of bloody socialist muggery. One sodding step at a time leaning on the railing, hoping it didn't break under his weight.

Stiff leg. Working leg. Stiff leg. Working leg.

Third floor. He flopped against the wall, right side, no blood smear on paint. He tried to keep it clean, maintain decorum. Gather breath. Focus. Prayer optional.

Buzzer. He couldn't reach the bloody button. Neither hand.

Elbow. Right elbow. He mushed around with his jacket sleeve until the point of the elbow brushed the button.

He heard a distant ringing.

Nothing happened. He tried again, three tries before contact.

Nothing.

It seemed easiest just to lean against the button, continuous noise, barely holding his body up against the door-frame.

He heard a muttered voice, inside, with the tone of swearing but no words. The door opened.

"Maureen . . ."

It was more of a groan than a word.

She just stood there with that damned gun in a firm

two-handed grip, centered on his chest. He couldn't tell if her expression was shock or hatred.

"Don't . . . call . . . police."

The barrel expanded into a tunnel and swallowed him.

# nine

—⚬—

THEY MET BY the peace fire in the Great Hall of Tara:
Dougal, Sean, Fiona. Afternoon sun shone through the
smoke hole in the thatch high overhead, burning a single
shaft down through the blue smoke and glancing off the
massive roof trusses. It barely lit the gloom: the dark stone
walls, the smoke-blackened wooden beams and purlins, the
dusty banners. A twin line of polished shadows marched
from one end of the hall to the other, oak-trunk columns
like sentries rooted in the flagstone floor.

No torches were lit for only three, no tables set out on
their trestles groaning with roast boar and bread and cheese
and wine—no bards, no Druids, no hopeful dogs underfoot. Peace and darkness ruled. *Dark for dark deeds,* thought
Fiona, with her usual touch of inner mockery.

Red firelight washed their faces. They sat close to the
central fire pit, where the flames just balanced the cool
darkness, no more than the few logs needed to hold coals
through the day. The peace fire burned from one Beltane
to the next, to die with the old year's night and rekindle
from the sun's first rays through a burning lens. The laws

of the Summer Country said matches would not work. Butane lighters would, simply flint and steel and flammable gas, but the sun made a more impressive ritual.

*Well,* Fiona thought, *this is what the Great Hall of Tara ought to have looked like, anyway. It's our vision of a regal barn huge enough to feast a thousand warriors of the Fianna at one time.*

A dozen fire pits stretched from one end to the other, all but one dark now and waiting for the great blazes that would magically drive the damp and chill from stone masonry without deviling her eyes and nose with smoke along the way. Instead, a wholesome smell of fresh rushes rose from underfoot, untainted by the dog turds, sour beer, and rancid table scraps historical accuracy would demand. It was a much grander, cleaner space than the cramped slum that human archaeologists had dug up in Ireland.

A neutral space to meet, that's what it really was. A DMZ, to use dear Brian's idiom. Few in the Summer Country felt the trust necessary either to give or to accept an invitation to another's keep. If three Old Ones came to Tara and only two were seen to leave, the rest of the Summer Country would move against those two. Because of this, what went on inside the Great Hall remained safe and secret.

Dougal poked at the coals with his knife, probably some esoteric *kindjal* or *hand-seax* or *hamidashi* she ought to recognize and praise. Dougal played at being an Authority on arms and armor, just as he played at being a Huntsman of all kinds of beast. The rising glow of the coals lit the hawk he carried, hooded, on his other arm.

When he looked up at her, the shadows hooded his eyes like the falcon's. "You seem to have failed again. What *is* this obsession you have with the Pendragon?"

"We each have our games. He's mine."

He showed his teeth in a parody of a smile. "I think I'd

rather train spitting cobras. You should kill him."

She glanced across at Sean, noticing the red glitter reflecting in his eyes. *Yes,* she thought, *you'd like that, wouldn't you.*

"Oh, such a waste it would be," she added, aloud. "Would you kill that hawk, love, just because it's dangerous?"

Dougal sheathed his dagger and smoothed the feathers of his bird, then adjusted the jesses to clear a twist.

"Falcon, my dear. Peregrine falcon. Never call a falcon a hawk. We'll think you ignorant."

"Different interests, that's all, love. Do you know anything of genetics?"

"Enough to breed hounds. That's all I need. We don't need those human games in the Summer Country. Life is good enough as it is. Life was good enough a thousand years ago, for us."

She smiled, a thin, slow smile she had practiced in a mirror for years until it spoke volumes about quiet scorn. "Good enough? Is life good enough for Sean, denied children by the dice of chromosomes? How many of the Blood live here, live in the Summer Country and know themselves for what they are?"

He paused for a moment, still caressing his hawk. "A thousand, more or less?"

She deepened her smile a calculated hairbreadth. "And how many of those are fertile, male and female?"

"Less than a hundred." He grimaced, and the hawk stirred under his hand, sensing tension. "You know the averages: fewer than one in ten."

"One in twelve would be more accurate. Such is the price of hybrid vigor. You think that this is good?"

"But there are the half bloods in the human world, ten times, twenty times as many. This one Liam hunted for me, her sister, others. We've held our numbers for centuries by picking and choosing just this way."

Sean stirred, across the fire. "Liam was a breeder. Lose one, gain one, where has the average been improved? You don't even have this Maureen woman yet, do you? She may end up mating with dear brother Brian. The walls between the worlds get thicker every year. Snatching strangers from the streets gets harder. Switching babies in the crib is not as easy when the crib's in a hospital, you know."

Dougal growled, and the bird roused on his fist, fluffing her feathers and loosening her wings for flight.

*Naughty, naughty,* thought Fiona. *Don't disturb the pretty murderess.* For an instant, she saw herself in the bird, saw herself in Maureen, and hated the sight. Dougal lived for domination. He really was a shit.

But sometimes a useful shit.

"You don't yet have Maureen. I don't yet have little Brian. Our two problems seem to have come together. Perhaps we can work a temporary alliance?"

Dougal rose to his feet, cocked his head like the falcon on his fist, and took two steps that carried him into a ripple of air like a desert mirage. He didn't come out the other side. Fiona yawned. Two steps to the human world, two steps back to the Summer Country—such travel was a gift the Old Blood gave them.

She guessed he was just checking on the questions at hand. All she really knew was that her agents had failed, that Brian had escaped them, and they were unable to follow. Where and how he'd left, and in what condition, remained mysteries to her.

She preferred a more distant style of management. Getting directly involved, either at the strip club or in the alleys, could be painful. She rubbed the back of her wrist in memory, the spot she'd burned to the bone by forcing Brian's trap.

Magical healing might erase the charred flesh and the scars, but it didn't cut the price he was going to pay.

Two steps carried Dougal from Tara to Naskeag Falls. He grimaced at the icy wind, the peregrine uneasy on his wrist.

*That's the price of an image,* he thought. *Damned awkward bird to carry on a night like this. And she's more than a nuisance here, if some nosy lawman asks to see my federal permit. That little weasel Sean was right about the walls between the worlds. Most of them are made of paper, or of laminated plastic.*

Time was such a strange thing, between the worlds. They knew of her agents' failure, Fiona and Sean and Dougal, days past in the golden afternoon of the Summer Country. And yet here was the Pendragon limping along under the streetlights, spreading the smell of fresh blood on the wind.

Dougal shook his head. He knew he could take Brian now, wounded as he was, but it would be ugly and dangerous—like following a wounded tiger into the elephant grass. He could take Brian now, but the only safe way would be to kill him. Little Fiona wouldn't like that. Oh, no, she wouldn't. Sean had made that *abundantly* clear. So revenge was out, for now.

*He's your tiger, Fiona dear. I track my own mistakes. I don't track yours. Not even for the blood of my own clan cousin.*

He watched from the shadows as Brian hauled his wounds up the steps of a run-down apartment building. Dougal sensed Maureen inside, sensed the power that had set Liam on her trail. So the wounded tiger considered this his lair? If the wind sat in *that* corner, Fiona's suggestion of an alliance made more sense.

Two steps took him back. Dougal drew the scene of Tara in his head—the fire and the shadows, the line of the sunbeam and Fiona's beautiful dark face glimmering in the firelight. The world bent around him and reshaped itself, through the half world of gibbering spirits and uncanny lights and a musty, boggy smell to the clean resinous tang of birchwood burning on an autumn afternoon. Sean had added two logs to the pile of coals while they waited.

The falcon settled again on his wrist, her bells tinkling quietly. She really was working out well. Such a *beautiful* bird. The woman would be next.

"Your children hurt him. He's gone home to Mother to kiss it and make it all better. Your toy appears to be playing with my toy."

Fiona wrinkled her nose. Such a lovely nose it was, on such an interesting face. It was too bad she had this fixation on her younger brother. It wasn't so much the brother thing. Dougal didn't care if people mated with their dogs in the middle of the street. But there were others she could choose. . . .

"Why this Pendragon? What's so important about him?"

She smiled her malicious smile, the one that made her look for an instant like the peregrine. "He's pretty, love. I've wanted him ever since he was a baby, you know. Not like you, with your nose like that hawk upon your wrist and your eyes set too close together and your neck stolen from a scrawny rooster. Sometimes I pity this Maureen: You're nothing much to look at, Dougal, as a man. No muscles to speak of, except those between your ears."

Sean stirred, reacting to a glare from Dougal. "She's just having fun with you. Our Fiona has a nasty streak. There's more to Brian than a pretty face. How many fathers of the Blood have two fertile children, even with the aid of different mothers?"

Dougal had to think. "Damned few."

The dark pools of Fiona's eyes grew remote. "Precisely. It's one of the joys of our hybrid ancestry. The ability to use Power is a complex of recessive genes. You have to get them all from both parents in order for them to show. The problem is, the Old Blood has both Power and fertility linked with a lot of lethal genes."

Sean snickered. "Not exactly a survival trait."

"So far, love, those genes have paid us back more than they cost. But that's one reason why you can recognize the Old Blood at sight. We tend to look alike because we don't have that many viable gene combinations."

Dougal's head buzzed with Fiona's human words. "Why do I need to know this?"

"Sean and I have done a little research, love. That's why we were poking around on the coast of Maine. You've heard of the Jackson Labs? Genetics research, mutant mice, tracing the genealogy of inherited disease? Sean's a wonder, you know, in the half world of the humans. He can even chase down grants."

Dougal grimaced at Sean. "Can you get her to stick to the point?"

Fiona dimpled, as if he'd just paid her a compliment. "Oh, we've done a little discreet gene-sequencing, love. Nothing that would allow another researcher to discover exactly what *species* we were studying. I'm afraid our notes are quite *hopeless* from a scientific point of view."

Sean shook his head. "What she's leading up to, in her nasty little way, is a mutation. She carries it, Brian carries it, I carry it but with a broken sequence and that stupid extra chromosome. Our father apparently was a most unusual man. Too bad he's dead."

Dougal sneered. "Too bad he got besotted with a woman of the Kamarei, you mean. It's hard to regenerate your way out of a stewpot. What's that got to do with us?"

Fiona smiled, showing teeth that were nearly fangs. "So, love, you earlier mentioned breeding dogs. If one of your wolfhounds has a trait you want preserved, what do you do?"

"Breed to the same trait in another."

Her smile deepened. He really disliked being the target of her smiles, the way they added barbs to her venomed tongue. He knew his mind wasn't as quick as hers—but then, few were. That was a human trait. The Old Blood had other tools.

"So, love," she went on, "isn't the same tail or nose or set of good sharp teeth often found in the same litter? Don't you often breed brother to sister for the purity of the line? Inbreed and then cull?"

"Yes."

Dougal nodded to himself, beginning to understand where she was leading him. So. Little Fiona looked to start her own selective breeding program? Given what he knew of her and of Brian, there probably wouldn't be that many culls to drown.

"Besides," she said, "he's awfully cute, love. Those beautiful blue eyes, that curly blond hair all across his arms and legs and chest. Those muscles. And he has some lovely scars. You should see him on a beach sometime."

Dougal thought Sean was going to pick up a hearthstone and chew on it, the way his jaw was working. *Sooner or later he's going to slide a knife between his twin sister's pretty ribs. Maybe,* Dougal thought, *just maybe I'll supply it.*


SEAN SWALLOWED BITTER rage. *Brian, Brian, Brian. It's always Brian with Fiona,* he thought. She could get what she wanted elsewhere. All of it: the genes, the sex, the worshiping. No, she wanted Brian. Maybe it was because she couldn't get him.

*Thou shalt have no other Goddesses before me.*

At least she still played with her twin, kept him close.

Every once in a while, when her other toys lost their appeal, she even invited him into her bed. Hope held him in a cage.

Brian or Dougal might call him "eunuch" as a calculated insult, but that wasn't accurate. He might be sterile, but he wasn't impotent.

"We need a plan," she said, and he dropped those thoughts. The Goddess spoke.

"View it as a Hunt, Dougal," she went on. "Apply your special talents. We have two specimens we want to capture, alive and in good condition. Breeding condition, if you will."

Dougal laughed. "Good condition? I could smell the blood all the way across the street. So much for working with your puppets."

She shrugged. "They forgot the rules. They'll regret it. For a short time."

Dougal's glance shifted from Fiona to Sean and back, as if sending some kind of message. "You'll enjoy that, won't you? You enjoy giving pain?"

"Pain is a tool, love. Terror is a tool." She waved a hand in dismissal. "Like wine, I can drink them or leave them alone. The next time I need some human tools, they'll have heard what happened to this set. They'll pay attention to the rules."

Sean met Dougal's gaze again, reading sympathy in those hunter's eyes. He seemed to be offering an alliance.

*The ugly little gnome is right: Why do I let her treat me like a worm? Is it some witchery she brewed when we were babes together, or even in the womb?*

Dougal shook his head. "Pain isn't always the best form of control, sweet Fiona. Not even with dumb oxen. Use too much pain on some animals, and they'll turn on you. That's dangerous, often fatal. Sometimes rewards work better. Food, shelter, sex, even just a chance to sleep. Find out what an animal wants and provide it when the beast does what *you* want."

They sat for a while, in silence. Sean traced runes forming and falling apart within the coals of the fire, reading omens, meditating on the unspoken message Dougal sent. "I know what you want," those eyes had said. "I know how you feel about this bitch. I know how you feel about that Pendragon."

Sometimes, when Sean was away from her, he dreamed of her face flushing purple, her eyes and tongue popping out with the force of his hands squeezing at her throat. Then she'd lift one finger, and his soul was hers. That hawk on Dougal's wrist had more free will. But when she sang . . .

Fiona leaned back against a polished tree-trunk pillar, scratching her back like some sleek sensuous animal. No wonder she kept cats.

"The three of us can control Brian," she said, "if we get him here. His injuries might even be useful: They weaken him. The woman is untrained, can't use her powers yet, has no idea what they are. Brian could teach her, if we give him time, or he could just draw upon her strength. We should move soon."

Dougal stirred. "We need them in the half world. We need them separate. Force isn't going to get us what we want. We need bait. We need a live-trap for dangerous prey."

"Ah," said Fiona, "but what's the bait, love? Brian's too smart to come here weak and unprepared. And the woman's strange. Before you set your heart on her, maybe you should study what's under that oh-so-cute red hair. She's nothing but freckled skin pulled tight over fear, with anger bonded to her soul. She went to shoot Liam before he even spoke to her."

Anger. Connections. Something clicked in Sean's memory. "You talked to her. Didn't your mention of a glamour set her off? When you hinted that Brian tampered with her feelings?"

"Yesss . . ." Her eyes slitted in the gloom, a cat accepting a chin rub.

"Wouldn't that mean his glamour worked? Untrained as she is, what worked once will probably work again."

"Ah, my lovely brother. Such a delightful snake you are."

Her words were sudden sunshine. She smiled on him, and the world was right again. For this, he'd do anything.

"I think we have our bait," he drawled. "Two sets of bait. A glamour set on Maureen to bring her here, then Maureen to bring us Brian. Tell me, Huntsman, will it work? Will it trap our prey?"

Fiona held up one finger. "Meet her in the light, meet her in public. Remember the fear. Liam died because of the fear, even though she didn't kill him. Dougal, love, you're going to have some problems there. The woman's strange."

"I suppose you think the rest of us are sane," Dougal answered. "I have ways to adjust her strangeness. But if I'm to cast a glamour on her and lure her to my bed, what do I need you for? Why should I help you trap your tiger?"

She laughed. "Dougal, Dougal, Dougal. A glamour's a weak magic. It works best where attraction's already growing. It can't swim against the tide. Forgive my rudeness, but you'd never do. I speak as a woman here, Maureen's tongue. We'll send my darling Sean to do it. He's much more suited."

Sean studied Dougal's eyes. A slight lowering of the brows told the whole story. "Get me the woman," those brows said, "and we'll work out a way to deal with this Pendragon. We'll have an alliance. I believe in rewards as well as punishments."

Sean nodded, one agreement for two distinct proposals.

Fiona's eyes glistened, hard rubies in the firelight. " 'When shall we three meet again? In thunder, lightning, or in rain?' "

" 'When the hurlyburly's done,' " answered Dougal. " 'When the battle's lost and won.' "

*A taste for cheap theatrics,* thought Sean. *Fiona loves making gestures. They won't always get you where you want to go.*

"That *won't* 'be ere the set of sun,' " he said. "And I hope we don't have to move Birnam Wood to do it."

Fiona smiled, her hard smile with the teeth in it. "Perhaps. On the other hand, I might like to play around in my gardens a touch. We'll see, my love. We'll see."

*And we'll see about a way to kill our younger brother, love,* thought Sean.

# ten

—m—

"COFFEE, COFFEE, COFFEE," Jo chanted, under her breath. She knew she shouldn't have drunk so much of that stuff at The Cave, but she didn't plan to get a lot of sleep tonight, anyway. Her fingers twitched, and she slipped her right hand into David's jacket pocket just to give it something to do. The buzz had her eyeballs ratcheting.

Tomorrow was Saturday. There'd be plenty of time for a lazy morning in a shared bed. They'd wake up sometime around three, have breakfast for two at sunset.

Midnight on an icy sidewalk in the heart of a Maine winter wasn't what she'd call a romantic idyll. No place to stop and smooch for an hour, no inviting patches of warm dry grass under the stars. And then there was the cold-hands problem. . . .

Jo snuggled tighter under David's arm. Nice thing about the chem-free club, he even smelled good. No stale cigarette smoke, no sour beer. Just warm male. Just enough fresh sweat left over from the gig to turn her on.

"You guys sounded good."

He squeezed her shoulder. "We need to sound better.

That one reel with Adam showed how *much* better we need to get."

"Pooh. It just proved how much better you *can* get." She extracted her hand from his pocket and herself from his side, to pook him on the nose with one finger. "Dump Mike, David. Either that or change to sea chanteys. He sounds like a Beals' Island lobsterman. No brogue, no lilt. With a good lead singer, you guys can make it. Look at Adam and Ish."

"He sounds like a Beals' Island lobsterman because that's what he *is*. His name is Mike *Beals*, you little cabbage! His great-grandpappy settled the place!"

David ducked to one side and scooped up a handful of snow. She dodged and retaliated. After a fast and flurrious skirmish they both ended up rolling in a snowbank with Jo on top. She shoved another handful of snow down his jacket.

"Peace, woman!"

"You surrender?"

"What terms?"

"Abject slavery."

He grew still. Staring down at him, Jo swore she could see the deep brown of his eyes even in the glow of the streetlights. He smiled.

"Done."

Jo stumbled to her feet, suddenly wobbly at the knees. She covered her confusion by shaking snow out of her hair like a redheaded poodle. Her tongue had decided it was time to go on strike.

"I think you mean that," she whispered, finally.

He lightly touched her shoulders, turning her to face him, then brushed snow from her cheeks.

"I do."

They hugged for some unknown length of time, just hugged through three sweaters and two layers of synthetic goose down. Somehow it felt sexier than screwing bare-ass naked on the seventeenth green of the municipal golf course under a full moon.

Finally, he pulled back and kissed her on the forehead. "I love you, Jo."

"I love you, too. David, you want to move in with me?"

God, *that* was a shivery thought, her tongue running away with itself. First it shut up like a clam, now it spouted things without asking her permission. She'd slept with ten or twenty men, but she'd never *lived* with one. It was a huge step, from making her body feel good to inviting a man inside her *life*, for Chrissakes. Jo felt like she'd just jumped from a plane with no reserve parachute.

"Jo, what about Maureen?"

The soft focus faded. She felt the sinking lump in her stomach that said the main chute had just failed.

"Oh, fuck Maureen." She stifled a giggle. "I mean, not literally. Oh, hell, yes 'literally.' Go ahead. If she says 'yes,' go ahead. I won't mind. God knows, she needs *something* in her life!"

She was blithering, covering up the Maureen Question. How much did she owe her baby sister? When did she get to have a life? She could talk with Momma 'til the cows came home, but the Maureen Question wouldn't go away.

"David, Maureen's more than just a roommate problem. She's stone-ass crazy. Clinically bonkers. Does that bother you?"

He took her hand and started up the slippery hill. She backed off to give him thinking time.

They paused for a traffic light even though there wasn't a car in sight. He drew her closer, wrapping his arm around her waist again.

"Honestly, Jo, it bothers me some. Not enough to matter. Even if your sister's cracked, *you* look sane to me. If you're thinking about kids, most madness isn't inherited.

Besides, like Teddy Kennedy once said, I guess I'll cross that bridge when I come to it."

Kids. Age thirtysomething, maybe she *should* be thinking about kids. David looked like good father material. He limited himself to two drinks a night, never snarled at her even when she was a bitch, willing to wash dishes and unplug a toilet and reach things down from high shelves. And he didn't snore. Everything she needed in a man.

Everything that Daddy wasn't.

Of course, he earned about enough money to keep himself in guitar strings. He'd make a nice pet, though, even if he wasn't a provider. *He followed me home, Mommy. Can I keep him?*

The light went from red to green to red again while they snuggled. A cop cruised by, slowing down before deciding they didn't look like a threat to public decency. Too cold for that.

They hugged and snuggled some more. Then she sobered and forced herself back to the subject at hand. She'd better get it all out in the open.

"David, Maureen's crazy. Dad's a drunken wife-beater. Mom's a religious freak: If she hadn't gotten married, I think she'd be a nun. I'm what you'd call an 'experienced woman.' You up to handling all that?"

"I don't have to live with the rest of the mob." He nuzzled her ear, again. "And I enjoy your experience. You're like Adam with his guitar: You don't get that far without some damn good teachers and a hell of a lot of practice."

"Stop that! Your hands are too cold!"

The hands stopped. They retreated. They left a tingling sensation on her butt, and she didn't bother to refasten the popped snap of her jeans. Hip huggers, they wouldn't fall off unless she asked them to. Which she probably would, but not until she'd walked another few blocks.

A hot shower for two would warm up those hands quite nicely.

She loved those strong musician's hands with the dancing fingers. Sometimes she felt jealous of his guitar strings. If he moved in, she could get him to play love songs at 3 A.M. and then proceed to the logical conclusion.

Yeah. He could play love songs at 3 A.M. with Maureen in the next bedroom.

She followed that thought to *its* logical conclusion and smiled up at him. "Maureen's got to go."

David blinked. "Just kick her out, like that?"

She pulled him across the intersection as if she was going to serve papers on her sister tonight. It was time to get this nonsense over with. Make a clean break.

"Lover, she's a leech. A twenty-eight-year-old dependent child, tantrums and all. If she can't put up with you moving in, she can haul her ass back to Mommy's apron strings. I'm not licensed to run a group home for the mentally ill."

David reclaimed his hand, then kicked at a lump of snow. He didn't look happy.

"Jo, I can find an apartment of my own, a place we can be private. Living with the band, that's kind of weird, anyway. Some kind of mystic brotherhood bullshit. Thought we'd practice more that way, build 'rapport,' fuse into one soul with five pairs of hands. All we needed was a magic well and the harp of Brian Boru to make it work. Let her stay."

"Screw it, David. I'm not Christian enough to be my sister's keeper. It's not just you. This has been wearing at me for years now, my own Chinese water torture. 'Watch out for little Maureen, dear, keep her out of trouble.' 'You're older, it's your responsibility, dear.' 'This wouldn't have happened if you'd been more adult, dear.' *Screw* it!"

David shook his head. "I'm going to hate myself for this, come morning. I can't let you kick Maureen out for me.

I'd feel like one of those damned seal hunters, clubbing little lovable white babies for their fur. She's got that same helpless look in her eyes."

"Helpless, *bullshit*! That little twit carries a *gun* everywhere she goes!"

David stopped short and stared at her. "A *gun*?"

"Frigging .38 Special. Sleeps with it, takes it to the john with her, even packs it with her swimsuit when we go out to the lake."

"Jeezum."

"You want to know what she thinks about men, watch her shooting silhouettes. She gets this look on her face like she's some kind of executioner. Scares the bejayzus out of me."

David rubbed his eyes. "What do you mean, how she thinks about men? Targets are kinda unisex, aren't they?"

"I saw her flat-out *shred* the crotch of a target—five shots, speed reload, five more shots. I could have put my fist right through the hole."

His hands dropped, instinctively covering the target area. "*Christ!* You keep talking like that, babe, you'll have me sleeping alone tonight. Maybe I need to take some time to think over that little question of yours. Yes, your crazy sister *bothers* me."

Jo blinked back tears. The weather they'd been having, she'd freeze her frigging eyelids shut. Even salt water would freeze, get it cold enough. Things were getting awfully cold around here, all of a sudden. She resnapped her jeans.

They trudged on through the snow, heads down and walled off in their own separate worlds. Jo felt like a yo-yo, up and down in the passion department. Even offstage, Maureen sure knew how to kill a party. Or maybe it was hormones.

David took her hand, kissing the back of her glove with

a courtly bow like some Renaissance poet. The yo-yo headed up again, spinning madly.

The streetlights picked up a tender smile. "You red-headed witch, it'll take more than that to break your spell. What do you know about that Brian character she was with tonight? Maybe we can patch things up between them, get him to whirl Maureen off into Never-Never Land. God knows, he's built like a knight in shining armor."

Jo shrugged, got her throat working. "Voice on the phone." She probably sounded like a crow, trying to talk after crying.

She swallowed and went on. "Never even saw him until we met at The Cave. Seems polite enough, good looking if you like the type. I kind of . . . maneuvered . . . him into being there, to take the heat off us. Never expected her to blow up all over the place."

*Maureen,* she remembered, *Maureen frothing at the mouth. Dumb-faced blond hunk of muscle jerking back in shock. The "R" word and instant rage. Genuine surprise.*

Memories.

*Damn.*

A curly blond, blue-eyed boy built like a brick shit-house. Did that ring any bells? Anyone she'd known?

*Oh, hell!*

Jo staggered over to another telephone pole and leaned against it, her head spinning. Shit, shit, shit, shit, *shit*! All her blood seemed to nose-dive to her feet, abandoning her brain to run on fumes. All it could come up with was a flickering montage of a red-eyed, red-haired child cowering in a corner, mixed in with flashes of Jo's first hormone-racked expedition into the wondrous Land of Sex.

*Buddy Johnson.*

Fucking *ghosts* from the fucking *past*. Brian looked a *hell* of a lot like Buddy Johnson. *That* was the missing link.

David gripped her shoulders, held her *up* by both shoulders. It was a good thing he did. Otherwise she'd be sitting in the snow with a strip of phone-pole splinters up her back.

Memories cascaded over each other: times she'd come home to find Buddy already there, times Maureen had moved funny, looked funny. Bruises Jo had seen when they were getting ready for bed at night, bruises she'd blamed on Dad. Maureen white-faced in the john off their room with blood on the toilet paper, years before she'd had her first period. She'd said she'd scratched herself. Things that never connected before.

"Jo, snap out of it! I had no *idea* watching out for her was that big a strain. We'll get you some help, move her into a group home, *something* . . ."

"David, don't pile anything more on that Maureen guilt trip. I've got enough on my conscience, already."

"Conscience?" He twirled her like a puppet until he was staring down into her eyes. "How in hell can Maureen be a load on *your* conscience? You program her brain when she was a baby, peel back her scalp before the soft spot closed and punch in the codes for some particular breed of mental bug?"

Those eyes. She really didn't want to tell him some things and look into those eyes while he thought about them. The far side of the street looked awfully interesting, right now.

"Not the schizophrenia, not all the paranoia, not talking with the trees. Her thing about men, especially men with a certain kind of hair, a certain build. That Brian she was with tonight, that look. Blond apes."

"So what's that got to do with you?"

"You saw what happened, heard what happened. She accused him of raping her. Typical spaced-out Maureen. Things just finally clicked. I used to go with a boy who looked like that. He could be oh-so-nice or he could be mean—*real* mean, a walking ad for a women's shelter. Sure cured me of my Electra complex damn fast, comparing him with Daddy. I . . . I think my first boyfriend raped my sister."

"And that makes *you* guilty?"

"I didn't protect her. I never even thought about that horny bastard alone with a ten-year-old kid. Too full of myself, fourteen and just found out *why* boys and girls were different. He raped her. I know he did. And I set it up."

All those years, and the little twit never *told*! And then another memory surfaced—her and Maureen whispering in a corner of the yard, and Maureen promising never to tell *anyone* about Jo and Buddy. . . .

The tears dried up, lost in the static-crackly air and leaving a scratchy feeling around her eyes. Funny how finding a key to Maureen defused the tension between her and David. Her focus changed from sad to mad. It was time to sort things out, rant and rave and throw things around a bit. Try some confrontation therapy.

She grabbed David's hand and hauled him along, stumbling over frozen ruts and tracks. She was *not* going to lose him to the family's skeleton in the closet. It had happened too damn many times. . . .

She wanted David. She wanted him *permanently.*

"Jo . . ."

He pulled back. She just latched down harder.

"Jo, what the *hell* are you doing?"

"We're going to have a talk, you and me and Maureen. She's going into therapy again before she screws up my life any further. Either that, or I move out and leave *her* with the bills!"

"Uh . . . okay. Look, Jo, slack off on the wrist. I'd like to be able to play again tomorrow. You've got strong hands, woman!"

She stared down at her fingers clamped around his wrist.

It felt like she was drawing power out of the ground and feeding it to a ball of fire on the end of her arm. She gritted her teeth and forced herself to relax. Her grip creaked loud enough to hear, and strength flowed out of the muscles, leaving them limp. David peeled her hand off and shook blood back into his fingers.

"Sorry."

"Jo, you looked like some kind of witch. Your hair stood up, and your eyes glowed like a cat's, and the world kind of turned sideways. You like to crushed my wrist. You're not *big* enough for that!"

"Momma cat defending her kittens. Lover, if I *have* any magic, I'm going to spend it holding on to you. I've never felt like this about a man before, and I'm not *about* to let you go. Maureen can sleep in a snowbank, grab a blanket down at the shelter, or curl up in the back of her rusty Tonka Toy. She comes between you and me, she's history."

David bounced along in her wake as if he trailed on a leash. Jo blinked against the pounding in her temples and tried to ease whatever she was doing. She wanted him with everything intact.

She felt a psychic tug when he stopped. What the hell *was* this magic thing, anyway?

"Jo . . . that gun. I'm not joking around. Maureen with a gun scares the living shit out of me."

She turned back, suddenly aware they stood on her front steps. It seemed like they'd covered two blocks in two seconds.

Jo stabbed a finger downslope, toward the river. "That gun's going for a swim, first chance I get. If she's asleep when we go in, we take it and heave it and tell her if she tries to get another, the police chief is going to get a call with some names and addresses he might want to contact. You're not the only one. My psycho sister ain't got no *business* owning a gun."

Jo turned and headed up the steps again. The ice looked like somebody had dumped coffee all over it, dark stains in the blue glow of the mercury vapor yard light. She had to watch her step all winter, what with the dogs and all.

Her glove stuck to the doorknob, wet wool on cold metal. And then inside she peeled it off and got some kind of gunk on her fingers. It was red under the hall light.

David ran a finger over the railing of the stairs and held it up for her. Red, again.

Blood.

"Somebody got hurt," he said. "Fall on the ice, most likely. You get cold enough, you don't notice it. When I was working construction one winter, about twenty below, I smashed my thumb and didn't even know it until I took a break in the warming shed. Blood like you wouldn't believe. Ruined a pair of gloves."

"Construction? You, working construction?"

He grinned at her. "Hey, even guitar players will work if they get hungry enough."

"Be careful of those hands, lover. I've got uses for them."

She climbed stairs, thinking more about Maureen and David than about which of her neighbors caught his finger in a door. It wasn't her problem. Sorting out things with her sister, was.

"Jo . . ."

She looked closer. The smears by the doorbell button were red and sticky. She looked down. Dark drops glistened on the floor, leading to a puddle smeared toward the door and across the threshold. Her brain slowed down.

About a teacup's worth of puddle.

Blood.

Maureen. That man . . . Brian.

Who looked so much like Buddy Johnson. Who knew where Maureen lived, who'd walked her home last night. Who left The Cave within minutes of his fight with Maureen, who easily could have gotten here before she did, who could have waited outside for her or called her and tricked her back outside. Who could have been just a little *pissed* at the things she said, the things she did.

Jo shivered.

Brian, who looked so much like the older Buddy when the pro trainers pumped him full of steroids and he damned near went to prison for pounding the shit out of a guy in a bar . . .

David stepped in front of her. "Jo, give me your keys."

The door stuck like it always did, jerky across the humped floor. Then Jo saw more blood—blood on the floor tile, blood on the white porcelain of the refrigerator, blood on paper towels wadded up on the table. She saw a man slumped in the corner between the refrigerator and the wall, head in his bloody hands, blood on his shirt, blood in his hair.

His curly blond hair.

Jo froze. She knew she should scream. She knew she should rouse the neighbors, call the cops. Instead, she growled deep in her throat like a feral cat.

She remembered, with a sudden flash, that she'd ended up *hating* Buddy Johnson—that sex between them had become war rather than love. Cops weren't good enough, personal enough; cops wouldn't allow her to tear this scumbag apart with her bare hands.

"You *bastard*, you've killed her!"

She flung herself past David, raging to claw the man's eyes out, sink her teeth into his throat, stomp his head until it popped like an overripe tomato and spilled his brains all over the floor. Her mind and sight and hands focused on a single thing.

Vengeance for Maureen. Vengeance for her baby sister.

Something grabbed her arm and spun her. A fist flashed at her face, a fist backed by red hair and a snarl.

# eleven

—◊—

MAUREEN'S GLARE NAILED David to the wall.

He felt like a frog that she planned to dissect, pinned to the wax bottom of the tray and spread out belly-up waiting for the scalpel. Alive.

Jo groaned and stirred, blood trickling from her lip, and David knew he should go to her, defend her, comfort her, help her up. The air smelled bitter with electricity. He couldn't move.

Insane.

Maureen *was* insane. It had just been a word, before. Here in the blood-spattered kitchen with a man's body slumped against the cabinets and a gun lying on the table, the words grew substance.

Psychotic. Demented. Deranged. Homicidal maniac.

Stone-ass crazy.

She had murdered that man. She was going to murder Jo.

And then the corpse moved. The corpse shoved itself up to sit against the wall and cradled its arm in its lap and groaned. The corpse wore undershorts and undershirt, not what a corpse should be wearing if it had forced its way into an apartment and gotten shot. Other clothing lay in a sodden heap in one corner, leaking a thin trail of red.

David's eyes finally passed details on to his brain. A long slash gouged across the man's left arm. Black thread ran up it in a ragged line of stitches. A bowl of red water sat on the floor. Little white boxes with red crosses on them lay scattered around. Gauze rolls and gauze pads and flesh-colored tape mixed among bottles, peroxide and iodine.

The static died, and he smelled a doctor's office, antiseptic and blood and freshly opened bandages. She hadn't killed him. She was patching him up. The poor bastard had gotten himself into a hell of a mess.

Maureen grabbed a lump of white and threw it at David. His fingers told him it was a roll of paper towels.

"Don't just stand there like a fucking idiot! Take some water and clean up that crap out in the stairwell."

Whatever pinned him against the wall vanished. David stumbled over to the sink, rattled a saucepan under the faucet, and splashed water in it. He *still* couldn't go to Jo. Maureen's aura forbade it.

He felt like he'd walked into a coven of witches. First, Jo damn near pulped his wrist with her tiny hands, then Maureen knocked Jo clear across the kitchen with one off-balance punch. Neither woman weighed more than a hundred, in winter clothes and sopping wet. What the *hell* was *with* these Pierce women?

Maureen told him to clean up, he went to clean up. No choice. Maybe Jo would wake up enough to battle her sister for his soul.

Blood and water and sodden red paper towels—it seemed like he wiped up enough blood for a minor war. A puddle of blood affects the eyes differently than a puddle of water, connects to different nerves, works deep on the brain stem. And the damned stuff spreads around like thick paint. One drop will smear to cover a whole floor tile.

It still was what Maureen or Jo would call a fucking mess, no doubt about it. Sometimes you could tell they were sisters from a typed transcript. Fucking this, goddamn that, assorted obscenities and blasphemies as add-on adjectives and adverbs at a rate of two per sentence.

His mother had always said that the casual use of profanity indicated a poverty of intellect. Someone with half a brain could come up with sharper and more compelling words that wouldn't blush a Baptist preacher. And besides, the way they used foul language it lost all effect. It faded into background noise after the first ten minutes.

Speaking of brains . . . where were his? He stared down at the saucepan full of thin spaghetti sauce and the wad of crimson paper towels. He was mopping up blood on the stairs while Maureen played EMT.

What the *hell* was she doing? That man needed an emergency room. Knife wound in the arm, livid bruises on face and shoulder and leg, the spaced-out pupils of a concussion victim—the guy was seriously hurt.

He grabbed everything and legged up the stairway two steps at a time, into what felt like psychic molasses. The closer he got to Maureen, the less absurd everything seemed. He wrestled with his sense of outrage, holding on to an image of punching 9-1-1 on Jo's phone.

The voice of reason yammered on in the back of his head. *Get professional help! Get some cops, some EMTs, anybody who can wade through this muck and bring some sanity to it!*

David swam against the current, into the kitchen. Maureen wanted the door closed. He closed it. Maureen wanted the bloody water dumped, both pans. He dumped them. What Maureen wanted, Maureen got.

Maureen crouched, tense, like a leopard strung out on speed, swabbing a scrape on Brian's forehead. Jo sat on the corner of the kitchen table, holding a soaked towel to her lip and glaring at her sister. David felt a crackling energy between them, like two storm fronts full of thunderclouds pushing against each other.

Just a quiet evening at home.

David forced himself to pick up the phone, sweating with the effort. Maureen didn't want him doing this.

"No calls." Her voice cut his resolve like a whip.

"Got to get an ambulance." His hand trembled. The phone went back into its cradle.

"No," Brian muttered. "Can't go to the hospital, can't see a doctor. My visa's expired. They'll deport me."

"Man, you need blood, you need X rays, you could have internal injuries or a cracked skull or anything! Maureen's just sewed up your arm with a darning needle and a length of binder twine. Tetanus shots, antibiotics—you name it, you need it. You got a death wish?"

"Be okay. Was a medic in the army. Told her what to do. Needle's clean, wound's bled enough to wash any crap out of it."

David surrendered to the pressure. It was the easiest way out.

"What happened to you, man?"

"Car. Hit-and-run."

"Bullshit. That's a knife wound."

Maureen's stare froze his tongue. "Shut up," it said. "Obey." That glare had nothing but imperatives in its vocabulary.

Charisma. *Beaucoup* charisma, *mon ami,* the commanding aura of the truly insane. Like maybe Hitler. David found himself wondering if Jo could do that. The idea ran icicles down his spine. It was something to think about. Something to *seriously* think about.

This family was *weird*.

*     *     *

MAUREEN JERKED HER attention back to Jo. "Stay away from us," she warned. "Keep your hands where I can see them. *Both* of you stay where I can see you.

"Don't even *think* of trying to get to the bedroom phones," she added, half to herself.

The knuckles of her right hand still ached from the punch. Served her sister right, attacking an injured man. First she stole David, then she waltzed in and tried to kill Brian. Who was the crazy one here?

She dabbed iodine on Brian's forehead and then the slash on his arm, still keeping half an eye on Jo and David. Brian winced at the antiseptic bite around the stitch holes. That was good. It proved he was still all there.

It was going to get a little involved here, wrapping gauze around that arm. She'd need both hands and some attention. She picked up the gun and set it on the floor, close to her knee, farther from Jo and David. No unnecessary risks.

Jo called her paranoid. Paranoid delusions didn't carve five-inch slices out of arms, didn't break ribs, didn't carry the rusty lengths of iron pipe she'd unstrapped from Brian's leg and tossed in the corner. God above, Maureen *knew* what paranoia looked like.

Her own fears had nearly pulled the trigger. He'd stood there filling the doorway, made some growling noise deep in his throat, and reached out for her. She'd cocked the .38 and was about an ounce shy of blasting five hollow points into his chest when she'd realized he was already falling. When she'd seen the blood.

The next instant, she'd been dragging that Neandertal carcass into the kitchen and swearing a blue streak at the damage she found. It didn't make sense. Or maybe it did. She stopped and stared at his blood, sticky on her hands.

*There's no way you ever could have met him halfway. You had to have control. You had to feel safe.*

But there'd still been that gap, when her instincts took control and overruled the terror. *Dissociation: temporary but drastic modification of one's personality.* Recognizing a symptom and naming it didn't make it a bit less strange.

It still felt odd, touching a man, wiping his skin, moving his arms and legs around like lumps of putty wrapped around a frame of sticks. The smell of blood, the smell of man, they ought to scare her. They didn't. She glanced at his crotch, at the lump in his underpants. That thing ought to scare her. It didn't.

Brian grunted as she moved his arm. Must hurt. She ran her hands down the muscles to each side of the cut, flowing cool energy from her skin into his. Weird sensation.

"Maureen, I'd help if you let me."

Jo winced back as if Maureen's eyes were daggers. *Good. Stay away from this man,* she thought. *You touch him, I'll kill you.*

Her mental critic pounced. *Sounds like the same thing you told him, two hours ago. A little paradox, girl? That glamour thing Fiona talked about? You call a man a rapist and then threaten to kill your sister to protect him? Why aren't you afraid of him?*

He'd come to her for help. He was hurt, in danger, alone, and he came to her for help. Nobody had ever come to her for help before.

He was too weak to threaten her. Besides, if he tried to touch her emotions, fuck with her head, she'd know it. Certainty.

*Voices again? Voices in your head, Maureen? No trees in here to tell you things. No trees to guard you. You're walking in the world of men.*

She didn't need trees. She could feel it in her hands. Brian wasn't dangerous.

Meanwhile, her fingers played ER nurse without her command. Gauze pads covered the wounds. Gauze strips bound them in place—wrapped two-handed, gently, only enough pressure to hold the bandage in place. It seemed her hands knew what to do. Her hands told her not to squeeze the wounds; it would be dangerous to slow down circulation.

"David, get *away* from that fucking *phone!*"

He jerked back as if he had touched a live wire.

The voices switched to strategy. She needed to ease up a little. Was she going to move this hunk of muscle into a bed all by herself? Going to cut the phone wires and hold them at gunpoint all night long?

She needed to try a bit of cunning here, soothe her bitch sister and that faithless fake-Irish guitar player. Maureen wasn't mad at them. Maureen was just protecting this poor man who had come to her for help.

"Jo, why'd you attack him?"

Glare met glare. "Thought *he'd* killed *you*, dammit! You had that fight at The Cave. Then we came in and saw all the blood. . . ."

"David, get her some ice to hold on that lip. Wrap it in a dish towel."

Jo glanced over to the gun and back to Maureen's face. Suddenly, she was five again, and Jo had found her playing with Dad's pocketknife. Such a pretty thing, and it cut so clean into the soft yellow wood of the scrap of lumber, such smooth pine-smelling curls. Trouble was, she didn't know to cut *away* from her body, *away* from her other hand.

She rubbed the thin white scar running from the knuckle of her left thumb all the way across to the center of her wrist. Memories. Maureen dropped her gaze.

"Sorry I hit you. Had to stop you, fast."

*Take a chance,* she thought. *Can't watch them all night, going to fall asleep sometime. Relax, people, it's just your little helpless hopeless wallflower sister.*

Maureen stood up, scooped up the gun, and tucked it back into her jacket pocket. Then she moved away.

"Brian's sleeping in my bed tonight. I'll sleep out on the couch."

She looked around, finally pulling her focus away from crisis. The kitchen was a mess: bloody towels, Brian's bloody clothes, melted slush, tag ends of bandages. The place looked like a *M*A*S*H* scene. It was time to pick up, mop up, get rid of the evidence. Besides, some physical activity might serve to calm things down. Nothing like mopping the kitchen floor to bring you back to reality.

She hauled clothes into the bathroom, running water in the tub to soak out blood before the stains set. She emptied his pockets first, and stared at a roll of bills about as big around as her fist. The outer one bore Ben Franklin's smiling face. Her hands shook at the thought of holding a whole year's wages in one lump.

Maybe it was reaction, but she felt like shit. The tendons in her right arm had turned to red-hot wires. She must have strained something with that punch. A headache centered about two inches behind her right eye and an inch below the scalp.

She moved back to the kitchen—mopping up bloodstains, David helping. Jo held that cold towel to her lip, gathering trash. Brian suggested using the black trash bags—opaque, he didn't want anybody seeing all that blood and asking questions. He didn't have enough answers.

Just one big, happy family. Just two women with their boyfriends on Friday night.

"Stay *away* from Brian, Jo. Not just cleaning up, I mean stay away from him *permanently*."

Jo's eyes widened. Such a look of innocence, you'd think she was an actress. Maureen thought she'd better get some clothes on Brian. Then maybe Jo'd quit running her eyes up and down his legs, across his chest, measuring his biceps.

Jo shook her head. "I don't need your new boyfriend, Mo. David's going to be staying here. He's gonna move his stuff in tomorrow. You don't like it, don't let the door hit you in the ass on your way out."

Maureen felt her skin prickle like she was charging up for a lightning bolt.

THE LIGHTS FLICKERED. Brian wondered if he was the only one who noticed. Both of them were doing it. Neither of them knew what she was doing.

He hoped they got this settled before they burned the apartment down around their ears or blacked out half of Maine. It was the most dangerous thing in the world, power in the hands of the ignorant. Like giving that pistol to a child just strong enough to pull the trigger.

Rage. Fear. Sexual attraction. Powerful emotions caused powerful responses. Whether they knew it or not, those were two powerful women. If they weren't balanced, one would have torn the other to shreds.

He was too groggy to handle it now. He tried to remember that pain was optional. He could use his left arm a bit, just stunned nerves. If he could get this background noise calmed down, maybe he could get some serious healing meditation going.

He was going to need to move again in the next day or so, fight again in the next day or so. Fiona never gave up on anything in her life.

And he made a mental note to never even *think* about touching Maureen's emotions again. Charged up the way she was, it would be like bringing a ten-pound hammer down on TNT. She'd notice, oh yes. She'd fry his eyeballs.

"Can't go back to my hotel. Following me."

Maureen paused and ran a cold towel over his head again. Her touch spread energy and soothing—unsuspected power. That woman needed some training. He'd better take her to St. Theresa's Abbey before Dougal got his hands on her.

"Stay here," she said. "If Jo can move her boyfriend in, so can I."

The lights flickered, and Brian felt the hair rise on his arms. It was a feedback loop, Jo reacting to Maureen reacting to Jo reacting to Maureen. He'd better get those two separated before they reached critical mass.

"Just tonight," he said. "Stay here tonight. Ask you to find me an apartment, tomorrow. Furnished. Buy some things. Find money in my jacket."

"I saw it." Maureen glared at her sister, at David. "If you don't mind, I'll find a place big enough for both of us."

Brian knew his brain was only functioning at half power, but some signs were printed large enough to read. One was, the look between Jo and David. Mixture of shock and relief. Said, "*This* is *Maureen*?" Said, "What the *hell* is going on here?" Said, "Good riddance!"

Undercurrents.

People with Power, people with the Blood, usually didn't fit in. They heard voices others couldn't, saw things no one else could see, touched and smelled and tasted and thought and acted outside the fences. Society pasted labels on them. Jo's face said Maureen wore a label. Jo's face said she was fed up with living with a label.

Jo's face still held worry.

"Maureen, I can't fucking *believe* you're moving in with a *man*."

Jo wanted her sister gone. She did *not* want her sister hurt. Brian must look like a very dubious case, judging by her frown.

"Take the money," he said, "find two apartments. There's enough."

"One apartment, two bedrooms."

The tone said, "Don't get any ideas. I'm your nurse, not your goddamned whore."

Maureen disappeared into the bathroom and returned, dumping his cash and keys on the kitchen table. David stared at the bloodstained roll of bills.

"You're a drug dealer." He edged toward the phone and Maureen's jacket—Maureen's jacket with the gun in the pocket.

The static charge in the room jumped a coulomb or ten. That man was going to get crisped if he didn't watch out.

"No. Swear it. I'm clean."

"The scars you've got, you've been carved up like a Christmas turkey. Street fights. Nobody but a drug runner carries his bank in his hip pocket."

Brian wished the debate club straight to hell. His fuddled thoughts weren't up to it.

"Drug runners and wetbacks. Can't use a bank. No plastic, no checks. That's my room and board for the next year, until I get home again. Think I'm going to leave it in a cheap hotel?"

Jo waved David back from the phone. At least she had the power to sense dangerous territory.

"Little Sister, what do you *really* know about this man? There's something screwy here. I've got some questions that need answering before I'd trust him behind *my* back."

The sergeant major was back, offering advice. *Don't get into what you really are, me laddie. Some of Jo's questions don't have answers they'd want to hear. Some of them cross the line into Maureen's territory—label territory. Maureen's already over there; she understands. The other two won't. Not unless they have their noses rubbed in it.*

Brian groaned. If Jo or David poked at Maureen one

more time, that bomb was going to explode. His head hurt too much to deal with it. "Maureen, let David take the gun. Lock me in your room tonight. You've got those old locks that use a key from either side."

He tried getting vertical. The walls turned into sponges under his hands, and the floor tilted to a twenty-degree list. Moving wasn't a good idea. It did get them off the topic, though. Pain spoke across a lot of gaps.

Hands and faces and shoulders and doorways and darkness and the blessed soft warmness of a bed. A bed that smelled of Maureen, the sweet musk of a woman with the Blood, overpowering and seductive. To sleep, perchance to dream—perchance to lust. Or heal. He set his body to concentrate on the bones first. They carried the rest.

The lock rattled and clicked. Taking no chances. They didn't know he could step around into the half worlds and be gone in two seconds. He'd have done that in the alley if he hadn't been sure Fiona was waiting for him to try, waiting under the Sidhe hill with her webs all woven. Traps within traps within traps. Now he didn't dare move until he had his strength back.

*Thought I saw Dougal out on the street: watching, waiting. Nobody else would be carrying a hawk around at midnight. He knows where Maureen lives. It'll be a hell of a problem if he comes here now.*

Darkness.

# twelve

—〰—

SIX-PACK OF DIET Coke, half dozen donuts, two packs of Slims: Maureen recited the Catechism of Commerce. Her fingers danced over the register keys—product codes and prices in the eyes and out the fingers without transiting the brain. Quick Shop. Mindless fucking job.

She gave the kids back by the magazines the hairy eyeball; keep your under-eighteen hands off the *Penthouse* rack, you little twerps. The number three monitor showed a potential shoplifter. That was her real job, the only one a barcode scanner with a price database couldn't handle.

Just watch out for trouble. Never trust anybody. Never relax. It was a good job description for a paranoid.

"Miss, I'm going to have to ask you for ID on the Slims."

The girl looked older than what Maureen saw in the mirror every morning, but that was the law. A kid could go down to the corner of First and Division and buy crack or grass or heroin any hour of the day or night. However, a beer or a pack of cigarettes underage brought down the full weight of the law.

The world was schizoid.

Just like Maureen.

*Jo's right,* she thought. *We had a little schizoid episode there the other night, didn't we? Maybe time to go in for a quick evaluation, get the medication adjusted? Somebody's not behaving normally here. Not even normal for Crazy Maureen.*

*Odd thing a lot of people believe, that nutcases don't think they're crazy. We know better, don't we? Knowing the definition of paranoid schizophrenia doesn't change its effect.*

The woman in monitor three started to slip a half-buck can of cat food into her pocket, then stared straight into the video camera. She put the can back on the shelf. Maureen slid her hand away from the call button and counted out change.

"Have a nice day."

Maureen switched her attention from the monitor to the real shoplifter. The woman wore a dirty brown coat down to her ankles, grease spots, tangled hair, worn army boots, a look to the eyes that said they saw into a different universe—probably "deinstitutionalized," homeless, planned to eat the cat food herself. Maureen looked at the woman and saw herself in another twenty years.

Tough shit. The woman could eat and stay warm in jail.

Quick Shop had security testers who came in looking to get caught deliberately, to check the cashiers. The same with underage buyers of alcohol and tobacco. Forget what's-his-name's question: Who's gonna watch the watchers? Quick Shop had it covered.

*Question: Who's the* real *paranoid here?*

Brian looked better today: bruises already yellowing, swelling going down around the stitches. He was moving more easily, walking again, breathing normally again. It made Maureen's skin crawl, just thinking about it. Uncanny.

It brought up major questions, though. When the man got healthy, what was she going to *do* with him? She wasn't equipped for living with a man. Physically, maybe, she had the usual female equipment of tits and ass, but mentally?

Move back to Jo's, her being shacked up with that lyin' cheatin' no-'count guitar player? Find a third apartment with Brian's money? Trust the lock on her bedroom door? Crazy little Maureen was sharing an apartment with a man she'd met three days ago. A man she'd called a rapist. A man she'd threatened to kill.

*Maureen's got a problem. Maureen's having flashbacks again.*

Girl, six-pack of premixed formula and box of disposable diapers, pack of condoms. Looked to be maybe sixteen, maybe not. Condoms? Now? Better late than never. Maureen counted out change.

"Have a nice day."

At least that's *one* thing hanging around with Jo had taught her. You'd never catch Jo without a condom in her jeans pocket.

Maureen's fingers danced their dance across the cash register, her eyes shifted from flickering gray monitors to prurient magazine rack in their paranoid patrol, her mind wandered the alleyways of sexual relationships. Maureen and men. Maureen and Brian.

Brian was behaving himself. She didn't know whether he was a nice guy or just a louse too badly hurt to show his true colors. He wasn't Buddy, anyway. She'd felt no sign of that suspicious warmth of his "glamour." He acted the proper British gentleman, not a word or gesture or touch out of place.

They played chess with an old wooden set she'd found when they moved out of Jo's. He was an unconventional player, brilliant but erratic. Sometimes the two of them combined for a grandmaster game, sometimes a total debacle. He tended to ambushes and sudden overwhelming power concentrated on a single point. She went in more for feints within feints within feints, with minor pieces or even pawns turning into devastating weapons when you least expected.

A shrink would have a field day with their different playing styles.

Sometimes, he'd overlook a simple mate in two because it was too obvious. Apparently his military life had been like that, flashes of brilliance mired in the retreat of a dying empire. The politicians called them victories, but most of his career sounded like one disaster after another. According to him, even the Falklands had been a total fuck-up. But you couldn't blame the bishop for being on the wrong diagonal when he was needed.

They watched movies, by preference old movies on the cable channels. Maureen liked knowing the ending ahead of time. Just like with chess, it helped her little problems if she knew the rules. Brian seemed to want a bit of predictability in his life, as well. Maybe he hadn't had enough of it.

They'd only spent a couple of days together, but time with Brian was strange. It went fast, and yet seemed far longer than it was. Seemed like they'd done too much to fit into the hours, and there were too many hours to fit into the days. Maybe that's where the fast healing came from.

Whatever it meant, she was getting used to having him around.

He was a good patient, too. Never complained when his inept nurse fumbled rebandaging or grabbed hold of the wrong piece of man when helping him out of a chair.

Twelve ninety-five for gas. She wiped the license number she'd automatically memorized when the car pulled up to the pump. If a car pulled out without paying, she either had the fucking license number or she ended up buying the fucking gas herself. Incentive plan.

She made change. "Have a nice day."

Half gallon of milk and the *Record Eagle*.

"Good evening, Maureen."

She jerked, almost knocking over the sign showing the Megabucks winning number. She'd been watching the gas pump, out the window. *Quit jumping like a Vietnam vet hearing a car backfire, you silly bitch!*

But she didn't *know* anybody in the store. Maureen's eyes snapped into focus. Sleek dark hair, dark eyes, olive skin: Fiona.

No.

It was her shadow, the other elegant cobra from the strip club: Sean. If he let his hair grow long and wore his clothes cut for a slim woman, he could pass for Fiona's twin sister.

He wore Fiona's face, molded into a kind of androgynous maleness. Fiona had said something about sterility. Brian had mentioned XXY chromosomes and the hybrid problem. Didn't that mean impotent? Maureen couldn't remember.

Where the *hell* had he come from? He hadn't walked in the front door. And then she remembered Fiona in Carlysle Woods, appearing and vanishing without a trace. Frigging magic.

Alarm bells jangled in the back of her brain. Sean and Fiona—Brian said they were behind his beating. Brian *said* they were dangerous. They had never hurt *her*, though. *Besides,* something whispered in her head, *you're safe here. Magic only happens in the alleys and the shadows. This is Quick Shop, the least magical place on earth.*

What was so dangerous about magic? Fiona had laughed when told Brian said the Summer Country was dangerous. And the real world wasn't all that safe. Maureen had seen Brian kill a man about four blocks from here.

Well, maybe not a *man*, according to what Brian *said*.

*Magic can't exist under fluorescent lights and monitor cameras. This tacky atmosphere would drive a stake through the heart of the strongest vampire. You're safe here.* It didn't really sound like her critic, but the voice was as persuasive as the snake in Eden. The alarm bells faded as if stifled in wads of cotton.

Her deep-rooted fear of men, of *everyone*, started to look laughable. This Sean, sterile, he couldn't be a threat. He'd be sort of like the harem eunuch—you could trust him around women. No chance of a glamour there.

Her automatic pilot counted out change for the milk and paper. "Have a nice day."

Their hands touched. Smooth. Warm. Electric. Like the touch of Brian's hand when they'd walked away from the fire. That had been nice.

"We need to talk," he said. "You shouldn't be afraid of us. When do you get off work?"

His voice had Fiona's soft Irish lilt but in a slightly deeper register. Soft Irish whiskey, it really was, golden and smoky and magic on the tongue, with a gentle liquid fire soaking straight into the throat and never even reaching the stomach. Brian's voice was gin, cheap gin. It would get you drunk enough, but you wouldn't enjoy the process half as much.

"It's past time for my break. Wait while I get the night manager out here to cover the register. We can talk outside."

She pushed the call button, one short dash that meant no trouble. One time she'd jammed the damn thing, gave the long buzz that said, "Call the cops." White cars and blue lights like you wouldn't believe. She'd smoothed it over with free cups of coffee and some outdated donuts that only would have fed the Dumpster in the morning.

Fred came out, glanced over the monitors, and punched his code into the register. He didn't even try to crowd her tits or brush his hand across her ass behind the counter. She felt calm and safe, as if Sean were guarding her against such threats. She grabbed her jacket, swinging it carefully so Fred wouldn't notice the lumpy weight of the Smith in the right pocket.

Sean took her arm, like a gentleman leading his lady onto the ballroom floor. It was a soft touch, a warm touch, a friendly touch—not something threatening. Faint unease raised memories of how Brian's glamour had felt the other night, how that slow gentle warmth had grown into frightening passion.

*Why be afraid of passion? Most people seek it out.*

*Besides, Sean's a sterile hybrid. He's no threat.*

The cold wind bit through that glow as soon as they stepped outside, an Alberta Clipper straight down from the Arctic Circle. She wiggled into her jacket and turned her back to the polar ice cap. Maine faced another month of winter before she could even *begin* to think about sun and birds and green, growing things.

And Mud Season. And then bugs. Someday she was going to move to a place where the weather was designed with people in mind.

"Fiona asked me to talk to you."

Maureen jerked her thoughts back from their vague wandering. Brian had told her this man was dangerous.

Sean didn't *look* dangerous. He stood in the frozen slush, wind tangling his hair, looking like an ad for some designer line of clothing: a Spanish don, somebody like Ricardo Montalban about to climb into a big Chrysler with butter-soft leather upholstery and a walnut dash. Even the garish orange glow of the streetlights suited his sleek, dark beauty.

"So talk." Maureen forced a hostile tone, fighting against the voice of the serpent. "What does Fiona want with me? Want me to poison her brother, perhaps? He's too big for me to beat him up."

Sean laughed, with a deprecating wave of his free hand. "Nothing so crude. She just wants you to remember that you have a home waiting for you with your people. A warm, green home in the Summer Country."

He gestured at the ice, the cold glitter of the winter stars, the tawdry beer signs flapping across the Quick Shop front. Maureen read the sweep of his arm. The store was flat-ass ugly: Marlboro's ragged vinyl banner, the stack of gallon bottles of windshield-washer fluid sadly depleted by the recent siege of slush, the Dumpster overflowing wet cardboard into the piles of filthy snow left by the plow truck. His arm swept on, to include the whole tattered, icy, dirty, dangerous, nasty scene of city winter.

Summer Country. The image was seductive, like the travel-agency ads for Cancún or St. Thomas, the cabin-fever getaway specials they trotted out right after a big storm. Somewhere around Groundhog Day, when the mercury in the thermometer congealed down near thirty below, half the state of Maine flew south. The other half wished they could.

"Why'd you guys attack Brian?"

Sean shook his head. "What makes you think it was us? Believe me, Fiona doesn't want him damaged."

For an instant, the golden warmth slipped, and Maureen caught a flicker of rage across Sean's face. She felt the sudden chill of danger and peeled her arm out of his hand.

"Not damaged? Just weakened? Weakened to the point where she can control him?"

He moved closer to her, bringing the warm glow back into the night. Sean might be dangerous, but not to *her.* Maureen focused on his eyes, the beautiful depth of his eyes in the light spilling out from the store windows. Anyone, man or woman, could fall into those eyes and drown.

"Brian is a ruthless man, Maureen. He has many enemies. Remember what he did to Liam. Brian has killed many Old Ones with many friends. Any one of those could be hunting him for revenge. Fiona wanted me to warn you. You are in great danger, living with Brian."

"And I would be safer in the Summer Country?"

Sean brushed a finger gently across her cheek, leaving a taste of delicious fire behind. "Safety is relative, my dear. Laws protect you in the world of men. We do not have laws in the Summer Country. We have customs."

The palm of his hand was impossibly soft and warm and gentle, caressing her neck. "You are a beautiful woman, Maureen, a powerful woman. When you come to the Summer Country, your beauty and the power of your blood will defend you. Men will fear you and adore you, laying their hearts at your feet. They will protect you, each from the other. There is strength in jealousy. This is our custom, strength balanced against strength."

His face floated, inches from her own—soft, dark, handsome, hypnotic. "We are not barbarians in the Summer Country. No man will take you against your will. Come with me, Maureen. Come with me to your own homeland."

She smelled the land on him—the warm earth, the green grass, the peat fires, the slow river waters flowing smooth and tannin-dark across the waterweed. The word pictures flowed through her head using Grandfather O'Brian's voice, the voice of safety. Sean's lips burned against hers without any trace of the cold north wind. Maureen fell into the kiss, losing herself, barely conscious of his hands drawing her body against his.

Something in the back of her head screamed terror and warning, but it was weak and far away. Her pulse buried it under the rushing, throbbing heat in her breasts and belly.

JO BLINKED AGAIN. Maureen had been right *there*. *Maureen,* kissing a *man*. And then Jo had blinked with shock, and the two of them were gone.

She must have stepped back inside the store. It could

have been a minute rather than a second, Jo's surprise being what it was.

Jo pushed through the icy wind and into the Quick Shop. Just checking, she reminded herself. She owed it to Maureen, she owed it to *herself*, to make sure everything was fine. She hadn't seen her sister since the morning she moved out. They hadn't ever thrashed things out about Buddy, either. There'd never been a chance.

The greasy little man behind the counter looked up and jumped. Jo had seen *that* look before: Maureen walked out and Jo walked in, different clothes on the same woman with no time to change. Sometimes they used to do it for a joke, just like real twins.

"Where's Maureen?"

The man's eyes narrowed as they groped their way up and down Jo's body. *Slimeball,* she thought. *Come out from behind that counter, and I'll kick you in the* cojones. *Freebie, special for Maureen, just for having to work with you.*

"Stepped outside a minute ago. She never told me she had a twin sister."

"She doesn't."

Jo pushed back through the door, right into a gust of wind that might as well have been liquid nitrogen. Her teeth felt like they were going to crack from thermal stress. Maybe Mo had ducked around the corner, hiding out in the shadows and a bit of shelter.

Smooching.

Maureen? No way in God's green tomato patch. Something was wrong here. The whole scene, wrong. It stank like a week-old road-killed skunk. If that Brian character had tangled her up in trouble, Jo would skin him alive with her fingernails.

She'd been right to check on Mo.

Jo closed her eyes. There was a trick they used to do, she and Maureen, it played hell with games of hide-and-seek:

find the sister. Get calm enough, quiet enough, and listen to the chunk of brain just on top of your spinal cord. If Maureen was anywhere within a couple hundred yards, Jo could find her. And vice versa. In some ways, they *were* twins. Nothing mystical or magic: Her back brain probably just knew how Maureen thought, where she was likely to go.

The wind nipped at her, and she drifted along with it, around that hypothetical corner into a calm eddy. No Maureen.

She quieted herself, relaxed, slowed her breathing.

*Center my self in peace.*

*Part of me is missing. Where is she?*

A faint echo returned, at the edge of her sister-sonar: Maureen, that way, around back. She might be embarrassed as hell, Jo catching her making out with a man. Tough shit. Jo wouldn't be able to sleep tonight if she didn't track her sister down.

Eyes closed, Jo turned and took a careful, sliding step. The feeling strengthened as the air fell still around her. Careful, careful, there was ice underfoot. Another step brought a touch of warmth to her face, and she opened her eyes, expecting an unseen vent.

Sweat jumped out of her spine and froze there.

She stood in formless dark. Phantoms played with the corners of her eyes, then disappeared when she flicked her vision after them. Faint whispers echoed sight in her ears, voices and words just beyond or beneath understanding. The damp coolness of a cave hung musty around her, mixed with some sense of graveyard earth. *Under the Sidhe hill,* she giggled hysterically to herself, *a waking dream.*

She was going crazy. She was following her sister straight into the loony bin.

Jo snatched at her only way out. Where was Maureen?

Calming breaths, again. In. Hold. Out. Relax back into

the center. Open herself to the void. Seek the emptiness in her mind. Seek the peace.

Maureen was *that* way. Now Jo was trying to save herself instead of her sister. Too late to back out now—she didn't even know which way *was* out. She was committed.

Another cautious step and Jo felt the ground firm beneath her feet, spongy with turf rather than the crusty winter muck coating Naskeag Falls. She opened her eyes again.

Grass. Trees. Green, rolling hills. Blue sky. Sun.

*This isn't real.* She blinked and shook her head like a horse tormented by flies. The impossible world mocked her confusion by continuing to exist.

Jo shivered even though she was no longer cold.

She stood by a fieldstone wall that separated pastures from ancient woods. The breeze caressed her cheeks, wiping the bite of winter away and bringing the sweet warmth of spring to her nose. Dazed beyond fear, she slipped off her gloves and ran cold-reddened fingers over the moss on the stone. Damp. Velvet soft. Coolness that felt warm by contrast with her touch memory of Maine ice. She brought fingers to her nose and drank in the sour wet smell of lichen eating stone.

It was real. Either real or delusions strong enough to make Maureen's look like sanity.

Starch leaked out of her knees. She settled onto a rock, grateful for its gritty reality under her butt. She'd always thought little Mo's babble about wizards from Grandpa's Summer Country proved she was ready for the butterfly nets.

Black dots swirled across her eyes, and she fought them down, continuing to breathe slowly against an urge to just give up and faint. She'd always hated those tight-corseted females who gave a theatrical groan and collapsed under a little strain.

Jo gritted her teeth and forced the world to settle on an

even keel. *Jesus H. Christ, Maureen, what* have *you gotten into now?*

Jo scanned the forest edge, picking out oak and birch and a huge glossy holly that dominated the field's corner like a god. This forest was *old*, radiating age like Stonehenge or the Sphinx. That pasture oak, it had to be older than Columbus.

This was no place in Maine, with old-growth forest right up against a pasture wall. The oak would have been firewood sent up a chimney a century ago. And she'd never *seen* lush grassland like this. Maine pastures tended to look like a terminal case of mange: bald spots of granite mixed with drifts of scrub juniper too tough and prickly for grazing.

The field wasn't just grass. Jo plucked a three-lobed leaf. Shamrock. Grandpa had given each of them one in a silver locket, when they were kids. Another hallucination. Ireland? Bullshit. Ireland would be in the middle of winter, just like Maine. The sky glowed blue from horizon to horizon, and the breeze felt warm and dry.

Meanwhile, where was Maureen? That was the question that brought Jo here. Maybe Maureen had some answers, her or that man she was with.

Jo could use an answer or two about now.

She scanned again, looking for an echo. Eyes closed, she concentrated on calm and centering. Calm would help a few other things, things like the sweat forming on her palms and trickling down her armpits in a most unladylike display of gibbering terror.

Calm. Centering got her into this. It could get her out again. She concentrated on her breathing. Where was the sister? Maureen knew the way here, she knew the way back. Simple.

*That way.*

Her compass pointed through the woods, a line near the ancient holly. There was a stile over the fence, flat stones set into the wall to make a set of steps no cow or pig could follow. Goats sure as hell could, but the Irish were never big on goats.

She decided just to go and call it Ireland, ignoring the sunshine. Having a name cut back on the terror.

A trail led away from the stile, back into the shadows under the trees. Jo followed it into a fairy-tale forest, dark and old and musty and watchful, full of ancient dangers. The trees wore faces crusted with lichen beards and split peelings of bark hair, drowsing faces with closed eyes and mouths. Jo thought she'd just as soon they never woke up. She remembered fairy-tale dangers and felt her fingernails digging into her palms.

Again, she forced herself to relax. After all, she wasn't big enough to be worth eating.

Well, she was bigger than the woodcutter's children. Fairy-tale forests had teeth. Big Bad Wolves, the Gingerbread Witch, the Black Dragon at the Ford—dangers lurked in the shadows and waited for lunch to walk into their jaws.

She scuffed her boots in the litter on the trail, rustling along through the dead leaves and branches, trying to substitute anger for fear. She was hot. Some of that sweat was earned, dressed as she was for winter in Maine. She stuffed her hat and gloves into a pocket.

What the hell was she going to do with this cold-weather crap? She'd need it again on the way home.

A hiss froze her in her tracks. Something large moved among the trees—something as big, as slow-moving, as confident as a bear or moose.

*Bears don't hiss. Moose don't hiss.*

Darkness filled the trail, a heavy glittering darkness that swirled and coiled like a twining anaconda in the Amazon jungle.

*Oh, shit!*

# thirteen

—⁂—

DAVID THOUGHT THAT somebody sure had wrung a lot of mileage out of a single set of building plans. Maureen's new tenement looked like a clone of the one she had shared with Jo, and there had been five others just like them in the blocks between the two. Typical three-story wooden rat palaces, all seemed to have been built within ten years of each other back around the 1920s. They were probably all owned by the same family of slumlords off in California.

He squinted against the sunlight, trying to see if the shades were up or down.

It looked as if *somebody* was awake. He hoped it was Maureen and not that freaky gangster of hers. Brian had never *done* anything hostile, but something about him reminded David of a police Doberman. Whether he was hurt or not, you moved carefully around him and kept your hands in plain sight.

Jo had said she was going to see Maureen, might be late. Noon was more than late. Noon was worry time.

He took the stairs two at a time, muttering about the

length of time that it took to get a phone installed. The apartment was wired already; he knew that from helping to move them in. It shouldn't be much more of a job than flipping electrons at the central office and assigning a number. So could Verizon do it in less than a week?

No. David knocked and waited.

He'd raised his hand to knock again when he heard the click and rattle of someone inside. Chains, bolts, shiny new dead-bolt lock—either Maureen or Brian didn't want surprise visitors, that's for sure. The little round eye of a spy hole in the door also looked new.

Brian answered the door. *Damn.* The gangster wore a tee shirt, jeans, bare feet, and a spectacular set of bruises, but he looked a hell of a lot better than he had a couple of nights ago. He barely limped, and he used both hands to reset the locks. That arm and shoulder must be healing.

"Is Jo here?"

That earned David a startled glance, followed by narrowed eyes. "No. I thought Maureen went over to your flat."

Double damn.

"I haven't seen Jo since last night. She went to the Quick Shop to check on Maureen. I thought maybe they both came back here and talked girl talk all night."

Brian sat down at a kitchen table that must have come from the same factory as Jo's. Hell, it looked like it had the same knife cuts in the plastic laminate and the same dents in the zinc edging. David hovered near the door and kept that table between him and the Doberman, just in case.

The kitchen smelled like a lab—or a hospital. Then details registered: Surgical forceps and a few scraps of black thread lay on the table, next to bottles of antiseptic and a scattering of chess pieces.

David blinked and shook his head in disbelief as Brian

snipped another stitch with a pair of tiny stainless-steel scissors. He swapped them for the forceps and teased more black thread out of his own arm. The wound looked like it was weeks old rather than two days, edges a deep purple with the shiny gloss of fresh-healed tissue and a few peeling scraps of dead skin.

"I heal fast," Brian said. "Runs in the family." He snipped the last two stitches, pulled them, and swabbed the arm with peroxide. It foamed gently in the holes left by the thread, spreading a thin tang of excess oxygen.

Brian cleared away the medical debris and wrapped his tools up in a green nylon field kit. "So they decided to take a girl's night out? They need a break from us, now and then. And vice versa."

David shook his head. "I called the night manager for the store. Maureen went out on a break and never came back. The man said to tell her she's fired. He said Jo came in a couple of minutes later and went out again, looking for her. He's pissed."

Brian got up and poured a cup of coffee, lifted his eyebrows at David to offer him the same, then shrugged.

"One other thing." David paused and drummed his fingers on the table. "The manager said Maureen left with this person, he wasn't sure if it was a man or a woman. Thin, well dressed, dark hair, dark skin. Not black, he said, more like Spanish or Italian. Good manners. Sound like anybody you know?"

Coffee splashed all over the floor.

"I guess the answer is yes." David stopped, rather than let his voice edge into the snarl he felt his face forming. When he could control his tongue, he went on. "Is she in danger? Is Jo in danger?"

"Maybe." Brian growled, the kind of sound you'd expect from a bear cornered in a cave. "Probably. Bloody pig-headed bitch wouldn't listen to me!"

David's heart turned over and froze. "Forget about cleaning up that mess! We're going to the police!"

Brian ignored him, sopping up blotches of hot liquid.

"What the fuck's the matter with you, man? Don't you care about Maureen?"

Wadded towels splatted into the trash can with a lot more force than necessary. Brian poured another cup and met David's eyes. *That* was the look—the one that made David think of fire and blood and sharp steel, the Doberman look. Brian's eyes had faded from blue to ice gray, and the thoughts showing through them were even colder.

"I care," Brian said. "The police just don't have jurisdiction in this case."

"What the hell you mean, *jurisdiction*? They aren't in Naskeag Falls? The FBI handles kidnapping! That's the fucking *jurisdiction*!"

"The FBI doesn't cover where Maureen and Jo have gone. Neither does Interpol. Please move: I need to get into that closet."

The alternative seemed to be leaving through a door without opening it first. Brian looked about as stoppable as an avalanche. David slumped into a chair, his knees suddenly unreliable.

Jo was in danger. Jo!

The closet spat out a mottled green knapsack covered with loops and pockets. A heavy web belt followed, clip-on canteen, and pouches. Binoculars—*expensive* binoculars, rubber-armored Leicas. Floppy jungle hat faded nearly white with sweat and sun. David cataloged the contents of an army surplus store as they piled up on the table. Where the *hell* had all *that* come from?

Brian noticed David's scowl and nodded at the pile. "Maureen fetched this lot for me, cleaned out a locker down at the bus depot." The gear had seen a lot of mileage. Some of it bore patched holes that looked suspiciously small and round.

A curved black leather sheath landed on top of the pile. Brian stood up with a grunt that was his only concession to leg and ribs. He unsheathed a heavy knife, like a short machete bent in the middle. Moving smoothly and quietly like a man performing a religious rite, he tested the edge with his thumbnail, pulled one of two smaller blades from the sheath, and used it as a sharpening steel.

The rasp of metal on metal sent icicles down David's spine. The dull sheen of the blade spoke of hours spent honing, honing, honing. Waiting. *Soldiers do that,* David thought, *soldiers waiting to go over the top, soldiers waiting to reach the drop zone or the beach, soldiers waiting for an enemy they know is just beyond this ridge. Waiting to kill or die.*

Those scars weren't from gang wars.

"My God, what *is* that thing?"

"It's called a *kukri*, the fighting knife of the Nepalese Gurkhas. I served with a special Gurkha scout unit in the British army. Little buggers preferred these knives to their rifles. There are tales of a single Gurk with a *kukri* taking out a Japanese platoon, one by one, to the last man."

David shook himself and beat thoughts back into his head. "What do you mean, even Interpol can't help us? You trying to tell me some crazy crap like they've been abducted by men from Mars?"

"Not Mars." Brian stopped, his stare measuring David. "Do you care enough about Jo to reset your brain? To throw out a lot of stuff you *know* is true?"

An eye of quiet settled in the middle of the storm. Images floated by: Jo talking, Jo skittering around the kitchen in her start-stop squirrel mode, Jo in sunlight and in moonlight, Jo in bed and Jo fuzzy-eyed and snappish and foul-mouthed in a ratty bathrobe across the breakfast table with her hair matted and tangled with sleep.

"I care enough about Jo to die for her. I've asked her to marry me."

That drew a blink and raised eyebrows. "We're not talking about pretty songs. You bloody well might *get* a chance to die for her." Brian seemed to think for a moment, then shrugged.

"Get the box of matches from the stove. Take one and strike it on the box. Strike it once and then hold it. Keep your fingers well away from the head."

David did as he was told. The head sparked but didn't light. He held it up, puzzled. There was nothing strange about that; normally he would have just struck it again.

Suddenly the match exploded in a single burst of light and heat as powerful as a flashbulb. David blinked. Through the sparkles of the afterimage, the head and half the wooden shaft had vanished. The remaining matchstick ended clean at a blackened line. There was only a faint wisp of smoke.

"Magic exists," Brian said. "You are not hypnotized. That was not a stage trick, not an illusion. The man who took Maureen from the store uses magic like you walk and breathe."

A suspicion crept into the corner of David's brain and whispered. *Words, weapons, healing, the magic show: What does this add up to?* David sat down again, *very* slowly, as if the Doberman had just growled and bared its fangs.

"You've dragged them into some kind of war, haven't you?"

Brian quieted like a cat ready to pounce. He studied the edge of the *kukri*.

"Not intentionally."

The Gurkha knife seemed huge, a bent sword. David saw his own blood on it. That thing could take a man's head off with a single stroke. He could be dead already. He might as well ask the rest of the questions.

"Just what, *exactly*, do you mean by that?"

"I mean, before I knew her, I was following some dangerous men. One of them chased Maureen into an alley. I took him out. That's where I met her."

David shuddered at the bald, terse statements. He suddenly wasn't sure if he was willing to live with any more answers.

"One of them . . . What about the others?"

"Another was the shark who took the bait. My half brother."

"What *right* did you have to risk Maureen?"

"That first time? I didn't even know who she was. She wasn't in danger until just before I moved. Last night was desperation. She refused to call in sick. By tonight, I would have been well enough to guard her."

"Where is she? Where the *hell* are Maureen and Jo?"

"Another world, the thickness of a sheet of paper away from you. Sean would take Maureen there. How Jo went, I can only guess. She may have tried to stop Sean, or she may have followed on her own. She has the Power. David, your lover is not entirely human. Neither is Maureen. Neither am I."

A cold knot formed in David's belly, the chill reaching out to his fingers and toes. However, things could be worse. Brian could be using that knife already. Apparently the big soldier thought David might help, or at least not get in the way.

*I suspected this. I called Jo a witch. I knew the other night was freaky.*

He swallowed his heart. "You're going after them."

"Yes."

"I'm coming with you. I said I'd die for Jo, and I meant it. I don't want to even *think* about living without her."

Brian shook his head. "No. You're not a fighter, and you don't have the blood to work with Power. Someone like

Sean would take you like a grizzly snapping up a trout."

David winced. The image was too vivid.

He gritted his teeth. "You take me along, or I'll call the cops on you. If nothing else, I can carry your pack. You're not fully healed yet. I saw you limping. And if you have something like a shotgun, I can at least *scare* those bastards."

A grim smile flitted across Brian's face. "Call the cops? Maureen wouldn't let you use the phone, and she didn't even realize what she was doing. Try to get out of your seat."

Stand up? Simple. But nothing happened. David cussed, silently. Nothing below his waist worked. He had feeling, he still balanced upright on the chair with all the unconscious adjustments an unstable posture needs, he didn't feel heavy or have any sense of magic glue holding him to his seat, but his legs simply wouldn't make the necessary moves.

And then his hand reached out and picked up the discarded matchstick. It turned and moved steadily toward his face, toward his right eye, and he couldn't move his head away, he couldn't turn his head, he couldn't stop his hand or drop the match or even blink his eyes.

An animal scream forced its way out of his throat, low and quiet but rasping with pain against clenched teeth. He smelled the char on the stick, he lost focus on it, he felt it brush his eyelashes, and then it stopped. His hand finally answered the scream and whipped the splinter of wood away from his eye. It bounced off the refrigerator with a *tick* that echoed in the quiet kitchen.

David collapsed across the table, his arms wrapped over his head in a vain attempt at shelter. He gasped for breath and fought against the instant replays running through his head, that blackened weapon inching toward his eye as if it was held in a drill press made of his own flesh.

"Sean wouldn't have stopped."

David looked up, still shaking. "I don't care. I have to go."

That cold, gray stare weighed him. Finally, it softened back into a faded blue.

"And guns don't work where we're going. I don't suppose you ever studied fencing or karate?"

David laughed, a bark just short of hysteria. "No. What do you mean, guns won't work? The laws of physics take a holiday?"

"Remember the match. The easiest way to see it, is think about a few additional laws. Say the Old Ones put a speed limit on oxidation-reduction chemistry. Without magic to help, nothing can burn much faster than a normal fire. It's kind of a 'union shop' clause in the way they run their world. They don't like paying attention to people who can't use the Power."

Brian hauled more gear out of the closet. He assembled a takedown bow and started to string it, and groaned with pain. Forcing the tip down toward the string, his hand wavered just as the loop caught. The bow snapped loose like a striking rattlesnake. Brian clutched the side of his face and sank to the floor.

The fiberglass tip had left a gouge across Brian's cheekbone. David wet a towel and swabbed at the scrape, then jerked his hand away in shock. The bleeding stopped, and a shiny film of healing spread across the wound.

Witchcraft. Healing like that was enough to get you burned at the stake. How bad had the earlier injuries *really* been, if Brian hadn't fully recovered yet?

Brian dragged himself upright and shook his head like a dazed fighter. Beads of blood had popped up along the stitch holes in his left arm, but it was his right shoulder he wiggled experimentally. He shook his head again, as if bothered by a swarm of flies.

Archery. Memories tickled David's fingers, and his left forearm stung in sympathy. "I might be able to use that bow. I practiced target archery in high school, got good enough to compete on the local level."

Brian's face froze with one lifted eyebrow. "How long since you drew a bow?"

"Ten years, maybe. At least I know the mechanics—a sight picture, the draw, a smooth release."

"You need muscles as well as skill, but it's worth a try. That's a hunting bow, twice the pull of a target bow even if you were in practice. String it and see if you can draw it."

David stepped through the bow, hooked it on his opposite ankle, and bent it. It was stiff. Damned stiff. He fumbled the string's loop onto the tip. Pulling the bow to full draw damn near cut his fingers off, but he managed. His hands trembled as he held it long enough to draw a bead on the bow sight. Then he slacked off, shoulders and biceps screaming.

It had been a long time. Too long.

Brian's face was still a mask. "The people I'm going to fight are stronger mages than I am. They like causing pain. I wasn't joking with that match. If I could draw my bow, I wouldn't consider bringing you along."

David met his eyes. "Jo is over there. Do you have a better chance at saving her with me or without me?"

Brian's smile looked more like a skull. "This isn't some damn fantasy novel. Are you seriously willing to be tortured to death? To be forced to watch while they torture *Jo* until she uses her powers the way they want?"

Torture. Jo. David swallowed bile.

"I have to. I couldn't live with myself if I didn't."

Grim sadness washed across Brian's face, as if he saw memories in the air between them. "Bards never *have* done well as warriors. They die a lot. Quickly or slowly, they die a lot." He shook himself like a wet dog. "Okay, you can come with me. We're going to need that bow."

A bow David could barely draw. "Don't expect me to hit a barn at more than fifty yards."

Brian grinned, a savage expression with too many teeth exposed. "I'm not too damned good with one, either. What I'm worried about is more likely to be in your face, ten yards or less. You'll be facing dangerous animals, ones you won't find in any zoo, and you won't get time for more than a single shaft. Don't worry about aiming, and just let the adrenaline do the work for you."

He rummaged around in the closet until he came up with another *kukri*. David caught it. It was heavy, heavy as hell. The blade looked to be a quarter of an inch thick.

"That's not a bad weapon for a beginner. Just hack at things. The balance and curve of the blade take care of the rest. Don't even think about stabbing with it. That takes practice. A Gurk, now, he could shave you dry and never leave a scratch, or slice you in two halves before you ever saw the steel. The buggers can even throw the bloody things. Little brown brother has lived with one since he was in nappies, see, knows it better than he knows his wife. He sees it a hell of a lot more often, that's for sure."

Brian's voice wove an atmosphere, the air of the military training camp. He had more accent, all of a sudden, and David felt like a raw recruit under the wing of an old soldier. There was a new depth to Brian, a sense of age far beyond his looks, the calmness of a veteran.

*He's doing it on purpose,* David thought. *He knows I'm scared. He's telling me he's been through this a thousand times before.*

Brian flexed his left arm, swung his right in a slow, exploratory arc, winced. "I'm glad you'll be carrying the bow."

*And that,* thought David, *is the closest you'll ever come to admitting how badly hurt you really are. The confidence rings a little hollow.*

"One suggestion," Brian added, "from a veteran. Bathroom. Don't take it as an insult, but the body has its own ways of dealing with fear. Anytime you have the chance, empty your bowels and bladder before going into combat."

David grimaced. They took turns at the plumbing, then filled canteens and empty plastic Pepsi bottles with water and tossed more dry food into Brian's pack. Brian rigged a quiver full of broad-head hunting arrows through the loops of the pack and adjusted the whole mess on David's back until it hung right and he could draw and loose without fouling on something.

David blinked. "Hey, I didn't put on my jacket first."

"You won't need it. I plan to put us on the edge of the forest, between Dougal's keep and Fiona's garden maze. Neither of them likes rain or winter. Weather is a matter of consensus in the Summer Country."

Speed limits on chemical reactions. Weather by consensus. Mages with the power to control someone else's muscles. David's stomach knotted at the picture.

Magic.

Maureen and Jo, the match, the psychic Super Glue: None of that really had the impact of feeling skin heal under his fingers. It had a kind of greasy heat to it, sort of like plastic straight from the molding machine. He wanted to wash his hands of the memory.

Brian grabbed his wrist, and they stepped from the kitchen into a darkness full of soft, slimy touches and the faint warmth of breath on his cheek or the back of his neck. David's nerves twitched at chittering noises on the edge of hearing and moist air warm and slightly foul in his nose. Brian's hand was an iron clamp pulling him through the darkness and into green light.

# fourteen

—⁓—

SEAN SMILED AT Maureen and nodded. His approval made a good decision better. Not just better, but imperative. She draped her jacket over a branch stub and left it as a puzzle for the squirrels. She felt warm in the forest, and she no longer needed that reminder of ice and slush— would not need it ever again. After all, this was the Summer Country.

She wasn't going back to winter. As for the gun, she had never needed that at all. Sean would protect her.

They walked on into paradise. A loaf of bread, a jug of wine, and thou beside me in the wilderness . . . Who the hell needed the bread and wine?

She clung possessively to Sean's arm, as if the warm, damp earth smells could prove more seductive than her woman scent. Not that they were any real threat: She felt powerful, secure in her sexuality. She was a woman, and he was her man.

Something rustled, and the brush parted to reveal great, yellow, slit-pupil eyes in a flat triangle of a head plated with black scales. She glared at the giant lizard, daring it to threaten her lover, and it retreated.

Then she noticed the man next to it, a brown-skinned, brown-clad little man who almost disappeared if she didn't stare right at him. He had the same general look as Brian and that Liam creature, but smaller, leaner, and almost primitive. Somehow, the name "kobold" seemed to fit him, even if he wasn't in a mine.

The apparition spoke grating syllables to the dragon, and it darted its forked tongue at her, testing, tasting, as if it needed to know her smell again. It slithered off into the tangled brush.

*"Tha i an so,"* Sean said to the funny-looking little man, and Maureen heard him say it and also heard "She is here," at the same time.

So Fiona had been right. This warm, green land gave people understanding of another's speech. It even told Maureen that Sean spoke Scots Gaelic with a Galway Irish accent, a feat that would have had her giggling if she could laugh at anything Sean did.

But she could not mock Sean. Not after he had kissed her body awake to a fire of longing and brought her to this beautiful place. She floated in the golden glow of the romance novels she'd snitched from her mother back when she was a kid. She waited impatiently for Sean to draw her away into some grassy bower, longing for him to strip her clothing away in slow delicious torture until he played upon her body like a harp and entered into her to give her release from this tormented ecstasy.

She loved Sean.

She loved him with the unquestioning devotion of a spaniel. He was her god made manifest. Whatever she felt for Brian faded into ghostly invisibility. She loved Sean and belonged to him, without reservation.

The strange little man studied her. She decided to call

him Rumpelstiltskin, a gnome out of fairy tales. He had too large a head on too thin a neck, gnarled muscles showing beyond short-sleeved shirt and shorts, a chest and belly dropping straight from shoulders to hips, dark hair standing out in tufts like some miscut field of hay. Scars ran all over him as if he had been built hastily from spare parts. It was such a funny way to make a man. Nothing like Sean's slim beauty.

*"Trobhadaibh,"* the man said. "Come here," she heard.

She stood still. Sean smiled his slow, mocking, lovely smile and shook his head.

"You don't want me to release her yet," Sean said, while her mind stepped between sound and meaning. "This exquisite little kitten has claws and teeth."

He turned to Maureen, and she melted under his gaze. "My dear, allow me to introduce Dougal MacKenzie, self-styled Laird of the Clan MacKenzie. He aspires to be your husband, your lord and master. I wish you joy of each other."

He smiled again, as if mocking Dougal, and her, and even himself.

"But . . ."

*"Bi samhach."*

Maureen's heart sank. She wanted Sean, not this strange caricature of a man. But Sean told her to be quiet, so she bit off the words and closed her mouth.

He turned back to Dougal. "She's under a glamour now. Unless you want to take up the reins of it, I would suggest something more substantial to hold her. She can be dangerous."

"I know how to handle dangerous animals," the little man rasped. "Padric, the irons."

Blinking, Maureen noticed a third man. She had centered her whole existence on Sean to the point she barely knew where she was standing.

Now she saw beyond her god, as if he had let her eyes loose to learn her new world. Padric, this one was called: tall, thinly muscular, dressed in a battered leather coat and a pair of green twill pants over worn black boots. His eyes looked sad under long blond hair, guarded, as if he was used to doing things he'd rather not talk about.

He carried circlets of iron joined by thin chains. They burned with a peculiar cold heat when he locked them around her throat, around her wrists in front of her, around her ankles.

Maureen jerked at the touch, eyes wide and appealing to Sean. Why did he allow this?

"Sorry, love, we have a deal. I give Dougal what he wants; he gives me what I want. You may be very beautiful, but I'm not prepared to take the risk of keeping you. Dougal likes living dangerously. I have other needs."

He turned away from her. "Dougal, old boy, I promised that no one would take her without her consent. I trust you won't make a liar of me."

"Och, no," the little man drawled. "She will ask me to bed her before we are done. She will beg me. And nothing we do will mark this beautiful maiden—no scars, no blood, no fire. Just simple discipline and training."

Sean gave Maureen a long look that drew flame to her cheeks. "Maiden? I think not. A virgin wouldn't have reacted the way she has to the glamour, wouldn't have such vivid thoughts of the smell and feel of a lover. Such complicated thoughts. She's known men before and doesn't like the species. She's more dangerous than your hawks and beasts. Don't blame me when you find her pulling your keep down around your ears."

The heat faded from Maureen's belly, leaving sour ice behind. The word "glamour" echoed in her ears. That was the emotional touch Brian had used, to calm her after Liam's death and the strip-club fire.

She was trapped.

Kidnapped.

Brian had tried to warn her. "Don't trust Fiona," he'd said. "Don't trust Sean. The Old Ones don't have what you'd call a conscience." What they *could* do, they *did*, no matter what pain it caused to others.

She snarled and threw herself at Sean, hands out and fingernails turned to claws. Her feet jerked out from under her, and she smashed full-length into the forest dirt. She rolled, spitting rotten leaves, scrambling to kick and scratch and bite the slimy bastard who did this to her, to claw his eyes out and loop her wrist chains around his throat and strangle him.

Her feet jerked away again and dragged her backward, twigs and leaves gouging into her bare skin where her blouse rode up along her back. The pull turned upward, and she swung by her ankles, head just clear of the ground, thrashing around and screaming at three sets of feet.

She finally calmed enough to see the thin chain hooked to the shackles around her ankles, then looped up over a low branch and held by Padric. A leash. They had her on a fucking leash, like some kind of dog.

Maureen spat, again and again, until she cleared her mouth of all the forest trash. "I'll kill you! I'll kill every single fucking one of you!"

Sean smiled that mocking smile again. "Too bad she isn't wearing skirts, Dougal. Pants just aren't as interesting in this position."

Maureen's blouse hung loose around her neck, and that fucking bra snap had popped open again so her breasts bounced free as she swung. She snarled and curled up, to reach the chain hooked to her ankles, but Padric yanked it higher and she fell back. Now even her hands didn't reach the ground.

She twisted, helpless, jerking like a hooked fish. She

didn't even try to cover herself, to hide her flushed breasts from their greedy eyes.

"Okay, you bastards. Go ahead and rape me! Three strong men against one woman, you should be able to do it!"

She glared at each of them, through her tears. If they'd just come close enough . . . Sean looked amused, Padric frightened, while Dougal licked his lips as if he was considering her challenge. She hoped he'd try. She'd strangle him with his own goddamned chains.

Sean's quiet chuckle broke the silence. "I warned you, Dougal," he said. "Now you begin to understand what you've bought. I hope you still plan to pay."

The gnome spat. "Oh, I'll help you capture your Pendragon. He'll come after her, right into our trap. And this little wildcat won't be that hard to tame. I've handled worse—bigger, stronger, and with *real* claws."

Pendragon.

Brian.

Trap.

She'd let her guard slip because her paranoia was more afraid of Brian than of real dangers. She'd turned off her fucking brain when she walked into the Quick Shop, and ended up in chains. Ended up as bait.

Dougal stepped forward, expertly snagged her wrists, and snapped a second chain to those shackles. Then he tweaked her right nipple with his free hand, spun her around to smack her butt like a horse turned out to pasture, and motioned Padric to let her down.

She thumped limp on the ground. *Brian!* she screamed, but only in her mind. The thoughts kept circling through her terror. He'd warned her. Now he was in danger because of her stupidity. And he was still hurt.

She rolled to her knees, shaking herself. Padric loosened the chain from the limb overhead, giving her an instant's slack. She flung herself at him. Her arms snapped around against her motion, nearly ripping her shoulder joints apart, and she thumped back to the ground. A scream tore loose from her throat.

Chains bit into her wrists. Chains chewed on her ankles. They pulled her taut between them, stretched helpless face-up on the forest floor. Fury gave her the strength to pull against them, and she gained an inch, six inches, a foot, before the raging fire in her shoulders stopped her.

She lay rigid between the chains, panting. Tears streamed from her eyes and matted the tangled hair across her face. Something blurry hung over her head, dark and calm and sleek.

"You'll only damage yourself, love," the blur said, with Sean's voice. "Dougal would be most upset if you scarred your pretty face. And those magnificent breasts of yours, so small yet womanly, so firm, so perfectly proportioned to your chest: You must protect them for the children you will suckle. You'll be a mother within a year, love."

Cold clarity struck through Maureen like a flash of lightning. "And you'll be dead before the full moon shines upon your face. Your own treachery will kill you."

"Ah, 'tis prophecy she's giving to us, Dougal. The witch blood speaks. You'll notice she even calls upon the sacred goddess of the night to witness her revenge. Do you have a fate to offer Dougal, love? Care to bring the heaven's wrath down on our unhappy Padric?"

Her throat made words, without her will; they echoed strangely. "Padric will bring his own fate upon himself. As for Dougal, if he dares to taste my body, its fires will burn his body into ash. Beware."

"The oracle speaks," Sean mocked her. "Maybe you should sell this lovely wench to a whorehouse, Dougal, her favors are so dangerous. That's an absurdly high price for a piece of ass. Find yourself another bitch to breed your bloodlines."

The chains pulled tighter. Maureen grunted, gritting her teeth against another scream. She wouldn't give them the pleasure of it.

"A week," Dougal said, yanking again, "two weeks at the most. No bird or beast has ever taken more. She'll dine at my table when there's no food elsewhere; she'll wear the clothes of a proper woman when her choice is to go naked. She'll sleep with me, willingly, when that's the only sleep she'll get. What woman has the fierce will of a hawk or hunting cat?"

*Father Oak,* she prayed, *protect me. That was your limb they strung the chain across. Drop it on Sean's head. Trip his feet with your roots, burn him with the acid of your bark and acorns, smother him in the litter of your last year's leaves. Call on the forest to lash thorns across his eyes, raise up the rotted dead to clasp his ankles, breathe poison from the flowers and fruits. Father Oak, protect me.*

Iron burned at her throat and swallowed her words. Her wrists and ankles caught an icy fire separate from the scrape of tension in the chains.

*Iron.*

Morgan had feared iron in White's tale of Arthur—the cold iron which had replaced the Old One's flint and bronze. Iron defeated magic. The shackles bound spirit as well as body.

So Brian had been right. She bore Power, the Power of the Blood, and the bastards trapped her Power as neatly as they'd trapped her body. They knew her better than she knew herself.

*Brian, forgive me. I've done this to you, led you to a trap. I've led you to your death.*

The chains slackened again, and she curled in upon herself. Her bladder burned with the pressure of her fear. She fought against adding *that* to her humiliation.

Dougal looked down on her, his form made even more lumpish by the blurring of her tears. "You can walk and have some dignity, or we can carry you on a game pole like a gutted pig. It's your choice."

"Carry me, you bastard!" Then words formed again in her throat, words that seemed to rise up out of the dirt pressing against her bare skin, words that were not truly hers but belonged to the land and to all women. Even the burning iron at her throat couldn't freeze her voice.

"May the axe turn in your hands when you go to cut the tree, may the falling trunk drive branches through your skull, may the bark blister your hands at the touching of it. May the sap poison you, may the splinters of the tree's flesh drive into your own flesh and fester there." She gasped for breath.

"I curse you by the forest, I curse you by the meadow, I curse you by the mountain and the river. I curse you by the bog and by the well and by the roof-beam of your fucking house!"

"Such a lovely tongue the lass has in her head," mocked Sean. "And I was thinking the Celtic blood ran thin in her."

Dougal spat, just missing her bare belly. "Padric, cut a pole."

She saw Padric hesitate before tying her ankle leash to a tree, with a glance at her that might have been fear if she could read his face clearly through her tears. He moved slowly and carefully, selecting a slim tree well free of any others. So a curse could truly bite, in this world?

Sean stepped away with a negligent wave of his hand. Frown-wrinkles ringed his eyes, though, as if even his mockery was troubled by the words using her throat. Suddenly, she saw blood in his eyes and strangling green fingers wrapped around his throat. His vision-mouth screamed in agony.

The vision faded even as she drank it in.

"Dougal, my friend, I will leave you to your ladylove. I must prepare a greeting for my beloved brother. You will remember to tell your pets to let me pass?"

The gnome chuckled. "If you are such a mighty mage, *friend*, none of my pets should be a threat."

"Oh, I just don't want to hurt them. You might be angry with me. Some of them would be so hard to replace."

Padric returned with a thick pole, stripped of limbs. No matter how she thrashed against the jerking chains, she couldn't fight them as they slipped the pole between her wrists, between her ankles. And then she was swaying, hanging, bumping against rocks and tree trunks and clawing thorns, with the cold iron rings gouging fiery pain into the skin of her wrists and ankles.

Warm blood trickled down her wrists, and she concentrated on the feel of it, struggling to block out the pain of its source. Fire stabbed at her shoulders as if muscles or tendons had torn loose in her struggles, and slowly ripped further with each bounce and swing of the trail.

"Pain is optional," Brian had told her, one time while she retaped his ribs. "You can overcome pain with an effort of your will and mind. Concentrate on something greater, on survival or on revenge, and the pain will go away. Pain is optional."

*Bullshit,* her critic answered. *Pain is nature's way of telling you that you just fucked up.*

Her head throbbed along with the beat of the trail—a dizzy, nauseated migraine of a hangover like her worst morning-after ever. Was it from Sean's glamour, or from her own thwarted Power, or just her raging hatred? She twisted sideways against the agony of her shoulders and vomited in great, racking spasms.

Dougal and Padric walked on, ignoring their burden. They followed a clear trail, beaten as if well traveled but by men or horses only. It was too narrow and rough for carts.

*Watch the path,* the voice in Maureen's head ordered her. *Ignore the pain; ignore the rampage in your belly. You are going to escape. You'll need to know your way through this forest.*

She marked down a rounded lump of rock through the woods, here, a massive grandfather beech, there. The path dropped into a gentle valley or glen, down to a brook crossed by a ford, the feet of the men splashing quietly. Then the trail rose again, through switchbacks on a steeper pitch, the ground rising as if Dougal had set his keep upon the heights, for a view or for defense.

Padric's foot slipped, and he cursed. Maureen matched him word for word and topped him, as the jerk lanced through her body and struck fire from wrists and ankles and shoulders and head. She vomited again, the twisting of her belly just adding to the white-heat agony.

*Pain is nature's way of telling you that you just fucked up. Fucked up, big-time.*

Maureen cursed between the jolts and the spasms in her belly, silently but fluently. She wouldn't believe one man who was kind of nice, wouldn't obey a rational warning. Now she was trussed up like an animal for a zoo. Now she was helpless, a slave to men who wanted to breed her like she was some kind of fucking cow.

*No, pig. Cut the mixed metaphors, Maureen. Hanging from a game pole like a gutted pig, the bastard said. Pigheaded Maureen.*

Heads floated into her nightmare.

She saw heads by the trail, skulls, on poles. The bastard decorated his path like a cannibal, for Chrissakes. They stared at her with sightless hollows for eyes, the same bleak stare her vision had placed on Sean's head just before he left.

The head was where the soul lived. She remembered Grandfather telling tales out of Irish legend, of heads talking even when severed from their bodies, living on for years and carried across the seas. Telling of trophies, the heads of enemies preserved and handed down from generation to generation as treasures of the family.

Maureen remembered Grandfather's face, the Dies Irae face when he'd seen the bloody welts across her back and couldn't do a damn thing about them because he was old and weak with the drink and had no place else to live. *I'll take some fucking trophies, dammit,* she swore to that helpless angry god. *I'll jam Sean's head on a stake shoved through his asshole. I'll nail Dougal's skull to his own goddamn gatepost.*

Hack it off like Brian hacked Liam's head free from his shoulders to roll around the alley in the snow. Before it burned.

Would the bodies burn, here in the Summer Country? She remembered the uncanny fire. That would rob her of her trophy.

She vomited again, racking dry heaves trying to rid herself of something that was not inside her.

# fifteen

—m—

"SHIT," JO REPEATED. "It's a *dragon*."

She closed her eyes on the blasted impossible forest, counted to ten, and opened them again.

It was still there.

"There ain't no such animal," she whispered to herself.

The beast was all hard and glittery and black, armored with scales as sharp as obsidian flakes. It wasn't a flying dragon, no sign of wings—at least her hallucinations weren't trying to get her to accept something physically impossible. It was just a snake with four stumpy legs about as thick as trees, a tail that went on forever, and a sharp head filled with even sharper teeth.

She stared at it, willing it to go away—willing the entire *world* to go away and dump her back in the stinking slush of Naskeag Falls. The world refused, listening to the part of her mind that said that warm was nice, that green was nice, that it was about damned *time* Maureen's psycho brain came up with something useful. If only her delusions didn't include so many teeth . . .

The dragon kept coiling and uncoiling like one of those

garter snakes Maureen used to catch in the backyard—a garter snake sixty feet long. With teeth to match.

Maybe it only ate virgins. Different taste or something. Then she didn't have a thing to worry about.

Her palms were telling her otherwise. She wiped the sweat off them, smelling her own fear, then gritted her teeth at the stupidity of moving and attracting attention. The dragon lifted its head slightly, but it wasn't the jerk of a startled animal.

It knew she was here. It was *smelling* her, with that long forked tongue as red as a fire truck and damn near half as big. If it wanted to eat her, she'd only be a burp by now. What the hell was it waiting for?

The dragon coiled and uncoiled like an Escher puzzle, no beginning and no end, wrapped around a huge, moss-covered boulder and some ancient trees bearded with lichen. It stared at Jo as if it meant to freeze her with its slit-pupil lizard eyes. She saw a mind lurking behind those eyes. Maybe she should try talking to it.

"Look, I was just following my sister, didn't mean to trespass, never owned a sword or lance in my life. Nice meeting you." She backed away, down the trail.

<How did *you* get here? The Master says you must stay with him.>

Its voice hissed in her mind, cold but curious, as the creature moved to cut her off. Scales glittered like black opals as the dragon flowed between the trees, as fast as running water, much faster than she. It looked like the slow-motion replay of a striking cobra.

She dodged away from the trail and through the forest, stumbling over roots, branches slashing across her face. The glistening ebony snake blocked her, never touching her, never hurting her, seeming everywhere at once. Once she thought she'd spotted a gap, only to run headlong up against the scaly nose itself. Jo smelled its breath, moist and acrid, and barely dodged the forked tongue. One tip was as big as her arm. The damned beast still didn't bite her.

<You must go back.>

Jo leaned back against another tree, panting, the coarse bark reassuringly solid. Sweat poured down her back, and it wasn't all fear. The forest was way too hot for her to be running around in a winter coat and sweater and insulated boots.

*Sister mine, maybe I owe you this for Buddy, but I don't think I'm going to follow you into your dreams again. I thought your fantasy world was more fun than this.*

She started to dump her useless jacket, then hesitated and held it like a matador's cape. The tongue flicked out, and the dragon's head lowered as if it was puzzled. Maybe dragons didn't shed their skin, the way snakes did. She shook the jacket and trailed it on the ground, offering it as bait.

*"¡Toro, aqui! ¡Toro! ¡Toro!"*

The beast's head was as big as a car. She flipped her jacket over one of its eyes and ran. Cloth ripped behind her. She hoped the dragon would stop to worry its prey a little before it realized the filling of the sandwich had run off.

Something smacked her to the ground, and the forest spun around her in a burst of green stars. She couldn't get up. A tree trunk lay across her body—a warm tree trunk, pulsing with life, ridged with coarse dry scales. It ended in fingers each as big as one of her hands, and *those* ended in claws like steel meat hooks. Eyes squeezed shut against the sudden brightness of the sun, she gently explored her ribs. Nothing was broken, and she *still* wasn't eaten.

<You must go back.>

It sure was a single-minded critter. Jo stared up into a single yellow cat eye bigger than a dinner plate. *Jurassic*

*Park,* that's what the scene was. The *T. rex* looking through the car window. Only thing the scene needed was night and rain. Who was going to be eaten next?

*T. rex* didn't say. Her brain raced. How good was she at riddles? Dragons were supposed to like the riddle game. Something she'd read said so. Win the game and she went free.

"How many Republicans does it take to change the lightbulb in the Statue of Liberty's torch?"

The eye blinked, first some kind of transparent membrane and then the charcoal gray lid. It looked as smooth as velvet, delicate, like the shoulder wrap for an evening dress. She felt a crazy urge to stroke it.

"None. They've turned off the power to save tax dollars."

No effect. Okay, so it was a damn poor joke. Jo tried to slither out from under the dragon's paw but found she'd have to leave her pants behind. One of those claws hooked right under the waistband, cold and hard along her belly.

"Look, you keep telling me to go back, and I'm trying to. I may be lost, but I *think* that's the way I came in."

<You try to deceive me. You may change your skin and disguise your smell, but I still know you. You must return to the Master's keep. These woods are dangerous. He will be angry.>

*Maureen.*

*T. rex* thought she was Maureen. Just like the slimeball in the Quick Shop, just like dozens of people they'd spoofed since Maureen reached Jo's height and grew breasts. Maureen had come this way with the dude she was kissing.

*She's at his castle. Safe. The watchdog was told to keep her safe. That's why I'm not looking at the wrong end of an after-dinner mint.*

"Okay. Okay. Just get off of me, you scaly St. Bernard. I can't get to the keep lying flat on my back."

Weight lifted from her belly, and she scooted away from

that golden eye. It watched her, suspicious. "Go the right way," the eye said. "Try to leave, and things will get nasty. I could use a snack."

The frigging animal acted more like a prison guard than a watchdog. Something smelled fishy here.

Her hands stung. They were covered with fine lines of blood, like paper cuts—must have tangled with those scales. She found the shreds of her ski jacket and wiped the blood away, winding strips of fiber batting over the cuts like bandage gauze. The dragon still watched her like a cat with a cornered mouse.

<The trail is clear. I must not leave our territory, or the Master will be angry.>

The dragon blocked one direction. The keep must be in the other. Like *T. rex* said, the trail was clear.

*Our* territory, it had said. There were more of them? Jesus, Mary, and Joseph!

Jo's hands shook. Hot and sweaty or not, her teeth kept trying to chatter. She could only keep them still by clenching her jaw so hard it hurt. Funny thing was, she also had this urge to laugh like a hyena. If she gave in to it, she'd probably never stop. Hysteria.

So she had decided to add manic-depressive tendencies to the family portfolio? Jo groped for a tree to lean against. She was going nuts. It had been months since she last smoked pot, ten years since that stupid mistake with acid. Nothing stronger today than coffee. She couldn't blame this scene on chemicals.

*Dragons*, she thought. *Talking dragons.*

She unwrapped one makeshift bandage and stared at the razor-thin lines of red. Fresh blood beaded up when she flexed her hand. Did hallucinations cut people?

But she could imagine the cuts, yes? Imagine the blood?

She shuddered. Find Maureen, that was the priority. Find the way out of this frigging nightmare. Ask her sister for a nice calming hit of Thorazine or whatever the latest chemical tranquillity was called. *Hey, Sis, know any good shrinks?*

Back to "Find the Sister." She was somewhere up ahead, both the Genetic Resonance Imager and the dragon said so. The dragon also said the forest was dangerous. Jo had to catch up before something with less brain or more appetite decided this "Master" was far enough away to forget about his orders.

Jo heaved herself up from the tree and blinked, waiting for the world to stop spinning. She shook her head and blinked again, trying to snap out of the funk. Scared was one thing, paralyzed was another. She just had to keep her eyes moving, keep her feet moving. At least she had boots on, instead of sneakers. This wasn't a sidewalk.

Branches, brambles, tree trunks, rocks—the forest poked and prodded at the trail, trying to reclaim it from the touch of man. Jo felt tension in it, felt an edge to either side of her, as if the trail was a wandering, wavering line through hostile territory, and the bushes on either side were mined. The dragon might have left, but Jo could still feel eyes out there in the shadows. They weren't friendly.

*Paranoia?*

*Just shut up and keep walking.* How far was it, to this place the dragon called a keep? Her legs needed to firm up for swimsuit season, anyway. Or no-swimsuit season, if they rented the Long Lake cabin again this year. God, wouldn't having David at the lake be great: swimming nude, making love on the dock by moonlight . . . swatting mosquitoes by moonlight . . .

She grimaced. At least that was *one* menace Maureen's hallucinations seemed to have left back in the Great North Woods. Jo sure didn't miss the cloud of biters that could turn a Maine forest into the seventh circle of hell—black flies, mosquitoes, moose flies, no-see-ums . . .

Living in the middle of a lot of water had its downside.
Lakes. Creeks. Water. Jo's mouth felt dry—maybe it was
fear. This place looked clean enough, but the New York
tourists caught giardiasis every year, thinking the pure
mountain streams and lakes in Maine were clean enough
to drink. Maureen had explained it: Moose and bear and
beaver don't use outhouses, see. Jo thought she was going
to get a little thirsty if she didn't find Maureen and her
man.

A flash of yellow gleamed up ahead. She bit her lip and
wondered what was next—a golden dragon? Maybe the
Sphinx, since she'd offered to play riddles? Whatever it
was, it wasn't moving.

Maybe it was waiting. Waiting for lunch. Come into my
parlor, said the spider to the fly. It was right on the trail.

Jo clenched her fists and forced herself to go on. The
pain from her cut palms served as an anchor, a handhold
on reality. She giggled, half-hysterically, at the unintended
pun.

*Just shut up and keep walking.*

It was a coat. Maureen's stupid ski jacket, hanging on a
branch stub. It proved Jo's psychic nose still worked. Maureen had come this way, got overheated just about as
quickly, but didn't have an argument with the guard dog.

She checked the pockets. Yep, Maureen's. There was the
stupid gun, stupid speed loader with five extra rounds.

And *that* was proof Maureen was happy here, walking
off and leaving her gun behind. When a paranoid tells you
there's no problem, you can believe it.

Jo thought about guns, thought about dragons, and
sphinxes, and griffins, and all the other dreamscape animals. She shuddered with a sudden chill. A lot of characters
in fairy tales ended up as lunch.

The gun felt solidly comfortable in her hand. If she was
going to pick up Maureen's delusions, maybe she should

go for the whole package. Jo felt like she'd slipped through the Looking Glass, where Little Sister was sane and Cynthia Josephine Pierce was the whacko.

She tucked the gun into her waistband. Odds were she'd need a smart bomb or guided missile to take out that dragon, but maybe some of the other nasties didn't come with homegrown armor plate. Some of the men in legends were mean sons of bitches, too.

Maybe she'd better take the jacket, also. There was no guarantee she was going to be sleeping under a roof tonight, and her sweat was starting to chill with fear.

The trail wound on through the woods, under low-hanging branches that seemed to clutch at her, past the startled tree faces formed by old branch scars. She passed through patches of sour foulness in the leaf-mold smell.

Probably animals.

Does a bear shit in the woods? She shuddered. She didn't want to even *start* to think about bears—this damned forest already had enough teeth and claws. Gnarled fingers of wood pointed back the way she came, roots twisted under her feet and stubbed her toes, the gentle breeze pushed against her face and seemed to whisper warnings into the summer leaves.

Maureen's trees were talking to her, the voices in her head that personified schizophrenia. "Go back," they said. "Flee, be afraid. This forest is not a place to be. Danger and death lurk here."

Maureen's whole package, indeed. Next thing, Jo would be afraid of men. She smiled at the thought and walked on, forcing the dragon and the outrageous impossibility of where she was out of her mind. After all, warmth and green leaves and the smell of forest dirt felt as intoxicating as three stiff drinks when compared with Maine in February.

The sound of a creek trickled through the woods, reminding her that she was thirsty. The trail crossed it through a muddy ford, and she wished she had some tracking skills, to see if Maureen had passed this way. There'd been a lot of traffic, but it was Greek to her, and over-written Greek at that. She followed the water upstream, looking for some stepping-stones to save her feet a soaking.

She stared at the water. Crystal clear. Did she want to drink and chance the raging shits? Or hold out for some nice safe wine or beer at this "Master's" place?

If in doubt, doubt. It was Rule One of food and water in the woods, laid down by Maureen. Jo didn't have any Halazone, and she wasn't all *that* thirsty yet.

She climbed back to the trail, puffing her way up the hillside through underbrush and dead leaves. She tromped through a patch of mushrooms and squashed some purple berries, wondering if they were all poisonous and if not, where the cleanup crew had gone—all the little critters that eat stuff in the woods. She hadn't seen any birds or squirrels or deer tracks.

Maureen was the one for wildlife and plants, the expletive-deleted forester, but even Jo knew the woods shouldn't be so quiet. Hair rose along the back of her neck.

She came out on the trail again. The way was more open now, blue sky overhead. Birds circled up there, three of them, big and dark. Vultures? Ravens?

Swell. She'd asked for omens? Look what she got.

Buildings lined the ridge ahead: a round stone tower, stone castle walls, and shaggy roofs of thatch tan against the sky. It had to be that "Master's" keep. It looked cold and clammy and dark, and she wondered if you could really keep an Irish rain out with a roof like that.

Walls and towers said there were enemies, armies, sieges. Jo reminded herself *again* that fairy tales were dangerous places. Maybe she didn't *like* this world Maureen was wandering in.

She turned back to the trail, chilled in spite of the stiff

climb through the forest. She felt like it would take just about one more thing to shove her off the deep end. Dragons and vultures and too-silent forests and dark towers on the crowns of hills: Adventure was something nasty happening to somebody else, far away. It wasn't fun when it started to get personal.

And last time she checked, her knight in shining armor was in another universe. Just her luck, he was off buying guitar strings when she really needed him to slay a dragon.

Or maybe Brian would be a better choice. This looked like his territory.

Maybe that was where Mo found him. Wandered around in her psycho nightmares, grabbed one, and made him real. Put *him* in a suit of medieval armor, and he'd fit right in.

She reminded herself to shut up and keep walking. They should have a well up there, and maybe she could ask politely for a cheeseburger and fries, hold the onions.

And then Jo's eyes connected with her brain, overriding the mindless blither that had kept her from screaming, up 'til now.

Those white things on posts, they weren't streetlights. They had eye sockets. Some of them had lower jaws. Some had wisps of hair still sticking to the tops and sides.

They were skulls.

They were human skulls, set up on stakes like the light globes placed along a rich man's driveway to create an inviting approach for guests. One had a raven perched on it, pecking at shreds of flesh. A dinner guest.

Jo ran. She ran silently, except for a panting moan that was her throat tightened against vomiting. She ran downhill, off the trail, through the clawing brush and tumbling and sliding headlong through the dead leaves and moss and rolling to her feet and running again. She ran, and inside her head, she screamed.

She hit water. She splashed into the creek, uncaring.

*Follow water downhill,* she remembered, *it always goes to civilization.* Second Rule of the Woods, courtesy of Maureen. Trails could go anywhere at all, but water went downhill, to the sea. Follow water, and you'd find man.

But she didn't *want* to find man.

That was man up on top of the hill. Man the headhunter, man the tyrant, man the rapist.

Maureen's man.

Jo held Maureen's gun in one hand and Maureen's jacket in the other and splashed her way downstream. Icy water soaked through her boots and pants, working up to her waist where it met the icy sweat working down. She shivered and thrashed on through the overhanging brush and felt knives stabbing her ribs where her lungs fought for air.

Water hid scent, didn't it? Washed out the tracks? They wouldn't be able to use dogs to trail her. She had to keep to the water.

She forced herself to slow down. How would Maureen deal with this? What would that paranoid cunning say? Jo shrugged her arms back into the jacket and stowed the pistol, to free her hands. It was time to get sneaky, time to worry about avoiding the dragon and all its friends.

Thinking paranoid helped, thinking about *Them* following her around. Paranoia eased through the brush, instead of breaking it: Broken branches were a trail, a sign pointing fingers along the way she went.

Skeleton fingers.

She was seeing skulls everywhere, rounded white domes of limestone in the moss and running water, the dark pits of eyes and nose in the rotted boles of trees, the grinning teeth in sunlight glinting off leaves. Skulls followed her, watched her, and laughed at her panic.

Jo's foot slipped, and she splatted on her butt. That jerked her brain back to survival. Wet moss was nearly as slick as a greased slide. She scrambled to her feet and continued downstream, along the creek bed running smooth over bedrock coated with green goo.

She groped for handholds, overhanging branches or protruding rocks. The makeshift bandages were long gone. She planted each foot carefully, thanking the hiking gods for the ridiculous vogue for Vibram soles on winter city boots. She grabbed another branch, easing across the stream and looking for her next foothold.

Something bit her hand, a sliver of bark digging into the dragon-scale cuts. Jo snatched the hand back, instinctively sucking it in the monkey fear of venom, tottered, and fell again. Her feet shot out from under her. Her wet jeans skidded across the slick rock, faster and faster.

Where the *hell* had all that slope come from?

She slid and slid and balled up with her arms around her head, fighting to keep her feet below her to catch the rocks before anything more delicate smashed into them. The water piled across her, cold as fire, and she fell into it and out of it and into it again.

Wet darkness closed over her head.

# sixteen

—⁓—

BRIAN'S GLANCE FLICKED from treetops to drystone wall to emerald fields, searching for the enemies he *knew* were out there. He saw too much cover, too much dead ground, for comfort. You could hide an army in the folds of Fiona's rolling pastures, and he wasn't even ready to take on a squad.

The problem with coming out between Fiona and Dougal was that it landed him squarely in the cross fire of their war. Whichever way he went, he was on the outside trying to get past their sentries.

He scanned the neat stone walls, waist high and so perfect for hiding archers, then searched the sky for stooping griffins, with their talons ready for a killing strike. Or maybe Fiona had set strangling ivy to lurk in the branches of the pasture oak overhead, ready to slither around his throat?

Nothing. He relaxed an inch, but he was still sure he walked headfirst into a trap.

The Summer Country always looked too damned innocent. In spite of all its dangers, this land felt like home.

Whenever he came here, something fused with his blood and told him the land was his, that he could mold it to his will.

The feeling was seductive, as if even the air of the place conspired to draw him away from the humans he protected and over to the Old Ones. Everything here reminded him of the blood he shared with Fiona and Sean. Joining them would be so much easier than fighting them. He ignored that offer, knowing that it lied.

The land might welcome him, but the people didn't. Dougal had a spike beside his castle gate, waiting for another skull, and Fiona . . . Fiona had Sean lurking behind her shoulder for whatever might be left of Brother Brian when she was through with him.

And David wouldn't enjoy what any of the Old Ones would do to him.

The pasture oak stood as a reliable landmark for travel between the worlds. It was the image he'd aimed for in Fiona's land, a marker on the edge nearest Dougal, where things tended to stay the same from moon to moon. In *that* respect, edges were safer, sort of neutral territory between the minefields.

Fiona found passive defense to fit her moods: her poison plants and the misdirection of a landscape that changed while your back was turned or even right before your eyes. Dougal liked his guards more active, active enough to threaten even their own master. Dougal lived for the adrenaline rush of danger.

Brian didn't. Apparently David didn't, either.

The young bard held an arrow nocked and ready, but his fingers were trembling, his face pale and beaded with the sweat of the green recruit. His mind was on Brian, not the battlefield.

Time for some fatherly advice from the veteran. "It's normal to be scared," he said. "The day I lose my fear of dying will probably be the day I die from acting reckless. I've been too many places where life or death was a shade of angle or a gram of force. Just don't let it paralyze you."

Fortune was chance and chance was fortune. Luck, not skill, often determined who survived a battle. So much for glory.

David forced a weak smile.

The bloody fool *trusted* Brian. That's what was new, the different fear. Brian remembered too many mistakes. He'd misjudged Fiona's devious plots, and the lengths Dougal would go to, looking for a mate.

Sean had taken Maureen. That meant an alliance between Fiona and Dougal. It had seemed about as likely as Joe Stalin pairing up with Hitler's Reich. Brian shook his head. Those who fail to learn the lessons of history . . . He'd left the idea out of all his strategy for this living chess game.

That boy shouldn't be in harm's way, untrained and untested. Maureen shouldn't be here, Jo shouldn't be here. If Brian had deserved their trust, they'd all be home in bed. Which was where he still belonged, no matter what face he put on for David.

Brian still felt like a wrung-out dishrag. He was trying to fight on the enemy's ground, weak and unprepared. He was reacting, not acting. It was one of the quickest ways to die.

He shook off the thoughts, limped across to the nearest wall, and peered over it. Nobody home. Normally he would have vaulted over it with knife in hand, but his leg and arm and shoulder weren't up to those heroics. He was getting too old and lame for this.

He climbed stiffly over the wall and waved for David to follow. "Sean took Maureen. That much we know for sure. Dougal wanted her. Odds are, we'll find Maureen at Dougal's keep. I'm just hoping we'll find Jo by looking for Maureen."

Brian studied the forest ahead. He saw a killing zone, perfect for ambushes. Snipers in the trees or in spider holes under bushes, trip wires, pit traps, you name it. It was as bad as the Malayan jungle, except for the leeches and the bugs.

Dougal didn't work that way.

David wiped his hands nervously on his pants, scanned the horizon, and turned back to Brian. "What should I be watching for?"

The *real* question was, what could Brian tell him without breaking the boy's nerve? "Dougal will have beasts on guard throughout his forest, vicious things he's caught and trained or broken to his will. He'll have some human guards as well, closer in where they'll be safe, because some of the animals he keeps will kill anything that walks."

In other words, Jo could die quickly if she was wandering alone. Brian didn't want to remind David of that.

"Watch the forest," he said, "not me. Man or beast, anything out there besides Jo or Maureen, is fair game. Kill it before it kills you."

Brian moved as if he patrolled alone: eyes ahead, eyes behind, checking out each tree, each rock, each step along the beaten leaf mold of the trail. He couldn't expect David to spot danger, couldn't rely on the boy to guard his back. The training wasn't there.

The damned leg and shoulder still hurt. His ribs still stabbed him in the side with an ice pick when he tried to breathe too deeply, and he had all the stamina of a week-old kitten. That was always the last thing you got back after wounds, the body's revenge for deadly insults.

Sean couldn't have waited another day, another week, to snatch Maureen. He *had* to do it last night.

Bastard.

Scraps of purple rip-stop nylon lay in the trail, mixed with white fluff. Brian squatted with a quiet grunt of pain and studied the pattern, automatically looking for trip wires or the evil little prongs of a contact mine. To hell with the fact that explosives wouldn't work here: Old habits die hard.

His fingers traced prints in the exposed dirt. Something big had walked here, something with scaly feet and claws. A whiff of vinegar mingled with the earthy rotting of the forest floor. He wrinkled his nose.

Dragon. That would explain the overgrown lizard tracks.

David grunted something inarticulate, and Brian scanned the forest for mythical beasts. Nothing moved. His gaze flicked across the young human, then back to him again.

The boy's face looked like pale ash, a mask. He was staring at the cloth and blinking.

"Jo. Jo's ski jacket. She was wearing that when she left."

Brian picked up a scrap and ran his thumbnail over one of the dark blotches on it. Part of the stain flaked off, reddish brown: dried blood. He looked around for more splashes and puddles on the dead leaves, the torn earth.

Not enough for death.

He teased at the stain again, sniffed it, tasted it: the heady musk of a fertile female of the Ancient Blood. It was definitely Jo's jacket, almost the same fragrance as Maureen. Maybe a day old, maybe more. Less than a week.

Time ran differently in the Summer Country than in David's world. Time even ran differently in one part than in another. Last night in the "real" world might be last month or tomorrow here.

His fingers traced the tracks again, then he looked up at David. Brian decided to give it to him straight and see if he panicked. Better now than later.

"It looks like a dragon caught her and didn't kill her. The beast may have a brood she's teaching to hunt, like a mother cat. Or sometimes Dougal wants to take prisoners.

That's not a thing you should be hoping for."

The fear had faded from David's face, replaced by white rage. He forced words past his clenched teeth. "Dougal. One of your Old Ones. What are his powers? Will these arrows work on him?"

Controlled anger was good. Much better than either blind rage or panic. Brian could use anger—could aim it and pull the trigger, could set a timer on it and leave it ticking on someone's doorstep.

"Arrows will work. He controls people and animals, not things, and he needs to be close to them for hours or days. He's a beast-master. The other side of the coin is, the control *lasts*. It's not like a glamour, where if you move away five feet, ten feet you lose your power. His beasts will obey him even if he doesn't see them for weeks."

"I think I'd rather strangle him. If he hurts Jo . . ."

"Just kill him the fastest way you can. You won't get a second chance."

David swallowed and nodded. At least the kid wasn't sputtering about dragons. Shake him loose from his mind-set once, and he was willing to take all comers. *Good. Very good.*

How would he act under fire? That was the acid test.

"If you see a dragon, aim for the eyes or down the throat. The only place your arrows'll pierce the hide is right under the legs, and you'll never get a shot at that. Most other stuff you see, go for the chest or belly. Slow down, stay calm, choose a target, remember the smooth release. Panic won't help Jo."

"Jo," David muttered. "Dragon. Eyes. Throat. Kill."

And he was off down the trail, stalking like a windup toy all stiff in the legs and with the bow held like a forgotten walking stick.

"Bloody raw recruit!" Brian swore, and hobbled after

him, struggling to catch the kid before he triggered one of Dougal's traps.

Dark scales glittered between the trees and swirled toward David, a wall of armor more than man high. He jerked the bow up and loosed an arrow that flew wild, the string twanging like a plucked lute. The shadow hissed like a snake imitating a Russian basso, then struck at David with a head the size of a small car.

Dragon. The kid was lunch.

Somehow, David rolled sideways from the teeth and bounced back to his feet, shedding bow and pack and quiver. The dragon whipped her tail around, sweeping her prey from his feet and into a tangle of brush.

<The Master said *nothing* about eating *you*.>

Brian jerked his *kukri* from its sheath and limped forward, working a stunning spell as he walked. Real dragons didn't have magical defenses—they rarely needed them.

"Hey, snake!" Brian shouted. "Stop to eat him, and I'll eat *you*!"

The lizard head swiveled back, teeth gleaming a mottled yellow in the sunlight. She needed a good dental hygienist. That and tartar-control toothpaste.

<Two. Most excellent. Hunting has been poor lately.>

She glanced at David, tangled and moaning in a hawthorn, and concentrated on Brian. Smart snake: She paid attention to the one who still had teeth. She tossed her head and shot a look behind her, as if something back there disturbed her.

Brian had to get close enough for the spell to work. Close enough, but not inside her belly.

He threw the knife at her right eye, the one toward David. She ducked to the opposite side, and the heavy blade clanged against the scales on her eye ridge, striking sparks and spinning uselessly away.

He still needed to get closer. She turned away from David and glared at Brian, warily. "Anything that dares attack a dragon deserves caution," her look said.

He circled left, drawing her away from the boy, clearing David's way back to the bow. She slithered after Brian, circling him with her body, her head weaving like a hunting cobra. He caught a flicker of motion in the corner of his eye and jumped. The whip of her tail caught his toes, and he flipped, but the force missed him. He rolled to his feet again, ignoring dagger-sharp pains in his injured shoulder and ribs.

His old wounds might be bad, but they were nothing compared to what those teeth and claws would do. His leg wobbled, on fire, but it held. The dragon slithered closer.

David was moving, clambering to his feet, running.

"Get your bow, dammit! Go for her eyes!"

All Brian saw of him was ass and elbows flickering down the forest trail. Goddamn bugout.

The dragon feinted, jabbing with her head, then snapping her tail. She acted like she was testing for traps, for poison in her prey. Brian limped closer to her head, and she flicked her tongue, smelling for illusions. She didn't believe it could be so easy.

Close enough. Brian triggered the spell. He felt the power flowing through his wrists, his palms, the blackness of the stunning spell leaping from his fingers. It splashed across the dragon's nose.

Nothing happened.

The transparent membrane flicked lazily across her eye, protecting it from any dirt or scratches when she struck. Brian swore she was smiling at him, the malicious smile of little Sean. So *that* was why she'd looked behind her.

<So kind of you to walk into my mouth. The other one will not get far.>

Brian dove for his *kukri* and fell, headlong, lucky, as claws brushed past his leg. He scrambled to his knees, and the snout thumped his shoulder with a missed strike and bowled him farther across the trail. He shook stars out of his eyes and focused on a single golden eye.

The eye of death.

She blinked again, lazily, a cat with a mouse pinned between her paws. Her sour, sharp breath flowed over Brian like a fog.

Mulvaney whispered in his ear, again. *You're going to die, Brian Arthur Albion Pendragon. Goddamned guitar player bugged out. Left you to save his ass. Never count on civilians.*

Brian's head still rang, and he played dead to gather his wits. The dragon tapped him with one paw, as if he was a warm chocolate candy she was patting back into shape before taking a dainty nibble. The tongue flicked out again, tasting, testing, slithering over him as coarse and rough as wet sandpaper. She still couldn't believe he was real, edible, no trick.

He stared at teeth as long as his hand, pitted and caked and slimy. They carried jagged edges, like the serrated blades of steak knives or the dental arsenal of a shark.

He pulled in his last reserves and tottered to his feet, the *kukri* back in his hand somehow. "You goddamned worm, go ahead and bite! I'll dive down your throat and carve your heart out from inside your gullet!"

The teeth jerked away, and something like warm jelly splashed across Brian's face. An orange-fletched shaft poked out of a deflating yellow beach ball overhead. The dragon spun away from him with a screech that shook the ground.

A second arrow skipped off her head. Brian staggered forward, focused on stabbing that other eye. Blind her, and they just might have a chance. . . .

The dragon screamed again, and something huge slammed Brian sideways into the air, tumbling, flailing, barely tucking into a roll that carried him to thump against a tree. Another shaft hissed by his head and buried itself in the ground up to its feathers.

He identified it, automatically. Soft orange vinyl fletching. Olive green aluminum shaft.

Real-world archery, not Summer Country.

His own arrows.

The dragon roared and howled, head lifted high, pounding the ground with her tail, shattering trees and throwing dirt. A man darted out of the bushes right underneath her snout, drew bow, and loosed in a single perfect flow of movement. Point-blank range, ten feet or less, he couldn't miss. The shaft drove straight up, through the soft skin under her jaw, and vanished.

Brian thought his head would split with the shriek of the injured dragon. She thrashed and rolled in a fog of blood and dust and splinters, claws gouging furrows in the ground as though she were plowing for some deadly crop. He saw the shadow-man flipping through the air like a discarded doll.

Brian's focus narrowed to a single thought—*Away!* Just get away. The bloody snake wouldn't die before sunset. One arm and the opposite leg obeyed him, and they dragged the rest along behind. Something heavy slammed to the ground close by, and he refused to look. Whatever it was, if it wanted to kill him, he couldn't stop it.

He bumped up against a pile of rocks, slithered into a crevice between two of them, and waited for the factory whistles of hell to stop their braying. Forget about sneaking up on Dougal. If the bastard hadn't been waiting already, they'd just well and truly rung the doorbell.

Dirt showered across him, and he jerked his mind back to survival. The dragon lay sprawled across the trail, twitching and twisted, silent, steaming blood dripping from her jaw. Her undamaged eye hung half-closed and blank. As he watched, one forefoot relaxed, and a clod of dirt dropped back to the ground in bits and dribbles from the clench of her claws.

It was a damn good thing they didn't breathe fire. Teeth and claws and muscles were bad enough.

He gritted his teeth and hauled himself upright against the sheltering rocks, swaying, trying to sort out the scene. It was a bloody mess, in all senses of the word: Dragon blood and human blood and British swearing splashed all over the shattered forest trail.

Brian stared at a gash through his pants and into the meat beneath, twice as long as his finger and slowly flowing red. A dragon claw had just touched him lightly. He swung his right arm and winced when it refused to rise above his shoulder, either way. He spat, saw blood mixed with the dirt he cleared from his mouth, and hoped it came from a cut lip instead of from his lungs. At this point, he couldn't tell.

First priority: look for weapons. His *kukri* glittered in the sun, half-buried by leaves and dirt. He hobbled over to it and knelt, one leg stiff to the side, rather than trying to bend over. The knife didn't seem damaged. Only thing that wasn't.

The dragon spasmed again, tail thrashing and rolling a boulder as big as a Volkswagen across the trail. He wondered if it had a supplemental brain to work the hind-quarters, like some dinosaurs were thought to have. He'd better stay well clear of the carcass, anyway.

Next thing was, find David. The freeze-frame picture of an archer right underneath the dragon's jaw stuck in his mind.

Brian ran the videotape back in his brain, coordinating the trees that still stood among the ruins. The man had stood *there*, was knocked flying in *that* direction. Whatever was left of him should be under *those* fallen branches.

The *kukri* made a decent machete, lopping off the thinner limbs even with Brian's awkward, half-strength swings. He moved carefully, clearing and stacking in jerky spurts like a damaged robot, then resting whenever his head threatened to spin off and fall into the mess. The fraction of Brian's brain that still worked kept nagging him against shifting the balance of the wreckage, against cutting flesh instead of wood.

Boot. Blue jeans. A broken bow, fiberglass, recurved, still clenched in a pale hand. Bloody shirt, both bright red human blood and the darker hematite of a dragon's. David.

David Dragon-Slayer.

He still lived. Brian ran practiced fingers over his head, prodding bruises and finding solid, undamaged bone. The pulse felt strong, breathing regular. He pried back eyelids, found pupils dilated but matching.

Brian cut away more branches. He added to the list: dislocated elbow, cuts, scrapes, bruises. Not bad for a rookie, to use the Yank phrase. A quick jerk and the elbow slipped back into joint. It was best to do it while the poor sod was already out and save him the pain.

He'd have to ask about other damage when the kid woke up. The Summer Country didn't provide portable X ray machines. Just hands and eyes and ears, the original diagnostic tools. Brian stood up, joint by aching joint, and spotted the familiar worn cloth of his backpack lying in the trail. It held water and bandages.

Cutting his pants away from the gash in his leg was hard. Wrapping gauze pad and Ace bandage around it was hard. Everything was hard with fingers that fumbled and shook, with joints that refused to work in the proper fashion, with muscles drained of glycogen and ATP and whatever other bloody chemicals the bloody scientists had decreed necessary for coordinated bloody movement.

When he limped back to David, the boy's eyes were

open. He stared up at Brian and slowly blinked, then shook his head.

"I ran."

"You came back."

"I'm a coward."

"You're a brave man. Running away makes sense. Turning around and coming back is harder than staying to fight in the first place. Now shut up and see if everything still works. Try things gently, one piece at a time."

A broken branch stabbed the earth right next to David's shoulder, and another poked the space between his thighs. Together, they propped up a limb thicker than a man's waist. Chance ruled again. Chance dropped the limb there and chance spared David from being skewered, and chance probably guided his arrows in the first place, both the shaft in the center of the dragon's eye and the later one that had missed Brian by a hand span.

David slowly dragged himself out from under the brush pile. He wiggled fingers and toes and sat up groggily. He groped around his right kneecap and winced. Brian helped him to his feet, and they both found their way to the comforting support of a tree trunk.

David stared at the dragon, the monster hulk still twitching fitfully as different parts of it learned that they were dead. To Brian's weary eye, it looked as if the damned thing stretched clear over the horizon.

"Jesus Christ," David whispered.

"Himself and all the saints, as well. You killed it."

"Should I eat its heart or something?"

"If you want to spend the rest of the day puking, go ahead and try. This isn't Wagner, or some stupid fairy tale. Dragon flesh will make you sick."

They leaned against each other and the tree, with about enough strength left between them to ruffle a kitten's fur. Brian's vision blurred for an instant, narrowing to a tunnel before clearing, and he wondered vaguely how they were going to rescue Maureen and Jo if they couldn't even walk.

"Such a touching scene."

Brian jerked his head around at the words. Black spots swam across his sight at the sudden move.

It was Sean. Behind him stood the squat ogre shape of Dougal. Brian felt his hand turn numb, and the *kukri* thumped to the ground. His muscles froze with Sean's holding spell.

"You killed my dragon," Dougal said. "That will cost you."

# seventeen

—⚡—

SEAN JUST STOOD there, lazily, next to a shattered tree, as smooth and sleek and darkly elegant as ever in the gray pullover and gray slacks that were nearly a uniform to him and to Fiona. His smile twisted gently at the corners of his mouth, and malice danced like firelight in his eyes.

Brian's thoughts jumped from Sean to Dougal to David to his *kukri* lying on the ground. He swore quietly to himself, even inventing a few new phrases when the accumulated vocabulary of fifty years of army life seemed to come up short.

Even if he broke the holding spell, neither he nor David could lift a finger for another fight. *And* Dougal was wearing chain mail over leather and carried an ugly clawed mace. Whatever else Brian might think about the misshapen troll, he recognized a competent and vicious fighter.

Cooling sweat stung Brian's eyes and trickled down his back and forehead. Flies buzzed his head, attracted by the spattered blood and eye jelly of the dragon, the sweat, and the dirt. He twitched a finger, trying to swat at them, but couldn't move. Somehow, the filthy little buggers bothered him more than the certainty that he was about to die.

"Darling Fiona's heart will break," Sean drawled. "Poor darling Brian. Killed by a dragon, a blow to the head even as the beast twisted in its death throes. It must have been a valiant fight between worthy opponents."

He took the mace from Dougal. "What do you plan to do with the other one, my noble ally? Add him to your collection?"

"He's a poor trade for my dragon," Dougal growled. "You wouldn't believe how much time and trouble the beast cost me. I don't know where I'll find another."

"Ah, yes. An endangered species. And I'll bet my dear brother didn't even file an environmental impact statement. He's left you with a lot of damage to repair."

Brian wrestled with the spell holding him. Power drained away as fast as he gathered it, water pumped into a bucket with no bottom. Where in *hell* had Sean learned that kind of trick?

But Brian was too tired and muddleheaded from the fight to really care. His tongue seemed thick in his mouth when he tried to speak, as if he'd swallowed dragon's blood and his throat was swelling up to choke him.

"Quit gloating and kill me, you scrawny little freak. Or don't you have enough muscle to lift a weapon? Wouldn't you prefer to have Dougal do the sweaty work and keep the nasty gore off your pretty clothes?"

Get the runt mad enough, he might lose concentration. If he just lost his grip on a single *thread* of the binding . . . Sean was the dangerous one; Dougal couldn't use that kind of spell.

"You can't goad me into hurrying." Sean smiled, running words over his tongue as if savoring a fine wine. "I've waited half a century to bash your brains out. A few minutes of triumph are small enough payment for all your insults and interference. Even Fiona doesn't really like you,

you know. She just has this genetic experiment she wants
to try."

"So shut up and kill me before I get enough strength
back to break your hold and then your bloody little neck."

"Temper, temper. Wait your turn. I was asking Dougal
about your human friend."

One of the flies landed on Brian's nose, and he hated it
more than he hated Sean or Dougal. He couldn't even purse
his lips to try to blow it loose. The only reason he could
talk at all was Sean's hunger for a chance to taunt him.
How could Brian twist that weakness into a weapon?

He had to keep a hope for Maureen and Jo. David had
been blooded now, he ran and then came back again. He
wouldn't run a second time. He knew how to fight, and
he truly cared. They couldn't both die here.

"David is a bard. His life is sacred. Let him go or bring
the curse down upon you both."

Dougal clenched his jaw, then bit off words like chunks
of jerked beef dried a touch too long. "I think you're lying.
But bard or no, he owes me blood. He owes blood to the
land. I can think of ways to get that without killing him.
He'll pay."

Sean's smile broadened. "You interest me. I hope you'll
let me watch, even if you don't want help. Things would
have been so much tidier if he hadn't killed your dragon.
Now I have to get all sweaty, as my brother with the
perfect genes so crudely pointed out. He might even splash
blood on me, and these pants are wool. My cleaners get so
upset if I make them take bloodstains out of wool."

He lifted the mace.

"I don't think you want to do that," said a clear soprano
voice. Fiona glided out from behind a tree. "Sean, love, I
am not pleased with you. Protecting the dragon against
your brother's magic—I could overlook that. It made the
fight much more interesting." She shook her head. "Killing

him yourself? No, I don't think I can allow that, love. He's worth much more to me than you are. Especially once I've prepared him properly."

Fiona. *That* explained the drain. It wasn't Sean, or some new skill Dougal had found late in life. Fiona.

The mace slipped from Sean's hand and thudded to the ground, barely missing his foot. Sweat beaded his forehead, but Fiona smiled and shook her head again.

"You're no match for me, love. You never were. Genetics, as you said. Those flaws express themselves in more than just your fertility. Among other things, they make you so predictable."

She glided across to Brian and ran a finger along his cheek and jaw. "Your brother, now, he's a different matter. Much more entertaining. If he weren't hurt twice over, I don't think you'd have held him. What do *you* think, Dougal? Wouldn't that be an interesting contest?"

Dougal grunted.

"Oh, come now, neighbor mine. You often pit your beasts against each other. What do you think the odds would be? Which way would you bet?"

The troll grunted again. "Weapons? Sean wouldn't have a chance. Barehanded? Even worse." He paused and narrowed his eyes. "Magic, I don't know. You'd be the best judge of that. I'd guess Brian has more raw power and Sean more subtlety and precision. Brian seems to rely on brute force."

She giggled. "True. Who else would try to stun a dragon? We'll have to try it later, when Brian's healed and well broken to the leash."

Now her fingers caressed Sean's face, brushing a smear of dust from his cheek and then straightening the collar of his sweater. "You didn't think I'd trust you unwatched, sweet twin? The way you so admire your brother? No, love, I am not pleased with you. While Dougal plots ways to punish a bard with impunity, I have to think of what to do with *you*. I think a touch of poetic justice is in order."

She started to hum, gently, a tune Brian recognized. " 'My object all sublime, I shall achieve in time, to let the punishment fit the crime . . .' "

She broke off. "Dougal, love, you do have other guards? It's not like you, to trust everything to a single dragon."

"I have other guards," he growled. "With such trust-worthy neighbors, I'd be a fool not to."

"Oh, I'm not asking you what they are, or where." She chuckled. "That sort of information is dangerous to both the giver and the gifted. I was just thinking I might leave my beloved Sean in your woods to play a while. Just like Brian."

She picked up the heavy *kukri* from the ground and jerked its sheath from Brian's waist. "*Exactly* like Brian. With nothing but a knife and with his Power blocked. A week, or perhaps a moon or even two. What do you think?"

Dougal actually smiled. "I think, dear Fiona, it should be entertaining. I hope you won't be upset with me if he gets eaten in the process."

"Of course not, love. Any blame belongs to darling Sean, for being such a stupid ass."

She examined the *kukri*, a vague smile on her face. "Dougal, love, you know so much about weapons. Isn't it considered bad form to sheathe one of these without its steel tasting blood?"

Dougal blinked. "I didn't know you studied weapons lore. Some believe that, yes."

"I've studied brother Brian, dear neighbor, everything about him. The strangest things can be a window to the soul."

The blade caressed Sean's cheek. Brian caught the sudden smell of fear on the breeze and saw the muscles tremble in his half brother's face as he tried to shrink away.

"I ought to carve your eyes out, love," she whispered. "I ought to cut off your ears and useless balls and feed them to you. You tried to trick me. You thought you could get away with it, and that is even worse."

Brian snatched at a glimmer of hope. With Fiona concentrating on the others, maybe he could break free. If she thought he was hurt worse than he really was . . . He reached out and touched the winds of Power flowing through the Summer Country and jerked back as if he'd tried to grab a live wire.

She didn't even turn around. "Brian, love, don't try that again, or it will hurt. I've finally got you, and I intend to keep you. You always were such a *beautiful* child."

She tipped the *kukri* up and laid its edge against the soft skin right under Sean's eye. A blink would bring blood, a twitch of her hand would blind him. Brian swallowed convulsively, as if the razor steel touched cold against his own skin.

"I'd love to do this, sweet twin. But"—she sighed—"I may need you again sometime. You can be such a useful snake." She lowered the knife. "Instead, I think I'll let you watch part of my spell-song. It may hurt just as much."

She turned the blade and slid it along the back of her own wrist, leaving a thread of crimson. One finger dabbed up a drop of her blood and held it to Brian's lips. His jaws opened of their own accord, and his tongue reached out and licked the salty finger clean. The taste burned down his throat and into his belly like a shot of whiskey.

His right hand reached out for the knife and mirrored her actions, holding his own blood against her matching lipstick. Brian watched the ritual like it was a movie on the screen, his body having no relation to his mind. Fiona had taken over her brother's spell as easily as picking up a book.

She frowned and turned to Dougal. "You *do* have that

redheaded bitch behind cold iron? She's left her finger-
prints all over Brian's lovely soul. This may take a little
longer than I thought." Dougal nodded, watching silently.

Maureen. Brian focused on memories of her face, her
gentle hands, her warmth and smell when she was holding
him in the innocent acts of nursing. "I love you," he whispered to the memory, raising it as a shield against his sister.

Humming filled his ears, a gentle vibration against his
skin that became music and then a song. Words coiled
around his head and blurred his vision until it was filled
with Fiona's face, her eyes, her hair. He still held the knife
within inches of her heart, but he couldn't have stirred a
finger against her will.

" 'S tú mo choill, coill, coill," she whispered, singing the
chorus of her spell-song.

" 'S tú mo choill gaineach ban.
" 'S tú mo ghiolla dubh ar luaimh.
"Os ar ucht tú 'bheith slan."

Brian heard the words in an obscure out-island dialect,
and their meaning whispered in his brain: "You're my love,
love, love, you're my loved one so fair . . ." He lost the
thread of the song, but the words mattered little anyway.
They merely held his ears and set his will apart from his
body, sleeping.

What mattered was her voice singing, her perfect clear
voice with a faint touch of fuzz to it like a warm kitten.
What mattered were her glance and hands and body caressing him, dancing close around him. He bathed in the
light of her face, the warmth of her touch, the intoxicating
fragrance of her smell.

The knife left his hand and found its sheath. She tucked
it in Sean's belt and turned her back on it, and Brian
wanted to cry out to warn her of her danger, but she never

asked. The smell of her filled his nostrils and woke fire in him and banished pain into another world.

"Don't even think about it, Sean," she sang, the words woven into her melody. "If you try for the knife it will turn in your hand and cut your liver out."

Her dance continued, close and intimate around him, as erotic through her clothing as if she danced nude. Every touch burned as though it left sparks of phosphorous behind, eating into his skin, and yet the pain of the burning felt like ecstasy.

Fiona loved him. He loved Fiona. She ran fingers through his hair and soothed away the scrapes and bruises like a mother's kiss, she ran her palms down his thighs and sealed the slash left by the dragon's claw, she gently wrapped her arms around him and the pain of his ribs vanished as if it had never been.

"Dougal, love," she whispered, "if you think you can do that without my noticing, then go ahead and try. You've had reason enough to fear me, all these years."

Brian wondered what she'd sensed, how Dougal had tried to manipulate his land and beasts to fight her. She never even looked at Sean and Dougal behind her. Such a wonderful witch, she was, to see so clearly all around her. So powerful and lovely. The strength she had, to hold three men while she enspelled a fourth. Why had he ever denied his love for her?

Her touch slipped away from Brian, and he ached with longing. Her singing told him all was well; this parting would be short before they came together in her bed. Her will was joy to him. If she wished him to wait, he'd wait forever.

"Dougal, love, you really ought to learn this. It's much more efficient than your training methods, and it will work on man or beast."

"My way works." His voice seemed as rough and crude

as sharp crushed stone after the honey wine of Fiona's song.

"Ah," she whispered, with a beautiful smile, "but it will be days before you can taste your bride, and you can never truly trust her. In spite of all your skill, sometimes the falcon does not return to your fist. Of course, I know that's part of the thrill for you."

"Falcons are animals," Dougal answered. "They have small brains and little understanding. I've never lost a person yet."

"Yet," she repeated, with a pause full of comment. "Yet. You've never tried to work Blood as powerful as hers or Brian's. This is no glamour I'm casting on him. Once I'm through weaving this fabric, darling Brian will never want to escape from me. Even casting the clay from a new-dug grave between us wouldn't set him free."

Dougal shook his head. "Once you're through?"

"Oh, there are a few more rituals to observe. I thought we'd finish in private, if you don't mind. Poor Sean would have a stroke if I forced him to watch."

She turned to her twin. "Sean, love, you are bound to this forest until I give you leave. Your touch on the Power is bound. Think sweetly on me and on betrayal until we meet again."

She waved him away. He turned as stiffly as Punch retreating from the Judy puppet, jerking his steps along the path, his hand on the knife but powerless to draw it or to turn. Fiona turned her back on Sean, dismissing him with a shrug. She eyed David, still leaning helpless against the oak.

"And what do *you* think about the things you've seen, young human innocent? You've walked from the streets of gritty reality into the pages of myth, you've slain a dragon against all odds and been captured by the evil sorcerer, you've seen betrayal and seduction and wait now for your doom to be spoken on your head. Such a poor fate for a hero out of myth. Such a puzzle we all must seem, to your virgin mind." She laughed, a harsh sound seeming to mix contempt for all of them together, then waved negation.

"Don't answer me. I don't really want to know." She turned to Dougal. "What *do* you plan to do with him?"

Dougal stared at the dead hulk of his dragon. His face grew hard. "If Brian isn't lying, I'd hate to chance the death-vengeance of a true bard. The Pendragons rarely lie. Yet this human owes me blood. My land needs renewing. As you point out, he *is* an innocent as our world reckons such things."

"Ah. You think of casting the Green Marriage."

"So quick you are," he smiled. "He will die but live, bringing spring again to my lands and thwarting the curse. We think alike, you and I. Almost I wish we could be friends."

"Our powers and our interests lie too far apart for that."

"Maybe. Or maybe our differences would make us better partners." Pain sat in his eyes, and longing. Dougal blinked away the weakness and gestured at Brian. "Can *he* understand what is happening? Will you permit him to see and hear and care? He deserves it."

"You *are* cruel, Dougal, love. And just. He brought the poor boy here. I'll let him care."

*Green Marriage*, Brian heard, echoing through his thoughts. *The sacrifice of an innocent.* The land would swallow David, draw him into itself, destroy him by splitting his life into atoms of feeling and understanding scattered through the root and branch of its own life.

It happened slowly. It happened with great pain. Moons from now, one with the Blood running in his veins would be able to talk to David through the touch of water and stone, the whisper of wind, the rattle of branch against woody branch in the stillness of the night.

Gradually he would fade, as the grains of a sand castle

crumbled in the rising tide, fading as his soul spread thinner and thinner until he vanished into the murmur of unthinking life, as the molded sand returned to the featureless sweep of the beach.

Brian's heart chilled at such a devious way of evading the death curse of a bard. He screamed in the distant locked closet of his mind that Fiona allowed him, the small space that let him care. Guilt crashed down on him and threw the charges in his face. *He* had brought the boy here, unprotected, untaught, brought this sacrifice as a crutch for his own injuries. *He* should suffer and die, not David.

He still owned a tiny fraction of himself. That fraction wailed with grief and remorse over David, over Maureen, and Jo, and even the simple hungers and desires of the dragon, so rare and beautiful and now so dead.

Dougal grabbed David's arm, the arm of the injured elbow, and jerked him across the splintered trail to a clump of greenbrier. The boy moved woodenly, stumbling as his feet chased after his balance and barely caught it before falling into another step and then another.

His last step failed to catch him, and he fell facefirst into the briars, arms flopping loose at his sides. The briars tore at him, and he screamed as if their touch was acid.

Tension and control seemed to flow back into his body, and he fought against the tangle, against the biting thorns and against the twisting, slithering vines that whipped around his arms and legs and throat and tied him like a bundle. Blood dripped from his bare skin and stained the cloth of his shirt and jeans where the vines touched him, as if each touch point was a wound and the briars sucked his blood through hollow needles.

He screamed, a harsh grating sound as if he tore the fabric of his lungs and forced it up his throat. Brian had heard such screams before, as men died in torment, and he'd never understood where they found the air to keep on so long.

The green coils tightened on David, wrapping again and again around him until he barely jerked. Dougal or Fiona kept his chest free; kept his throat and tongue and mouth free enough to howl his agony. But the thorny fingers invaded his nose, his eyes, his ears, writhing inside his clothing until Brian knew with sickening clarity that they penetrated bowel and bladder as well and sucked at the fertility they found there.

Brian pounded against the door of his closet, trying to escape, to regain his body, to find the use of hands to plug his ears and cover his eyes. The sight, the sound, the thought of David's torture reached into Brian and grabbed his gut and twisted. Fiona held him, dry-eyed, rigid, a spectator. She turned to him and smiled, showing teeth as sharp as any vampire's, and he knew she saw inside his hidden corner and loved what she saw there.

Briars root where their canes touch fertile soil, where they bend down and meet the damp earth under matted leaves. The briars rooted in David's body.

They cased him in green. The roots ate into him until a green man lay still on the forest floor, a shape woven of living wicker. The screaming finally stopped.

Brian hunched over his stomach, and Fiona let him vomit. Then the fog returned, even in his hidden closet.

# eighteen

—◦◦◦—

THE CELL MEASURED eight feet by ten feet, Maureen guessed. She was a shade over five-two and couldn't quite lie the length of her prison twice. It worked out to five paces plus turning space, anyway, with the shackles on her legs. Call it five hundred lengths to the mile. She did ten miles one day, five thousand lengths, and blistered both her feet with the constant turning.

Then they took her boots away, "to prevent an infection." The bastards had taken her clothes away, too, "for cleaning." That seemed like weeks ago.

So she ruled eighty square feet, more or less. She shared it with one iron bunk hanging from iron chains set into the stone wall, one iron-sheathed door with a peephole just about big enough to put her hand through, and one electric light high overhead that must be powered by the solar panels she'd glimpsed when they carried her in. She also owned one stinking hole in the floor that she only used when she was about to burst because it required squatting in full view of the peephole, and they never gave her any toilet paper.

Stone paving covered the floor, ninety-seven random-sized rectangles, and the prime number bothered her. She thought she'd prefer a smoother number, maybe ninety-six. Eight times twelve, or four times twenty-four, so many ways to factor it: Ninety-six would be a satisfying number. Either that, or the sixty-four squares of a chessboard.

In some perverse way, all this macho rapist shit was better than living with the endless fears of paranoia. Dougal and Padric were real, here and now. She could kill the slimeballs, if she could just figure out a way. They weren't Buddy Johnson, always giving her the finger from behind the protection of her nightmares, always lurking in the shadows and vanishing when she tried to pin him down.

She smiled grimly to herself and settled deeper into the dissociation that was the only good thing insanity had ever done for her. All these things were happening to that other woman, over there. The dissociation helped Maureen hide within her head, helped her wait and study and scheme.

Meanwhile, numbers and mental chess games comforted her. They kept an elemental purity that didn't change with the whims of her jailers.

She had saved the counting of each wall for next week. She could spend a day on each one, counting and recounting the patterns of dressed-stone masonry that looked like any classic dungeon complete with the rusty iron staples and hanging chains that should have held a shackled skeleton, forgotten. She hadn't even tried gouging out the mortar with her own irons: That would be a waste of time and energy. Maybe she'd save that for next week, too.

She wondered if weeks held any meaning. They had taken her watch right at the first, and there wasn't a window to give her hints to day or night. The light dimmed on an unknown schedule but never went completely dark. Sometimes she felt as if her life had been twisted onto one of those endless loops she'd made in geometry class in high school.

All her meals were identical, and their timing didn't seem to have any relationship to the light. No clue there. All Padric ever gave her was small fragments of brown bread and hard yellow cheese and a cup of murky, flat-tasting water—about what she'd eat for a light snack at home. She didn't need that hole in the floor much; nothing was left over when her gut got done with the crumbs.

The cold iron ate at her wrists and ankles, gnawing red sores when she paced. Dougal worried about them, during his infrequent visits—asked her not to hurt herself, not to scar herself. He healed them with a touch, whenever she held still enough for him to touch her. Padric was her real jailer, and he only sneered at her. Whatever fear her curse had laid on him was now dead and buried. He'd seen how weak she was, unable to back up her words with action.

She shivered. She took the coarse wool blanket off her bunk and wrapped it around her shoulders, huddling her warmth to herself. The fabric scratched her bare skin, itchy and crawling with her own filth. The stone cell was far too cold for a bra and panties, but Padric refused to give her back her jeans and shirt. He told her she could wear a dress like a proper woman or wear nothing at all like the whore she was.

Dougal and Padric played good cop, bad cop. She'd read enough stories to know the routine. One cop beats the poor slob senseless with a rubber hose, the other one comes in and screams bloody murder at his partner and gives the suspect a cup of coffee or a shot of booze from a smuggled pocket flask and wants to be a friend. Repeat and vary, as needed.

Guess who got the alleged perpetrator's confession? Next prisoner, they swapped roles.

Of course, what Dougal wanted was her ass. She'd see

him in hell, first. If only they'd let her sleep . . .

The lock snapped behind her, and Padric filled the doorway, snarling. "Blanket stays on bed! You know rules!"

He pointed toward the corner of the cell, the one with the hole in the floor. Bath time again, with a bucket of water that always felt like it came from the bottom end of a glacier. As usual, he carried some harsh soap, a scrap of towel, and a brush fit for scrubbing elephants. She was supposed to strip and wash, wash *all* over, while he watched.

It was calculated humiliation, just like shitting and pissing in full view, like an animal. She wondered what would happen when her period started. At least *that* would give her a measure of time men couldn't steal.

Padric could talk better than his ape-man impersonation. She'd overheard him, once. The whole fucking thing was an act, Dr. Frankenstein's Igor.

She turned toward the corner, her shoulders slumped in submission, and then spun back using her chains as a flail. One link caught him across the cheek, and she saw a glint of blood before his fist smashed into her breast, setting it on fire. She staggered back against the wall, whimpering. Another fist in her gut drove the breath from her body, then a third blow caught her just as she started to gasp. The stone floor jolted her knees.

He hit her with precise, scientific blows on nerves and muscles, using a sadistic sense of what hurt worst for a woman. *He's an expert,* her mind stuttered through the pain, *a fucking virtuoso. Bastard must have trained under the Nazis or the KGB.*

Everything seemed calculated just short of permanent injury. Most of it wouldn't even leave bruises on the surface. Just deep, like on her kidneys, her liver, and her ovaries. She screamed, hoping there was *somebody* within hearing that wasn't part of the conspiracy.

Thoughts vanished into the roar of pain.

\*      \*      \*

SHE WOKE COLD and naked and wet. Her underclothes lay in a stinking puddle, soiled. So *that* was what they meant, about getting the shit beaten out of you. She never knew it was literal. She hurt all over, not just the beating but raw skin that told her Padric had scrubbed her while she was unconscious. The idea of sleep pulled her so hard she closed her eyes again and ignored the pain, ignored the thoughts of what else he might have done. They weren't important enough.

*Sleep.* " *'Sleep no more! Macbeth does murder sleep,' the innocent sleep, sleep that knits up the ravel'd sleave of care, The death of each day's life, sore labor's bath, Balm of hurt minds, great nature's second course, Chief nourisher in life's feast'* . . . She drowsed with memories of Drama Club and the sense that if she didn't move, nothing would hurt. Where was good old Macduff when you really needed him, someone to kill this fake Scots Thane of Cawdor?

"Wake up, you filthy bitch!"

Ice water slapped her again and soaked at her until she realized the cold flowed up from the puddle beneath her. She lay on the stone paving, and some of the pain was bruised skin caught between protruding bones and the floor. She'd never *had* much padding, and here she was losing weight. That was a hell of an idea for a diet. Next best-seller, *The Torquemada Diet*, guaranteed to slim you down or the Inquisition would know the reason why.

"Get up and get dressed. The Master wants to see you."

Maureen peeled one eye open and sorted out the blurry shadows into Padric leaning over her with a towel. "Go 'way. Le' me sleep."

The towel cracked like a whip, and her ass caught fire. She rolled, groggily, and another snap lit pain in her right breast. She kept rolling until she cowered under the iron bunk, whimpering and shivering and curled into a ball with her butt pressed against the cold stone wall.

"Get up and get dressed, I said! The Master invites you to dinner."

"Fuck you," she muttered, but her mouth betrayed her by watering at the thought of food.

"Eat with him or starve. Your choice."

"Gimme back my clothes."

Something green landed above her, and she focused on it. He'd pulled the thin mattress off the bunk to see her through the metal springs and strapping. Velvet. It was a velvet dress, green with golden trim. Damn thing would go well with her hair and skin.

Not too good with bruises, though. Levi's and her white blouse would set *those* off better. She reached around the edge, tugged the dress down, and threw it into the filthy puddle in the corner. The cold gnawed at her: Velvet was *warm*.

She glared out at Padric from her hole, baring her teeth. Something warmed, deep in her belly, at the sight of a ragged scab and bruise across his left cheek. At least she'd given him *that* much back.

"Then you go to him naked," he growled. "Save time when he beds you."

He reached under the bunk and grabbed her wrist, jerking until she banged her head on the iron frame. By the time the stars cleared, her butt was dragging across the stone flooring of the corridor outside. The rough edges and surface sandpapered skin off her ass.

Something roared and then formed words. "What the *hell* do you think you're doing?"

Maureen shook pain out of her eyes and found Dougal looming over her. Something cracked like a rifle shot, and her arms dropped to the floor. Another crack and she saw the short whip flash across Padric's face. A savage joy boiled up in her belly as the whip sounded again and again, driving Padric down into a cowering huddle.

"How *dare* you treat my lady like this?"

"She refused to come, Master," Padric whimpered.

"Of *course* she refused to come, you idiot! Are you too stupid to see she's naked?"

Padric kept his head covered and muttered to the floor. Dougal hit him again, the whip drawing a line of blood across the protecting forearms.

"Speak up, fool!"

"She refused the dress you sent her," Padric spat. "She threw it in her own filth."

"Then . . . get . . . her . . . the . . . clothes . . . she . . . wants!" Dougal punctuated each word with a blow of the whip.

Padric scuttled away down the corridor like a frightened crab. "She demands those man-things she wore when she came here."

"Then bring them before I take every inch of skin off your miserable carcass!"

Dougal reached down as if to soothe her, and Maureen twisted away from him, huddling against the wall. She didn't even try to cover her breasts and crotch: Modesty was the least of her problems, right now. Besides, she had the perverse idea that if he raped her, she'd win at least a moral victory. She wouldn't have surrendered.

Padric scuttled back, cringing, blood oozing from whip cuts across his face and arms. He carried her jeans, her shirt, and clean underwear draped over one arm. His other hand held a dry towel.

Dougal flicked his whip again, pointing. "And get those stupid chains off her, you idiot! All we need is the iron rings, to control her Power until she learns how to do that for herself. She's the Lady of this castle now! Act like it!"

Locks clicked, and the chains rattled to the floor. Maureen snatched up her clothing and turned her back to the men, mopping herself dry and regaining some poise along with her pants. It was amazing how helpless nakedness made her feel. She'd always wondered why people thought it was sexy.

Padric followed like a humbled ghost as Dougal led her down the hall. He opened the door and waved her into a large room, dark like a cavern and lit with candles. It felt warm and smelled like heaven: a bakery with charbroiled steaks and flowers. She lost the petty details when her eyes locked on a long table.

Standing roast of beef. Potatoes. Steaming rolls. Sweet peas. Her stomach wrenched, and she nearly drooled down her shirt at the thought of food, hot food, good food, endless quantities of food. Wine, red wine, sparkled in crystal goblets.

She grabbed the wine and gulped it, eyes closed in bliss. God, she'd needed a drink. She didn't even care if they'd drugged it. The fire of the wine sent golden warmth through her body and splashed a rosy glow over the room. It ironed the kinks out of her bones and made the bruises seem less urgent. It even made Dougal look good for an instant.

He smiled and refilled her glass. *Wine. Would booze, by any other name, smell half as sweet?*

A plate materialized in front of her, a slab of roast and potatoes swimming with butter, and her hunger took control of her body. She didn't eat, she inhaled. In mere seconds, her plate gleamed as if she'd licked it clean of every scrap and drop of red meat-juice. Maybe she had. She couldn't remember. All she knew was that she'd only stopped when her stomach couldn't take another swallow without puking.

She had a knife in her hand, a sharp knife only slightly greasy from the roast as if she'd even licked that in her frenzy. Where was Padric? He was out of range in the shadows. She turned to Dougal, across the table, and her head swam for an instant. *Wine. Several glasses of wine, starting on an empty stomach.*

He smiled at her, politely, and nodded as if he often dined with starving tigresses. She measured the distance across the table and put down her knife. Whatever happened next, she'd at least had one decent meal, and she had her own clothes back. Now, if they'd just let her *sleep* . . .

"Maureen, you must become my wife."

"Why don't you just rape me, you bastard? Don't you have the balls?"

He studied her quietly, as if he was measuring her hatred and weighing how much to let her know. "You must become truly the Lady of this castle. I want you to bear my children. Unless you come to my bed willingly, you could cast out any seed I plant in you. This is the Summer Country. You wouldn't need a doctor or an abortion. A woman of your blood has such power and more."

*Abortion.*

The word sent shivers down her spine, waking memories of the grisly pictures Father Donovan used to carry when he led his parishioners on the picket line down at Planned Parenthood. Mom had always dragged her daughters along, forcing them to study the horrors while they knelt on the gritty pavement and prayed for the souls of dead babies. Those were such *lovely* images for a child of five to worship.

Amazing how deep the programming went. Maureen hadn't been to Mass in years, but the word "abortion" and the memories still made her sick. What did that bearded patriarch on the Sistine Chapel ceiling have to say about the child of rape? Don't punish the child for the sin of its father? Bullshit!

"What makes you think I wouldn't lie to you, spread

my legs, and then strangle you in your bed?"

He smiled again. It wasn't a friendly smile this time. "I'd know. This is *my* magic, if you will, the magic by which I train hawks and hounds and dragons. If you said 'yes' today, you'd be lying. I wouldn't trust you. The day will come when you'll mean it. I'll know."

She stared into her wine. The alcohol and lack of sleep combined to tangle her brain. Dangerous. Good cop, bad cop. He'd whipped Padric after ordering him to beat her. When she gave in to Dougal, he'd probably kill Padric just to make her happy. Torture her jailer to death, gouge out those leering eyes that had feasted on every inch and opening of her body and rip the nails from his filthy brutal probing fingers, and she'd be watching every minute to cheer him on. Padric was nothing more than a tool to Dougal.

The wine, the dinner, they were nothing more than tools to him. He'd starved her to set it up. He knew she needed the booze. He knew she was an alcoholic, a binge drinker. The whole scene gave new meaning to AA's "hitting bottom," didn't it?

*When* she gave in to him. Not *if*.

A growl formed, deep in her throat. "God damn you straight to hell!"

The wine flew across the table, glass and all, splashing his face and chest and arms. He only smiled as Padric pinned her arms and lifted her bodily from her chair. The grip on her arms was an iron clamp as hard and fiery as the bracelets that shorted out her rage.

Words took too much energy. She spat catfight noises and kicked the empty air. Padric just carried her back and dumped her in her cell.

\*    \*    \*

SOMETHING SHOOK HER shoulder again, and she burrowed deeper under the pillow. The luxury of smooth clean sheets and a warm comforter were nothing compared to the simple joy of sleep. She'd just gotten to sleep. *Deprive a person of sleep long enough, and she goes crazy,* she muttered to herself. *Even just interrupting dreams will do it. And you weren't sane to start with.*

The rude hand shook her again and pulled the pillow off her head. Bright light flooded through her eyelids.

"Fuck off," she muttered.

"Maureen, wake up. You've got to help me."

It was a man's voice. There was a man in her bedroom, and she remembered she was sleeping in her underwear— some frilly transparent stuff more suited for a honeymoon or a whorehouse than for comfort. She clutched the bedclothes around her and forced one eye open.

She faced a stone wall. She was still in that damned nightmare dungeon cell. Her head pounded with the revenge of the wine, her gut boiled in an uproar over her rampage through the dinner table, and that goddamn hand on her bare shoulder had to be Padric or Dougal.

She spun around with her hand in a claw, trying to rake his eyes out or at least smack him with the iron bracelet. Dougal caught her wrist, effortlessly. His face was inches from hers, and for an instant she thought he was going to kiss her. She bared her teeth, ready to bite.

"Maureen, you've got to help me."

"Why don't you just go off in a corner and fuck yourself?"

He shook his head. "This isn't for me. Your sister followed you here, and she's in terrible danger."

"Fucking liar! How the *hell* would she get here? Did that slimy shithead kidnap her, too?"

"I don't know how she did it, but she's out in my forest.

I didn't bring her here. You've got to help me find her before something eats her."

Padric stood behind him, looking worried through the bruised welts of the whipping. *Hide-and-seek. Find-the-sister.* She tossed the comforter to one side and swung her legs out of her bunk, sneering at the fact that she gave both men a full-beaver shot of her crotch through those stupid panties. *Dream on, you rapist bastards.*

Her jeans slipped on over her vanishing hips, much too easily. She ignored the urgency of her bladder and tugged at the zipper. The damned thing jammed, just like usual. Did anybody here sell Calvin Kleins?

"There's just one thing," Dougal said, blocking her reach for her blouse. "I can't let you leave the keep without agreeing to be my wife."

Maureen screamed and threw herself at him, teeth and claws and toenails. One flailing hand connected, first the iron wristlet and then her fingers raking across his cheek. She felt his skin ball up under her fingernails, and she growled like an enraged jaguar tasting blood.

An arm clamped around her neck, lifting her off her feet to kick helplessly. Her vision blurred and turned into a dark tunnel. Her body went limp. She dove into darkness until the arm relaxed and let just enough blood through to her brain to keep a thread of consciousness.

"Stupid woman," a snake's voice hissed in her ear. "People you care about are in great danger. Your sister is lost and hunted by my animals. Fiona has captured Brian and holds his soul in her deadly little hands. The land is eating David, plants rooting in his flesh and sucking his life out through his sightless eyes. Only you can save them."

"*You* put them in danger." She could barely whisper, couldn't find enough breath to rain curses down on his head. "Only cowards take hostages."

"You can command this castle. You can be mother to

mages and witches powerful beyond your dreams. *You* can be powerful beyond your dreams. What is so bad about sleeping with a man, about bearing children? Motherhood is the true birth of a woman."

The arm relaxed a shade further, and she could see again. She spat at the face in front of her and ground her teeth when she missed. Too far. At least she could see blood trickling from three parallel scratches across his cheek.

"I'd sooner fuck a warthog."

Dougal shook his head in disbelief. "What kind of a woman won't even help save her own sister? Padric, take all these silly luxuries away. The bitch doesn't deserve them."

This time they chained her to the wall, standing, so she couldn't sleep. They wouldn't even let her use the hole first, so she had to soak her pants and hang there, stinking, wet, and shivering again, with her arms tearing out of her shoulder sockets.

Jo. Brian. David. Some sixth sense about lies said that Dougal had been telling the truth. That bastard had drawn them into this cesspool and dangled them like swords over her head. He gave her such lovely choices: "Fuck me or Jo dies. Bear my children or David will be eaten alive by some damned plant. Bury your own mind in the darkness of my will or lock Brian away from light forever."

Maureen wept. She wasn't sure whether they were tears of rage or grief or pain, or just her eyes rubbed raw by lack of sleep, but she wept until her cheeks burned from the salt.

# nineteen

—⁓—

"FOLLOW WATER AND you'll find man. Great advice, sister mine," muttered Jo. "Great advice when you've got reliable Maine granite under your feet. No damn good in limestone country."

She stared up at blue sky, bright beyond the dark over-hanging walls of the sinkhole, and at the shadows of trees. Her sinkhole—the Cynthia Josephine Pierce Memorial Sinkhole, she called it, about thirty feet across and thirty or forty deep. Say it was thirty feet to freedom. That was the width of her apartment. It might as well be a mile.

Viewed objectively, it was just about the prettiest place she'd ever seen. A Japanese garden's plunge pool sat under the waterfall, lapping at moss-covered rocks. Ferns and del-icate bushes draped the walls and framed the outflow where the clear stream dove underground.

Even the rocks were beautiful, if she forgot that they had damn near busted her head when she fell in. She'd *thought* they'd busted her left arm, but it had healed too fast for that. Must have been sprained, instead.

The only thing the scene lacked was an elevator. There was no way out.

How long had she been down here? Three days? Five? They were all running together, as if somebody had photocopied yesterday and handed it back to her this morning, claiming it was a new assignment.

Back into the endless loop. She traced out another possible climbing route zigzagging up the sinkhole, from split stone to lump to gnarled root. Every try so far had ended with her stretched across the wall like a splattered spider, groping hopelessly for another hold while her leg muscles imitated a sewing machine from exhausted tension. Then she'd fall and try to turn it into a jump out into empty air, to miss the rocks and splash into the dubious cold cushion of the pool below.

Speaking of work. "Bet you're unemployed by now, girl. Rob may believe in flextime, but he likes people to call in if they aren't going to show up. *Especially* with a deadline coming up this week."

She was talking to herself, just to hear something besides the whisper of wind and the hissing water endlessly falling over the lip of her world and flowing away into darkness. Talking to herself, just like a bag woman wandering the streets.

Staring at the sky made her eyes water, so she shifted her gaze lower in case something new and interesting had appeared in her gloomy realm. Like maybe a ladder.

Rob was the least of her problems. He wasn't even her worst problem back in the real world. David would have the cops out dragging the river by now. She shook her head. She'd spent all night worrying about that. Not a damn thing she could do about it, so she saved her energy for important things. Like food.

She gnawed the last shreds of flesh from the backbone

of her last baked trout, then sucked on the bone for any trace of juice or flavor. She'd never thought that unsalted, unbuttered, half-raw, half-burned smoky fish could taste so good she'd hoard the bones.

Unless some others lurked inside the black mouth of the overflow cave, that was *it*. Even so, five trout were probably too many for a pool this size. She shook her head with amazement that she could catch the ones she did.

It was wonderful what a little patience could do for her. She just moved slowly, like she was no threat at all, and slipped her hand up behind the fish and snagged it by its tail. Then she gutted and cleaned the trophy with her Swiss army knife and stuck it over the fire of driftwood the stream had washed into the sinkhole.

She was burning the last of *that*, too, except a few chunks too rotten to even smolder, and she was lucky nonsmoking Maureen had carried a Bic lighter in her coat pocket along with the useless .38. Otherwise, Jo would've been eating raw fish and shivering.

Or she would have been dead of hypothermia days ago.

She flexed her left arm for the thousandth time and made a face at the lingering ache right under what passed for muscle in her forearm. It was time to try the wall again.

A seasoned rock climber would laugh at her and walk out like a fly, she knew. Probably take two minutes, max. Those idiots could stick to hand- and footholds you couldn't even see, stick to coarse sandpaper glued on over-hanging rock. She'd seen it on TV.

However, she was a city girl. Her idea of climbing was the escalator up to Casual Corner out at the mall. And as far as bodybuilding was concerned, her version of pumping iron involved bedsprings.

At least she didn't need a bath. A zillion falls into the pool took care of that. Her hairdo was shot to hell, though, and she couldn't guess where to find the nearest electric outlet and blow-dryer.

Sore arm or no, logic told her to climb now. Then there would still be some coals and scraps of wood to warm her up after she fell in the pool again. She shoved the gun, the knife, and the lifesaving Bic lighter into a pocket and zipped it tight. If she did make the top, it was damn sure she wasn't coming back for anything.

Climb now. If she didn't make it out today, she never would.

This time she tried the other side of her prison, working on the pigheaded theory that if it looked worse for climbing, it really must be better. She'd done a lot of things like that in her life. She'd gotten away with most of them—so far.

The first part was easy. The first part was *always* easy, just clamber up some loose rock fallen from the walls above as the water ate the limestone.

"Just don't be under the particular part that wants to fall today," she muttered. "You're known for being thick-headed, but that ain't good enough."

Those TV rock climbers used helmets as well as ropes. She ran a tentative finger over the hot raw lump above her right eye, the track of a chunk of sinkhole that had turned into a portable handhold.

She looked down. Just like every time before, the hole gave her eight or ten feet for free, high enough to really drive her ankles up her nose if she fell. What she saw wasn't pretty: One reason she'd avoided this side was that the pile of rock stretched farther out. The pool sat off center; if she fell now, she'd splatter instead of splashing.

She looked up. No fun there, either—the wall overhung her head maybe four feet, five feet in the distance up to the shadow-cut rim. She'd have to hang from her tattered finger-nails. She reminded herself that she was the girl who couldn't do a single pull-up in high school gym. Thin was in.

But she thought it might be better to bash out her brains on the rocks than starve to death. This was talking about thin like a sub-Sahara refugee camp, bones sticking out and dry crinkly hair and skin like a banjo head and bug-eyed alien faces. Not pretty. Not chic.

She saw a ledge, big enough to stand on or even sit, up above her head. *That's* what she needed to keep her muscles working, some place she could slack off and relax. Half of her exhaustion came from tensing up, from her own muscles clenching against each other. Shit, last time her *jaw* had ached worse than her legs after the climb, from gritting her teeth.

She could fit a boot into *that* rough spot, wrap her hand around the gritty, chalky knob of stone over *there,* shift weight onto them, and lift the other foot a few inches, rather than trying to swallow the whole elephant in one gulp. She'd gotten herself into trouble just last night, stretching for a foothold about half an inch too high.

She closed her eyes and concentrated on friction, dragging her boot up the rock face to search for a little nubbin just big enough for the edge of her sole. Her free hand groped blindly into a faint scratch in the stone, a line like the scoring of a cat's claw where the water had flowed and etched the lime away. It ran vertically and she pulled sideways against it, moving the first hand higher.

Keeping her eyes closed helped. She couldn't see a damned thing, anyway, the stone was so close she had to go cross-eyed to focus on it, nose rubbing its tip raw against the dirty chalk that leaned out as if it wanted to French-kiss her right tonsil. Maybe she could use *that* for support.

Her right hand found another crack, and she risked jamming her fist into it rather than wasting the energy of a fingerhold. She groped around with the left, banging up against a dangling root and following it back to the lumpy base of a shrub, then clamped on like she planned to strangle the bastard.

Her boot toe snagged on a lump of limestone, going up, then hunted around for the top of it coming down again. *Gotcha, you mother.* Her other foot inched up, found a hairline ledge, and twisted sideways, to stick by sheer inertia. She shifted weight from point to point gradually, never committing to any hold before she tested it, just moving one thing at a time. It was a dance, a vertical tango with her bod spread all over her gritty lover. Get to the top, and it would be orgasm time.

She ought to find that ledge any move now, that wide place in the road that would look like downtown Boston in comparison with the microscopic holds she'd been using. Her right hand relaxed and backed out of the crack, fingertips exploring for her lover's hot spots in the dark. There was the swell of the ledge. She turned her head sideways to look up for the best approach.

The movement pushed her body out from the rock, maybe half an inch. Her left hand jerked, and pebbles rattled down the cliff. Jo plastered herself against the stone again, holding on by body friction and feeling the coarse surface against cheek, breasts, belly, hips. It flowed past her, grain by scratching grain, then her boots popped loose from the wall, and she was falling again.

Her head snapped forward, and she looked into a surrealist parachute ride, the tumbled boulders floating up to her like bubbles in a scuba movie. "Don't land on *that* one," the image said. "It's sharp and unstable."

Suddenly she felt like a flying squirrel gliding sideways to hit the one over *there*—it was solid and smooth and firmly rooted. She planted both boots just *so*, broke her fall with bent knees, threw her weight back just *so*, and kicked out into a backflip that carried her into the soft cradle of the pool again.

The cold water smacked her in a belly flop that burned from her toes right up to her forehead. She snorted water and gasped, flailing her way to the edge of the pool and crawling over moss-slick rock to lie dripping and panting at the bottom of the hole. Again.

Right under the frigging waterfall. That was appropriate. The land showed its amusement by pissing on her head.

Back to square one. She didn't even have enough breath to do a decent job of cussing.

She also didn't have a clue about what she'd just done. That dreamlike sense of flying *couldn't* have been real. But it had saved her ass again. She reminded herself to quit asking questions. She might not like the answers.

Something tangled with her left hand. The fucking bush. She still had her latest portable handhold, about four feet of scrub, dripping wet and bleeding clear red sap from its mangled roots. No wonder she couldn't swim worth a damn.

It was probably poison ivy. She didn't know what that looked like, but it would just fit right in. She tossed it on the remains of her fire and glared at it. Traitor bastard plant.

Water sizzled from the coals of her fire, and the bush sparked into flame. She blinked at the apparition. It shouldn't burn. It was green and soaking wet. It steamed and spat and smoked like a smoldering rag pile, but it burned. Maybe it was her hatred burning.

She crouched over its heat, stripped off Maureen's jacket, and gave three cheers for modern synthetics. If it had been goose down, it would have cost twice as much and turned into a sodden worthless mess when it got soaked. Polyester fiber didn't absorb water, and it had held enough air to act as a life jacket when she first fell into the sinkhole, hurt and stunned.

She wrung out the water in streaming sheets, stripped

off her sweater and did the same, then the boots and socks, then the pants. Shivering, she danced naked around the fire to warm up, cussing the world in general.

"You would be the sister."

Her head jerked up with shock at the voice. A thin shadow moved against the sky, and her first thought was, *I'm saved!*

Her second thought was, *That's a man's voice.* She blushed and grabbed her pants and shoved legs into cold wet denim. Yecch. Ditto for the clammy top. At least her embarrassment would help to steam the water out. *Literal em-bare-ass-ment,* she giggled to herself. Soaking wet, her sheer underwear gave about as much cover as Saran Wrap. Well, a free show was a cheap enough price for a rope out of this hole.

Minimally decent, she looked up again. All she could see was a silhouette, dark against the afternoon sky, hands casually in its pockets. Watching.

Her ears burned again. "Do you have a rope?"

She sat on a rock and squeezed water from each sock, again, before putting them on, then squished her feet into the sodden boots. The silence hung a little too long for comfort.

"Oh, I could probably conjure one up. I think my sister left me that much power."

The shadow didn't move. Jo felt the hair on the back of her neck start to prickle. What the *hell* was wrong with the schmuck? This smelled like one of Maureen's paranoid psycho daydreams, enemies all around.

"Look, I fell in here and can't get out. I'd really like some help."

"It looked to me like you were doing fine: a little flying, burning wet wood with a glance, that sort of thing. Why don't you witch your way out?"

"Left my broom back at the gingerbread house," she

muttered. Then she raised her voice again. "A rope would be a lot easier."

The shadow shrugged, and a coiled snake flipped down, splashing in tangles across the water and rock. She stared down at salvation, lying at her feet. Jo relaxed for an instant before she realized something was wrong.

Both ends of the rope had come down. Bastard had thrown the whole thing. Hadn't held on to one end, hadn't tied it off or looped it around a tree or anything.

Her teeth chattered for an instant, and it wasn't just the wet clothing. First dragons, then Skull Alley, finally Norman Bates with a rope: This version of Never-Never Land really sucked. It really *was* one of Maureen's nightmares.

"Why don't you want to help me?" Her voice came out like a whimper. She couldn't help it.

The shadow shook its head and laughed. "Around here, help is never free. *Nothing* is ever free. What's in it for me? What are you going to give me, in return?"

*Men,* she thought. *Ninety percent of them think with their balls. Like Momma always said, they only want one thing. 'Course, a lot of women think with their gonads, too. I've been known to do that.*

It depended on what he looked like. She was past her fertile days for another month, and she'd promised herself an orgasm at the top of the climb. If he was ugly or smelled bad, she had Maureen's gun.

"What do you want?" she yelled up.

A bitter laugh drifted down. "My sister's head."

Jeezum!

Norman Bates, indeed. Jo shuddered. Fairy tales were like that, she remembered, the real ones that Disney hadn't tidied up for the kiddies. Blood and irrational hate and rape and incest and *extremely* dysfunctional families.

"I've got nothing against your sister!"

"Oh, don't you?" He chuckled. "Fiona's the one who

lured Maureen here and gave her to Dougal for a brood-mare; she's the one who wove a spell to bed brother Brian and gave your handsome young David as a blood sacrifice to the land. I'd think you'd have plenty against darling Fiona. More than enough to help me."

Her blood froze. "*David!* What's *he* doing here?"

"Dying, my beautiful drowned rat. Dying, inch by inch, as the strangling python of thorns sucks his blood, his breath, his very soul out of his body and spreads them through the land. Dougal wanted to bring springtime back to his corner of the Summer Country, so Fiona gave him an innocent to kill."

"Oh, God," she gasped. She collapsed on the wet rocks, face in her hands. "David." The worst of it was, she *knew* that bastard was telling the truth. She could feel it through the rocks.

And then rage took her. Steam rose from her jeans and sweater as her chill vanished. If Fiona could drag David into this, she damn well could drag David back out again. This mocking shadow could have his sister's head, just as long as Jo could ask the bitch a few questions first, perhaps with the emphasis of twisting her guts out of her belly and strangling her with them.

"Get me out of here," she snarled.

The laugh floated down again, harsh as fingernails on a chalkboard. "Maybe I don't want to. Dougal has Maureen to gloat over, naked and starving in his deepest, darkest dungeon. Darling Fiona holds Brian in the palm of her hand, or perhaps between her thighs would be a better choice of words. All I have is you. Maybe I'll leave you down there and watch you die."

"I'll help you kill your sister."

"Ah, can you now? I wonder. Do you have the Power? If I have to help you out, how much use can you be to me?"

<Jo, don't trust him!>

David's voice whispered in her head, bringing all the threads of her anger and suspicion and fear together.

That slim shadow, where had she . . .

"I *saw* you! You were kissing Maureen in front of the store!"

The shadow bowed.

"You bastard, you helped your sister do all this!"

He bowed again. "I've decided to change sides, my dear. My bitch twin stabbed me in the back once too often." He paused and chuckled. "The question is, are you strong enough to be worth the trouble? Prove yourself by getting out of there, and we'll be allies."

Cold clarity flooded through her. Maureen's gun nestled comfortably in her hands. "If I don't need you, the *real* question is, will I let you live?"

Mocking laughter floated out of the silhouette. "I can't help you kill Fiona if you shoot me. Besides, that thing won't work. This is a land of magic, not of chemistry and physics. Go ahead and try."

She hadn't drawn the gun, hadn't consciously unzipped the pocket and reached in and pulled it out and aimed it. Just, suddenly it was there, steady in both hands, sights notched on the heart of the shadow overhead.

"Then," she snarled, "think of *this* as magic. Instead of gunpowder, these bullets hold rage and hate and are capped with the poison of betrayal. This isn't a gun, it is the Spirit of Death. Your death."

She squeezed the trigger, smoothly, steadily, just like against the black man-shapes on the target range.

The gun bucked soundlessly in her hand. She brought the sights back in time to see the shadow stagger, and squeezed again, and the sights jumped away again with the same recoil she had felt practicing on the range, silently.

The rim of the sinkhole hung there, empty against the glare of the sky, and she lowered the gun. Mechanically, she flipped the cylinder open and dumped two empty cartridges into her hand. They stank of rotting meat instead of the sweet headachy perfume of burned gunpowder. She slid two fresh rounds out of the speed loader and into the cylinder, and snapped it shut.

A slight rustling overhead brought the gun back up. Jo squinted the sights against a lump on the sinkhole rim and found an arm dangling over the edge, out of the light and into shadow where she could see details. The fingers slowly clenched into a fist, then relaxed.

The gun burned like cold fire in her hands. She stared at one palm, then the other. Red prints matched the line of the metal on her flesh, the frame between the wooden grips across her palms and fingers, a negative and reversed Smith & Wesson logo printed on one thumb. The marks ached like frostbite.

She felt empty, as if the rage had burned through her and hollowed out her guts. She'd killed a man. What had it gained her? She was *still* down in this frigging hole! David and Maureen and Brian were *still* in deadly danger.

That man up there might have been a Grade A bastard, but he was *still* the only person who knew where she was. Why didn't she just shoot herself, instead?

"Rope," she reminded herself, aloud. "Now I have a rope." What could she do with rope that she couldn't do before? It was time to quit weeping like a baby and pull her head out of her stupid ass. She stowed the pistol, re-zipped its pocket, and sat down to study the rocks and trees overhead.

More Maureen-thoughts crossed her mind. *It was too damn bad that bastard didn't fall into the sinkhole when he died,* the paranoid voice whispered. *I could have eaten him.*

<Jo.>

David's voice touched her mind again. The shock of it dulled her ears, and she ignored the faint rustle as the hanging hand clenched and relaxed again.

# twenty

—◊—

THE TEAL ARROWED in from green marshlands and across the pasture, wings blurred by its speed. High above, a shadow paused and dropped like an avenging angel. Fast as the duck flew, the falcon dove faster. The teal sensed death reaching out with icy fingers, and it dodged frantically for the trees and safety.

Shelter was too far away. The falcon swerved as though drawn to the duck by magnetism, flipped her talons forward, and struck with the force of a rifle bullet. Feathers exploded from the teal. Its body tumbled into the loose unmistakable cartwheel of death, and the killing scream oof the peregrine split the air.

Dougal closed his eyes and replayed the scene, a hard, predatory smile full of teeth turning his face into a cousin of the falcon's mask. The stoop, the kill—they were beautiful. The peregrine met all his hopes and dreams, and more. His heart pounded with her excitement and bloodlust, the fierce exultation of her power and deadly speed. He licked his lips and let his mind feast on her flight again.

She didn't even land on her kill but circled back to his

fist to land with incredible delicacy. Those talons could drive straight through his gauntlet and into the flesh beneath if she tried, but she barely gripped him. He could probably fly *her* from his naked fist.

"Ah, you are so lovely, my dear," he whispered. His free hand offered her a chicken wing to tear, the blood and meat and destruction her pounding heat demanded. Her eyes gleamed with predatory fire as if she thanked him for the chance to kill. They were partners.

The bird's power and nature married to his own will, that was what turned falconry into something sexual. When the peregrine killed for *him*, he trembled just short of orgasm. Now, he relaxed into the afterglow as he carried his feathered assassin across the soft grass and looked down on the crumpled body of the duck.

Common teal, male, he named it automatically, one of the smallest ducks. It was such a prosaic name for such a handsome bird, with its mahogany head and soft green mask sweeping back from the eye, with its green wing patches glowing iridescent against gray and brown flight feathers in the afternoon sun. The falcon had broken his neck, swift beauty brought down by swifter beauty.

Dougal soothed the peregrine with his fingers, caressing her lovely chest. As always, he thought out loud when alone with his falcon, the sound of his voice helping to maintain the spell of her manning.

"Yes, my pretty one. You are such a deadly beauty, just like my darling Maureen. She is almost ready to come to my fist, come to my bed, my feathered assassin. Soon I will fly *her* against Fiona, against Sean, against my other enemies in the Summer Country. The truce is over. She will leave my wrist and fly free and strike the prey I choose for her, then return willingly, to me, as you return."

The falcon preened on his wrist, cleaning duck down

and a scrap of skin from her talons. The chicken wing had vanished into shreds.

Such beauty. Such power. His. As Maureen would soon be his.

He sensed it. The girl fought on, longer than he had thought possible, but she weakened. Her need to save her sister, that would push her over the edge, that would be the final straw. That had been nothing but chance, chance he wove into his plan when it floated by. Without it, he would still have succeeded. Success was only a matter of time and will.

"Time and will, my lovely one." He smoothed the feathers of her crown, and she rubbed against his finger sensually, like a cat. "Even the humans understand it. Boot camp, brainwashing, tough love: Call it what you will. I take the person apart and reassemble the pieces the way I want them fitted. Sooner or later, the subject does what I want, says what I want, truly thinks what I want her to think. Sooner or later she comes to obedience. And then I reward her."

Because he was who he was, time compressed for him. What took humans tiresome weeks, he achieved in days. His own peculiar skills added the special touch, the little nudge that pushed the creature beyond obedience into love. Maureen teetered at that edge. He felt it, clearly. Soon she would become his newest, deadliest falcon.

One of his serfs approached, and the peregrine swiveled her head, cocking it first one way and then the other, as if considering the man as prey. The Old One smiled at the sight. A man was far too large for his falcon to eat, but she could actually kill him with a lucky strike of her talons. And she would try, for her Master.

"Take the duck to the kitchen. Tell them to hang it until it is well aged, then roast it with apples and cloves. My bride will still be hungry when it's ready. She will want such dainty snacks." His face hardened, again. "Remind the cooks: tender and juicy. If they keep overcooking game, I will roast one of *them* for dinner."

The man bowed silently, knowing better than to laugh; it wasn't a joke. He added the teal to his game bag. Two hares, a pheasant, and a duck: not a bad afternoon. Dougal had been delighted when the peregrine showed she would take hares. Birds were her natural prey. She would eat well, back at the mews, and sleep.

"Yes, my love. You will eat well, but not as well as you might wish." The falcon's eyes relaxed, lulled by the sound of his voice and the power of his Blood behind it. He didn't need to hood her.

"Yes, my precious killer. Just like Maureen, I must keep you sharp. A well-fed hunter is a lazy hunter. If you fed on that teal, you would gorge yourself, and I could not hunt you again tomorrow. Just like Maureen, you must always want that little something more that only I can give you."

Her eyelids drooped, and she dozed on his wrist, bathing in the joy of killing and the calm warmth of his presence. Food, and sleep, and the fierce exultation of deadly flight: These were her world.

He gave them to her. She had forgotten that he had first taken them away. He was her god.

Soon Maureen would see him the same way. Then he could use her to attack those keeps of renegade slaves and the traitors of the Blood who sheltered them, carve the human cancer from the belly of the Summer Country. Then he could quit twitching every time Fiona looked up from her cottage and her nasty little games.

He frowned and shook his head. Balance Maureen against the loss of the dragon, and he still came out ahead. However, he would have preferred not to pay so high a price for her, no matter how great her power and beauty.

The dragon, too, had been beautiful.

Dougal turned and took one last glance over the fields, breathed deep of the rotting marshes. Again he spoke to the falcon, and himself. "Those are Fiona's fields you flew, my darling. In human terms, you and I were poaching her preserves. Our truth is a little deeper than that, isn't it, more like a reconnaissance? Testing an enemy's defenses? I'm sure she felt my footsteps on her grass, knows each time we probe and where. It's all part of the game we play."

Fiona being who she was, he needed to check the edges on a regular basis, see what plants she might have sent creeping along as advance scouts of an invasion. The marsh was one way he fought back, wild land conquering her pasture. In Scots terms, they were border lairds, never truly controlling any ground their troops did not stand on with weapons bared.

One of his troops materialized out of the brush, licking his paws. Blood spotted Shadow's nose and cheeks, and the fastidious cat groomed it out of his charcoal fur. Dougal saw a rabbit in the leopard's thoughts, and Sean creeping through the forest, and Maureen's sister by a pool. He thought about setting the cat to hunt down one or both of them, and shook his head. He never discarded tools before their usefulness was done.

Instead, he told the cat to prowl, and started the climb back to his keep. *I need more guards,* he thought. *Losing the dragon leaves a hole in my defenses. Shadow should stay in the keep, with me.*

*Perhaps Liu Chen would discuss the cost of importing another worm from the Celestial Temple. Chinese myth holds such exquisitely dangerous animals. No one else would have exactly what I need, the hunger and the cunning and the beauty.*

Or maybe the dead dragon's mate would succeed with that clutch of eggs. Only time would tell.

He climbed through the tangled, dangerous wildness of

his forest, testing his eyes and ears and Blood against the defenses he'd set. Finally, grassland opened out around his keep—the open hilltop that provided a clear view of anyone approaching, a clear shot at anyone approaching.

Padric waited, summoned by guards who knew better than to let *anyone* approach the keep unnoticed and unmet. The master falconer took the peregrine gently on his arm and smiled as if the bird was his, the training of it was his, the pride of mastery was his. Sometimes Padric stepped above his station. Dougal didn't think he was a harsh master, but he insisted that humans know their place.

"She missed one stoop on the pheasant, and was slow to come back for the second. Have you been feeding her too much?" The accusations were half-true, at best, but they would serve to remind Padric of who ruled the keep and mews.

Padric's smile vanished. "No, master. Only the standard working ration." He quickly ran experienced fingers over her legs, her crop, through her flight feathers, down her back and tail. If she had a flaw or injury, those fingers would know. The peregrine studied him in return, as if she questioned *his* fitness for the hunt.

"And how is the woman doing?"

"Not well, master. She wastes away. She loses weight much faster than she should."

Dougal nodded. "That's her magic wrestling with mine. Make sure she gets no meat, no fats, no sweets—nothing with energy or blood in it, nothing to feed her powers. You've only given her the skimmed-milk cheese?" Starvation was a two-pronged weapon in his strategy, weakening both her will and the power flowing in her veins.

"Exactly as you said."

"Good. And the rest?"

"She mutters. She talks to people who are not there, sees things that are not there. Now that we've unchained her, she sits and rocks back and forth, staring at the walls. The last time I checked on her, she didn't even see me. Her eyes were open, but her mind was far away."

"Good."

"I was happier when she tried to hit me." Padric raised one hand to his cheek, to one scab among the many on his face. Something lit in his eyes then, as if her defiance meant hope for him. Then sorrow followed, the thought of where the woman was now bound, and what was planned for her. Padric's eyes dodged Dougal's.

*Ah,* Dougal thought. *It starts with pity and grows into admiration, just like with the cats and falcons. You've lost your heart to our prisoner. I can let you love Shadow or the hounds, but we can't have that with the mistress of the keep. Such a powerful witch, she is. She's spelled you away from fealty, without you knowing—without even* her *knowing what she's doing. So great she'll be, once I've trained her.*

He reached out with the Power, running fingers over Padric's emotions as he had soothed the peregrine with his touch. Padric was a valuable tool. Dougal couldn't afford to lose him yet. Not *quite* yet.

He felt the loyalty build, the warmth, the trust. He felt Padric break loose from the thin net of Maureen's weaving, felt the ragged bindings of obedience grow strong again.

Dougal wrapped his control in steel and set a watch on it. He shook his head in wonder. The signs had been there to read, and he had nearly missed them. Now he would be on guard.

"Remember, she must believe. If she thinks you're acting, the moment will pass. I would be *most* displeased."

"She won't break. She'll try to claw your eyes out when you come to rescue her, just like she did two nights ago."

Padric's eyes still glistened with unshed tears. Dougal scowled at the sight. "Shadow tried to claw both of us during the training. Now he serves me gladly. The peregrine bated until she nearly died from exhaustion. Those were only stages we had to pass. Keep to the plan."

"Master, if we keep this up much longer, she will die."

"No. She'll give up. No bird or beast or woman can stand against my skill."

Padric swallowed something bitter. "Remember Ghost."

Dougal remembered. Shadow's littermate, a female, black-on-black and a slimmer, deadlier grace: Ghost. She'd fought. When Dougal came to her cage, she'd throw herself against the bars—clawing toward him rather than away. She'd known why she was caged. She'd known who had caged her.

"True. Some animals can't be tamed," Dougal murmured. "Ghost preferred to die rather than obey." He shook his head. "Fiona isn't that strong."

"This isn't Fiona."

Dougal blinked at the reminder. Sometimes he confused the two women, the captive he held in his dungeon and the one he wished he held. But Maureen would be better: stronger and more beautiful. Maureen wouldn't haunt his nights with dread and failure and mockery. Maureen would help him destroy Fiona, destroy the fear and the acid laughter.

"No, she isn't Fiona. And because she isn't, she has no training in her power, no understanding of what she does. That is why my way must tame her, turn her to my will. That is why she'll surrender. My Blood is stronger."

Maureen would be the most powerful witch in the Summer Country. Dougal would control her. That was his revenge, revenge on all the Fionas of the world.

"My Blood is stronger," he repeated.

"Why don't you take more part in taming her, if your powers would make such a difference?"

"The woman isn't a hawk. She has a memory. Shadow is our smartest beast, and even he remembers poorly. We want this woman to love me, rather than just obey me. Everything that she hates must come from you, not me. I must be her rescuer. If she learns to hate me, it could slumber like banked coals and rekindle moons from now."

Padric stood, holding the hawk and thinking. Dougal read his face. Pain sat there, and confusion, and fear. *Yes, my slave,* he whispered to himself. *You are building hatred in the heart of a powerful witch. You, personally. Think about what that means. Just don't think too much.*

"Do exactly what I told you. This will be the final stroke. She hates and fears all men. You will strike to the heart of that fear and push her straight into my arms."

Dougal read obedience in the slump of Padric's shoulders. The human turned away, carrying the peregrine back to the mews, carrying his own burdens back to the dungeon and the last act of Maureen's training. Dougal smiled and shook his head.

The dragon had been rare and beautiful. Humans were not rare at all, and few of them were beautiful. Padric was worth far less than the dragon. His value had been part of the balance from the very start.

Dougal waved those thoughts away and considered dragons, planning his approach to Liu Chen. For the moment, Maureen sat lower on his priorities.

Padric must do what needed doing until the final scene.

# twenty-one

*"DAVID!"* JO STUMBLED to her feet, twisting around to look for his familiar form. He'd sounded close.

"David?"

No David. Not down in the sinkhole, not silhouetted against the afternoon sky, not poking his head out of the dark, secret, frightening cave that swallowed the stream. No rescuer. No rescue. She was still stuck in this fucking hole.

She slumped back on her favorite rock, inhaled the smell of damp stone and rotting leaves and a faint cinnamon trace from the ferns, and sighed. Nothing had changed. It even sounded the same, the ceaseless thin hiss and burble of water cascading down on rock.

Only the rope was new, and the lump with one arm draped over the rim high overhead. She'd never even known his name. She felt unreal, looking up at him, the sort of dissociation from her actions that psychos were supposed to feel.

And she'd thought *Maureen* was the homicidal maniac.

Schizoid or not, her sister had never *killed* anybody. Here

Jo went, shooting a total stranger who might be her only way out of this goddamn pit. And she'd complained to Momma about a little round of talking to the trees?

Maureen. The whole mess was her fault. She'd come here with that mocking shadow, made this place real with her schizoid delusions. She'd dragged Jo after her, and Brian and David, dragged all of them into danger. Jo felt like strangling the little twit. All this bat guano was *her* fault.

"David?" She whispered his name again, almost praying.

Her only answer was the hiss of falling water, like an AM radio tuned to a station so weak it was just a voiceless pulse in the static. It formed vowels and consonants and even syllables at times but never a coherent word. She shivered.

The passing rage had left her cold as well as hollow. She pulled Maureen's damp jacket tight around her and huddled closer to the dying fire. The waterfall muttered behind her back, and she quit trying to force words into its voice. It wasn't David.

The stranger had said David was a blood sacrifice, not dead but dying in some obscene gift to the land. The thought turned her knees to jelly and left a throbbing knife-sharp headache in its wake. She couldn't do a damn thing about it, trapped in the bottom of a fucking hole.

*Damn* Maureen!

She closed her eyes, tired of forever seeing the same rocks and clumps of moss, the same rough dark circle cutting off her vision overhead. She had to relax and recharge and make one last try at climbing out. Maybe she could loop the rope over a protruding lump of limestone, or tie a rock on the end and see if she could snag it somewhere up above like a grappling hook.

Just relax. She had to let her mind ride on the pulsing hiss of falling water. Forget about Maureen, forget about David, forget about the lump with the dangling arm. She

let her empty mind search for the mystic's center, calm in
the heart of storm.

Relax.

Listen to the water.

<Touchhh> formed out of the water's song.

<Ssssomething> followed, a hissing tumble of syllables.

<Livinggg> echoed with a sigh.

The voice of the water sounded like David, like his whispered thoughts at three in the morning when they both
hovered on the edge of sex-drained sleep. Their words
would tiptoe around the edges of telepathy, single thoughts
or words or half-formed noises completed in the other's
brain.

She opened her eyes, and the sound became falling water
once more. *Touch something living*, it had said. She sat on
bare dry rock. The wet moss glowed faintly in the light
from overhead. Crimson-and-gold edges drew fine lines
around the fronds of the ferns, as if they shone with an
inner light that leaked out into a static corona.

It had to be refraction in the mist, an underground rain-
bow from the afternoon sun. Her vision buzzed like she
had just downed three cups of coffee.

*Touch something living.* Her hand reached out, tentatively,
to a clump of ferns, as if her body had given up on impossibility and the rational forebrain that sneered at such
foolishness. Next thing, she'd be reading fiery letters carved
in tablets of stone, hearing voices from the burning bush.
It was time to call for the men in white coats—maybe
they'd pull her out of here.

Her fingers tingled.

<Jo.>

The word jolted her like an electric shock. Concentrating, she reached out again, felt the tingling again.

"David?"

<We are here.>

Her hand jerked away. *We?*

She gritted her teeth, touched the ferns a third time, and closed her eyes. Something brushed her mind like butterfly wings, then left the memory of a kiss on her forehead.

<*Muirneach.*>

Beloved. He'd scrounged half of his scanty Gaelic vocabulary out of songs, a dozen dialects from the Shetlands to Cape Breton. You'd think the man would take lessons or at least buy a language tape if he hoped to make a living as a Celtic musician. . . .

"Where are you?"

The signal dissolved into hiss again, spurting out scattered words. < . . . all around . . . everything . . . alive . . . >

Terror knotted deep in her belly. This voice spoke with Maureen's madness and the strange fire that had burned through Jo's hands into the gun. She didn't dare look in the water of the pool. She'd see insanity looking back.

<Do not be afraid.>

Sure. That was what the voices in the Bible always said. Jo whimpered and managed to form her fear into words.

"What's happening to me?"

< . . . already know . . . of magic . . . you . . . power . . . blood . . . bend land to your will . . . >

"Bullshit. If that was true, I wouldn't be sitting in the bottom of a hole."

< . . . fall because you expect to fall . . . > came through a break in the static.

*Yeah,* she thought, piecing things together.

And the gun and lighter worked because she expected them to work. And she caught fish because she expected to catch fish, but there were only five because that was the most she could believe in.

"Why are you speaking with David's voice?"

The signal strengthened, as if David-ness needed to

think of her to pull itself together. <We are David. We are his blood, his breath, his thoughts. The land is David, and David is the land.>

Ghost fingers walked down her spine and touched her twitch spot, the freaky bundle of nerves that caused a jerk she couldn't control. David sometimes played with it to tease her, and *that* was one of his less lovable habits.

"Cut that out, you bastard!"

<You did not believe that we were David.>

"Why do you fade in and out?"

< . . . scattered . . . lose focus . . . distraction . . . >

"So now you've got somebody to talk to as you die," she muttered, half to herself. "Sometimes. Big help."

<Climb . . . waterfall.>

She'd avoided the rocks next to the waterfall. Coated with wet moss and lichen and the same slick green algae that had greased her drop into this hellhole, they were treacherous.

*Remember the rope.* She grabbed one end of the rope and hauled it in, forming a loose loop between her left elbow and hand. The stupid thing looked like some kind of gaudy shoelace, a purple-and-orange woven sheath of synthetic yarn. It felt soft, dead limp, and pliable, and it gave a little like a stiff rubber band when she snagged it on some rocks, before she jerked it free.

It was a specialized climbing rope. She'd seen them described on that TV sports show about competitive rock climbing. Frigging synthetic climbing rope designed to absorb the impact load of falls. The bastard had conjured it out of thin air.

Great. Now that she had it, what the hell was she going to do with it? Throw? What she needed was a nice thick pole across the sinkhole, a fallen spruce or something like it. Then she could loop the rope over it and climb out, hand over hand.

Thirty feet of pull-ups, she reminded herself. She was the girl with no biceps.

Besides, there wasn't any pole, and she couldn't see anything else to hook a rope on. If that slimeball had just tied the damn thing off before throwing it down . . .

The right side of the waterfall seemed to carry more of that eerie glow than the left. A sign from David? She slung the rope across her body and clambered over to that side.

She reminded herself to *test* each hold before she trusted her life to it, to lodge her feet *behind* the boulders so she couldn't slip off the greasy tops. One thing she'd learned from the last few days was to keep her weight over her feet. If she leaned forward, the angle would force them to slide. Up, up, five feet, ten feet, past the easy stuff, she stepped gently and gripped the rounded, cold, knobby, slimy handholds.

She tried to split the difference between dry bare rock and the pounding shower of the stream, climbing in the cold mist but not getting soaked and blinded. Looking up and squinting through the spray, she saw something she'd never noticed before. The stream had carved a notch in the rim, cut the overhang back into the rump-busting slide that had first caught her. The water actually curved, spiraling down into the sinkhole, and the notch was hidden from the floor.

$<$ . . . left . . . $>$ came crackling through the static. Left moved her farther into the wet, into ice water splattering on her head and sluicing down her neck.

The water had carved buckets in the limestone, leaving fluted honeycomb shapes like ice melted out from under a dripping downspout. Her feet felt sure, her hands strong and deft, her balance serene and relaxed. She'd found a rhythm to her climb.

"Where the hell were you when I was climbing before?"

$<$ . . . lost . . . found anger . . . focused . . . $>$

So the slime was alive enough for David to whisper through its life. She paused in a secure stance and scouted her route. She guessed she had about ten feet to go, closer to the rim than she'd ever climbed before. A rounded lip crowned her view, a smooth-humped sheet of water with an undercut below it, then a ledge that must have been harder stone.

She couldn't see beyond the lip. Jo shrugged; whatever was up there couldn't be any worse. "Famous last words," she muttered under her breath.

*Shut up and climb.* She quit worrying about a fall. From this height, she'd either hit the pool like the first time, or smash her head. Each of her moves found a hold, each gentle probe with fingers or toes. She felt like she was floating up the wet rock, even making love to it, instead of fighting it.

Her right hand reached the ledge, then her left. She had to hoist a knee up on it because there were no higher hand-holds below the rim. Slowly, delicately, in perfect balance, she brought her final boot up and moved her weight to it and stood up. Her head rose above the rim.

Shit.

Shit, shit, shit, shit, *shit*!

The rim came just below her breasts. The rim was the bottom of a funnel. Now she knew what an ant lion saw, lying in wait at the bottom of his cone of sand. A trap. Jo stared up a wet sheet of rock, smooth and sloped and coated green with algae and slick as a TV game-show host.

She tried pressing her palms down on the slope, and they slipped right back to her sides. Her boots had perfect footing. She could stand here all day, she could even lie down and take a frigging nap using the frigging rope as a frigging pillow, but there wasn't another hold within ten feet of her.

The edge of the stream flowed across her belly and trickled down her legs, cold and indifferent. *It* had a way out. She scooted carefully sideways, away from the water, and her right toe found empty space. End of the ledge, end of the road. She shuffled back again. If she went in the other direction, the stream would wash her right off the ledge. No thanks.

Twenty feet away, trees crept up to the edge of the slick green limestone. It might as well have been a mile. Lumps of rock poked through the dirt and tangled roots, ranging from beautiful hand- and footholds up to boulders big enough to moor the *Queen Mary*. Beyond them, dirt and forest stretched away to level ground and safety. Jo felt tears running down her cheeks.

"Damn you, David! This is even worse than sitting on the bottom and waiting to starve!"

Her fingers brushed coiled rope and gripped it so hard her knuckles cracked. What did she think it was, a fashion statement?

Jo whacked herself on the forehead. Sometimes she was just *stupid*. Time to play cowgirl. She made sure of her footing and shrugged the rope off her shoulder. Three tries at a slipknot for a noose persuaded her that Scouts and sailors had different kinds of fingers than she did. Anything she tied that slipped did it much too enthusiastically to trust with her life.

Finally, she just shook out a loop of doubled rope. Swinging it around her head, she heaved it at a likely-looking nub of rock and saw it land about ten feet to the left.

"Some cowgirl you make," she muttered. "How the *hell* do you throw a snake?"

Swing again, miss again. This time, the rope splatted down about fifteen feet to the other side. She retrieved it, fingers slimy from the green goo the rope picked up in its slither.

"It's okay," she muttered. "Take your time. We aren't going anywhere."

Leaning up against the rock lip cramped her movements. "It would be real nice," she added, "to just step back a pace and be able to get my shoulder and hips into the throw."

She looked down and scratched that idea. There were a lot of rocks between her and the water. *Sharp* rocks. How the *hell* did she ever miss those things the first time?

Swing, throw, miss. Swing, throw, miss. Swing, throw, *hit*! The rope draped over a lump of rock, and she twitched gently on the two lines leading from her hand. The damn thing lay doubled, the woven sheath construction too limp, too pliable, to form a nice wide loop like a good cow-rope noose. The rope curved and her pull dragged it off the nubbin again and it slithered back into the wet grease.

Swing, throw, miss. Swing, throw, miss. Swing, throw, hit, slither. Swing, throw, hit, slither.

Jo gritted her teeth. Son of a bitch rope was damn well going to land on that nub of rock and it was damn well going to loop over it and it was damn well going to catch and hold. If she could make wet green wood burn with a glare, she could damn well breathe a little stiffness into a rope.

She narrowed her eyes and hefted the doubled climbing rope again. Anger seemed to trigger whatever it was she did, and she was seriously working on getting angry, right now.

She swung the rope again, threw it, controlled her glare. The noose floated out into a beautiful curve, the two threads separating into the prettiest loop she'd ever seen. They settled like a pearl necklace around the nubbin of rock, and she pulled tight against it, feeling the strength of her anchor in the deep thrum of taut, springy rope.

Heat boiled in her belly and flushed strength into her arms. She pulled herself up and over the final lip and slid, hand over hand, through the slimy algae and up the funnel of rock until her knuckles bumped the rough bark of tree roots. Gently, one hand at a time, she shifted from the rope to firm rock and still more distant holds. She brought her knees onto grit instead of grease and finally gathered her feet under her body to stand, hugging a dry cedar as if the spiraling bark was her lover's body.

"David, I'm out," she whispered.

< . . . >

No words. She barely imagined the faintest hint of exhausted thought, buried under the long slow dreams of trees and the bright darting quicksilver of whatever squirrels used for brains. David had scattered again, now that she was safe.

Jo slumped against the tree, exhausted and hungry, her legs so shaky she slid down the bark and thumped her butt on a lumpy root. *Some food would be nice, right now,* she thought. *Double cheeseburger with fries. A half gallon of Ben & Jerry's finest. Flaming kebabs down at* The Riverside, *with a pitcher of dark ale and a basketful of garlic bread.*

Useless thoughts. She ran through her list of assets: one revolver with eight remaining bullets and some kind of a hex she could overcome if she got mad enough, one Bic lighter maybe half-full, one Swiss army knife, one yellow ski jacket covered with green slime, the clothes she stood up in. To hell with the rope: that thing was *heavy.* Besides, from now on she was damn well going to watch where she put her feet.

She had to find David. Whatever was happening to him, she had to find him and stop it.

< . . . dragon . . . > barely rose above the background noise of forest life. She remembered the great obsidian snake with its cryptic references to a Master.

She could follow water back the way she came. The

stream crossed the trail, and the trail led back to the dragon.

If that Master was behind David's problems, the scumbag had better watch out. She had just gained one additional asset: a belief in magic and a faint but growing sense of how to control her powers. Somebody's ass was about to get fried, and she didn't think it was hers.

*Damn* Maureen!

SEAN FOLLOWED HER touch on the forest gently, gently, in his head. He didn't dare to *think* of moving until she was well out of sight and hearing. One more bullet and he was dead.

He coughed quietly, the jerking muscles rousing knife-sharp pains in his chest and side. Something lumpy scratched at his throat, and he coughed again, spitting out blood. *Bitch.* She'd blown a hole in his lung and another in his liver. That was bad enough, but her curse really *had* put venom on the bullets.

"I wish you joy of each other," he muttered, remembering his jesting words to Dougal and Maureen. Mixing the two quests, Fiona for Brian and Dougal for Maureen, began to look like a mistake similar to letting a pyromaniac loose in a fireworks factory. Sean had thought he'd find an ally against his damned half brother, and *look* what he got, instead.

The older one, Jo, was farther away now. Sean allowed himself to curl around the stabbing pain in his gut. He'd just stood there in shock after the first bullet slammed into him. Then the second tore through his belly and out his back. Only instinct dropped him out of the line of fire and froze him into faked death, before she'd witched a third.

Witch blood. The genes of Old Ones and humans mixed unpredictably. Besides the sterility thing, Power skipped and surfaced in chaotic variations. Even untrained, this red-headed witch was dangerous—nearly as dangerous as Fiona.

He coughed again and spat out a deformed lump of copper and lead. The poison and his instinctive antidote had tarnished the bright red metal jacket to the green of a weathered statue.

Sean needed to follow the woman, follow her *carefully*. The Power of the Summer Country would pull her back to Brian and her sister. He could use her for revenge, use *her* against Fiona and Brian before he passed his pain back to the bitch with added interest. She was far enough away now that he dared to move.

He forced himself to his hands and knees. Healing tissue screamed at him, and he panted for air. Racking coughs cleared more blood and torn tissue from his lung.

He reminded himself to just move *very* carefully. All his energy must concentrate on healing. He was in no condition to challenge the bitch right now. After she'd fought Dougal and maybe Fiona, she'd be weaker. And besides, he couldn't leave the forest until Fiona released him.

That would give him time to plan.

Something else detached itself from the shadows and followed the woman—Dougal's mutated black leopard. It was about as big as a lioness.

Lovely. Now he had to hide from *that*, as well. Sean squandered some of his precious hoard of Power on masking the scent of his blood.

The cat stalked Jo for about a dozen yards. Then it shied away from her trail and looked for safer game.

# twenty-two

—◊—

MAUREEN PLAYED CHESS against Brian. The position seemed surreal, like her life since Liam and the ice-storm alley. This pattern of pieces hadn't grown from any normal opening and development, but she made the best of what her dream offered to her. At least the rules for moving remained the same.

She'd schemed and even sacrificed her queen to force a passed pawn and advance it to the seventh rank, protected by a rook. Brian ignored the threat because he had his own attack, and the potential queen was blocked from direct view of his king.

He picked up his own queen and moved it three squares along the black diagonal. "Mate in one move," he said, with Dougal's voice.

She looked up. It was Dougal on the other side of the board, not Brian. She hadn't noticed the switch. His sly smile implied a double meaning to the threat.

She glared at him with her teeth bared. Chess was not a game. Chess was war. Chess was domination. Chess was a battle of wills in which your opponent must be destroyed—not just defeated, but destroyed.

Chess was life.

She ignored Dougal as she looked over the position, noting his forces that backed her king into a corner and the single bishop's move that would force the checkmate. Queening her pawn would be useless. None of her other pieces could intervene, could even move to a point to interpose their bodies in sacrifice. Dougal was sure of his win.

She smiled, and advanced her pawn. Dougal shook his head and reached for the replacement queen.

"Knight," she said. He blinked. "Check."

The knight reached out with his crooked move, the only move that could fly over another piece, and attacked Dougal's king. The king retreated one space. Dougal's threatened mate still hung over the board.

She advanced another pawn, the single-space and diagonal threat of the weakest piece on the board. "Check."

If he moved his king farther, to capture the undefended pawn, he'd be even more exposed. She could draw with perpetual check. Instead, he captured with his queen, dividing his forces and removing the checkmate threat. Maureen could cover her king now, and battle on.

Instead, she moved her bishop along the white diagonal. "Check, and mate."

Dougal's queen sat on his only escape square.

Her dream faded back into the stone walls, taking the inlaid marble board and the ivory chessmen with it and leaving cold, damp loneliness behind.

Those were her favorite strategies, the feints and the unexpected moves, the misdirection. Offer her enemy a goal juicy enough to tantalize and make it just one move further off than her own attack would take. Sacrifice, even her most valuable pieces. Then strike for the throat, with a force so weak it was easy to overlook.

Too bad life wasn't a fucking chess game.

\* \* \*

"*DAMN JO!*" MAUREEN'S voice was a weak mutter, barely audible even to herself.

"Damn Jo and Brian and David, damn them *all* for following me, for making such a simple thing so complicated!"

Maureen sat on her thin mattress on her iron bunk in her cold stone cell and stared at her hands. They were skeletal and dirty, with a translucent pallor under the grime as if she didn't have enough blood to spare to turn them pink. They trembled with cold and with exhaustion.

Padric never gave her enough food. Dougal invited her to feasts, but Padric starved her. She muttered to herself about the "good cop, bad cop" routine, but that part of her brain was shutting down. Right now, she didn't fucking *care* where the food came from, just as long as it came.

Her eyes blurred. She suddenly saw twenty fingers instead of ten. Her head sank to her chest, and she jerked back with a grimace and rapid blinks to clear her sight. Her eye sockets felt as if they were filled with gravel.

Now each finger was ringed with a thin halo of purple light. At least there were only ten of them.

Her skin itched as if things crawled on her, either the layers of her own sweat and the filth of the cell or bedbugs and lice. More likely, it was just the lack of sleep and food fucking with her brain, twitching her skin's nerves with another kind of hallucination. Or maybe it was the DT's, the snakes and bugs of alcoholic withdrawal. Padric wouldn't give her a goddamn drink.

Dougal offered her fine wine.

She didn't think it was lice. Dougal wouldn't want extra wildlife in his bed. He wouldn't want *her* in his bed without a bath. God knows she stank. Since she'd thrown that wine at Dougal, Padric hadn't even given her a bucket of ice water for washing. Not what you'd call a dream date, by any means.

Her head sank down and jerked back again. She stumbled to her feet and forced herself to balance against the swirling of the walls and floor, the black dots swimming across her sight.

She thought it was low blood pressure. Brain not getting enough oxygen. Not just balance, not just eyes—screwed up her thinking as well. Logic went to hell, went to sleep, even if *she* couldn't.

"Can't go to sleep," she muttered. "Not sleep time."

If she closed her eyes Padric would be there in an instant, always that bastard Padric. He was just outside the spy hole, watching, she could hear his breathing. Close her eyes, and the fucker would hang her up by her wrists again, drench her with icy water, beat the soles of her feet with his goddamn rubber hose, take her clothes away so she was too goddamn cold to sleep.

But she could beat them. She was strong enough. The problem was Brian and Jo and David. Hold out, and David dies, Jo dies, Brian lives on for years as a brainless slave. Not fair.

Fucking liar Dougal. All she had was his word. Everyone else could be safely home in bed. Everyone else could be pigging out on greasy pizza washed down with pitchers of beer. They'd abandoned her, the bastards. They didn't care.

Not their fault. Fiona caused this. Sean caused this, the traitor bastard. Dougal promised he'd help her get revenge, help her save Jo and David and Brian. Dougal promised he'd help her learn how to use her powers, the Power in her genes. Dougal told her that she could wash her hands in Sean's blood. All she had to do was sleep with him, bear his children.

She'd see him in hell first, take him on a guided tour.

"Give in, you get a bed," she mumbled, under her

breath. "Give in, you get food. Give in, you get warm, you get clean clothes, you get a bath. So what if your bed includes a man? Men have slept with women ever since sex was invented.

"Sleep. Right now, you'd sell your *soul* for a good night's sleep. What's this big thing against selling your goddamn *body*?"

Nothing was going to happen to her that hadn't happened before. She'd survived. Saga of Woman: She survived.

Dougal wasn't all that bad. She'd never sleep with Padric. Padric was an animal, while Dougal was a gentleman. Dougal never hit her, never chained her naked in her filth, never took food right out of her hands because she'd done something wrong. That was Padric. Always Padric.

*Good cop, bad cop,* whispered the dying voice in the back of her head.

All she remembered of Dougal was him beating Padric with a whip. The finest meal of her life. Clean clothes.

So what if she'd prefer Brian? One man was much like another, a bunch of muscles fronting for some sperm. They were all pricks, when you came down to it. Jo sure didn't pay much attention to the differences.

Dougal was an Old One, and he chose her, chose *her* out of a million women. She was special. It wasn't his fault Liam screwed up when he came to talk to her. If things had gone the way Dougal had planned, she would have come here as a princess rather than a prisoner.

When Liam screwed up, she got tangled in Fiona's plan for Brian. All this nasty shit was Fiona and Sean, not Dougal.

He wasn't all that ugly. Hell, walk through the mall sometime and look at people. Really look at people. They aren't actors, they aren't models. Beauty was a crock of shit,

an airbrush fantasy. Even centerfolds got retouched to perfection.

Her knees wobbled underneath her, and she slumped
back on the bunk. A corner of the iron frame dug into her
leg, and the pain served as a last anchor to reality.

Somewhere, out of the last depths of her soul, she
dredged up the strength to pry her eyes open and glare at
the peephole in the door. The eyes on the other side
blinked and vanished.


"Go 'way." Maureen couldn't even find the will-
power to shake her head or open her eyes.

Something lifted her. Seconds passed before the pain in
her scalp made sense. The bastard was hauling her up by
her hair. Fingers clamped her earlobe in a vise and squeezed
until tears ran out under her eyelids. The pain shifted to
her breast, her left nipple. She still couldn't care.

"If you're that sound asleep," a deep voice growled, "I
can do whatever I want with you. You'll never tell."

She bounced against the rough stone wall and slithered
down to sitting. Hands fumbled with her snaps and buttons, her zippers, tugged at her pants, forced her bare legs
apart, groped between them.

Her mind flashed across the years, thrown by that touch,
those hands. Buddy Johnson was back. He'd never really
left. She whimpered in the darkness behind her eyelids.

The door clanged again, and she heard a scuffle and
curses followed by blows like a boxer pounding on a side
of beef. Gentle hands wiped the tears from her cheeks.

She pried her eyes open. It was Dougal. Buddy Johnson
cringed in the corner, fresh blood flowing from his nose.
His hair seemed longer than she remembered.

Dougal helped her with buttons and zippers and snaps,
not even wincing at the touch of her filthy, greasy clothing,

her filthy, greasy body. He helped her to her feet. He picked her up as if she weighed nothing, carrying her like a child in his arms. His face hovered just above hers.

"Maureen, I've got to save you from all this. Come away with me. Be the mistress of my keep and bear my children."

He'd draped her arms around his neck. She left them there. "Yes."

His hands tightened around her body, gently, protectively. One of them pressed lightly on her left breast, the one Buddy had pinched, and warmth flowed from him to soothe the ache. She snuggled closer to the warmth and power.

Her glance drifted across Buddy, still cringing in his corner. He'd lost weight since she'd seen him last. Tears stained his face—tears that looked more like loss and sorrow than pain. Dougal carried her out of the cell and kicked the door shut behind them, locking Buddy in, locking him out of her life. Savage glee flooded through her.

*There will be a reckoning,* she whispered to herself. *You will suffer ten times what you did to me.*

Slowly, gently, Dougal carried her down stone corridors and up stone stairways into brighter, sweeter-smelling, warmer rooms. She lost herself in his arms, drowsing even though she didn't feel half as hungry and tired as she had before.

His encircling arms felt so warm, so strong, so protective. They were the arms of a warrior, her warrior, to fight for her and for her friends. She smelled his maleness, and it wasn't threatening. He wasn't Brian, but at least he was the right species.

"Brian. Jo. David. Danger." Talking was an effort.

"It's night now. We'll start our hunt in the morning."

Good. Sleep first, then duty.

Warm moisture tickled her nose, touched with lavender

and soap and a faint resinous burning smell like incense. She opened her eyes again. He had carried her into a smaller room, tiled, warm, softly lit. Vivaldi played quietly in the distance.

She blinked with surprise. It was a frigging California bathroom, with huge spa tub recessed into the floor and skylights that showed a moon nearly full and towels that looked like they were about an acre across and three feet thick. Some castle her lover kept, bidets and surround showers and full-length mirrors framed by sweeps of ivy climbing to the beams overhead. Stereo speakers hung high in the corners.

The room even had a goddamn fireplace in one corner, lit with fresh birch logs to scent the air. She blinked again and shook her head, trying to chase the illusion away.

He smiled down at her. "You were expecting an outhouse? We're not the Sassenach here, not barbarians."

He helped her undress and kissed her again with a gentle caress that warmed her belly and made her cheeks tingle. Then she settled into the absolute bliss of hot water and soap.

When she surfaced again, he was sitting on the tiles by the side of the bath, smiling quietly, holding a glass of beer and a genuine, nonmirage, Swiss-and-ham-on-rye sandwich. She grabbed for it with a sudden lurch and splatter of suds, but he gently pushed her hand aside and fed her himself, alternating bites of sandwich and strong kosher pickle washed down by sweet dark beer.

The beer seemed to go straight to her head, bypassing her stomach. It called out for more, loud enough for him to hear, but he shook his head.

"You shouldn't eat or drink too much, too suddenly. It will make you sick. Tomorrow, the day after, you will build up gently. This is all you should have, for now."

She splashed him. He dunked her head underwater, and

she got soap up her nose. He massaged shampoo into her hair and washed her back and gently, erotically, teased other parts of her awakening body. Maureen floated in a warm, fuzzy bliss.

"Time to get out."

She shook her head, not denying but trying to wake up. The whole scene felt like a dream. She stood, climbed out of the tub, felt soft warm towels fold her to their heart. Her hair dried itself. She caught a glimpse of something slim and pink and elegant in one of the steamy mirrors. She preened and posed for an instant, thinking that stranger didn't look at all bad for an escapee a few minutes out of Buddy Johnson's dungeon.

A heavy door opened directly into his bedroom, a huge space of stone and wood panels and richly embroidered drapes and arched beams overhead. Weapons and animal heads hung the walls and furs warmed the wooden floor. She stood on one, kneading it with her bare toes and soaking up the sensual bliss.

Dougal lifted the towel robe from her shoulders, and she wondered at the warm air on her naked body, such a contrast with the stone and the gloom and damp she'd always associated with castles. Such a delight, magic was, to allow both comfort and grandeur.

Then Dougal took her in his arms again, lifting her gently and carrying her to his bed. Darkness stirred at the back of her head, a fear long felt and fought.

Man. Bed. Sex. He was going to make love to her. She had feared this, struggled against it. It was something painful and evil. She had sworn to kill, to die, avoiding it.

But that was all Buddy Johnson. Buddy was locked behind cold iron, in the dungeon.

She relaxed. Dougal wouldn't hurt her. He loved her. Sex between a man and woman who loved each other was sacred, not evil. Even Father Donovan had said so. Sex was a sacrament of God.

His kisses were warm on her breast, gentle, and her nipples hardened as if they were something independent of her mind and body. His fingers probed and caressed, below, a delicate and knowing touch. Dougal kissed her belly with a final, tender promise before he stepped away from the bed to undress and join her.

She closed her eyes, waiting for him, trusting in him, and fell sound asleep.

# twenty-three

—◊◊◊—

JO FELT INVULNERABLE, and it scared her shitless.

She *knew* there were things out there that would love to munch her up like a cocktail olive. The dragon was one of them. And here she was actively looking for it instead of beating feet in the opposite direction like a sensible woman. So why did this damned forest act like she was a frigging rhino with PMS?

She crawled out from under the holly tree where she had spent the night, squinted at the morning sun, and walked to the stream—scratching and yawning and generally unlovely, picking dead leaves out of her hair. The great outdoors rated about 3.5 on a scale of ten, as far as she was concerned. Unlike Maureen, Jo preferred civilization.

She wanted coffee instead of water from the creek. She wanted a hot shower and some clean clothes. She wanted a pizza with anchovies and mushrooms and sausage and green peppers, washed down by a big frosty pitcher of dark beer.

She wanted toilet paper.

*Nobody has ever written an ode to toilet paper,* she thought.

*One of the greatest inventions of modern man, and it goes totally unnoticed. I'm going to buy a ton of it when I get back.*

Her fire was dead ash and charcoal on scorched stone. She didn't need to light another one: There was nothing to cook. Oh, she could catch some more of those terminally stupid trout. Half-charred fish for breakfast sounded *really* great. It just needed hunger for a sauce.

Make that starvation.

She splashed cold water on her face and scrubbed her hands with sand from the stream after fertilizing some bushes. So much for morning rituals. She thought she should find the trail pretty soon. She hadn't run *that* far downstream after panicking.

That hadn't mattered after climbing out of the sinkhole. She'd only been able to walk for maybe five minutes before her adrenaline ran out.

She tugged Maureen's jacket closer around her shoulders, snuggling against the morning chill. Another problem with the Great Outdoors was the lack of central heating.

Or maybe she always felt cold because she was always hungry. She looked at her wrist and tried spanning it with her other hand. She was definitely losing weight. She'd never had much body fat to start with, and those trout weren't keeping up. Better find that dumb man and take him out for pizza before she faded into an Irish ghost.

Jo laid her hand on a rough-barked old willow and listened with her inner ear. All she got was that static hiss pulsing quietly as if she was listening to the blood rushing in her own ears. The land lived, and somewhere in that life, David wandered.

*Scattered,* he'd whispered. He'd only focused on her fear and anger. Now that she was out of immediate danger, he'd gone cloudy again, lost in the slow drift of the forest.

The agenda for the day was move upstream, find the trail, and follow it back to the dragon. Anything beyond that was beyond her horizon. She didn't even want to *think* about those teeth and meat-hook claws, those razor-edged scales, those cold yellow lizard eyes. But they were tied to David, and she had to go.

The stream burbled quietly, talking to itself like a contented baby playing with his toes. She followed it upstream, dodging tangles of briar and deadfalls and wet nasty-smelling patches of the forest floor that threatened to suck the boots right off her feet. She was amazed at what she had run through on the way downstream. Had run right straight through and never even noticed.

Suddenly, the forest thinned, and the trail cut across the water. Arguments that had been tickling at the back of her head forced their way forward and gained a voice. Just what *exactly* was she doing? Why didn't she just sit down for a minute on that nice convenient moss-covered rock and meditate on her actions before they become fatal?

She was going to find out what was happening to David and stop it. If that dragon was part of it, she was going to chop it up into pâté and spread it on crackers.

With a Swiss army knife?

With a frigging piece of chipped flint, if that's all she had. She was *hungry*.

She could get seriously dead trying. She remembered a *Nature* program Maureen had watched last month on PBS, they had a parental advisory at the start of it. Remembered what the tiger's fangs did to that cute little deer. Ugly. Jo reminded herself that she was female, about five feet two inches and a hundred pounds *before* she went on a diet, and used to shriek at creepy-crawly things and ask Maureen to kill spiders.

But she'd just killed a man, yesterday.

Did she? Who did she think had been following her?

*Oh, shit!*

Jo broke out of her funk and grabbed the gun. She

twisted from side to side, nervously checking the shadows under rocks and the distant trunks of trees, but saw nothing dangerous. She shoved her left hand into the forest dirt and felt the same vague sense of something cold and angry watching, something afraid and staying just beyond sight.

The chill of it had forced her into hiding. The holly tree had been her natural barbed wire, a guard no man or animal could sneak past without making noises in the dark. It had welcomed her, as if it had turned its barbs aside to let her in and then closed the gate behind her. David's work, she'd thought, but when she tried to talk to him through the trunk all she'd found was the same static heartbeat. The forest protected her but wouldn't speak to her.

David.

Was David worth dying for? She wasn't talking metaphor. She was talking about the thing she'd called *T. rex*. With cause.

She was talking about *David*. She was talking about the best all-around lover she'd ever found. She was talking about the only man who'd ever got her thinking about cribs and diapers and maybe tossing the condoms in the trash.

That was just her biological clock ticking. Men were men, interchangeable parts. She'd quit counting how many she'd screwed.

No, she hadn't. The number was fifteen. That was just practice. That was just a large enough statistical sample to tell her how special David was.

Special enough to die for?

Jo sat on her rock, chilled. Dying. Not having David in her life. The two feelings left her equally empty. At least with the dragon, dying wouldn't take all that long.

Special enough to die for.

She stood up, pulled the pistol out of her pocket, and walked quietly down the trail.

The forest watched her. She felt it, the mixed fear and protection all around her, the mixed fear and rage behind her. Whatever, whoever, was following her—it hated her but wasn't about to tangle with her. The fear was stronger. The forest told her that.

Raucous cries filtered through the trees ahead, caws and croaks that even a city girl could identify as crows. Jo slowed down, a cold lump forming in her chest. Crows and ravens were scavengers. A mob of them usually meant dead meat.

The chill spread down to her fingers and toes. That was how they always found the bodies in the Westerns, she remembered. By following the vultures. Grandpa used to tell his tales about the war, about the crows over the battlefield, picking at the dead. He'd talked about rats, too.

David.

The stranger had said David was dying. She was too late.

The cold turned her heart to ice. Jo staggered off the trail and pressed her forehead against the rough bark of a tree. *David. Dead.* She felt the corrugations of the trunk biting into her skin and wanted to pound her skull against them until the blood ran and her head split open and the pain ended in oblivion.

*David. Dead.*

Instead, she dug her fingernails into the bark as if she were a cat, sharpening them. Fiona, the shadow had said. Dougal. The bastard and bitch who ran this freak-show world. Her rage started to burn through her fingers, and resinous smoke rose where she touched the bark.

"Dougal and Fiona," she growled. Somebody should tell the ravens, dinner was about to be served in some other locations. Jo snarled. A part of her froze at the sound, so like a hungry lion stalking the African plains.

< . . . not . . . dead . . . >

The whispers returned to mock her. David's voice rose

from the tree, from the sticky pine sap gumming her fingers where she had gouged straight through to living wood.

She stared at her nails, at the grooves cut into the bark. Some bear must have done that. She couldn't have done *that*; she hadn't even split a nail. She'd just put her fingers where a bear had already torn the bark.

< . . . anger . . . >

She gritted her teeth and snarled again, this time with words.

"You want anger, I'll show you anger! I'll turn this goddamn tree into a torch! I'll burn your forest flat, your fucking vampire forest living off of David's *body*! I'll roast your god-almighty-damned land alive for taking my man from me!"

She cranked the Bic up to maximum flame and held it against the resin and bark. Her rage glared into the dampness, forcing steam to curl out and then smoke and then flame as the green wood spat into fire against its will. She drove the heat of fire deep into the heartwood of the pine. *Burn, baby, burn!*

<*No!*>

David's voice screamed pain as if it was his own flesh in the fire. Jo shuddered, and she beat the flames into silence. Boiling pitch clung to her palms and hardened. She peeled it off, leaving clean undamaged skin behind. Illusions.

*The land is David, and David is the land,* whispered the remembered voice. She'd taken that as metaphor.

She'd joined Maureen in the world of delusion, of voices in her head, of strangers following her around. Had she ever shot that man, been in the sinkhole, run screaming from the avenue of skulls? Was the dragon real?

< . . . real . . . >

David.

The crows still called their brothers to the feast. Jo stared at the charred circle of bark on the pine, the claw marks matching her fingers, the thin white scars crossing her palms where the dragon scales had cut her.

Those cuts had healed too fast. This was a land of magic.

If David was dead, she had to see his body. She had to bury him. Then she would go and meet the owner of this forest. Debts would be paid.

With interest.

The cold anger carried her down the path, into the thin smell of death that grew into a garbage reek so thick she almost had to lean against the air to walk. Nearer and nearer came the raucous cackle of the crows, until they pounded her ears and the hiss of their wings filled the spaces in between their calls.

There were too many birds. You couldn't feed that many crows from the fields of Armageddon. And then she saw the long, low lump ahead, crawling with a buzzing horde of flies and suddenly realized the flies were the crows, and what she saw was huge.

It was the *dragon*. The frigging *dragon* was dead, not David.

She gagged at the thick stench of rotten meat and the maggot-crawl of crows and ravens. They tore threads of meat from the carcass, fought, swirled overhead, waddled around like overweight ducks with the gorge of carrion in their bellies.

She wrestled her stomach back into line. Damn good thing she'd skipped breakfast. To hell with what *killed* the dragon. The question she wanted answered was, Where was David?

She saw scraps of cloth on the ground, fragments of curved fiberglass, a scattering of arrows. She forced her way through the heavy air and found a discarded backpack. She found a tangle of hooked-thorn greenbrier wrapped into the wicker effigy of a man David's height and weight.

The icy lump in her chest spread to her lungs and blocked her breathing. She forgot the racket of the crows. She forgot the stench. She knelt by the green man and stared at it.

David.

The forest told her that was David.

She touched it. The thorns writhed away from her hand as if they refused to bite her. She touched the leg of the form and could see blue denim between the vines. David was inside.

The denim was warm, even though the trees shaded her. If she watched carefully, a slight swell and fall moved the briars around the thing's chest. David was still alive.

She fumbled the knife out of her pocket. She split a nail opening it. She slipped the blade under a single stem and cut carefully, delicately, away from David's leg.

The scream jerked her hand away—the deep piercing scream of torture as if she'd lit bamboo slivers under his fingernails. The cut end of the briar writhed like a snake, away from her, away from the knife. It dripped the thick crimson of human blood.

<I'll die if you cut me loose. I'll be trapped outside my body.>

The clarity of David's voice jerked her out of her robot movements. He was here. He was focused.

Fire had hurt *him*. The knife had hurt *him*. Jo sat back on her heels and stared at the vines. She could kill them with her eyes, she knew. If she could burn wet brush with her glare, set fire to a living tree in springtime, then she could scorch those vines into ash and charcoal.

And David would die.

She touched the vines again. "How can I set you free?"

< . . . master . . . >

Now he'd gone fuzzy again, just the single word coming

through the static. Just before, he'd even said "I," not that goddamn "We."

"I'll fry your *Master's* liver for lunch," she muttered. She reached for another vine of the briar, and it twisted away from her in fear. The knife flashed in her hand.

<*NO!*> The mental scream was deafening.

David's pain wrenched her guts. Another vine leaked drips of blood onto the dry leaves. "Can't *do* that," she hissed. "Fucking blood loss will kill him even if the pain doesn't."

< . . . leave . . . >

He was fading. Even with her hand on the stems wrapping his arm, he was fading into the static. Heedless of the thorns, she dug down underneath the briars and touched the skin of his wrist. His pulse beat weak and slow, and she felt only the faintest echo of life and thought.

It was as if his soul was spreading out, like those drops of blood were mixing with the water of a pool, starting out pure red and gradually thinning away to purple smoke, then the merest dark haze before disappearing completely in the blue reflection of the sky. Another day, maybe another hour, and he would be gone beyond recall.

She dropped the knife. She squatted on the forest floor, staring at the vines forming the effigy of the man she loved, and thought.

David was dying. She was his only chance.

Every thought led back to the same point: The forest's hold was too strong and too intimate for outside force to work. She could only see one place where it might be vulnerable, one place she could fight it. She could force him to focus and hold him together, waiting for a miracle.

Slowly, gently, as if she was reaching for one of those overtrusting trout, she captured one of the rooted vines. The thorns twisted away from her flesh, and she jerked suddenly to force them to cut her palm. Her own blood touched the green stem.

"I will follow you," she whispered. " 'Whither thou goest, I will go; and where thou lodgest, I will lodge.' " She felt her face set into a grim mask of stone.

"I will track you to the ends of this land and gather every bit of you and bring you back. I will search every hill and hollow, every root and branch, I will search the rock and soil and water and the very sky if it be necessary. I swear it by the sun and moon and all the stars above." She paused for breath and emphasis.

"I will bring you back or die with you."

<Jo, *don't*!>

Slowly, gently, precisely, as if she was arranging flowers for a Zen master, Jo draped the vine three times around her wrist and forced it to scratch the skin. She held the stem against her blood. She felt it root. She sent her mind into the thin filament joining her to the land and asked the darkness she found there to bring her David.

The wordless hiss touched her hand and embraced her. She wrapped herself around its fog and squeezed it into the semblance of a man and held it. She looked around for her body and the daylight of the forest.

Darkness surrounded them.

<David?>


SEAN LEANED AGAINST a tree and coughed again, gently, the noise buried under the ravens' calls. He'd heal so much faster if he didn't try to move.

But then he'd lose her.

That bitch was his weapon against Fiona and Brian. That bitch owed him blood. He tried to weigh the balance. Revenge would be satisfied, either way. He fingered the heavy knife Fiona had taken from Brian.

The woman knelt there by her lover. She didn't move.

He stared at her back, willing her to move, willing her to speak, willing her to smell or hear or feel him through the land, willing her to notice him and pull out that ugly piece of human metal that never should have worked.

If she sat there much longer, she'd make his decision for him. He knew how to find his dearest siblings without her help.

His gut ached. His gut refused even the thought of food. The simple act of drinking water felt like it tore his chest and belly into shreds. Maybe it would be easier just to die, like a gut-shot deer in the woods.

*As the humans would say, "Up yours!"* he thought. Next week, he'd be better. The week after that, he'd be back to normal. He'd been through this before. He *would* survive.

Survive. He smiled. The full moon would rise tomorrow night. So much for Maureen's prophecy. Live one more night, and he would break the doom she'd laid upon him.

The sister still knelt there, her back toward him. Sean drew the knife and stole forward, as silent as a cat. Who needed magic when his enemies were fools?

Something snagged his ankle, and he fell. Instinct and training tucked his fall into a roll, but his gut stabbed him and broke the silent flow. He staggered to his feet in a rustle of leaves and cracking twigs.

She still knelt there like a statue.

Sean shifted his weight to move again. A vise tightened around his leg, and he jerked his concentration away from her defenseless back.

It was a vine. A green vine wrapped around his ankle and up his leg, its tendrils questing upward. He snarled and hacked the vicious thing loose from the ground, ripping its thorns out of his pants and flesh. Red blossoms of blood tracked the cloth where it had twined.

Even cut loose, the thing twisted like a mad snake in

his hands. He shuddered and threw it across the clearing.

The dead leaves rustled as if disturbed by a thousand insects. Smooth green curls and loops twisted out of the forest floor, searching. Sean knew they searched for him.

He backed away. Gritting his teeth with concentration, shuffling his feet to avoid hidden traps and snares, he edged farther and farther away from the silent figure kneeling amid the briars.

The forest quieted.

*So*. Sean chuckled silently. He'd wanted a balance. He hadn't been able to decide between his hates. Now it looked like Brian and Fiona had just moved up to the top of the list.

And it looked like Dougal didn't own this part of the forest anymore. Sean wondered when the bastard would find out. And how.

# twenty-four

—◊◊◊—

ALL MAUREEN COULD do was run. Buddy Johnson was stronger than she was. He was faster. Above all, he was meaner, and she fled through the backyards of her childhood. Sweat drenched her. Hedges tore at her skin and lashed her eyes. Again he caught her and dragged her into the overgrown yew bushes behind the Fords' old carriage house. Again he stripped off her shirt and shorts and pinned her naked body against the peeling clapboards and rough fieldstone of the empty building.

And then it changed, as she stepped aside in a surreal jujitsu move. Time and again, she cycled through the pain and terror of the chase until he caught her and groped her and forced her down on the prickly dead needles under the yews. Each time, she turned into mist and slipped away.

Heat boiled in her belly. Her power flowed across the years and she seized him like a doll, pulling one leg from the other until he split from crotch to forehead like a wishbone. "Make a wish," she whispered savagely, in her dream. "Make a wish."

She threw the bloody pieces away and twisted her world onto a new path.

MAUREEN WOKE SLOWLY to warmth and softness. Images floated through her head, the fragments and remains of dreams—hot, wet, erotic dreams of Brian's touch, Brian's kisses, Brian enfolding her and covering her naked body with his. She smelled the sharpness of his male sweat, felt its touch on her skin, felt the drying sticky residue of him on her bare thighs.

Her thoughts drifted in the place where such things were possible, away from the panic his actual touch would bring. In her dreams, she controlled things. She made the moves. She made the rules. *She* acted on *him*. That killed the memories.

She stretched lazily, like a cat, basking in the feel of silk sheets on her bare skin. A bed like this was a work of art.

Then her stomach growled and disturbed the peace.

She opened her eyes. Dark beams arched overhead, alive with the deep golden brown of ancient varnish. Sunlight in tall windows shot beams of warmth across the room to fall on match-board mahogany paneling, splashing light on the steely gleam of hanging swords and lances, bringing out flashes of glittering blue and green in the tapestries, firing red sandstone into glowing coals.

Dougal's bedroom.

Tapered columns of golden oak stood at the four corners of the bed. The canopy and hangings they had once supported were gone; magic or technology took away the need to wrap the sleepers within a tent, as if they were camping inside the cold, damp castle. Her bathrobe hung, waiting, on the nearest post, and she smelled the fresh birch smoke of a new-laid fire in the bathroom. She even sniffed a hint of coffee. *Good* coffee.

Coffee that she didn't have to make, didn't have to wait for. Servants were a *wonderful* idea.

Dougal grunted beside her, rolled over, and settled back to the slow, steady breathing of sound sleep. She turned to him. He lay faceup, naked and half-covered by the sheets. Her eyes narrowed, comparing him to her dreams of Brian. She shook her head, gently so she wouldn't wake him. He *still* looked like a shaved chimpanzee stitched back together after a bad car wreck.

So it was done. She remembered dreams, but her brain had shoved the rest off into a corner and walled it up with stone. Somewhere deep inside her belly, sperm and ova played their game of blindman's bluff with the calendar. She studied his face, relaxed in sleep. What kind of children would he father? Not that it would make any difference. . . .

She quietly lifted herself up on one elbow and looked down at him. A sardonic smile touched her lips as she remembered his arrogant trust in his powers.

Then she drove her fist into his throat.

Every ounce of her weight and will rode behind the blow. He gasped, and his arms clutched at her. She rolled away, but one hand snatched her left arm and squeezed her biceps in a vise. Fire shot straight up her shoulder to her neck. The other hand groped for her, and she slashed her own right hand across his face, sinking her fingernails deep into his eye sockets. A rasping scream forced its way out of his throat, and he let go.

She tumbled to the floor, smashing first her elbow and then her head on the wood. Dazed, she rolled through a black tunnel shot with the fire of her hurts. Something smacked her bare back, and she shook black spiderwebs from her eyes.

She stared at the bed, half-stunned. Dougal coughed and spat red on the sheets. More blood seeped between her fingers where they covered his eyes. He tried to shout for help, but the noises came out more like a pig squealing than like words.

Maureen staggered to her feet. Weapons. Weapons lay all over the fucking place. She needed something with range. She didn't dare let him get his hands on her again. Her head still spun, and her left eye refused to track with the right.

She groped around the brown lump supporting her, knocking a lamp and other trash to the floor. Her knuckles brushed something heavy and cold. She hefted it for throwing before she found a hilt nestled in her hand.

Blinking, shaking her head, she forced her eyes to work. The damn thing looked like Brian's knife, the heavy bent one he had used to kill Liam. They must be more common than she thought. She jerked it from its sheath, gripped it with both hands, and made her legs cooperate well enough to stagger back to the bed.

"Got to stay clear of the arms," she muttered to herself. "Hit-and-run."

His head tracked the sound. She swung at his leg and spun away with the weight of the heavy knife. Blood splashed like a fountain. Instead of either attacking or defending, Dougal dropped his hands and stared at her with ruined eye sockets.

"How?" His crushed larynx turned the word into a croak.

"Schizophrenia," she grunted. The heavy blade chopped into his groping arm.

"Depersonalization."

He jerked again. Fingers flew loose in a red spray.

"Dissociation." The words spat out of her mouth with each gasping breath of effort.

"Delusions of persecution and conspiracy." The blade stuck in his chest. She threw her weight against it, snarling the last word, to pull it free.

"Blunting and incongruity of affect." The steel glanced

off his skull, laying bone open to the sunlight.

"Hallucinations." One of his hands flopped to the floor.

"Withdrawal from reality." The knife carved through his belly and swung her like a spinning discus thrower with its momentum.

She stopped, gasping for breath. "Also . . . occasional . . . violent . . . behavior . . . against . . . authority . . . figures. You really should study more psychology."

Hands on her knees, she panted and cleared her head. Her inner voice told her she should have waited and regained her strength. She was almost too weak to kill him.

*Almost,* she snarled back. She straightened up and studied the carnage.

Splatters of gore painted a Jackson Pollock canvas across the bed and floor. She traced a line of teardrop spots up the wall, arcing across where they had been flung by the swinging blade.

*Death as Art,* her critic offered. *Performance Art.*

The canvas included her body. Her arms dripped red to the elbows. Splashes and smears of blood covered her breasts, her belly, and her thighs. She ignored the scratching noises of a severed hand twitching on the floor, and swabbed blood out of her eyes with her bathrobe from the night before.

Dougal was still alive. Arms and legs spouted red, great gashes tore his chest and ripped through his belly, but he still lived. She was a lousy killer.

She straddled his slippery body like a lover and hacked at his neck until his head sprang loose in a gush of blood. She snarled in triumph, grabbed his hair, and held the head up like a trophy, miming Perseus with Medusa's crawling snakes.

Then she flung the blade away and stood up to carefully set the head on one corner post of the bed. It hissed and rattled its teeth at her as if it still tried to talk with no breath to form the words. Staring into the gouged eye sockets, she smiled.

"Welcome to *my* reality, Dougal MacKenzie."

Her wrists burned from the iron bands, and her ankles, and her throat. Where had the bastard hidden the keys?

She wiped her hands and feet: She didn't want red smears to disturb the impromptu beauty of the bedroom, didn't want to leave anything to show her wandering through the scene. Just Dougal's corpse, and the bed, and the splattered blood, with his severed head presiding over all. Art.

His clothing lay, cleaned and neatly folded, on a chair. Servants, again, coming and going without waking her. Once the bastard had finally let her sleep, they could have marched a frigging brass band through the room, and she wouldn't have twitched an eyelid. She didn't even know if she'd slept one night, or two, or a goddamn week.

The keys were in his pants. She clicked the locks free, using a mirror over one dresser for the one around her neck. Each ring of steel left red circles behind, like narrow bands of sunburn.

Even the mirror wore dots of blood from the slaughterhouse. She stared at her face, at her naked body, at the drips and smears of blood painting her, and suddenly the slimy feel and smell disgusted her. She staggered to the bathroom, weak and vaguely sick.

*Bath,* she thought. *Rinse his blood, his touch, his semen from my body.* She knelt by the tub and spun knobs, splashing the first hot gush of water over her arms and letting the crimson tendrils swirl down the drain before setting the plug.

" 'Yet who would have thought the old man to have had so much blood in him?' " she murmured, flashing back to Shakespeare. She flopped back on her heels and waited for the water to rise.

Coffee twitched her nose again. An insulated pot waited, on a marble counter by the fireplace. Her clothes lay on a chair nearby, cleaned and folded. They'd even cleaned her boots. She drew a cup of caffeine, hot and black, and swallowed the heat of it to settle her belly, and stared at the fire.

*Fire.* Her memories of Brian and Liam, of the winter alley, played like a videotape in her brain. With all she'd done, was Dougal really, truly dead? He hadn't burned, and those teeth kept clacking curses at her. . . .

She rummaged through cabinets and drawers, dumping towels, bottles, tins, and boxes on the floor. Oil, scented, for massage, and rubbing alcohol. A shelf of booze: brandy, whiskey, rum, vodka, unopened bottles without tax seals on the corks. She carried armloads of bottles back into the blood-drenched room—once, twice, a third time—and smashed them on the bed, the wooden paneling, and the floor.

Swinging the knife with grunting frenzy, she hacked chairs into splinters and piled them over the body. The severed hand tried to clutch her when she threw it on the pyre. She buried it with drawers jerked out of a tall oak dresser.

The water had nearly filled the tub when she dropped the knife and sheath on the bathroom floor. She shut the taps and searched in vain for matches. Finally, she growled in frustration and grabbed a flaming log from the fireplace. The coals didn't even warm her hand.

The alcohol caught fire with a greedy surge of flame, leaping blue tongues spreading across the soaked cloth and dripping to the wooden floor. Yellow flame joined the blue as the oil caught, and the silk, and the wood. She stared at the hungry blaze for a minute, as the pieces of Dougal twitched in the pyre. Smoke billowed up, and the smell of burning hair filled the room.

She turned and studied the bathroom door. Nearly three inches of ironbound cross-ply oak and a frame set in solid stone, it looked like it was designed to hold against battle-axes. She closed it behind her and set the latch. Fire could gnaw on that for hours before breaking through.

Blood. Her reflection in the mirrors disgusted her, the sticky runnels and smears of drying crimson. Soaking in that would make her puke. She flicked levers in the shower and felt the water grow hot immediately, and sluiced Dougal from her body, out of her hair.

Muffled thuds shook the wall, as if something had exploded in the bedroom beyond the stone. She thought of windows blowing out and letting in fresh air, just like *Backdraft*.

Let fire purify his bed of the stains of rape.

She shut off the shower, dumped bath oil in the tub, and slipped into the lavender-scented water. She looked up, through the skylights, and saw tendrils of black smoke drifting across the morning sun.

She scrubbed, and scrubbed, and scrubbed, Lady Macbeth and her spots of blood. And then she realized it wasn't his blood she sought to wash away.

She stared at her belly, underneath the foam. Nothing she did to her skin would cleanse that.

Was she pregnant?

The crackling fire beyond the door answered her. It said, "The moon is right." It said, "You can ask your body, ask the flow of blood to your womb and the balance of your glands." It said, "You have the power to cleanse yourself of his seed, just as you have purified this room."

Something scratched at the door, as if that severed hand was fighting to escape from the flames. A crash shook the floor, and the scratching stopped.

She climbed out of the tub, steaming, only half-clean. The outer half. The part the world could see. Dripping on the tile, she finished her coffee and stared at the mirror. Maureen stared back, pink and naked and defenseless.

Smoke seeped around the door to the bedroom, puffing

and sucking back as the fire searched for fuel and oxygen. *There* was a solution. Open the door and let the fire burn her clean of him.

Father Donovan's voice joined the chorus in her head, the babbling of schizophrenia. "Suicide is a mortal sin," it said. "So is abortion. The baby didn't rape you. The instant egg and sperm are joined, the soul is formed. You have a human child inside you. Thou shalt not kill."

Her coffee cup smashed the mirror.

"This! Baby! Isn't! Human!" The growl of the fire swallowed her scream, turning it into a whisper.

She dried herself, and dressed herself, and shoved the sheathed knife into the waistband of her jeans. The cold leather rode against her belly, against the unanswered question of her womb. Meanwhile, Padric still waited for her, somewhere out in the tangled stone of the keep and outbuildings. She refused to look at the unbroken mirrors. The woman they showed was a victim, not an avenger.

The other door was still cool to her touch. She braced her foot against it and slipped the latch, nervously. Dougal might yet laugh at her from the flames, if the fire had spread to block her other exit.

The landing yawned at her. Worn stone stairs spiraled down around a central column, no handrails, irregular treads guaranteed to trip any stranger trying to fight his way up. No connection into the bedroom. The stair should lead to the kitchen, to where the coffeepot lived.

And to the dungeons, as well, the faint cold distant dampness told her.

She paused at the next landing, hand on the lever latch, unease tugging at her mind. She couldn't remember the way they'd come. How many landings had they climbed, how many sets of stairs, how many twists and turns?

Smoke seeped through a crack and tickled her nose. She

looked up. The door lay directly under the landing to her bath, back into the tower.

*No thanks.*

Down two more flights of stairs, a heavy door led off the opposite side. She tested it, gently, blocking with her foot, and found cool, clear air. A breeze blew into her face, and she thought she heard a growl overhead, the sound of a predator seeing fresh meat: more oxygen to the fire. Chimney effect. People who expected sieges shouldn't live in perfect chimneys. She closed the door behind her.

A short passage brought her to the kitchen—to empty chaos of food half-ready and pots boiling over on the wood-fired ranges and crocks of milk and flour dropped on the floor by fleeing cooks. She carved off a chunk of fresh bread and layered it with butter, chewing on that while gathering dried sausage from a hanging garland and tossing apples into a cloth bag for a picnic lunch. Cheese, and bottled water, and more bread followed. God, she was hungry.

Wine. Bottles of wine waited, racked, probably for cooking, but she wasn't picky. Maureen grabbed one, the memory of her thirst wakening and calling out for alcohol. She dragged the cork free with her teeth and swallowed red nectar.

And suddenly she realized the urge was weak. Wine was nice, yes, but not necessary. Maybe Dougal had forced her through withdrawal and out the other side. She set the bottle down and lifted both her middle fingers to salute him.

She stared at her wrists, at the red circles that had grown into welts like warming frostbite. The iron bands had drained her power, bound her soul. Dougal wouldn't have taken them off until he was sure she'd use her power for *him.*

Now they were gone. She felt different, free, as if she

was emerging from a dark, damp tunnel into daylight. She wasn't afraid. She didn't *need* the drink.

She remembered a time like that once. A time when she thought and acted like a normal person. A time when the world smiled at her. A change had started when she unlocked the iron bands. The magic of the Summer Country seemed to blend with her mind and was working to heal her madness.

*This is where you belong,* she thought. *Madness is like a weed, a plant out of place. When you march to a different drummer, the world calls you crazy. Your blood tried to change the world into the Summer Country and retreated into madness when it failed.*

Doors led into pantries, into twisting stone passages, into damp stone stairways that probably led to wine and root cellars. Maureen fumbled her way out through a labyrinth of afterthoughts and additions until she finally found sun and sky and an open yard. She looked up.

The round stone tower of the central keep loomed overhead, four or five stories of defiant fortress. It belched flame and smoke like a blast furnace. Chimney, indeed. The idiot had built a chimney and filled it with fuel and lived in it. *That* was why so many real castles had cold stone floors and arrow slits for windows. It made them damned hard to burn.

Something rumbled deep inside the tower, like bolts rolling around on a kettledrum. Sparks fountained into the sky, and then the smoke thinned to gray instead of black. More air, she guessed, less fuel. For all the smoke and burning, she still smelled the lavender of the bath, the onions and garlic and roasting meat of the kitchen. The tower carried the smoke straight into the sky.

Men and women bustled around the yard, hauling buckets of water and spraying thatched roofs with garden hoses against the slow rain of embers. She wondered why the hell they fought to save their prison, then realized it was probably the only home they had.

Someone spotted her and grabbed another's arm, and a spreading pool of faces turned toward her. They backed away, dozens of them, fear written in their wide eyes. "That's the one," she heard them whisper. "That's the red-headed witch who killed the Master. What kinds of pain will *she* bring to us? What are the games *she* plays?"

She shook her head and turned toward the castle gate and the forest beyond. She didn't want to think about the slaves. She didn't want to think about her belly, either. She'd only done what she had to do.

A man stepped out of a stone outbuilding and jerked to a stop, breaking her funk. She blinked twice before the picture registered, the mixture of terror and resignation on his face. It was Padric.

He carried a peregrine on his wrist, a beautiful huge bird of slate gray and a white breast mottled with black. He carried a pair of heavy scissors. He stared at her bare wrists and neck, and sweat beaded on his forehead. He crossed himself with his free hand.

Maureen pulled the knife from her waistband. The cold hiss of steel sliding out of its sheath overwhelmed the roar of the fire and the crowd fighting it. She felt the greasy warmth of blood on her hands, felt the frenzy of hacking Dougal into chunks of crawling meat, and almost vomited. Could she kill again, without the madness driving her?

He studied her face and blinked at what he saw there. "Please let me free all the birds, Lady, before you kill me." He snipped scraps of leather from the falcon's ankles and flung her into the air.

The peregrine circled, puzzled for an instant, and then climbed steadily into the sky. It was beautiful. It was free. Maureen followed it with her heart, until it dwindled into a speck and vanished in the smoke against the morning sun. Her eyes blurred.

Tears. She remembered tears in Padric's eyes last night or the night before, when she'd surrendered to Dougal. She remembered the blood on his face, and the scars from whipping. He was a slave.

She'd had to kill Dougal, to save her own life and soul. He'd left her no other choice. No one was forcing her now. She didn't have to kill again.

"Let the birds go, Padric. Then leave. You're free. We're all free."

She turned her back on him and sheathed the knife, knowing she was safe, and looked down from the hill into the tops of trees. It was good to smell trees again, and grass, and the slow fire of rotting leaves. The forest echoed the swells and hollows of the land beneath, spreading out on either side, and encircled a distant checkerboard of fields and gardens. Fiona's place, she guessed. Where Brian was.

*Brian!*

The name sent a jolt of fire through her and left icy darkness behind it. Brian, and Jo, and David. She'd forgotten them. They were out there, somewhere, all of them in danger. Whatever else she might think about Dougal, she didn't think he'd lied about that.

She turned back for Padric. The man was a tracker, a gamekeeper. He knew this forest. He could work off some of his karma finding them.

He was gone.

The door of the building stood open, empty. She stepped inside, through some kind of a clerk's room of books and tables and piles of records, and found nothing but an outsized chicken coop lined with wooden perches and a workbench covered with scraps of leather.

The only man who could help her was fleeing for his life.

From her.

# twenty-five

—⚬⚬⚬—

THE FOREST SET Maureen's teeth on edge, like some-one scratching fingernails across a chalkboard. She felt weirdness twisting over her skin as she walked along.

A battle raged under the deceptive calm, as if the wild grapes tried to strangle the squirrels and the pines staged root warfare against the foxes in their dens. The forest touched her and yet did not, reached out to her and pushed her away at the same time.

It was like setting her against Padric. That was how Dougal had ruled his land. He'd twisted the balances until the forest was at war with itself. It even smelled wrong.

Her nose wrinkled. The stench of death touched her again, thick and sickening. She angled farther upwind, giv-ing some colossal heap of carrion a wide berth.

Whatever the crows fought over here, she didn't need *that* adding to the queasy feeling in her stomach. Maybe it was the result of eating too much after starvation. Either that or it was psychosomatic morning sickness: Her belly thought vomiting could purge it of poisons that came in the other way. Too early for the real thing.

Her hand kept returning to the cold hilt of the knife, then slipping off to caress the skin of her belly. Was she pregnant? *Half of that baby is me,* she thought. *Half of it is Dougal. Yang and yin, black and white, Ahriman and Ormazd battle in my womb. The forces of darkness wrestle with the forces of light. Do I damage my soul more by joining the fight or by staying neutral?*

*I don't even know if there* is *a baby,* she answered.

*That's because you're afraid to look,* the whispers muttered. *You're hoping the moon and your body's tides are wrong, you're hoping for implant rejection or a defective egg or the side effects of starvation, you're hoping for any one of the thousands of reasons why women don't get knocked up every time they fuck.*

*You're hoping for a spontaneous abortion so you don't have to create one yourself.*

She gritted her teeth and reminded herself to let the dead past bury its dead. Or cremate them. She didn't have to decide anything for weeks or even months. Like, maybe, eight of them, and then there were adoption agencies for after that. Right now, she had more urgent worries: Brian, and Jo, and David.

She touched a tree, a smooth-barked beech with a kind face wrinkled into its gray elephant's hide, and asked the way to Fiona's land. <Straight to the morning sun,> the tree said, clearly. <Go through the woods and across the pasture. You'll see the roof and chimneys over her hedges, and the top branches of the house-rowan spreading against the sky.>

Fiona.

Dougal had said the dark-haired woman was his enemy. He'd blamed Fiona and Sean for the dangers to Brian and David and Jo. Sean, yes. Maureen could believe Sean poisoned Socrates, crucified Christ, and shot Lincoln and both the Kennedys one morning before stepping out for lunch.

But the one time Maureen had talked to her, Brian's sister hadn't seemed all that bad.

Kinky, yes. Who the hell wanted a baby by her brother?

Ruthless, yes. Fiona had used a street gang to try to kidnap Brian.

Brian had explained that as a lack of any moral sense, of conscience, as if the Old Ones lacked souls. Brian was an Old One. It sounded like a philosopher's paradox.

*You are an Old One,* Maureen's mental voice reminded her. *You have the powers to prove it.*

She shuddered. Walking down the hillside from the smoking chimney that had been Dougal's keep, she had touched each mounted skull as she passed it. The bleached bones had powdered into dust, giving up a sigh as if each touch released a bound soul.

Souls, souls, souls. Did she even *have* a soul, she wondered? What percentage of human blood made a soul? *There* was a question for Father Donovan and his black-robed Jesuits.

Enough. She needed to keep track of priorities. Find Brian, free him: He knew this land. Find David and Jo with his help. Get the fuck to someplace safe before her legs gave out and dumped her on her ass. Anything else was secondary.

She touched another tree, a rough-barked ancient European maple her professors would have graded as a prime veneer log and valued by the inch. Did trees have souls?

*Brian,* she asked it. *Have you seen Brian?* She closed her eyes and called up an image of his stocky body, his shaggy blond hair, his blue eyes as deep as a mountain sky. Her heart felt strange when she thought of those eyes, and the warmth of his hand seemed to touch her arm.

Her pulse beat through her fingers into the bark, and pictures returned: Brian in the forest, Brian and David and Dougal and Sean, and then Fiona. Fiona danced around

Brian, rubbing against him, singing words Maureen didn't understand in a voice that tore her soul.

*Seduction spell,* her growing sense of witchcraft said. *You can't understand the language because it's weaving magic as strong as the land itself.* Fiona had spun a web of words to bind Brian to her.

*If you want him, you'll have to fight for him.*

Maureen's eyes snapped open. A faint aroma teased her, just above the dry bitterness of the bark and lichen under her nose. Her memory flashed back to Jo's apartment, and she stood weeping over the rumpled sheets of a bed. Lust and sweat blended with the paired scents of Jo's Passion-flower perfume and David's aftershave, the morning after she'd met Brian.

They were here.

She spun around. Nothing. The scent faded as her hand left the maple. She turned back to it, touched it, and grabbed the barest hint of the scent returning. She smelled them through the tree, through the breath of the forest.

What she smelled was magic: the magic of her blood, the magic of this land. It called to her—seductive, dark, and private.

<Trees have souls. You have a soul. Everything alive has a soul, and some things that have never lived.>

Maureen's hand jerked from the bark, as if the tree had tried to bite her.

<Not that slow sleeping chunk of firewood, woman with fur like mine. It thinks in pictures only. If you want words, I'd recommend an oak.>

Maureen traced out the speaker, a muzzle and sharp, bright eyes and radar ears separating out from the shadows of the undergrowth. It was a picture puzzle, an illusion of camouflage in which bush became fox and fox became bush, each time she shifted her eyes. Once she saw the animal, she wondered how she'd ever missed it.

<You only see me because I wish it. The forest wonders about you. What better animal to satisfy that curiosity than a fox?>

A thrill of joy ran down her spine and out to each finger and toe. She'd always thought the fox was the spirit of the forest, the expression of its soul. She'd only seen glimpses of them in Carlysle Woods or out in the Experimental Forest. They were as shy as ghosts.

Cross fox, her mental catalog named it: *Vulpes fulva,* a color variant on the more common red fox, known by the dark cross-marking on the back. Reddish body, light underside, white tail tip, and dark legs.

<You have the naming sickness. Wild magic doesn't work that way. Putting a name on me doesn't give you power.>

Without moving, it vanished into the shadows.

Maureen jerked as if waking from a dream. She started to search the brush for a den entrance, then shook her head at the image of following Alice down into Wonderland. A fox's den probably wouldn't lead to the same sort of place as the Rabbit Hole.

"Come back," she whispered, half to herself.

<How can I? I never left.>

And the fox mask poked out of the forest gloom, in the same briar-tangled shadow underneath a kind of dogwood Maureen didn't recognize. She traced out the body, with lumps down chest and belly. It was a vixen, with recent kits hidden somewhere near.

Maureen willed the fox to stay, to continue this blessed instant. Talking with a fox was almost worth the cost of Dougal.

"I don't name things to gain power over them. A name helps me to think about you, remember you, gain understanding of how you live and what you need and how you affect the forest in which you live."

<You killed the Master.>

How could she condense kidnap, torture, and rape into something a fox would understand? "He kept me in a cage."

<Ah.>

The fox settled into a sphinx pose, almost like a cat. Maureen wasn't fooled: Twitch a hand and the vixen would vanish without a sound.

"What does the Master's death mean to you?"

<It depends on what replaces him. He was a hunter. I understand hunting. Life and death are two sides of the paw. The Master did more. He controlled. Are you one of those?>

Maureen closed her eyes and shuddered. "The falcons are free. All the cages are broken. The skulls are empty dust."

<Ah. And you—are you predator, or prey?>

A fox *would* think that way.

Maureen opened her eyes again, forcing them against her need for sleep. She was so tired. . . .

"Humans eat anything. You know that. Omnivores."

The vixen held a dead chipmunk between her paws. That was the forest: One of the cutest critters on God's green earth was also just another snack.

Maureen could live with that. Simple hunger was so clean compared to the fear she'd carried all her life.

<I spoke of mind, not food. Are you predator, or prey?>

"I was prey. I'm done with that. But I *refuse* to turn into Dougal MacKenzie."

<In this forest, there is no third choice.>

Maureen's gaze devoured the fox, marveling at the flick of one pointed ear identifying a distant sound, the twitch of whiskers, the clean daintiness of the paws. Sight had to substitute for feeling the warmth of her red-brown fur, smelling her sharp animal musk. Maureen's fingers itched to caress that fur and soak up the pulse under it.

The fox radiated *alive*.

"I'm a watcher. I'll *make* a third choice. Steward. Keeper of the balance."

She paused, then went on as if she was justifying herself to a human listener. "I love chipmunks alive, and I love chipmunks turned into fox. I love this tree standing in the forest, talking with the wind. I love it formed into planks to make a table, glossy with hand-rubbed oil and the careful strokes of a cabinetmaker's tools. I love it burning in a fireplace, or in a hot black woodstove with the cold January wind howling music down the chimney. And I would love to climb it, if I was feeling strong enough."

<You claim to be a poet?>

"You claim to be a fox?"

The vixen tossed the chipmunk into the air with a flip of her head, caught the body, bit. Bone crunched. No chipmunk.

<If I am not a fox, what ate that noisy little windbag?>

"You've got an awfully big vocabulary for a fox."

A red tongue wiped the spatters clean. Then wicked eyes sparkled up at Maureen, mirroring the foxy smile.

<Who better? Although many things in this land are not quite what they seem.>

Maureen stared at emptiness where the fox had been. This time, she did step forward and kneel to touch the ground. She felt warmth, and her fingers found blood and chipmunk fur, but there was no sign of a den or burrow.

"I wish you hadn't left."

Damp cold touched her ankle. Maureen swallowed a scream and looked down. Yellow eyes glinted back at her. She felt almost as if the animal was teasing her. Or—courting her?

Slowly, carefully, she reached back along her leg and touched the cold nose. Her fingers traced the wiry whiskers and caressed the ridges over the vixen's eyes, then moved on to scratch between the ears. Soft fur, smooth fur, silken fur cool at the surface and warm beneath, delighted her fingertips. The vixen closed her eyes, like a cat, and gently leaned into Maureen's touch.

She felt a pulse, racing at twice the speed of her own. And then the fox vanished.

*I'm hallucinating again. Got to get more sleep.*

Maureen sniffed her fingers. Nothing—no smell of fur, no pungent fox-reek almost as strong as skunk.

<And the forest? Is this a waking dream as well?>

The fox looked down on her from a huge moss-covered boulder. The vixen licked one paw and cocked her head as if listening for a mouse.

Maureen listened.

She heard the wind brushing the tips of leaves, she heard the stealthy scuffle of beetles under bark, she heard the chitter of a distant squirrel. She heard her own pulse.

She didn't hear cars, or the thumping National Guard helicopters that made the Naskeag Falls airport their base. She didn't hear the constant background hum of civilization that might as well be distributed on utility poles along with electricity and phone.

No matter what time of day or night she went into Carlysle Woods, she never heard only forest. Even out in the puckerbrush beyond the last straggling villages of backwoods Maine, there'd always been the distant roar of jets overhead and log skidders growling over their prey two ridges to the west.

Camped out in the middle of the mountains, you could hear the Maine Central diesel air horns at midnight grade crossings twenty miles away. The voice of man was noise.

Not this. This was the way forests had sounded before the first machine. Maureen felt peace wash through her. God knows, she'd earned it.

"I've dreamed of forests like this."

<The land is yours, if you choose to claim it.>

Maureen studied the forest, opening her professional eyes. Coming here, the land had been a blur—first the theater backdrop to Sean's glamour, then something vague, red-tinted through her rage and fear. She'd never *seen* it.

She saw lichen an inch thick on the trees, carpets of reindeer moss on the ground between the bunchberry and the bramble, dens and rocky labyrinths and damp pockets of rotting leaves spiked with lycopodium. Oak. Beech. Maple. Birch. Others she did not know the names of or the uses, European trees she'd never learned. Fir and pine and cedar and spruce. Young trees, old trees, giants, and scraggly dwarfs. Beautiful trees, trees with heart and history and character.

This land waited for her touch, her understanding, and her healing.

How much land had Dougal held? The view from his keep had shown forest for miles in every direction—rolling green out to the distant tilled fields and the pastures. She traced the furrows of watersheds in her mind, almost stroking their leafy fur with her hand.

This land was damned near empty. The Old Ones were loners, distrustful of each other and of humans, almost like Daniel Boone and the other American wanderers. It was time to move on when you could see the smoke from your neighbor's chimney on a frosty morning.

She remembered Fiona in Carlysle Woods, talking of the Summer Country. "Think of it as clay on the potter's wheel, and you the potter."

The fox offered her a forest to tend, tend by her own rules.

Old trees to talk to. New trees to learn. The mystery of that wrongness she'd felt, to solve and correct by careful stewardship—psychotherapy for an ecosystem.

No one to call her crazy when she talked of the soul of

a tree. No stockholders to complain when she guided her decisions by what the land needed rather than by numbers on a ledger.

If some land-management firm in Maine had offered her this job, she'd have killed for it.

*I already have.*

She found her hand on the knife hilt again and jerked it away. The fox vanished.

Magic. Maureen wondered if it was the mundane magic of a red fox startled by her movement, or the true magic of the Summer Country.

She felt like a mystic blessed by the touch of God.

<Next time you come here,> the fox whispered, <bring your wooden flute. You'll find it plays a different kind of music in its true home.>

# twenty-six

—〰—

MAUREEN STRUGGLED TO separate reality from illusion.

Had she conjured the fox out of sleep deprivation and a week of fasting? Could she hold a clear and rational conversation with a beech tree if she was still on medication?

*How does this world define sanity?*

First things first. She had to find Brian. He understood this crazy place.

She strode off through the forest, straight east. Her hand went to the hilt of the knife again and massaged her belly underneath it.

A low stone wall divided the forest from rolling pastures, divided the smell of old leaves and damp forest moss from a breeze full of fresh green grass and wildflowers. Maureen sensed another boundary there, as well, as if she'd be crossing into enemy territory when she climbed over the line of fieldstone.

Her paranoia revived: *They* were watching her. She found herself chuckling at the notion. She hadn't realized how much the magic of the land had changed her until the old feeling returned. Now every blade of grass had eyes and ears.

Maybe this time it was true.

She sat on the fence, chewing on an apple while she rested her legs. Her queasy stomach welcomed the food, so she pulled out a chunk of cheese and gnawed on it, then followed up with slices of dried sausage. The warm sun tempted her to lie down in the grass and sleep. A short nap, say a week or maybe two, seemed just about right. Wake up and eat, then sleep again.

Recover first. Brian could wait. She leaned back against an oak—an ancient white oak rooted firmly on *her* side of the stone wall—and closed her eyes.

<That's Fiona talking,> the oak whispered. <You're at the edge of her territory now. She's far more skilled than Dougal was, more subtle. Let the paranoia rule for a little longer. Even paranoids have real enemies.>

Maureen jerked awake and shook herself. Father Oak never spoke *that* clearly. He tended to be more like a Greek oracle, all enigmatic and vague. She looked over the land-scape with a fresh eye, looking for trouble.

A chimney poked out of green lumps, a mile or so away. Maureen studied it, picking out the rounded line of a thatched roof pale against the spring shrubs. She'd expected something more impressive, more defensive, something cold and tall on a hill, like the castle she'd left in flames.

Fiona seemed to keep a lower profile than Dougal had. Basic psychology said it meant she was more confident—probably with good reason.

Maureen heaved herself upright again, groaning quietly. Spending a week or so in a dungeon hadn't done anything good for her stamina. Her legs were sore. She felt more tired than she had any right to be after walking only a mile or two.

Also, she seemed to have done something nasty to her

right shoulder in the process of hacking Dougal into bits. That was typical. Every time she tried something new, like canoeing, bicycling, or simply killing people, she seemed to find muscles she'd never used before.

There was no way to hide, so she went openly. The fields spread out around her as she walked, neat stone-walled pastures like velvet lawns with no sign of any cattle or sheep to keep them mowed, no smell of the barnyard, no meadow muffins. The grass was part of a picture, she decided, a setting rather than a working farm. Fiona had said that she kept gardens.

The hedges around the house mirrored that casual perfection. Tangles of hawthorn and wild rose laced together with briar and grape; they built solid walls with the precise and studied wildness of a Japanese garden. The hedge hummed with bees floating from one sweet pink rose to another.

Maureen remembered a history course, Patton's armor cutting through France after D-day. The hedgerows there could stop a tank. These looked like they would even stop a rabbit. She circled the house, warily, in and out around the wanderings of the green fence.

Finally, she decided it really was a castle—one made of soft, living stone that would bend but never break. You'd need an army to get in, flamethrowers, bulldozers, a commando assault team with blasting charges, if you weren't invited.

She wondered what protected it from the air. Long odds, you couldn't just fly in.

An orange cat lay sunning his belly by one of the two white gates. Maureen held out her hand for sniffing and learned that a chin scratch would be appropriate toll. She spent a few minutes at the task—you never knew when you'd need a friend in a tight corner. She was rewarded with a purr like an idling Ferrari.

It was a damn shame the apartment had a "no pets" lease. The world was a better place with cats in it. And if Fiona kept a cat as her gatekeeper, she couldn't be all bad.

Cats, plural, Maureen amended, when she opened the gate and slipped inside. A gray-and-white female joined them, tail up in a greeting question mark. They were probably sentries. She'd just rung the doorbell, but she was too tired to really care.

The hedges apparently formed a maze. Just inside the gate, she faced a blank wall of green and the option of right or left down a flagstone path. Each way ended in a sharp turn that blocked any further view.

Even if she'd been desperate enough to climb the thorny hedge, it arched over to form a barbed-wire tunnel. Fiona's defenses might be prettier than Castle MacKenzie's, but up close, they looked just as strong.

*The thorns are probably poisoned as well,* she thought. *Or maybe the pretty blossoms breathe out narcotic vapors, like the poppy fields on the way to the Emerald City, or the bees carry stone-fish toxin in their stingers. Brian told you the job was dangerous when you took it.*

She had two choices. She could follow the right-hand rule or follow the cats. If she looked like a person who might operate a can opener, the cats would probably lead her straight to the kitchen. Humans were as obsolete as *Homo habilis* if cats ever evolved an opposable thumb.

*More likely they'll lead you straight over a pit trap set for human weight,* her paranoia answered. *They are Fiona's cats, after all, familiars of a powerful witch.*

The cats went right. Maureen went right, accompanied by a round of ankle polishing. It was either that or flip a coin, and she'd left her purse at the Quick Shop, back in another world.

Right again, the gray-and-white led, and Maureen shook her head. The hedge hadn't bumped out in that area. She turned around and checked behind. From this side, the turn still went right. Her head spun—the hedge looked like a mirror rather than "real" life.

The orange tom leaned against her leg, and she scratched his ears. He looked up with eyes filled with lazy scorn at her insistence on the laws of physics and geometry. She shrugged.

Right again, and right again, and right again, she followed the cats. Maureen gave up on mapping an impossible spiral. The hedge shrank down to just above her head, open now to the sun and the butterflies. She had a sneaking suspicion the walls would be just above *anybody's* head, even a seven-six NBA center. It would always be high enough so you couldn't see where you were going.

Then she caught up with the cats. They sat in a pool of sunlight, daintily washing their paws, at a blank dead end.

Maureen turned around. Instead of the path she had walked between the hedges, she faced another dead end. Butterflies and bees danced across a solid wall of green dotted with pale pink roses. The hedge had boxed her into a trap.

She squatted, nose to nose with the orange tom. He went back to washing his ears with one paw, a study in calm confidence.

"Okay, fuzz-face, what gives?"

"You wouldn't have gotten this far if the cats thought you were dangerous."

Maureen jerked at the voice, nearly falling backward into the hedge. A face formed in the leaves, sort of a Cheshire Cat in green, and smiled at her. It could have been Fiona.

"I've always hated answering machines, love," the face said, "so I've decided to make mine more personal. I'm not in, right now, but you can leave a message. What makes my service more personal is this: The message will be you. You can't leave until I release you."

Something furry butted Maureen's hand, and she supplied scratching service automatically. Then she realized she could still see two cats. A third had joined them, a gray tiger-stripe. She couldn't see any gaps in the hedge around her.

"If," the green voice went on, "you're anybody I really want to meet, you'll figure out how to get on to the house and have a cup of tea while you wait. Otherwise, too bad."

The hedge face melded back into the wall of green, from the edges inward, leaving a smile. Somebody had been reading too much *Alice*.

"Oh, by the way," the smile added, as the eyes returned. "I wouldn't recommend touching anything purple, love. I've decided the color doesn't go with my complexion."

The face faded out completely. Maureen shook her head and looked around, at a sunlit box of greenery and three smug cats grooming themselves. Bees hummed from flower to flower, then rose up to float away south, probably to their hive.

Purple? What the hell had she meant, don't touch anything purple? Poison?

The gray tiger-stripe batted at a butterfly, leaping up with paws spread wide. She missed, landed with a flip of her tail that said, "I meant to do that," and cocked her ears at the fluttering cat toy. The yellow ribbing of the tiger swallowtail turned purple. It wavered its way past Maureen's ear and into the bush, where it perched on a purple rose blossom, sipping nectar.

All of the blossoms were purple, now. They had been pink a minute ago.

Another purple swallowtail fluttered across Maureen's nose. She brushed it away. Fire flashed up her arm, and she stared at the red blotch left on the back of her hand. It throbbed like a hornet sting.

Hot coals touched her neck and arm, feathery touches

that left acid running up her nerves. Butterflies flitted across, an inch from her eyes, brushing her ears, lighting on her knees to fan their wings. She felt the heat of them even through the denim of her jeans.

The hedge inched closer. She could have lain down crosswise in the path, before, and never come near the bushes. Now she could touch the thorns on each side with her outstretched arms. More blossoms spattered the walls with purple. More butterflies filled the air. Maureen huddled in on herself.

The cats ignored it all. She wondered how they judged which visitors were dangerous and which could pass into the maze. Two of them sat in loaves, with tails and paws tucked in, watching her like feline Buddhas. The third, the orange tom, had vanished through a cat door into a parallel dimension.

*Poe, not Lewis Carroll,* she thought. Fiona had created her own version of "The Pit and the Pendulum." The problem was, nobody was going to show up to arrest the Inquisition.

Purple, that was the problem. Nothing had happened until the first butterfly turned purple. She glared at the lavender roses. *Pink,* she screamed in her mind. *You were pink!*

They stayed purple. She singled out one, ignoring the heat of a score of fiery butterflies perched on her blouse and pants. Something brushed her cheek and left a swelling welt. She squinted against the pain and tears, thinking of nothing but the single blossom. If she couldn't return to the past, maybe she could change the future. . . .

She snarled at the flower. "Okay, dammit, you're yellow. I'll paint all you bastards yellow, like the cards in *Alice* painting the roses red."

Maureen leaned closer, her eyes crossing as she held the blossom centered in her sight. Her breath rustled the leaves and shivered the fragile petals of the rose.

"Yellow," she whispered. "You are a yellow rose."

Her vision narrowed to a tunnel, and she lost touch with her body. The burning coals died in the darkness. The hornet stings left her flesh. The humming bees and the whisper of wind through the hedge died out of her ears, the warm green smells of grass and tree and earth abandoned her nose. All that remained was rose—the glistening velvet petals of the flower, the golden pollen on the stamens, the soft perfume of the nectar.

Time froze around her. "Yellow," she repeated, as a mantra. "You are a yellow rose."

She reached out and set her thumb and forefinger between the thorns. She flowed her will into the stem. She plucked it.

It was yellow.

Her vision opened out again. The roses around it were yellow. The swallowtails were yellow. Golden sunlight poured down around her, splashing on golden sandstone under her feet.

The cats unfolded themselves and stretched, lazily, as cats do when they want to show they are granting you a favor. The gray-and-white female padded daintily back the way she had come, through space that had been hedge a moment before, and turned left. Maureen followed.

They walked into grass and open sun. A thatched stone cottage sat in the midst of daffodils and azaleas and tulips, walls whitewashed into a travel brochure for the Emerald Isle, waiting. The orange tom lay on a windowsill, basking in the only sunbeam falling on that wall. The rest was shaded by a tall rowan tree guarding the side porch.

Maureen opened the door, nervous, expecting further traps. It squeaked heavily on its hinges but showed her nothing except a tiled entry and an arch back into a modern kitchen. The cats scalloped past her ankles and strode inside.

Have a cup of tea, Fiona's leafy face had said. Jimson-weed? Or water hemlock? It would take a brave woman to brew tea in a witch's kitchen. Maybe there would be milk for the cats. That bastard brother of Fiona's had been buying milk at the Quick Shop. But he'd left it there, on the counter. . . .

She stepped inside. Brian sat at the kitchen table, reading. He looked up when her shadow crossed his book, a smile breaking across his face. Then the smile died, replaced by blankness.

Maureen understood, with a chill. He'd expected Fiona. She wasn't Fiona. That was the end of it. Nothing else mattered.

He didn't look as if he even recognized her.

# twenty-seven

—⚶—

BRIAN PAID NO more attention to her than to the cats. He didn't speak. He acted as if Fiona had reached inside his brain and frozen part of it.

Maureen shied away from him, her own thoughts scattered and useless. She groped for something to do, something to say, a way to break the wall of ice between them. She glanced out the window, at a thin plume of smoke on a distant hill. Maybe that was where Fiona had gone, squabbling with her fellow witches and wizards over the spoils Dougal left behind.

Instinct had said, "Go to Fiona's place." As far as Maureen was concerned, instinct could damn well continue making suggestions. Besides, if she had come with some kind of plot in mind, had come looking for a fight, the hedge and the cats probably would have kept her out. Sometimes improv was the only way that worked.

Other than Brian and the cats, the house seemed empty. And it *was* a house, even a farmer's cottage, not a castle or a palace. Maureen had seen no sign of servants, another difference between Fiona and Dougal.

The orange tom rubbed her leg insistently and padded over to a refrigerator purring in the corner, reminding her of milk. The machine seemed vaguely incongruous in the old cottage kitchen, but it held a stoneware crock of milk with a thick skin of cream floating on the top. She found three saucers, filled them with cat bribes, and drifted into irrelevant questions to avoid thinking about Brian. He was still ignoring her. The cats gave the cottage more of a lived-in feeling than he did.

Electric refrigerator and microwave oven—Fiona had to have some solar panels on the roof, like the ones Dougal had. But the woodstove, oil lamps, marble countertop with slate sink and hand pump, and lines of cabinets with buttercup yellow paint worn back to bare wood along the edges and knobs made a comfortable mix of old and new. It looked as if centuries of feet had worn the slate floor smooth and darkened it to ebony. Bundles of herbs hung from the blackened beams of the ceiling, perfuming the air with sage and tarragon and rosemary and more exotic scents. It didn't feel like a dangerous place.

A black laptop computer lay in one corner of the counter, somehow less clashing than it should have been. Maureen smiled at a vision of Fiona keeping her spells in a database, maintaining inventory on her eye of newt and toe of frog electronically to make sure she always had fresh stock—a thoroughly modern witch, perhaps with her own web site.

Brian sat at the table, ignoring her, reading. The damned man could at least say good afternoon, nice to see you, beautiful day we're having. She'd been counting on him.

*You're suffering from Snow White Syndrome,* her critic snarled. *Once Prince Charming is in the picture, he should take over and everything will be Happily Ever After. Ain't a-gonna work that way, this once-upon-a-time.*

This time, it was the Handsome Prince who'd eaten the poisoned apple, and the Princess had to wake him. A simple kiss probably wasn't going to work.

Her hand was rubbing her belly again. Maureen jerked it away, bumping against the hilt of the knife. She pulled the heavy blade, sheathed, from her waistband and dropped it in the middle of Brian's book.

"I think this might be yours."

He didn't even look up. He *did* pick up the knife, running his fingers over some scars in the black leather of the sheath, then showing a couple of inches of steel to read the maker's mark.

"It looks like my spare," he said to a point somewhere beyond her left shoulder. "Where did you get it?"

"Dougal had it. I killed him with it, this morning."

He blinked. "I gave it to David before we came here. Dougal must have taken it from him."

That was all the response she got? Chop the villain into stew meat and burn down his castle after spending a week or so naked in his dungeon, and all the man did was *blink*?

*Hey, girl, you've got a serious problem here. The man's a zombie.*

"Where's David?" she asked.

"Dougal bound him to the land. He's in the forest, near the dragon." Brian put the knife down and turned back to his book.

She snatched the book out from under his nose and threw it into a corner. Cats scattered and glared at her. Maureen glared back, and they vanished.

Brian still stared at the table. She grabbed a fistful of hair and pulled his face up to meet hers. "Goddamn you, *what* fucking dragon?"

"David killed a dragon." He spoke slowly and patiently, as if he was talking to a young child. "It belonged to Dougal. Dougal bound David to the land in a blood sacrifice, for revenge." He reached up and squeezed the sides of her hand, forcing her fingers loose from his hair and driving white-hot pain into her pinched nerves.

So *that* was what was rotting in the forest. Maureen stared into his eyes, forcing him to recognize her. "Take me there. Help me set David free." She massaged her hand, wiggling the fingers until they all worked again.

"Ask Fiona. If she says I can go, I'll show you where he is." He paused for a moment, frowning as if he was almost starting to notice the woman standing in front of him. "If you killed Dougal, you own his lands by right of conquest. That's the law of the Summer Country, as much as there is any law. If David is still alive, you can set him free without my help."

Maureen exploded. "Damn you, I want to find David and Jo and get the fuck out of this freaking place! I need your help!"

"Ask Fiona."

She backed away from him with a sick feeling in her gut. She remembered the tree's picture show: Fiona dancing around Brian, singing to him, enslaving him.

*If you want him, you're going to have to fight for him,* the whispering repeated in her head.

*How do I fight for a man?*

The answer only added to the flip-flops in her belly. She was going to have to seduce him. That was what Fiona's dance had done. Maureen was going to have to turn into Jo. Maureen, the woman who was afraid of men. Maureen, the woman who had just killed a man for raping her. If she wanted Brian's help, she was going to have to break this spell.

The only way was with a spell of her own.

*You slept with a monster, to get a chance to kill him. Why the hell can't you seduce the man you love, to save him?*

Her head hurt, and her eyes refused to focus.

*You. Must. Bed. A. Man.*

Just thinking the words made it hard to breathe. Dougal didn't really matter. She knew it had happened, knew a time bomb might be ticking in her belly, but she remembered nothing. She'd switched off that part of her brain and slept right through it.

She remembered Buddy with perfect clarity. He was huge. He was on top of her. He *hurt* her.

She remembered his face hanging over hers—panting, red, sweaty, the glazed look of animal hunger in his eyes. She remembered sweat dripping off that huge flat caveman nose like scientists always showed on their Neanderthal sketches.

Brian had that nose. So had Dougal, and Liam before him. Sean didn't. Maybe that meant it was for tracking female Old Ones by their smell.

Fear condensed into her bladder. It felt like it would explode any minute, reminding her of the night in her apartment, walking down the hall away from Brian's fading glamour. She remembered how she'd nearly killed herself in the tangle of insanity afterward, how she'd hated him for tampering with her emotions. And now he ignored her.

If Fiona used a hand pump, she probably had an outhouse. Maureen tried doors in the vain hope for an indoor toilet and found one, just off the kitchen. She emptied herself and sat in the universal refuge, arguing with the voices in her head.

*What do you want?* they asked.

*I want him to help me find David and Jo. I want him to help me find a home. I want him to talk to me. I want him to smile at me. I want him to touch me.*

*What are the first three words of all those sentences?*

*I want him.*

*What was he doing in your dreams, last night?*

Maureen clenched her fists, staring at the white knuckles standing out under her flushed skin. *He was kissing me,* she answered. *He was running his hands over my naked body. He was . . .*

*And you liked every bit of it, in your dreams. Those weren't exactly dreams. Those were Dougal. He didn't hurt you. He didn't even really wake you up. You aren't ten anymore. Your body knows something your brain doesn't. You're a woman now. Most women enjoy sex. We're programmed that way. It's how the species survives.*

She wiped cold sweat off her forehead. *Give me time,* she whimpered.

*You don't have time,* the surly voices muttered. *Fiona will be back here, soon. Once she's here, you've lost him. Lost him forever. If you want him, you'll have to fight for him. You'll have to break her spell.*

*You're going to have to bed him.*

She stood up and peeled off unbleached toilet paper and searched for a flush lever before noticing it was a composting toilet. Maureen shook her head, unable to visualize *très élégante* Fiona shoveling out a year's load of composted shit. The Old One probably witched it directly to her rose beds.

*Shut up and quit stalling!*

" 'If it were done when 'tis done, then 'twere well it were done quickly,' " she quoted. " 'But screw your courage to the sticking-place and we'll not fail.' " And then she shuddered at the unintended pun.

How did a woman seduce a man?

*Do what Jo would do,* her voices nudged her. *You've called her a whore often enough. You've seen her at her work. Learn from the pro. Turn into your evil twin. Let her possess you.*

Maureen studied herself in the mirror. How would Jo wear those clothes? *You've tried to imitate her all your life, worshiped her, even learned to talk like her, hoping it would help. What would she do, fishing for a man?*

First thing she'd do, she'd show a lot more skin. Maureen gritted her teeth and unbuttoned her blouse, top and bottom, until it was barely decent and then one button farther, and tied the shirttails across her belly. She tugged her bra down an inch beyond her comfort limit. She unsnapped her jeans and slipped the zipper and settled them on her hips, until white lace showed below her belly button in an open invitation.

Jo looked back at her from the mirror, Jo in her tomboy temptress phase. They matched except for the hair. Maureen borrowed Fiona's brush and flipped hair forward until curls half covered one eye.

That took care of the outside. What the hell could she do about the inside? Last time she checked, you still had to get close to a man to screw him. If she tried that, she'd go catatonic or grab for that knife.

She gagged at what she *did* remember of Dougal, his arms enfolding her naked body, his kisses on her breasts, his hand between her legs. She felt filthy again.

*Think of some other man,* the voices prodded. *Think of a man you aren't afraid of. Think of a man who gave you joy instead of sorrow.*

A tune floated through her head, and she started singing softly to herself, remembering a child's nonsense song learned from her grandfather long before Buddy Johnson clouded her horizon. It was the only bit of Gaelic she'd ever learned, and she didn't know the meaning of half the words—if they even had meanings other than mouth music and a lilting rhyme. She did remember *dúlamán* was a kind of seaweed.

"Dúlamán na Binne Buí, Dúlamán Gaelach,
"Dúlamán na farraige, 's é b'fhearr a bhí in Éirinn."

Grandfather O'Brian was always warm and gentle and friendly, even when he reeked of Irish whiskey. She'd loved him. She still did. He'd never hurt her. She tried to visualize him as the handsome charmer he must have been when he was young. She'd marry a man like that in an instant, booze and all. She'd bed him without the blessing of the priest and to hell with contraception.

Maureen stepped out of the toilet and met Brian's stare. He looked at her, not at the table, and she saw something in his face no man had ever aimed at her before. It was the way men looked at Jo. The look punched her in the gut, and she stopped singing. His eyes lost their focus. She forced herself to start again.

> "A 'níon mhín ó, sin anall ne fir shúirí,
> "A mháthair mhín ó! cuir na roithlé go dtí mé."

Gentle warmth flushed her face and hands, not a blush but a reminder of her sexual dreams. She washed up at the sink, his gaze on her back again, and she remembered her vision of Fiona in the forest. The dark witch had been singing as part of her spell.

*So this is magic. How can it feel so natural?*

Now came the hard part. She had to retreat into her padded cell and let Jo take control. She walked over to Brian, conscious of a different sway to her hips. His eyes focused on the top of her zipper and the lacy cloth showing there.

> "Tá cosa dubha dúbailte ar an dúlamán gaelach
> "Tá dhá chulais mhaol ar an dúlamán gaelach."

Her hands, Jo's hands, caressed his cheek and slipped inside his shirt. The heat of his body felt scorching to her, and his warm male smell twisted her nostrils. She took his hand and pulled him out of his chair, led him to the next room, pushed him to the floor where there was a rug and room to work.

He moved like a putty doll—pliable, inert and yet living. "Zombie" was the word.

His attention was riveted to her body, but he wasn't aroused. She knew enough about men to know that. Her hands, Jo's hands working without command, unbuttoned her blouse and slipped it off, slid her zipper fully open, performed the rest of a slow striptease. Her magic controlled her as much as it did him.

"*Rachaimid go Doire leis an dúlamán gaelach,*
"*Is ceannóimid bróga daora ar an dúlamán gaelach.*"

The voices in her head echoed Fiona's words in the frozen forest. *He smells you,* they said. *You lead men around by the nose. You can make a man do anything you want.*

Her hands, Jo's hands, slipped down her body and probed the moisture between her legs. She brought a finger to Brian's nose and his nostrils flared. His body stirred against the spell that bound him, and she pushed him back to the floor.

Jo's fingers deftly opened buttons and buckles, slid cloth over skin, laid his body bare on the rug. Maureen's stomach clenched at the sight, and she forced herself back into the song.

"*Bróga breaca dubha ar an dúlamán gaelach,*
"*Tá bearéad agus triús ar an dúlamán gaelach.*"

He groaned. It came out as a word, "Maureen," and he reached for her.

"Shut up and lie still," she hissed. "The only way I'm

going to get through this is if *I* do *everything*. Be a god-damned crash-test dummy."

His eyes widened, but he obeyed. *Of course he obeyed,* the voices muttered. *You're making him your slave, just like Fiona did.*

She straddled him, forcing herself to look only at his eyes. His eyes lived now. They saw her. A mind sat behind them.

Memory forced itself forward, pain and exhaustion and slick sweat and the stench of blood. The last time she was in this position, she was chopping a man's head off while his dying reflexes vainly tried to screw her. She fought the image back and reached down beneath her, concentrating on the simple mechanics of alignment rather than exactly *what* she actually was doing.

' *'twere well it were done quickly'* . . .

She lowered herself on him, and she felt the Power of the Summer Country throbbing through her blood to focus on the fire growing beneath her belly. She moved on golden light and wept.

SHE STOOD AT a window in Fiona's parlor, naked, with her back to Brian. Their mingled fluids chilled her thighs, and she ought to wipe herself, but she couldn't care. Enough of the magic still glowed in her body.

*I'll fucking kill Buddy if I ever see him again,* she swore. *He stole at least ten years of this from me.*

*You're not out of the woods yet,* her critic muttered. *What are you going to do when Brian comes to you? What are you going to do when he wants to be on top?*

*That,* she answered, *depends on Brian. Right now, I'm in a mood to negotiate.*

She heard him stir behind her. She continued to stare out the window without seeing. The orange cat appeared out of nowhere and settled on the sill. She rubbed his shoulder, and he sprawled into her kneading fingers.

"Someone hurt you very badly, a long time ago." Brian spoke just above a whisper, as if he was allowing her some space even in her ears. "Someone long before Dougal."

"Eighteen years ago."

He stood up. She felt the movement more than heard it, and he didn't come any closer.

"Is he still alive?"

"He's still alive. I'll kill him myself, thank you. How did you know?"

"That night in your apartment, the things you said in The Cave, watching you just now. Few women regard sex as torture. At worst, they are indifferent. You forced yourself into this like it was surgery for cancer. Something, somebody, had hurt you deeply enough to scar you to the bottom of your soul. Logic said it was a man, when you were still a child."

He wasn't getting dressed. Her old fears stirred, as if she'd stunned them but not yet killed them dead. There was going to be a problem in another minute or so, if she didn't get dressed. She couldn't clean up, with him between her and the door. She couldn't turn around. He had her trapped, as much as if she was back in chains.

"Tell me about it, sometime. Wait until it comes naturally. I've heard a lot of pain in seventy years. I think you'll feel better if someone else knows what happened to you."

That was one of the basic principles of psychotherapy or the confessional, she remembered. Pain shared was pain diluted.

"Maureen, is Dougal really dead?"

"I cut his head off. I burned his tower with his body in it. If that isn't enough, I don't want to hear about it."

"I love you, Maureen."

*Oh, God.* "Of course you love me. You don't have any fucking choice. Ten minutes ago, you loved Fiona for the same reasons."

"No. I've loved you since the night we met. You just wouldn't have listened if I told you. Besides, Fiona used a different spell than you did. I obeyed her. I didn't love her. You broke her spell and left me free. You ripped your own soul apart to do it. I love you."

"I did the same things she did. The forest showed me."

"Maureen, magic power is not a cookbook. You had a different intent in your heart, so the spell changed to meet your needs. You bound yourself to me more than me to you."

He stepped closer, slowly, as if he was approaching a hurt and frightened animal. She felt the heat of his body on her back. The muscles along her spine crawled.

"Men and women don't have to hurt each other. You set the rules. You set the limits. I promise you, I'll stop. 'No' means no."

She smelled him—smelled his musk, smelled her own sweat on his body, smelled the mingling of his semen with her mucus where their bodies had joined. She gritted her teeth against the urge to vomit.

Maureen's hands clamped the windowsill, bracing herself to spin and flee or fight. He wanted to touch her. He wanted to hold her. She shouldn't give control to Jo this time. But it was too soon. . . .

*Don't live in the past. Don't live in the future. Do it now, while you still remember how good it can be.*

*Brian loves me. I love Brian. What he is offering me is a sacrament between a man and a woman. He wants to give me joy, not pain. He is sharing his body, not using mine.*

*Bullshit. He just wants to fuck you again. Once isn't enough for him. Buddy was like that. Goddamn rabbit, one afternoon he had you twice and still screwed Jo when she got home. At least he used a rubber for her: He never wasted one on you. You weren't old enough for sperm to hurt you.*

*But his prick could. I bled after the second time. Bled for three days. It hurt to pee.*

She swallowed a scream and forced herself to hold still, sweating, trembling, eyes scrunched shut. She couldn't breathe.

*Brian loves me. I love Brian.*

His hands touched her waist, and she felt his hips snuggle against her bottom. She leaned forward and pushed back against him, and her world caught fire again.

# twenty-eight

—◊—

"MARMALADE CAT, MARMALADE cat, how do we leave?"

Maureen stared down at the orange tom sprawled across her lap. She scratched his ears and repeated the question silently in her mind. How the *hell* could she get them out of this trap?

She closed her eyes and slumped back against the smooth bark of the rowan by Fiona's kitchen door. Just doing *nothing* felt so damned good. The day had drained her, and it wasn't done yet. They had to get out of here. They had to find Jo and David. Somewhere out there Fiona and Sean waited for her.

Especially Sean.

The cat answered both her questions with a rumbling purr she felt deep in her belly. He was comfortable. If she left, who would provide a lap, scratch his ears, pour out cream on demand? Why should he help her leave?

His paws kneaded the fabric of her jeans, claws slipping and catching gently. Possessive little beast. Everybody in the whole damn world thought they owned her lap, and all the appurtenances thereto.

She wondered how long human sperm remained viable in the female body. Was Dougal waging a posthumous war with Brian for her womb?

She shook her head. That would have been part of Freshman Health in high school, sex education for hormone-ravaged ninth graders. Mom and Dad wouldn't sign the permission forms for either of the girls. They seemed to think Jo and Maureen would stay virgins forever if nobody mentioned the fact that men had penises and women had vaginas.

Odd idea, and a little late in either case.

The cat shifted on her lap, redirecting her hand to his left shoulder blade. She wished she could be that simple and straightforward. Cats didn't have any of those body hang-ups. If a cat wanted something, either food or sex or a warm sunbeam on his belly, he went out and got it. If he wanted his shoulder scratched, he told you which one and how long. Hedonist. Mister Marmalade had his harem and his windowsill and his milk; all was right with his world.

Brian appeared around the corner of the house. He saw her and shook his head.

"Nothing?"

"The hedge is a solid wall. Fiona tells it to open when she wants to leave. Right now, it isn't even playing dead-end maze with me."

Shit.

"Can't you cut a way out with that knife of yours?"

"That wouldn't be wise. The hedge has defenses."

"Can't you magic it open?"

"It's my sister's pet." He grinned down at the cat. "You seem to have better luck seducing them than I do."

She blushed. Her quick smile faded as fast as it came. "What happens when she gets back?"

"I don't know. Fiona's a wild card. She might say she's bored with me and let us go, or she might turn you into a toad. You'd make a very lovely toad."

Somehow, she didn't think he was joking. Maureen shuddered.

"Isn't there any way we can fight her?"

Brian chewed on his lip for a moment. "Again, I don't know. She drained my power. My mana, if you will. It'll be days before I build up anything worth mentioning. I have no idea what *your* strength may be. It's obviously greater than Dougal thought, or you wouldn't be here."

She closed her eyes. "I'm tired. Don't expect much from me. If this tree wasn't behind me, I don't think I could even sit up straight. Last night was just about the first sleep I've had since I left our apartment. You don't want to ask how I got it. And I haven't been eating much, either."

"I know how you got it." His voice was gentle. "What I don't know is how you held out as long as you did. How did you escape?"

She decided to put it in the simplest possible terms. He deserved to know.

"I'm crazy, Brian. I'm schizophrenic. I turned him into a delusion and stepped aside into one of my private little worlds. I've had plenty of practice. Anyway, it fooled him into thinking he'd won. This morning, I just unchained the paranoia and let my own personal Doberman have him for breakfast." She opened her eyes, and met his glance, and held it. "Still interested in sleeping next to me?"

He waited long enough for her to know he understood.

"Yes." He grinned. "You'll keep me from getting bored." Then his expression sobered. "Maureen, you never told anyone about the rape, did you? Not even a priest or therapist?"

Cold fire shot through her like a lightning bolt. "I didn't say it," she whispered, too quiet for him to hear. "Jo, I *swear* I never said it. God as my witness, I didn't break my promise. I never told."

"No," she added, aloud.

She shook her head. She had to learn to be honest with herself, even about this. *Jo would skin me alive if she knew what I've covered up. She was just scared of Daddy, scared of what he would do if he ever found out about her and Buddy.*

*But I couldn't say what he did to me without Daddy finding out about the rest. . . .*

Brian squatted down so she wouldn't have to squint up at him against the sky, and spoke softly. "There's something you ought to think about, something the psych-boffins are always sniffing after, in combat veterans like you and me. It's called posttraumatic stress disorder. Some of the symptoms are damned close to schizophrenia. I've walked that road myself. As you Yanks would say, 'Been there, done that.' "

Maureen froze. She knew about PTSD. They'd had months on it, in her various psych courses back in college. But *that* hadn't applied to *her*. That hadn't explained the voices, hadn't explained the things she saw that no one else could see—hadn't explained the ways she had been "different" long before Buddy Johnson stalked into her nightmares.

Her mind filled the gaps with its own added diagnosis. *That's the Blood, magic, a whole world the shrinks won't admit exists. A lot of "crazy Maureen" has always been the power in my blood struggling with a world that doesn't believe in magic. Advice from trees was a strength, not a symptom.*

Brian seemed to read her thoughts. "Nobody here would call you crazy. You deceived Dougal by using your power.

You killed him by using your power. In this world, you're not schizophrenic. You're a witch."

She felt calm washing through her, the cool relief of a lanced boil draining pus. She hadn't told Brian, but he knew. The years of hiding were over. She'd never dared admit the true problem, even to herself.

"My delusions are real?"

"They aren't delusions."

"I really *was* talking to the trees?"

"How do you think Fiona controls her hedge?"

Her glance dropped to the cat in her lap. Her hands had switched to rubbing his cheeks, pulling his eyes shut in an ecstasy of attention.

"The rest was just Buddy Johnson?" She spoke softly, to the orange fur, as if naming her fear could summon it.

"Buddy Johnson." Brian repeated the name. He sounded like he was underlining it, in his memory. "I wouldn't say 'just.' Men like him have crippled other women for life. You've survived both him and the battle of living in the wrong world. That takes incredible strength."

"I really *can* talk to trees?" She picked up the limp cat, hanging his nose in front of hers. "Marmalade cat, take us out of here."

<Can't.>

She dropped him, in shock. The cat tumbled off her lap and glared at her, shaking his ears until they rattled. His tail switched indignantly.

"Ingrate. I gave you cream and scratched your ears all afternoon, and now you won't do us a little favor. You brought me *in* here, you must know the way out."

<Mistress won't let us.>

"And a *cat* lets a *human* tell him what to do?"

<Mistress commands us.>

Maureen shook her head and looked up at Brian. "Can *you* hear him?"

He smiled at her, tolerantly, not as if he thought she was nuts but more like he was amused at her confusion. "No. I told you I was drained. Obviously, you aren't."

*Jeezum!* A human commanding a cat? Somebody had better get the morals squad down here. *That* sure fit the definition of an unnatural act.

Suddenly, little oddities clicked in Maureen's brain, and she looked around herself with fresh eyes. The rowan overhead held the orange berries of autumn against the unblemished leaves of spring. Daffodil bloomed next to chrysanthemum next to climbing rose, ignoring their proper seasons. An apple tree held both blossoms and five kinds of ripe fruit.

Fiona did *too* keep slaves.

She was less obvious about it than Dougal, was all. She forced her plants and animals out of their natural ways to perform at her whim, like the hedge maze and her answering service. Maureen laid her hand lightly on the grass next to her and felt pain. It wasn't *allowed* to grow beyond a golf-green carpet height.

They weren't talking land ethic and Wicca here. To hell with the unbleached toilet paper. This lady lived on the earth, not in it. Nothing around Fiona's cottage marched to a different drummer. Things stepped out smartly on her beat, or they didn't march at all. She'd break their kneecaps.

How did she control the land? How did she speak to it?

"Brian, what did Dougal do to David?"

His face turned grim. "You've read about the offerings that archaeologists find in bogs? The gifts to the land, to bring fertility?"

She nodded, and he continued. "Sometimes those offerings included human sacrifice. A priest would strangle a man with leather cords, slash a woman's throat. Then they'd give the body to the bog. Most times, the person was a criminal, an outcast, someone condemned to death for good reason. This way, their death could serve a higher purpose.

"Archaeologists love the practice. The acid in the bog embalms the offering, and you get to find all sorts of perishable artifacts, wood and leather and cloth."

He grimaced. "I'm wandering. Sacrifices. In really bad times, the sacrifice needed to be more powerful. An innocent was killed, sometimes even the leader or 'king' had to die to serve his land. Their blood was more potent. It fed the land, soothed the anger of the gods. Even gods have bled and died to renew the world. Jesus held no monopoly on that."

A black pit opened in front of Maureen. "Dougal killed David? To feed his land? My land?" If that was true, she could never speak to the fox again. David's death would always stand between them.

"Worse. David is still alive. The forest is drinking his blood and soul, slowly. The longer he takes to die, the more powerful his sacrifice."

She swallowed sour bile. Suddenly, chopping Dougal into dog food looked less ugly. Do unto others what they *have* done unto others.

"Blood is powerful?"

He nodded. "Blood is *very* powerful."

"Give me your knife."

Memories swam out of decades back, a book about a man who kept an otter. A vengeful lover had cursed his rowan tree. The rowan held the soul of the house, the seat of happiness or sorrow, the magic of threshold and hearth. Maureen twisted around and laid her palms against the tree trunk behind her.

"Rowan, do you bless this house?"

The answer came clear, heavy with anger.

<No!>

She cut her left palm and barely felt the sting. She smeared her blood on the trunk of the rowan. She leaned her forehead against the cool smooth bark and drew strength from it, drew strength up from its roots and the hidden waters below and the rock beneath it all. Her blood trickled down the bark and dripped from her hand into the soil.

Again, the mirror of another time entered her, the sense of having been here before. Maureen felt words force themselves between her lips.

"Rowan, I curse this house. I break its hold over you. I sever the threads that bind you to it. I free the plants and creatures of this land from bondage to this house and to its owner. I call the earth below to witness this. I call the sky above to witness this. I call the winds to speak of it, I call the rains to write it in the dust, I call the sun and moon and stars to shine upon it. I curse this house. You stand free."

Again the feeling came to her, the way she used to hear Father Oak speaking silently.

<Yes!>

A whip cracked in her ear, and her eyes snapped open. The worn stone threshold under Fiona's door had split in half.

Dark spots wove through her sight. She fought to hold her balance. She felt Brian take the knife from her, then he knelt beside her, wrapping his arms around her, loaning her warmth and strength. She sank into it, gratefully.

"Remind me," he whispered, "to stay on your good side."

"Beloved, right now you *are* my good side." She shook her head, trying to clear the daze.

Rough wetness rasped over her cut hand. She pried one eye open and forced it to reconnect. Cats. Marmalade Tom licked her blood, then Tiger Stripe, then Gray Spot. Animals licked wounds, didn't they? To keep them clean?

Maureen staggered to her feet, using the rowan as a guide to vertical. Her head spun and her knees seemed to lack some essential parts.

"I thought being a witch was more fun. Don't I get to lure children into my gingerbread house and bake them for dinner?"

"I don't know. I've never been a witch. Some of the noises you made earlier seemed to imply pleasure."

She blushed. "I think we can talk to the hedge now."

Brian was staring at the cracked threshold. "Leaving behind a house filled with turmoil and strife. You don't mind smashing a walnut with a sledgehammer, do you? My dear sister may find it easier just to move someplace else. How did you *do* that?"

"I don't know." Shivers danced along her spine. "Words came to me. The blood, the rowan tree, the words, all came to me. Power seems to use *me*, more than the other way around."

He shook his head. "With the Blood, as with other things, power is a matter of will. *Most* of us have to learn spells as a focus."

<We go now.>

The cats strolled across the lawn, tails up, stopping to sniff this and that as if to imply total mastery of the situation. Maureen found the strength for a faint grin. It was such a typical cat attitude: "We're leaving now. You may follow us if you wish. Take it or leave it."

Brian tucked an arm around her waist, and they accepted the offer. She leaned on him in a pose that might have been a casual snuggle but actually was nine-tenths of her support. Her hand dripped red into the grass, and she watched each drop fall, fascinated with the way the ground drank it in without a trace. Her sight pulsed with fatigue, the grass approaching and receding as if the ground was a heart beating in time with her own.

The cats padded quietly into a gap in the hedge and turned right, where no gap had stood a minute earlier. Right and right and right again they turned, impossibly, just like entering, and then they faced the dead end again.

This time it was Fiona instead of a blank wall of hedge.

Maureen blinked twice to be sure. The hallucination spoke.

"So *that's* what set off the alarm. It *would* be you," she said. "With Dougal dead, it *would* be you. I warned him."

Brian's hand twitched toward his knife, then froze. Maureen's heart froze with it.

"What are *you* doing here?" she asked, embarrassed by her stupidity even as she mouthed the words.

"I live here," Fiona answered. "What's your excuse?"

"I came for Brian."

Fiona laughed. "He's not yours, love. You didn't want him, when you had the chance. Now you've changed your mind, but you're not strong enough to make it stick."

*Strong enough?* Maureen thought. *I'm not even strong enough to stand. Brian was holding me up.*

She felt his rigid hand slipping up along her waist, across her ribs, brushing past her breast. She felt like Jell-O oozing out of his grip, down the length of his body, unable to even lift a hand to grab him like a tree. She slipped to her knees and then toppled sideways in a quiet thump. Even the flagstones of the path felt soft and inviting.

She looked up into Fiona's face and saw pity there—pity and detached amusement. *This isn't Fiona,* she thought. *This isn't magic. I'm just used up. No food. No sleep. Long day. Tired.*

She reached out with her cut left hand and grasped the stem of a rose in the hedge. *I tried to set you free,* she thought. *You, and the cats, and the rowan tree, and Brian. I'm sorry. I just wasn't strong enough.*

<Kill!> echoed in her head, the only answer.

Maureen tried to snatch her hand back from Fiona's trap. The muscles wouldn't obey. Her whole arm just flopped into the tangle of stems and roots at the base of the hedge.

The rose didn't follow it. Blood still beaded on her cut palm and oozed slowly down to drip into the soil, to touch the grass at the edge of the path and vanish into the land. Maureen followed a drop along that road, and then another, and another.

*Strange,* she thought. *It isn't clotting right. Women don't get hemophilia, they just transmit it. Must be short on vitamin K or something.*

A sound like wind rustled through the hedge, followed by grunts of pain. She tore her attention away from the minor magic of her own blood and refocused higher, on Fiona battling with strands of thorny green.

Maureen blinked, woozily. The hedge was attacking *Fiona.* She stared at it, unbelieving. *I'm not doing anything! Brian's not doing anything! She's still fighting for her life!*

Green whips lashed at the dark witch and shriveled into black powder, only to be replaced by new legions. Vines clutched at her legs and sought her throat. Tufts of wool stood out from her sweater, and scratches lined her face and arms. Her face snapped from side to side, flaming with rage but with a touch of frantic madness. Even her hair stood out in tangles that mocked her usual cool elegance.

Brian stirred. His hand reached his knife, drew half an inch of steel, an inch. Sweat popped out on his face and dripped to his chest. Fiona screamed some inarticulate noise of power.

His hand froze, then retreated, eclipsing the steel in its sheath. The hedge attacked with a fresh spasm of vines and thorns.

Maureen forced herself to stir, to drag herself to hands and knees, to crawl across the rough stones of the path. She grabbed Fiona's ankle. She couldn't reach higher. She pulled her face up against the cool silk of Fiona's stockings and bared her teeth and bit down, hard.

She tasted blood. She couldn't tell if it was hers or Fiona's.

She tumbled sideways, her head ringing from a kick and Fiona's scream. When her eyes cleared, Brian had his knife clear of the sheath.

Maureen fought her way back to a crouch and scraped up the strength to speak. "You've . . . got a choice," she gasped. "You can fight . . . the hedge and me . . . or you . . . can hold Brian. The hedge . . . wants to kill you. Brian . . . will probably . . . let you live. Make up . . . your mind."

She grabbed the trunk of a hawthorn and thought of earth and rock and water. "Strength," she whispered. "Give me strength. Give me the strength that splits rocks and drives roots deep and sends leaves to the sky. Build a wall of the stone heart of the earth to block Fiona's power, weave a spell of life around her and draw off the essence of her blood and leave her helpless. Loop vines out to seize her wrists and ankles, thread the hooked thorns of her roses against her own throat and eyes. Hold her."

<Kill!>

The copper taste of Fiona's blood filled Maureen's mouth. She couldn't tell if it was from her own bite or tasted through the hawthorn's sap.

Blood. *"Yet who would have thought the old man to have had so much blood in him?"* She stood over Dougal's bed, drenched in clotting gore and with the knife heavy in her hand. She spread her own blood on the rowan's trunk, and dripped red on the grass. Everything was blood. Everything was death. She had to find another way, if she was going to live with her memories. Dougal had given her no choice. Here, she had choices.

Power seethed through the blood in her mouth, searching out its differences, hunting for any weapon she could use against Fiona. She unraveled the cells, and something in the traces spoke to her.

Fiona was pregnant. The child was Brian's. It was a girl.

<Kill!>

"*NO!*"

Maureen dragged herself upright, using the hawthorn as a crutch. It didn't scratch her.

"Don't kill her," she whispered.

Brian's knife pressed against Fiona's throat. The hedge held her pinned against its green wall. Tendrils locked her arms and legs, encircled her waist, threaded through her hair. Her skin shimmered as if she was wrapped in some kind of supernatural plastic film.

"Don't kill her," Maureen repeated, searching for an argument that even rage could hear. "Let the baby live."

Brian blinked and shook his head, as if Maureen had punched him between the eyes. Then he relaxed a fraction. The plants eased their hold. Fiona's eyes opened, locking with Maureen's in a glare of fear and rage and cunning.

Maureen forced words through her exhaustion. "Do you yield?"

The archaic phrase nearly made Maureen smile, but she couldn't waste the strength. Still, it sounded right.

The cunning shone brighter. "What are your terms?"

Amazing. Hanging on the edge of death, and the woman wanted to bargain. So be it.

"Brian leaves. I leave. The cats go where they will. We have a cease-fire. That's all."

"Cease-fire. If I don't bother you, you won't bother me?"

Maureen blinked, slowly, forcing her eyes to keep working. Her knees wanted to quit, too. *This is the Armistice at the end of World War I,* she thought. *Both sides are dying, bled dry, but one is just a shade drier than the other. If you take too much, you set up another war. And I can't* kill *her.*

"That's what I meant," she said.

Fiona gave her a sly, calculating grin. "I can live with that. Besides my own belly, I've got enough of my dear brother's sperm in liquid nitrogen for a few decades of selective breeding. You may find him kind of useless for a few days, love. I've been making him work hard."

"Exercise builds up muscles," Maureen heard Jo's voice shoot back. "I found his performances satisfactory."

Fiona's eyebrows quirked up. "Performances, love? If you must know, I thought he was kind of boring."

"Ah, well." Maureen shook her head. "As the fox commented, those grapes were probably sour, anyway. You had his body, but you didn't have his soul. There's a difference, *love*."

"Meow. Now that we've got past our little catfight, love, will you please let me go? This is a touch uncomfortable."

Brian tested the vines around Fiona's wrists and ankles. "I don't think so, sister dear. It's not that I don't trust you, it's just that I don't trust you. I think we'll leave Maureen's bindings on your body and your Power, at least until we're safely off your lands. You have a nasty reputation for treachery. Nearly as bad as your twin." He sheathed his knife, apparently satisfied with what he found.

Maureen felt the last of the adrenaline wash out of her and take every trace of starch with it. Her eyes started tracking things that weren't really there. She sagged away from her hawthorn crutch. Brian caught her, lifting her in his arms as if she was a doll. *Neanderthal,* she thought. *Or something close to it. He's designed for carrying mastodon quarters back to the cave. Sometimes it comes in handy.*

She forced herself back out of the warm grayness of fatigue. "One last thing on our agreement. The cease-fire doesn't cover Sean."

Fiona smiled faintly, and her eyebrows lifted in a way that said Sean was totally expendable. "I never thought it would."

# twenty-nine

—⁓—

BRIAN SHIFTED MAUREEN gently in his arms, resting one set of muscles by throwing another to the wolves. His eyes measured the distance to Maureen's forest and relative safety. No matter how he added it up, the answer depressed him.

When he'd first stepped outside of Fiona's hedge, he'd wanted to dance like a demented gypsy in celebration. The world glowed. He owned his mind again. He owned his body again. He was *free*!

Instead, he walked slowly and smoothly, with a sleeping woman wrapped in his arms. She snored quietly and snuggled tighter against his chest.

It made a romantic picture. Problem was, whoever posed the scene had never needed to carry a body for miles, cross-country. Flaming tension spread across his shoulders and ice picks stabbed his biceps. He couldn't carry her all the way. At least not as he was.

Brian sneered at his self-image. He wasn't modeling for the cover of a novel, ripped-shirt masculinity cradling the swooning heroine in his embrace. He shifted her into a fireman's carry across his shoulders. It might not be as elegant or as comfortable for her, but life was like that. If she didn't like it, she could consider the alternative.

She didn't stir. She didn't even whimper. He felt her heartbeat against his neck, felt her breathing, so she hadn't done something soap-opera stupid like dying in his arms. She was warm, and her body smell wrapped itself around him, a reminder of intimacy and a promise of reward.

Maureen's hips poked into his shoulder, bony, no padding. He could wrap one hand around both her wrists. He thought about her eyes, sunken in purple hollows above knife-blade-sharp cheekbones. Her skin was as thin as parchment, and her clothes hung on her like rags on a stick scarecrow. What it all boiled down to was, he was carrying a warm skeleton.

She was starving. She had been all lean tension when he'd first met her. Now she'd blow away in a light breeze. It wasn't just missing meals and sleep. Her body had burned itself to power her magic.

She really weighed too little to be slowing him down this much. He'd carried backpacks weighing more—carried them all day long, twenty, thirty miles through the Malay jungle or over the sodden moors of the Falklands. This tiredness was Fiona's gift, her theft of his Power. He couldn't draw on it to aid his legs, his back, his shoulders.

Where had Maureen found the strength to do what she had done today? If Dougal weren't dead already, Brian would have killed the bastard three times over.

Every few paces, he stole a glance back at the hedgerow and the ridge of Fiona's roof, half-expecting to find his sister strolling casually along behind them. Those vines and Maureen's binding wouldn't hold forever, and his sister could give new meaning to the word "vindictive."

It would have been simpler just to kill her. Maureen said no. She'd spared Fiona, because of the baby his sister carried and because Maureen wasn't crazy anymore. She'd spared Fiona because she didn't want to kill again.

"I love you, Maureen."

She stirred and settled into a different curve around his shoulders. She was still alive. He was still alive. She might even love him. Those had to count for something.

Not that he deserved it. After all his mistakes, she'd still escaped, she'd found him, she'd broken the spell that held him—set him free and defeated Fiona on her own ground. What it had cost Maureen to break that spell, to rise from butchering Dougal in his own bed to seducing a man, he'd never really know. How does a woman overcome something like Buddy Johnson?

"You remind me of the Gurkhas, love," he whispered. "You're like them, small and tough and indomitable and dangerous way out of proportion to your size. If we get out of this alive, I'll take you to Nepal sometime. We'll stay with Lobsang Norgay in a dirty stone hut and drink buttered tea spiked with Jamaica rum. He was my old corporal, saved my ass a dozen times. He wanted me to marry his daughter. He'll like you."

She made a quiet noise in her sleep. It might have been agreement. He wondered if Lobsang would see her magic: Those mountain shamans were used to some truly strange things.

A sudden chill caught at his heart. She'd walled off Fiona's Power. That was how they'd finally won. But Fiona's Power bound Sean to the forest, blocked *him* off from Power.

With Fiona bound, Sean was free. Sean had his Power back. Sean knew Maureen wanted his head.

The forest edge waited, a hundred yards or so ahead. It didn't look as inviting, now. It looked dark and sinister, like an alley in a bad neighborhood at midnight.

Brian guessed he had just about enough Power to goose

a grasshopper. Maureen might as well be in a coma. She was as fit for a magical duel as she was to run a marathon.

He had to sneak Maureen through that bloody forest without running into Sean, get her up to whatever was left of Dougal's castle. The people there would help her. They'd have to. They owed Maureen their lives.

Ancient strategic principle propounded by Sun Tzu: When your enemy is strong and you are weak, avoid battle.

*Brilliant observation, Mr. Sun. Now let's see if I can implement it.*

He climbed the stile over the stone fence and entered the forest. They were off Fiona's land. A chill ran down his spine as he carried Maureen into the shadows.


SEAN CLENCHED HIS fist around the feeling of Power and chuckled quietly. Fiona had released him. Fiona had forgiven him. He was strong again.

His fingers caressed the tree next to him, feeling the life pulsing underneath the bark as he had not been able to feel for the last endless week. The tree spoke to him again. The forest felt alive again. He touched Power again.

The tree nipped at his hand, trying to catch his fingers between the ridges of its bark. *Ah, yes. That would be Maureen's sister. There's a lot of hostility in that family.*

He threw back his head and laughed. The noise ricocheted out into the forest and died. The forest wasn't in a mood for laughter. The forest told him Dougal was dead. The forest waited for its new mistress. The forest waited to digest its latest meal, wondering what price it would pay.

It was time to leave this forest.

That other redheaded bitch would be coming down from her hill, looking for him. She did not love him. She had destroyed Dougal. This land would obey her. Better to face her on his own terms.

No more skulking around the woods, no more slow, painful rebuilding of his lung and liver using the traces of Power that trickled past Fiona's walls. He stood up and stretched, lazily, completely, like one of Fiona's cats.

There were debts to be collected. People owed him blood.

He picked up the knife and pack—Brian's knife and Brian's pack. How generous of Little Brother to provide both food and weapon. Now Sean had to return them with proper thanks.

He relaxed his mouth into his slow, mocking smile. Fiona had a short attention span. A little nudge here, a touch of irritation there, the suggestion of some new novelty to be investigated, and he could move against Brian.

He glanced across the forest glade. Maureen's sister still sat there, briar wrapped around her wrist. When he killed Maureen, he'd own this forest. The sister wasn't going anywhere. She could wait. She was last on his list of chores, payback for the lingering ache in his side and the shortness of breath. Brian first, then Maureen, then tidy up the forest.

He drew Brian's knife and chopped a gouge out of the nearest tree, baring the sweet white sapwood underneath. A small payment on the older bitch's account. If he cut a tree, she bled. If she hadn't reminded him of where she lived, he wouldn't have found the need to blaze a trail.

He moved slowly through the forest, lazily, slashing vines and carving deep into the bark of trees, feasting on the tingle of inflicted pain that ran up his arms with each cut. What was her name? Jo? Jo owed him. This could be fun.

A twig snapped ahead of him, toward Fiona's, and Sean froze. If Dougal was dead, his pets might do almost anything. That rotting dragon hadn't been the worst thing in the forest, not by a long sight. At least it was rational and curious, as well as hungry. Most of the other beasts were just hungry.

Something moved between the trees, and Sean crouched behind a bush to watch. The shape resolved into a man, a big man, a man carrying something heavy.

Brian.

Brian walked free, through the woods, carrying a woman across his shoulders. Sean caught a flash of red hair from the draped body.

Brian and Maureen. They had come from Fiona's cottage.

Fear washed through Sean, followed by rage. His twin was dead. *That's* why he was free. Brian and Maureen coming from Fiona's cottage meant Fiona was dead.

Caution chilled his rage before he could move. Brian was dangerous. Maureen was dangerous. Attacking them together called for an ambush to crush them without any chance of defense.

Sean loosed a tendril of Power, the merest wisp of fog testing his enemies. It would just be more of the forest's uneasy watchfulness, to Brian or Maureen.

Fierce joy flashed through his veins. He sensed nothing. Brian carried no defenses. Maureen felt as if she was barely even there.

Was she injured? Was that why Brian carried her? Had their battle with Fiona left both of them so weakened? Sean smiled to himself, allowing the faintest beginning of a plan to warm his heart.

He pushed gently at Maureen and felt her stir. She slept. She seemed unhurt but exhausted, and he sensed absolutely no reserves of Power. Either she was the greatest actress since Hepburn, or she was helpless.

How about Brian? Sean's touch found weariness and hope. The Pendragon was still strong, too strong for any kind of physical fight. But magic? Sean felt nothing. His brother, too, seemed helpless against Power.

Sean's eyes narrowed, and his grin widened. His heart raced with anticipation. He slipped from bush to tree trunk to rock, curving in behind Brian and creeping closer, thirty feet, twenty, ten.

A twig cracked under Sean's foot, and Brian spun around. The Pendragon dumped Maureen like a sack of grain, drawing his knife.

Sean shook his head, in mock sadness. This was all too easy: no artistry, no drama. He loosed a stun-spell and felt it break across his brother. Brian toppled like a felled tree, all in one stiff piece, and a fierce joy flashed through Sean's blood. It felt like an orgasm without foreplay.

"Fiona won't save you this time, my brother. Nothing will save you. I'm not even going to waste my time gloating."

He lifted his knife and stepped forward and smashed to the ground. Sean spat curses and rolled over against the tight cords binding his right ankle.

*Vines!* He slashed at them, felt them twang like bowstrings, and jerked away, only to find brambles crawling up his left arm. Fire woke in his ankle, and he saw blood blossoming through the cloth of his pants. He hacked again and again, chopping to right and left, but the ground crawled underneath him and thorns tore at his flesh.

"Fiona!"

The forest swallowed his shout. The forest tangled him. The forest threw vines and brambles around him to drag him down, to drown him, to suck his blood as it had sucked blood and soul from the others. Now both legs and his left arm burned in agony, as if tendrils ate the flesh from his bones. Sean thrashed in panic, triumph turned to terror.

His thoughts raced. Dougal had set this forest as a guard.

With Dougal dead, it was an unchained monster. Sean called on fire to cleanse the land but felt his Power draining away with his blood.

"*Fiona!*"

But his sister was dead. She couldn't save him. Sean hacked frantically, sweat flying from his arm. For every vine he cut, three took root in his flesh and sent acid along his nerves. Brambles looped around his throat and bit him, forming sucker roots that pierced into his veins and drank. His brain fuzzed.

One thought still loomed through the fog. *Kill. Kill before I die.* Brian lay a few feet in front of him. Maureen lay to one side. Both were helpless. Sean hefted the knife.

Brian.

Sean pulled all his hatred, all his fading Power together, and aimed the knife. His hand drew back for the throw. Something jerked at his wrist, and the knife dropped. He forced his head around. Green briars spiraled up his wrist.

"*FIIIOONNNAAA!*"

His scream died off in a strangled gargle, and he sank under the waves of pain. His thoughts splintered into sparkling atoms and fled like a cloud.

Darkness took them.


MAUREEN PUSHED HERSELF up, groggily. Trees. Brian. Noise. Stench. Pain. Hunger.

She squatted on hands and knees. She sorted out her senses.

The noises stopped. The stink didn't. Rotting meat. She'd smelled that before. The forest. She shook her head, trying to focus. Blood dripped from a bundle of vines and briars a few feet from where Brian lay. The bundle twitched once, then twice, then settled as if whatever hid inside it had lost all tension.

"What? Happened?"

Single words seemed to be her limit. Her head pounded, and her left hand throbbed in time with the beat. She focused on the hand. A red line crossed it, a half-healed wound. It wasn't still bleeding, she noted with relief. She might have gotten around to worrying about that, sometime.

Brian stirred. His head rolled from side to side. He sat up, jerkily, as if parts of him rejoined the whole like pieces of a puzzle. He shook his head again, a groggy owl staring around. He peered at Maureen.

"I could have sworn you were asleep."

She stared at him. "What happened?"

He waved at the bloody bundle. "Sean attacked us. You killed him."

She shook her head. "I didn't do anything."

"Bugger that. *I* bleeding well didn't. That leaves you."

"Bullshit. Last thing I did was faint into your arms like Scarlett O'Hara. I dreamed I was strangling Sean. Jo and David held him down. Then I woke up with a bump on my head. Whatever happened to him, *I* didn't do it."

Brian stood up, moving slowly. He shook his hands and feet as if they tingled from returning circulation. He knelt and poked at the wrapped form that must have been Sean, using the tip of his knife.

"Dead." He looked up at her and studied her face, as if he was reading the mixture of fierce joy and loathing she felt. He shook his head. "You seem to think Sean was your worst enemy. That poor sod may have been a nasty piece of work, but he was really just a puppet. Fiona's the one who made him, and you had to leave her alive behind our backs. Alive and *very* angry."

Maureen stared at the bloody vines and refused to worry about Fiona. She was tomorrow's problem. "Is that what Dougal did to David?"

"No. This just killed him, fast. David may even still be alive."

"Show me."

He offered her a hand and pulled her up. Maureen leaned on him again, tucking herself under his arm. He felt hard and warm and reassuring, support she could rely on. It felt like leaning on Father Oak, only with a heartbeat.

The dragon still stank like the devil's own cesspool. Crows and ravens and vultures perched all through the trees, too gorged to fly. The birds barely even followed the two of them with their black, sated eyes.

Brian stopped. "My God!"

Jo sat there, next to another bundle of vines. She didn't move. Maureen traced the greenbrier looped around her sister's wrist and saw the fine rootlets bonded to her skin. Her eyes were open but blank. A faint breath stirred her chest, then another.

Maureen remembered a vegetable in a nursing home, fed by a tube. Psych class field trip. Catatonic withdrawal. Lights on, nobody home.

She vomited. She barely had enough strength to keep the vile mess off her clothes. A part of her body snarled at the silly waste of food.

Brian held her. Brian spoke soothing noises. Finally, the noises made words. "Jo found him. She forced herself into the bond, to track him through the land. They're both alive."

She forced a whisper. "How do we get them out?"

"I don't know if we can. I don't know if anybody ever has broken this kind of bonding. Their bodies are here, but their thoughts are scattered throughout the forest. They've *become* the forest."

The flash of insight felt just like a cartoon lightbulb. "Jo and David killed Sean. They saved us. We've got to save them."

Brian shook his head. "Maureen, you may be the most powerful witch in the Summer Country, but you're damn near *dead*. You have to rest. You have to eat, and sleep, and rebuild your Power before you're ready to try anything like this."

"No." She knew, with cold hard certainty, that Jo and David couldn't wait. She felt it. They'd die. "You said I own these lands? I take over from Dougal because I killed him? All that feudal shit of *force majeure?*"

"Yes."

"Then I'm going to be a feudal lord." She found some strength, somewhere, and staggered over to the nearest tree. She stared at the trunk, too exhausted for emotion, thinking about the spells she'd worked.

The Power didn't come, this time. The words didn't force themselves on her. She didn't have the strength.

The bark of the beech was smooth under her hands. She'd asked a beech for directions, earlier today. She hoped it wasn't this one. If she'd just walked right by Jo and David . . .

"Give them back to me. You've got Sean. You've got your blood. In their place, I swear to act for the good of this forest. Give them back." Nothing happened.

"I don't have the strength or time to argue with you. I am the ruler of this land. I command you to give them back."

Still nothing. This world seemed to require threats.

"If you don't send Jo and David back into their bodies, I swear I will burn every last tree and bush and clump of moss in this forest. I will burn this land as bare as the knob of rock where Dougal set his tower. It may take me the rest of my life to do it, but I *will* do it, as surely as the sun rises in the morning.

"Ask Dougal MacKenzie's ashes whether I am patient enough to do it. Ask Sean's blood whether I have the foresight. Ask Fiona's hearthstone and threshold whether I have the will. Give them back."

Her vision throbbed again, pulsing with her heartbeat. The cut on her hand had reopened and left a thin red smear on the gray bark of the beech. It looked like a brushstroke of Japanese calligraphy, signing a contract.

The forest stirred around them. Something tapped Maureen on the ankle. She glanced down, slowly, without the strength for more than idle curiosity.

One of the briars looped its way around her leg. The tip turned black, curled, and dissolved into powder. A second branched off and quested upward.

Maureen watched a slow-motion video of Fiona's battle with the hedge. It was happening to someone else. She wondered how it would come out.

# thirty

—✳—

<THE PRICE HAS been paid. The pact is signed in blood.>

Ghostly bindings unraveled. Misty fragments of Jo's soul floated free and reached out to each other, gathering.

She had been vast. That echoing voice seemed to trap her, compress her, and stuff her back into her skull. The claustrophobia of her own body was unbearable.

Images flickered back into her eyes, a scuffed patch of dirt and roots replacing the pattern of life for miles around. Rot offended her nose, and the harsh croak of ravens buried the song of leaves rejoicing in the sun. The caress of the earth and sky, the water and the rock, died away to the scant range of her own skin. She plunged from riches into poverty.

Worst of all, she'd lost a bond to David deep enough to make all-night sex seem like a picture postcard from Detroit. Now that was gone.

A dull hatred simmered in her, residue of the land's fear of fire. It left her looking for the thief who had stolen bliss. She tried to move, to punch something in frustration, even just to vent her anger in a burst of pungent swearing. Nothing worked. Her body rebelled, demanding toll for the days of abuse she'd heaped upon it.

Jo coughed. Her throat felt like cracked mud in a dried-up creek bed. Her wrist stung where the vine had rooted, her knees and hips ached like someone had cut them open and sewn burning coals inside, and her eyes were full of the sand of hours of unblinking sight.

A scream broke into the tangle of her anger. She sorted out the clashing images and found a focus.

It was David.

She forced her muscles to move and staggered to her feet. She managed one jerky step and fell facefirst in the dirt. Her feet were numb, no feeling from her knees down to her toes. She blinked and cursed and crawled over to David, to the cage of vines that held David.

They shriveled into brown ash before her eyes, giving up a smell of burning foulness. Her hand reached out, then jerked back, afraid of what it would find under the dust. The forest had eaten him. Could a half-digested meal be human? Could it even *live*?

She looked at her own wrist, where the briars had joined her flesh. Red dots like a healing rash speckled her skin. She gritted her teeth and touched David, brushing the dust away from his face, from his closed eyelids and nose and cheeks, daring to look.

He was David. He'd lost weight, and his skin shone waxy pale under the angry red welts and pockmarks of what looked like the aftermath of the world's worst case of poison ivy, but he was David. He was alive.

His screaming stopped when she touched him. She felt his recognition, as she had felt it when she dove into the forest's web to find him and bind him and draw him back.

She'd won.

She'd wrestled the forest for his soul and won.

Someone offered her water. She drank it greedily, the cold wetness soothing her parched throat. She cradled David's head in her arms and dribbled water down his throat and held him against the racking coughs as he rejoined the human race.

His hand jerked and twitched, then steadied as he reached up and stroked her cheek. "Jo," he croaked, and then, "I love you."

"Hush." She held his head against her breasts. She felt a shivery warmth there, not sex but mothering. She wanted to open up her blouse and suckle life back into him.

Feet intruded into the Madonna scene. She traced them up legs to find Maureen and Brian.

"Where the *hell* did *you* come from?"

They shouldn't have been able to sneak up on her through the forest. The forest saw *everything*.

Then she remembered, hazy through the fading bond.

She remembered their coming into the forest, and she remembered the skulking bastard she'd shot creeping up on them, and she remembered the fierce hungry thrill when she and David had hurled the forest's rage at him and tripped him and swallowed him alive. She also remembered Maureen's threats.

The forest had wanted to eat them both, Maureen and Brian. The forest hated fire and feared everything on two legs. It had reached out for them, and Jo and David fought it back. The battle was vague in her mind, but a fox was bound up in it, and an oak almost as old as the hill on which it stood. Both had fought on Maureen's side.

"Goddamn you, why couldn't you just leave us alone?"

Maureen blinked. "Leave you trapped here? What kind of a bitch do you think I am? You're my *sister*! I *had* to get you out! Either that, or die myself!"

Jo gritted her teeth. "I should have let the forest eat you. We were happy. You've got no idea what it's like, joining the land. It's all your goddamn fault, anyway. You dragged all of us into this fucking mess."

Then the last threads of the spell finally broke. Jo shuddered, staring into the black chasm of what she'd done. She had nearly died. *David* had nearly died, and the land had made death seem so inviting that in the end, both of them had nearly reached out for it.

Maureen's eyes rolled up, and she collapsed into a heap of dirty clothes around a stick doll. Jo jerked with shock, finally noticing details: hollow eyes like bruises in her face, wrist and elbow bones standing out so sharp they almost cut the skin, pallor that made her freckles stand out like spattered paint.

That was her *sister*. Someone had done that to her *sister*!

Fear surged through Jo, then cold rage. Maureen looked like one of those survivors in the photos of Dachau.

"Brian, what the *hell* did you drag her into?" Jo felt something dangerous pressing against her eyeballs. That clone of Buddy Johnson stood about an inch from getting his ass fried.

He seemed to know it. He held up a hand and knelt to gently ease Maureen's position. "Peace, woman! I'm just carrying her to a place where she can get some food and rest. Ask David. He and I were both captured within minutes of coming here. She set me free this morning. She'd already killed the man who did this."

Jo fumbled her way out of Maureen's jacket, took the lighter out, and tossed both of them to Brian. "Get her covered. Make a fire, warm her up. Get some water into her. You know this goddamn place, for *Chrissakes* get her some fucking *food*!"

He just stared at her.

"Goddamn you, *move* your ass! Do I have to light a fucking *fire* under you?"

David shook his head, still groggy, and looked up at

Brian. "Sisters," he said, as if he was cussing. "They fight like cats, but God help you if you dare threaten one of them."

The pins and needles of her waking feet proved that she was alive. She was alive and held a living David in her lap.

She noticed a briar next to David's hand, green and wiry and covered with thorns. It moved. Rage took her, and she ripped it out of the ground—a foot, three feet, five feet of rooted horror. It broke loose and shriveled in her hand. She threw the blackened remnant into a bush and hoped David hadn't seen.

She stared at her shaking hand. The rash throbbed with her racing heartbeat, and she thought of asphalt. Nice, safe, dead asphalt.


MAUREEN TASTED BLOOD. She must have cut her lip when she fell. Damn fool theatrical stunt to pull, fainting in the middle of a fight. Debate Club wouldn't permit it, but the Drama Club might. The world fuzzed in and out, balancing on the foggy edge between reality and dream.

*Blood,* the little worm boring in the back of her mind muttered. *Remember the taste of Fiona's blood? Remember what it told you? Do you have the guts to run a blood test on yourself?*

Was she pregnant?

The thought formed ice in her belly. She lay there, limp, eyes closed, and wondered. Words echoed around in gray emptiness, bouncing off the walls of her future. Was she pregnant? If so, who was the father?

And, what would she do when she found out?

Three questions. Three questions about *her* goddamn belly, not anybody else's. Not the pope's, not Father Donovan's, not even Sister Anne's back at St. John's School.

She'd asked how long sperm remained alive inside the

human woman. Memories stirred, rolled over, and sat up. The past spoke to her in the dusty words from a medical text on anatomy a high school friend had stolen from the library. *Adults only!* the circulation stamp shouted in heavy red ink. Black-market Sex Ed. It showed clinical detail to curious teenagers who had no other source. *That* was where she had found out about puberty, about why Buddy had used rubbers with Jo but never wasted one on her.

*Sperm remains viable for up to three days inside the human female,* said the dry, clinical voice of the pages. The translation was, Dougal's slime still swam around in her, mixed with Brian's seed. Her skin crawled at the thought. For a moment, she thought she'd puke again.

*An egg can be fertilized for anywhere up to twenty-four hours after ovulation.* So a woman had a four-day range in any cycle of the moon, to become pregnant. Russian roulette is what it was, one bullet in seven chambers. Basis of Rhythm and Blues, a highly questionable method of contraception endorsed by Father Donovan. Like he'd really *know*.

And women tended to be more interested in sex when they were fertile. That was Nature's little joke, but then, remember She's a Mother.

*Thirty hours from zygote to mitosis, three days for the embryo to migrate to the uterus, one week to implantation, all rough figures that change from one woman to another.* Fiona must have gotten herself knocked up the first day she had Brian, to taste like that. Witch's luck, or witch's skill.

All Maureen would have would be a fertilized egg, at most.

Did she have the guts to look? Did she have the guts to live with the answers?

Maureen tasted the coppery salt in her mouth. When would a lab test know, she wondered. When would the proper hormones and other changes show up in her blood, her urine?

Not for weeks. There was another way. The dirt she lay in told her of it, lent her power. It was her land. It obeyed her. It supported her. That was the only reason she still lived.

<Look inside yourself,> it said. <A witch has more ways of sight than eyes. You don't need a crystal ball.>

She lay in her half faint, voices murmuring around her, feeling warmth, feeling wetness in her mouth washing away the blood, feeling the gentle touch of concern. Brian, she knew. Brian held her. Brian cared for her.

She'd fucked him. Twice. She'd been too busy wrestling with herself to pay much attention to him in the process. Next time, she'd try to do better. Someday, she might even be able to kiss him.

*You're dodging,* the worm said. *Are you a coward? Does the witch who killed Dougal fear to learn the truth? She can bind Fiona but can't control her own belly?* As Maureen thought about it, sweat turned clammy on her skin.

She looked.

She found an egg. It had been fertilized. The helix strands of DNA said Dougal was the father. Maureen's stomach twisted like a writhing snake.

Abortion? Adoption? Tough it out? She could kill the fragile life with the slightest touch of Power. . . .

She had started to turn her thoughts down those tangled alleys before she noticed another minute blob of protoplasm. Twins. Different eggs, released at different times. Brian had wound the chromosomes in that one.

Twins, by different fathers. One she ached for, one she had hated enough to kill. God was such a joker. There hadn't ever been twins in her family, as far back as she knew the tree and all the monkeys swinging in it.

*The Pierce women,* she thought, *the O'Brian women, both sides, we're small. We're skinny, we're flat-chested. None of those big-hipped big-boobed earth mothers who can birth twins and then go out to finish plowing the back forty with one baby hanging on each tit.*

The irony of it all sickened her. *Thanks a hell of a lot, God. I've just swept eighteen years of ghosts out of the fucking madhouse and You go and dump a new load of trauma in my lap. Some people can't stand the sight of happiness.*

And then she let her inner eye wander, through the rest of her belly, the rest of her body, and realized neither baby ever could be born. Her body would reject them. Her body simply didn't have the strength for pregnancy—didn't have the fats and sugars and whatevers floating through her bloodstream to build placenta and nourish one baby, let alone two.

She'd lost too much weight, between the dungeon and the magic. She'd barely been able to ovulate. Dougal had killed his own son. Brian could try again, next month or the next. "Feed up good and you can still be a mommy," her body said.

*God's own abortion,* she thought. *Even He takes steps to protect the mother's life. God aborts embryos and fetuses all the time.* She remembered an obscure statistic from Dendro 202: Something like 90 percent of the fruit set on an apple tree got aborted, every year. *No matter when it starts, life isn't nearly as sacred as some people like to think. There's always more of it than the world can hold.*

*Never count your chickens before they hatch.*

Relief jangled with pain and loss. She wondered what they would have looked like, what they would have grown up to be. She thought she probably always would. *I'll cry for them,* she thought, *sometime when I can find the strength for tears.*

The worm stirred again in her brain. It asked, *What would you have done? To hell with chickens. Would you have flushed a baby away with a used Kotex?*

*Don't know,* she thought. *Damned glad I won't have to choose.*

She opened her eyes and stared up at Brian. She smiled, weakly, through tears.

"Sorry."

He shook his head. "I *told* you to save your strength. Wait here. I'll get some people and horses down from the castle. They'll carry all of you up the hill."

Maureen blinked her eyes, puzzled. "Why should they help us?"

"They need you. This land is still feudal. People band together around power, for protection. You're their protector."

She swallowed bitterness. "I don't want slaves."

"Then don't treat them like slaves. They'll stay."

"Brian, will *you* stay?" She held her breath.

He bent down and gently kissed her forehead. "Yes. I think it's time I retired from the hero business. The Pendragons have gotten fifty years out of me. Whatever's left is yours."

She could breathe again.


MAUREEN WATCHED BRIAN'S back disappearing through the woods. "Castle," he'd said. Her home. She lay in the dirt and leaves of her own bonded land. She could feel it in her bones.

The stench of the dragon hung over them like a cloud. As far as the forest was concerned, the rotting meat was just so much food and fertilizer. The way she felt now, though, the stinking hulk revolted her. She was too damn tired to take the larger view.

David stirred in Jo's lap. "Is that guy really dead?"

"Which one?" Maureen's voice came out as a whisper, nearly as hoarse as the croaks of the ravens in the trees.

"The one we grabbed. The one over there."

Jo answered. "He's dead. He isn't held in limbo, like we were. I felt him die."

David looked like he wanted to vomit. "We ate him."

"He deserved to die," Maureen whispered. "Treacherous, murderous, conniving bastard, he deserved to die. He would have killed all of us. Don't lose sleep over Sean."

Treacherous, murderous, conniving—those adjectives all fit the land, as well. She could feel it. She had some work to do, some attitudes to change. She'd leave enough dangers in, though, to serve as guards against Fiona.

But her blood belonged here. Brian had talked to her about Power, about Blood, about Old Ones, but the words hadn't really stuck. After all that had happened, all that she'd done, that sense of belonging finally said it all.

She and Jo weren't even human.

"You're staying?" David aimed his face at Maureen, but he looked like he was afraid of *Jo's* choice.

Maureen answered, anyway. "I'm staying. I'm not crazy here." She shot a glance at Jo. "I can talk to trees, and nobody calls the shrink. And if I think 'They' are out to get me, it's probably true."

Jo stroked David's forehead. "You're a hero in this land, darling. You've killed a dragon. Bards were always powers in Celtic legend. You have a place here."

David suddenly looked even paler. "I'm not a hero, Jo. I ran away. I only came back and fought because there wasn't anyplace to run to."

Jo laughed and stroked his forehead again. "I'd prefer to live with a *smart* hero, any day. I've got no use for a *dead* one."

"You can stay at my castle until you find another place," Maureen said. "Fiona told me there was lots of room around here, unclaimed land. Of course, she *is* Sean's sister. He was a champion liar, too."

Jo stared down at David, her face suddenly a mask. "I don't know."

*She's waiting for something,* Maureen thought. *She wants him to tip the balance. What does* he *want to do?*

"Jo," David whispered, "Jo, I *like* living with four seasons. Let's go home. Otherwise, every time I touch a leaf, I'll wonder if it's going to drink my blood, suck the marrow out of my bones, eat my soul. Even the dirt is hungry here. I feel it. You may be born to it. I'm not."

A faint smile eased Jo's face. "Thanks, dear. This land scares me." She hesitated. "No, I'm lying. *I* scare me. I'm afraid of the woman this land creates in me."

She finally looked across to Maureen. "You say you aren't crazy here? Well, I *am.* I don't like being crazy. I *enjoyed* killing that creep. I even did it twice, it was so much fun."

Maureen nodded. "I never belonged, back in Naskeag Falls. You don't belong in the Summer Country. We're not twins. We never were twins. We're some kind of mirror between the worlds. It reverses our souls, not our faces."

The orange tom had reappeared from wherever cats go. She caressed him, snuggling him under her filthy ski jacket and ruffling his fur. "Marmalade is walking between worlds, too. He and his harem seem to be moving in with me. Fiona wouldn't let them just be cats. Maybe you can ship us some cases of tuna or sardines."

She looked up at Jo again. "Come and visit. Both of you. I promise to make the forest behave itself."

A tiger-stripe butted Jo's hand, demanding attention, while a gray-and-white feline settled against David's side and started to wash her paw. The three cats purred in counterpoint harmony, almost loud enough to shake her bones.

Maureen heard voices and the thump of hooves. *Brian,* she thought, she hoped, she prayed. *It had better not be strangers. The cats could put up a better fight than we could.*

It was Brian, leading three horses and two women with

food and wineskins. They hoisted their patients into saddles, funny little saddles without any horn to grab hold of,
and Maureen had never sat on a horse since summer camp.
They handed up three cats, to perch neatly in loaf-shapes
crosswise behind the saddles as if they rode every day. Each
walker took a set of reins and led the horses off through
the woods.

All she had to do was keep her butt on the horse. Big
as it was, the beast seemed placid enough, rocking along
in a slow walk suitable for small children and fools and
invalids, and she didn't have any reins to worry about, so
she concentrated on wine and cheese. Good wine. Good
cheese.

Maureen looked up from a bite, and the skin along her
spine prickled. A red-furred shape stood sentinel on a boulder beside the trail, underneath a huge oak tree. Maybe the
forest had forgiven her threats of fire.

The fox didn't stir a hair as the parade ambled up, close
enough to touch it. Maureen reached out for it with her
thoughts.

*Thank you. Thank both of you. How did you keep the forest
from killing us?*

<We told them that they could be ruled by you, or by
the black-furred witch who tortures trees. Even briars can
understand a choice as simple as that one.>

Maureen nodded to the fox, and the fox nodded back.
They had a contract.

<Welcome home.>

It vanished into the bushes.